DEADLY CROSSING

A Thriller By

R. E. McDermott

Published by R.E. McDermott

Copyright © 2014 by R.E. McDermott

ISBN: 978-0-9837417-1-8

For more information about the author, please visit
www.remcdermott.com

Layout by Guido Henkel, **www.guidohenkel.com**

Printed in the U.S.A.

To Our Sons
Chris and Andy

Each passing day makes me prouder
to be your dad

Acknowledgements

With each new book, the number of people to whom I owe thanks grows, and my greatest fear is that I'll unintentionally leave someone out. I suppose that's inevitable, and I could take the less perilous route of issuing a generic and non-specific thanks, but that doesn't seem quite right somehow. Therefore, I'll give it my best shot and issue a preemptive and generic (but nonetheless sincere) apology to anyone I might have missed.

First I owe thanks to my wife, Andrea, always first reader and sounding board. Readers owe her thanks as well, for she's rescued you from more lame plot twists and tortured sentences than you'll ever know.

Captain Ken Varall again read an early draft (on a very tight deadline) and provided valuable input. Sean Killian helped me keep my US Coast Guard scenes technically accurate and within the realm of the believable. My friend and old roommate, Captain Seth Harris, lent his many years' experience as a container ship master to the cause, reading the shipboard scenes and making valuable suggestions to improve both their technical accuracy and plausibility. (I might add at this point that Seth's excellent note-taking ability got us BOTH through our undergraduate years.)

Also from the fraternity of ex-sailormen, Captains Andy Lavies and Chris Allport weighed in from the far side of the pond, saving me from a couple of potentially embarrassing errors relative to British terminology and geography. Nor were they my only British contributers. As she has with previous books, Barbara Elsborg read the early manuscript multiple times, making terrific suggestions with each iteration. Roy Brocklebank RAF (retired) also gave generously of his time, offering needed corrections and suggestions, and researching and nailing down details. If my Brits sound like Brits, I suspect it has more to do with my British friends than the efforts of this Texan.

On the publishing front, Neal Hock took on a new role finding the weak spots in the story and then helping me strengthen them. And just when I thought the multitalented Jeroen ten Berge couldn't possibly match his previous efforts, he delivers yet another stunning cover. I think this is his best one yet.

And last and far from least, over a hundred readers of my previous books volunteered to read the advance review copy of *Deadly Crossing*. Space prevents me from mentioning each by name, but you know who you are, and you have my profound thanks.

Any errors made, despite all this excellent help and support, are mine and mine alone.

Thank you for taking a chance on a new author. I sincerely hope you enjoy *Deadly Crossing*. If you do, please consider the links to the other books in the Tom Dugan series listed at the end of this ebook. And if you'd like to be notified when I release a new book, please consider signing up for my mailing list at this link.

PROLOGUE

PRAGUE
CZECH REPUBLIC

Karina shifted in her sleep and groaned, dragged by pain to the edge of consciousness. Her eyes flew open to stare into the darkness, and her heart began to pound like that of a captured bird. Had they heard her? If they knew she was conscious, they'd come back. Then it would all start again. She squeezed her eyes shut and willed herself to sleep. Just another hour, or even another minute. Anything to escape, if just for a moment.

But sleep would not come, and she lay still, listening for approaching footsteps. She heard none, and her pulse slowed, then spiked again as she turned on the bare mattress and pain shot through her naked body. Despair washed over her, and her shoulders began to shake in silent sobs, but there were no tears, for there were none left.

She thought again of killing herself, but that was impossible, even if she had the means. They had warned her what would happen to her sisters if she defied them.

Then there were footsteps in the hall, accompanied by laughter. She curled into the fetal position and trembled, dreading the squeak of the opening door.

CHAPTER ONE

LONDON, UK

"Whatever is wrong with you?" asked Anna Walsh in the back seat of the taxi. "You've been behaving strangely for days, and now you're sweating. Are you ill? Perhaps we should skip dinner."

Tom Dugan smiled to cover his unease. "I'm fine. I'm just preoccupied with work—and it is a bit stuffy in here. Besides it's your favorite restaurant, and we've had the reservation for a week."

He gave her hand a gentle, and what he hoped was reassuring, squeeze. Anna nodded but appeared unconvinced. He leaned over and kissed her, curtailing further discussion. One kiss led to another until she pushed him away, laughing.

"Yes, well, we best stop this and give you a chance to cool down a bit before you have to be seen in public. Otherwise, we'll have to turn the cab around and go home straightaway."

Dugan glanced down and moved back to his own side of the backseat with some reluctance. He gazed out the rain-speckled window, at the lights of London refracted through the drops clinging to the glass, and was soon lost in uneasy thoughts.

The source of his unease rested in his jacket pocket, a small black velvet ring box. He'd wrestled with 'popping the question' for weeks, but as the moment approached, he was beset by doubts. There was the age difference, of course, and the demands of her career and his, and a dozen reasons why their relationship shouldn't work. The fact that it had worked for the last three years was a source of continual amazement to him.

But what if she said no? She'd never even hinted at marriage, and if he crossed that line without invitation, the dynamic between them might be subtly but forever changed. Perhaps he was being greedy, wishing for more happiness when he already had more than any man deserved.

His reflections were interrupted by the trill of his cell phone, and as he fished it from his pocket, he reminded himself to turn it off before they got to the restaurant.

"Dugan," he said into the phone.

"*Dyed*, I am sorry to disturb you, but we need your help," said a familiar voice.

"Andrei?"

"*Da*, it is me, and I need to talk to you urgently," Andrei Borgdanov replied.

Dugan glanced over at Anna, who arched her eyebrows in a question. "Okay, I'll call you back in a couple of hours. I'm a bit tied up at the moment."

His reply was met with a momentary silence before the Russian responded. "Very well, *Dyed*, but please hurry."

Dugan sighed and suppressed his irritation at being addressed as *dyed*, Russian slang for 'gramps.' Borgdanov had given him the nickname at their first meeting, when they were far from being friends. Their relationship had changed, but the nickname was apparently here to stay.

"Okay," Dugan said. "But where are you? I thought you were still in the Indian Ocean."

"We are here."

"Here? As in London? Where?"

"In lobby of your building," Borgdanov said. "I tried to go to your apartment, but man at desk stopped us. He called your apartment to see if is all right, but he got no answer."

"Shit," Dugan said. "Pass the phone to the doorman. Wait a minute. You said 'we.' Who's with you?"

"Ilya."

"Okay. I'm going to have security let you in to the apartment. Make yourselves at home and wait for us. Now pass the phone to the guy at the desk."

"Security," said a voice.

"Walter, this is Tom Dugan. Do you recognize my voice?"

"Yes, Mr. Dugan."

"Great. Could you please escort these two gentlemen up to our apartment and let them in with your passkey?"

"Yes, sir."

"Thanks, Walter. We'll be home in a bit." Dugan hung up and slipped the phone back into his pocket.

"So Borgdanov is at our apartment," Anna said, "and there's someone with him?"

"Ilya Denosovitch, though damned if I can figure out what they're doing here. It's not like them to just show up out of the blue, so it must be something pretty serious."

"And something we'd both spend dinner worrying over, so we best go find out." She leaned forward and told the driver to take them home.

"That's probably the right call." Dugan felt the ring box in his pocket, and relief washed over him, along with a bit of guilt at his own reaction.

DUGAN AND ANNA'S APARTMENT
LONDON, UK

"But how do you even know she's in London?" asked Anna.

"We don't for sure," Borgdanov replied, "but we have information she is probably in the UK, and I think London is logical place if she is in hands of bad people."

"That's another thing," Dugan said. "Why do you think there's foul play? I mean, she's nineteen and out on her own for the first time. Maybe she's just caught up in the adventure of living life and has been too busy to write or phone home. It wouldn't be the first time."

"*Nyet!*" Ilya Denosovitch said. "My niece is good girl and very devoted to family. And even if she would be so cruel as not to contact my sister and brother-in-law, she is very close to her younger sisters and little brother." He shook his head. "If she doesn't contact family, can only mean she cannot do so, and that she is in trouble."

"Okay. Let's go over it again," Anna said. "You say she left home two months ago?"

"*Da,*" Denosovitch said. "Besides being beautiful girl, Karina is very smart. She speaks very good English and also French and German. She also loves children and is very good with them. She applied for job with agency in Volgograd. This agency places Russian girls as…" Denosovitch looked to Borgdanov for help. "How you say *nyanya*?"

"Nanny," said Borgdanov.

"*Da*, nanny," Denosovitch said, continuing. "This was two months ago, and little Karina flew to Prague, where there is training school. She told my sister there is one month training course, and then she gets assignment in Western Europe or the UK, or maybe even USA. My sister got a phone call from her when she arrived in Prague, and Karina was very happy and excited. Since then, nothing."

"And your sister wasn't able to contact Karina?" Dugan asked.

Denosovitch shook his head. "After one week with no word, they tried calling number in Prague, but it is disconnected. Then my brother-in-law goes to the office of the agency in Volgograd, but office is closed, like no company ever exists. Police in Russia are no help, so my brother-in-law goes to Prague, but he has no address. He tries police there, but they have no record of the company. He tries many days but is difficult for him because he does not speak Czech. He goes everywhere, showing Karina's picture, but no one knows anything. Finally, he goes home to Volgograd. Then my sister contacts me, but I am with the major"—he nods at Borgdanov—"providing security on ship transiting near Somalia. It was ten days before we could leave ship in Aden; then we come straight here."

He looked down, composing himself. He was a blond giant, six foot five in his bare feet, and tipping the scales at two hundred and eighty pounds, none of it fat. Yet when he looked up, he was the picture of helplessness. His hands were trembling, and his eyes were wet with barely concealed grief.

He turned to Dugan. "Can you help us, *Dyed*?"

Dugan reached over and laid a hand on the big man's shoulder. "We'll do everything we can, Ilya."

The room grew quiet for a long moment before Anna broke the silence. "You said you had information Karina was in the UK. What kind of information?"

"Under the circumstances, I think it is clear that Karina was taken by the *mafiya*," Borgdanov said. "It seems only logical answer. I know a few ex-*Spetsnaz* that work for mob. I do not like what they do, and we are not friends but we are not enemies. I put out discreet inquiries, and one fellow told me that normally when the *mafiya* steals girls and takes them to Prague, final destination is usually the UK or USA. They have many clubs here, and they force the girls to…"

Borgdanov glanced over at Ilya, who was sitting with his jaw clenched and hands curled into fists.

"…to work in clubs. I think you understand."

Dugan and Anna nodded, and Borgdanov continued. "Maybe she is in US, but I figure we start here first."

Borgdanov looked at Anna. "We were hoping that maybe you could use your contacts to help us, and if we have no luck here, that maybe *Dyed*, could help us in US. We have nowhere else to turn."

Anna nodded. "Officially, of course, MI5 can do nothing regarding a personal matter that has no impact on national security. Unofficially, you'll have all the help I can give you, and if we do have to make inquiries in the States, I suspect Jesse Ward will make some very 'unofficial' inquiries as well."

"I think you can count on that," Dugan agreed.

"Thank you," said Borgdanov, relief in his voice.

Denosovitch merely nodded, not trusting himself to speak.

"But I think there's another person you haven't considered who may have some helpful contacts," Anna said, glancing at her watch. "Tom, would you please ring Alex and ask if we might all pay him a visit?"

KAIROUZ RESIDENCE
LONDON, UK

"And just how long has this been going on?" Alex Kairouz demanded, his face flushed.

His wife, Gillian, hesitated. "Almost a year, though Cassie only confided in me a month ago."

"A month ago!" Alex's face grew redder still. "You've known a month and you're just getting around to telling me?"

"And with good reason, obviously. I knew you'd overreact."

Alex glared. "I'm not overreacting. You know Cassie is vulnerable, and she's far too young to be romantically involved, even if she were… she were…"

Gillian's eyes narrowed to slits. "Even if she were what, Alex? Normal?"

Alex wilted under her gaze and slumped in his chair.

"I didn't mean it like that, and you know it. I just don't want her hurt, that's all."

Gillian shook her head. "I know you THINK that dear, but the problem is you really did mean it that way. You're so intent on protecting Cassie you can't see her as anyone except a flawed and fragile child. But she just turned eighteen, Alex, and the cognitive rehabilitation therapy has worked wonders over the last three years. She's come further than we ever dared hope. She tested low normal on the last battery of tests. That's low NORMAL, Alex. We can't keep her wrapped up in some sort of cocoon, and if we try, we'll only ruin her chances for a happy life." Her voice hardened. "And she WILL have a happy life, Alex, even if I have to fight you to achieve it. I promised that to Kathleen on her deathbed, and I keep my promises."

Alex softened at the memory of his dead wife. "I know you do, dear. And God knows no one's worked harder to give Cassie her chance in life. It's just so unsettling. Who is this boy? Where did she meet him, and how have they been seeing one another? She's hardly had the opportunity. She's always attended all-girl schools, and we've never allowed her to date."

"Apparently they've pursued their relationship through emails and texting."

"My God! She met him online? What if he's a predator!"

"I didn't say she met him online. I said they pursued their relationship online. She actually met him face to face last year. So did we."

"What? Where? Who is he?" Alex demanded.

"Do you remember when we all flew to the shipyard in Korea for the christening and delivery party for the *M/V Lynx*?"

"Yes, what of it?"

"Do you also remember the handsome young cadet that escorted Cassie and I on a private tour of the ship while you and Tom conferred with the captain?"

"Vaguely," Alex replied, awareness dawning.

"Well, evidently young Nigel Havelock was quite smitten with Cassie, and the feeling was reciprocated. He apparently slipped her his contact information, and they've been communicating ever since." Gillian paused. "Cassie told me proudly that 'her Nigel' is now third officer on the *Lynx*."

Alex exploded anew. "The bloody cheeky little bastard! Chatting up the boss's daughter in hopes of currying favor, is he? We'll just see about that. I'll sack the little bugger!"

"Alex Kairouz, you will do nothing of the sort. And quit being a pompous ass! Why do you think it's all about YOU and your company? Are you blind to the fact that our little girl is not so little any longer? She's a warm and beautiful young woman, and you best learn to accept that."

Alex sputtered, at a loss for words, and Gillian continued.

"And besides, you've often remarked on how Kathleen had an uncanny ability to read people and that Cassie inherited that gift. If this boy's feelings weren't genuine, don't you think Cassie would have seen through him by this time?"

"I suppose," Alex said, the concession grudging, "but if it's to continue, I insist we engage our security consultants to run a background check on him."

"Don't be ridiculous!"

Alex colored. "I'm NOT being ridiculous! And I would think you would be the first…" He stopped mid-sentence and looked quizzically at Gillian, a smile tugging at the corners of his mouth.

"You've already done it, haven't you?"

It was Gillian's turn to flush red. "It seemed prudent," she responded primly.

"And?"

"And he's just what he seems to be," Gillian said. "A nice English boy from a solidly middle-class family. No skeletons in the closet as far as the security people could determine. He got full marks through school and glowing recommendations from your own captains while he was a cadet. He seems a fine young man."

"Perhaps," Alex said, somewhat mollified, "but I think we should—" He was interrupted by the ring of the phone on the table beside him. He glanced down at the caller ID.

"Thomas," he said, reaching for the phone, "whatever can he want at this time of night."

"Yes, Thomas," he said into the receiver. "What? Borgdanov? Here? Yes, yes, of course you can come over. We'll see you in a few minutes." He hung up.

"What's that all about?" Gillian asked.

Alex shrugged. "I haven't a clue, but Thomas and Anna are coming over with Major Borgdanov and Sergeant Denosovitch. Thomas said it was urgent."

CHAPTER TWO

An hour later, Gillian sat in the comfortable and well-appointed living room of the Kairouz home, across from Dugan, Anna, and the Russians. Beside her on the sofa, Alex addressed their guests.

"Of course, we'll do anything we can to help," Alex said, "but I honestly don't see much we can contribute. I'll contact our security consultants and put them at your disposal." He looked at Anna. "But surely Anna's MI5 colleagues and her contacts at New Scotland Yard will be of more use."

The Russians nodded their thanks, but Anna cut Borgdanov off before he could respond.

"Actually, Alex," she said, "I was hoping Gillian might be able to help us."

"But whatever can I do, Anna?" asked Gillian. "As Alex says, surely your sources are far superior to any contacts I might have."

"Yes and no," Anna replied. "First thing tomorrow I'll start working those contacts, but if, as Andrei suspects, the Russian mob is involved, they've likely covered their tracks pretty well. I'll start with the UK Border Agency to check on work visas and immigration records, but if the girl IS here, she may be under a fictitious name."

Gillian looked unsure. "Well, of course I'll do anything I can to help. But again, what can I possibly do?"

Anna hesitated, obviously searching for words. "I'm interested in any contacts you might have from… from the time before you were a nanny. Do you keep in contact with any of them?"

Beside Gillian, Alex stiffened and took her hand. He glanced at the Russians and then across at Dugan and Anna.

"It's all right, Alex," Dugan said. "You can trust Alexei and Ilya."

"Well, it would seem Anna's given us no choice," Alex said. "And I fail to see how any of this—"

Gillian cut him off. "It's all right, Alex. I don't mind helping in a good cause."

"It's NOT all right! They've no right to ask you—"

Gillian reached over with her free hand and gently put her fingers to his lips. "I know you want to protect me, and I love you for it, but this really is my decision."

Alex slumped back on the sofa and glared at Dugan and Anna as Gillian continued. "What do you want to know, Anna?"

"Tomorrow I'm going down to the Clubs and Vice Unit of the Met to see what I can find out about Russian mob operations here in London. However, most of their officers are undercover, and they aren't likely to want to jeopardize ongoing investigations by sharing intel for a very 'unofficial' inquiry. That problem is compounded by the fact that I don't have a strong relationship with anyone in that unit. I'm really clutching at straws a bit, but I thought if you still have any contacts in that world, it could help a great deal. You might be able to provide some insights that even the Vice Unit fellows don't have."

Gillian gave a hesitant nod. "I may know someone who can help, but it might take a day or so. I'll get on it straightaway in the morning."

"Thank you, Gillian," said Anna.

The room grew silent, permeated by Alex's brooding disapproval, until Anna rose from her chair.

"Right then," she said, "we'd best be off. Thank you both for your help."

Dugan and the Russians echoed Anna's thanks, but Alex only looked at them and scowled before Gillian walked them to the door. She returned to find him standing at the sideboard, pouring himself a rather large measure of brandy.

Gillian sighed inwardly and joined him at the sideboard. "I'll have a small one, please, dear."

Alex nodded and reached for another snifter.

"Are you going to continue to sulk, or shall we discuss this like adults?"

Alex faced her and exploded. "They've no right to ask this of you. Your past is just that—past. Daisy Tatum is long dead and buried, and you're Gillian now. My wife and Cassie's mum. Delving into the past benefits no one, and this Russian mafia is dangerous. Who knows what they might—"

Gillian cut him off by wrapping her arms around him and pressing her cheek to his chest, hugging him tight until his anger dissipated. She turned her face up to his.

"You know I love you both beyond measure, and you've given me a wonderful life. I count my blessings each and every day. But you of all people should understand that I can't refuse this request. This poor girl may be suffering as I did, and I couldn't sleep at night knowing I might have helped her and didn't." She paused. "And neither could you, dear."

He took a ragged breath. "I suppose you're right, but I can hardly abide thinking of what you went through, and I'd spend the last breath in my body to shield you from having anything to do with that sordid world again. Were it in my power, I'd erase those horrible memories."

She touched his cheek. "I know you would, and I love you for it. But you can't, really, and I wouldn't let you if you could. Daisy will always be part of me, a hidden part perhaps, but always a source of strength. As the saying goes, what doesn't kill us makes us stronger."

Alex returned her hug before speaking.

"So are you going to see her?"

"You needn't say HER as if it were an epithet, dear. You know she's always been a staunch friend."

"That she has," Alex agreed, "and I owe her a debt I can never repay for rescuing you and giving you a new identity. I just can't agree with her lifestyle."

Gillian chuckled, the tension broken.

"Gloria has larceny in her DNA, Alex. The fact that she spurned your multiple attempts to set her up in legitimate businesses shouldn't be held against her."

"I was rather thinking of the time she DIDN'T spurn my offer and ended up fleecing one of the fellows at my club out of ten thousand pounds."

"It serves you right. She told me it was the only way she could think of to keep you from your incessant attempts to force her to go straight. And you made good the loss, so everything ended well," Gillian said, barely containing her laughter. "Besides, you said yourself that Clive Falworth was, to use your words, a wanker of the first order."

Alex sighed. "I suppose there's no way I'm going to win this argument?"

"Not a chance." Gillian kissed him tenderly before pulling her head back and staring up into his face.

"However, perhaps I can make it up to you. Cassie's spending the night over at her friend Ingrid's house. Does that suggest anything?"

CLUB *PYATNITSA*
LONDON, UK

Arsov sat at the end of the bar and surveyed the dim interior of Club *Pyatnitsa*, the flagship of his new London territory. It was quite a step up from his old territory in Prague, a dozen clubs and half a dozen high-end brothels in flats scattered throughout the city, owned through various front companies set up by the *Bratstvo*'s highly skilled London solicitors. Competent legal representation had been a problem initially, but the Brotherhood always sought out the best representation in each specialty. Those firms without sufficient moral flexibility to appreciate the extremely generous fees involved soon reconsidered after home visits from the more 'persuasive' members of the Brotherhood. Surveillance photos of solicitors' families as they went about their daily lives, coupled with detailed descriptions of possible fatal accidents (along with graphic photos of previous 'accidents'), never failed to do the trick. After all, the world was a dangerous place, and who could fault the attorneys for wanting to make sure their families were protected?

The solicitor arranging the real estate and business transactions had been particularly skillful. Arsov controlled his territory from a well-appointed office here at the rear of Club *Pyatnitsa*, or Club Friday, but nothing connected him to the other locations. He was a powerful spider, sitting in the middle of a web visible only to the *Bratstvo*.

His move from the *Federal'naya sluzhba bezopasnosti Rossiyskoy Federatsii*, or FSB, had been a natural one. As head of an FSB task force charged with controlling organized crime, it hadn't taken him long to realize the hopelessness of the task. Corruption was endemic in the government, and the *Bratstvo*'s tentacles reached deeply into the very agencies charged with controlling it, and had since Tsarist times. Ever the pragmatist, Arsov had soon decided that if he couldn't beat them, he'd join them, and quickly moved from taking the odd bribe to becoming a willing recruit.

He smiled at his new surroundings. The Brotherhood had given him more power and money than he could have ever acquired as a servant of the state (even a corrupt one), and the techniques he'd introduced in Prague had raised both the efficiency and profits of their trafficking operations tenfold. His reward had been London, and in the six weeks he'd been here, things were coming along nicely.

"That's Katya, there," said the man beside him, nodding to a girl clad only in a thong prancing onto a spotlit stage. The girl began a wildly erotic dance as rock music blared in the background.

Arsov watched a moment. "She looks too young."

"I'm following your new guidelines. She's completely legal. She turned eighteen last week, and I've got the documentation. I've sent all the younger girls out of sight to the brothels, just like you ordered." He hesitated. "But if you ask me, it will cost us business."

Arsov shook his head. "You have to understand the psychology of the clients, Nazarov. Men come here for a fantasy. Middle-aged men, with receding hairlines and expanding waistlines, who manage to convince themselves that a young woman who looks like a starlet cannot live until she has given them a blow job in a curtained booth. They want to feel strong, virile, desirable. But if they see a girl here that looks like their own teenage daughter, some percentage might feel guilty, maybe even call the police."

"It was never a problem before. We have lookouts on the street to alert us to the first sign of cops. We get the young ones out of here before the cops even get to the door."

"And how many men do you tie up standing around watching for the police? Two? Four? Now multiply that by a dozen clubs," Arsov said. "It is a huge waste of manpower."

Nazarov grunted noncommittally, and Arsov continued.

"It is all about knowing your customers, Nazarov. There is a different dynamic for the men who patronize the brothels; there is no illusion of romance. And a man who arrives at a brothel with a specific request to fuck children is unlikely to suddenly be stricken by a crisis of conscience." Arsov smiled. "Besides, customers with those particular tastes will pay a lot more. Why should we let them satisfy their urges here in the back rooms at the same price a normal john pays?"

"All right, I'll give you that, but I still don't like the other changes. London isn't Prague, and what we were doing before worked just fine."

Arsov suppressed a sigh. "Fine as opposed to what? As far as I could tell, you never tried anything different. You hooked all the girls on drugs and then managed them by close confinement, withholding the drugs, and beating them from time to time for no apparent reason. You may think a glassy-eyed, bruised and drugged-out whore is sexy, but I suspect it doesn't help sustain our clients' fantasies particularly well, to say nothing of the cost of the drugs. We turn a much better profit by distributing those drugs instead of using them to control the girls."

"That's another thing since you brought up control. I don't like this new plan at all. I think you're giving them too much freedom."

"On the contrary, we're making them control themselves, AFTER they've earned some freedom," Arsov said.

19

Nazarov looked unconvinced, and Arsov wondered if he'd have to replace the man. Some resistance was to be expected and tolerated, given that Nazarov had obviously been expecting to be promoted to head the London operation. However, Arsov had his limits.

His main concern was his new underling's refusal to grasp the obvious—his resistance to the new control plan being a case in point. The concept Arsov had perfected in Prague was brilliant in its application of psychology and elegant in its simplicity. Breaking a girl's spirit and perfecting her acting skills was only the first step—she still couldn't be trusted out of direct supervision. And even then, there was always the possibility she might convince some sympathetic customer to contact the police.

Arsov's solution was preemptive action. Though she didn't know it, among each new girl's first paying customers were *Bratstvo* men in disguise, alert to any attempt the girl might make at outside contact. If the girl passed that passive test, a *Bratstvo* 'john' would then actively attempt to gain her trust and offer to make outside contact for her. If the girl accepted, the fake john would reveal himself to be one of Arsov's men and the girl would be punished by repeated water-boarding and other torture that left no physical marks. Testing in a controlled club/brothel situation was repeated until the girl was deemed trustworthy enough to advance to the next level.

At the next level, a girl was allowed some limited freedom to run errands or perhaps go to lunch at a nearby fast-food restaurant. However, and again, all was not what it seemed. The girl was under continual close surveillance. If she attempted to escape or to contact anyone, she was immediately captured and summarily punished.

Girls who passed this challenge were tested even more stringently and given an errand that took them right by a uniformed policeman on patrol, one of Arsov's men in disguise. The imposter would stop the girl on a pretext and engage her in conversation, giving her ample opportunity to ask for help. If she did, he would appear sympathetic, then put her in his car and deliver her back to captivity. The fake 'policeman' would be given a large cash payment in front of the girl, cementing the idea that the police were in Arsov's pocket, and the girl would receive even harsher punishment, ostensibly for incurring the cost of the policeman's bribe.

'Graduates' of Arsov's program went from being unsure who to trust to being absolutely sure they could trust no one, even the police. That, along with frequent reminders of what might befall their loved ones back in Russia and of their videotaped porn sessions and interviews in which they waxed enthusiastic about their new life in the sex trade, served to destroy all resistance. The girls were free to come and go as they pleased, because there was no longer hope of rescue.

But it didn't stop there. After Arsov had broken the girls to his will, he proceeded to reshape them. Top producers got special privileges, good food, and lavish gifts. Less enthusiastic girls were ignored, and if they failed to earn the minimum set by Arsov, they were punished. Repeated failure to meet quota meant a girl would be 'sent away,' which was rumored to mean she'd be sold to a brothel in some Third World shit hole that would make even her current lot seem wonderful by comparison.

Arsov was the first to admit the process was time consuming, but he prided himself on taking the long view. After a girl was trained by his methods, she had a much longer working life than those controlled with drugs, and made much more money. Additionally, he needed almost no muscle to control the girls, and he could devote that manpower to growing other areas of the business. He could always use more manpower in the drug trafficking, and loan-sharking to the small but growing Russian expat community was an expanding business as well.

"What about the new girl, Karina?" Nazarov asked, breaking into his thoughts.

Arsov smiled. Beria had done a good job with that one, considering. She was by far the most challenging project he'd seen to date. Perhaps if things went well, he'd have Beria transferred here to London; he was a much more competent Number Two than this idiot Nazarov.

"I'm enjoying little Karina, but I think she needs a bit more seasoning. I'll keep her in my flat another week or so before she starts earning her keep."

BELGRAVIA
LONDON, UK

Gillian Kairouz released the button as she heard the muffled sound of the bell chiming through the closed door. It wasn't a harsh buzz or rapid 'ding-dong' but a slow, stately chime, totally in keeping with the upscale building in which she found herself. She heard footsteps inside, and then the door opened to reveal an attractive woman of somewhat matronly aspect and indeterminate age, her faced wreathed in a broad and welcoming smile.

"Gillian, love," the woman said, stepping into the hall to fold Gillian in a tight embrace, "it's been far too long."

The woman released Gillian and stepped back, holding her at arm's length. "And let me look at you! Father Time has been kind to you, I see. You're as lovely as ever."

Gillian laughed. "And you're still the charmer, Gloria, and looking well yourself."

"A girl does what she can," the woman said, guiding Gillian through the door. "But come along. Let's have a spot of tea and catch up."

Gillian surveyed the apartment as Gloria closed the door.

"Belgravia no less. You seem to be doing well for yourself."

Gloria laughed again. "Appearances are everything, love. To be successful, one must first LOOK successful."

"I'm not even going to ask exactly what you're successful AT," Gillian said, moving through the well-appointed living room to a love seat Gloria indicated with a wave of her hand.

"Oh, this and that. Just this and that," Gloria said with a sly smile as she took a seat across from Gillian and busied herself pouring two cups of tea from the silver tea service that sat on the coffee table between them.

"And how's Cassie?" Gloria asked.

"Wonderful, thank you for asking. She's more lovely every day, and she scored absolutely brilliantly on her last battery of tests. She tested at the low end of the normal range."

"Well, bugger the tea!" Gloria stood and moved to an antique sideboard. "That calls for a toast!" She returned with an ornate cut-glass decanter and two brandy snifters on a tray.

"I really—"

"Just a small one," Gloria replied, brushing aside Gillian's objection and pouring a healthy measure into each snifter. "It's not every day I hear such good news, and we mustn't tempt fate by seeming unappreciative."

"Very well." Gillian took the proffered snifter.

"To Cassie." Gloria raised her glass.

Gillian joined the toast and set her glass on the coffee table after taking a small sip. Across from her, Gloria settled back in her chair, snifter still in hand.

"And is Cassie excited?" Gloria asked.

"Very. It's a heady time for her. She's even started something of a relationship with a young man."

"Well, good for her."

"Yes, I think it's healthy, but Alex is, of course, less excited."

Gloria snorted. "And how is His Nibs?"

"He's fine. And he sends his best, by the way."

"Yes, I'm sure."

"Really, Gloria. Alex is a good man."

Gloria nodded. "I never doubted it for a moment, but you have to admit he's a bit rigid."

"He is," Gillian replied, "and that's unlikely to change. He is who he is and so are you, and I've the rare privilege of loving you both. But I didn't come here to discuss Alex. Were you able to find out anything?"

Gloria's face clouded, and she leaned forward and put her glass on the coffee table before settling back in her chair.

"Aye, enough to concern me. Are you sure this is something you want to get involved with?"

"It's not a matter of wanting, Gloria. Sergeant Denosovitch has nowhere else to turn, and I couldn't live with myself if I didn't help him do everything possible to rescue his niece. Not after what I... not after—"

"I know, I know, love. But these Russians are orders of magnitude nastier than our homegrown British bastards. I just want to make sure you understand what you're getting into. To be honest, I'm a bit nervous to even be nosing around."

Gillian was taken aback; she'd seldom seen Gloria more tentative. "Go on."

"Well, the Russian mob is like an octopus with a lot of tentacles. The preeminent group at the moment seems to be called the Brotherhood, or *Bratstvo*. They're into everything, from legit businesses to every criminal enterprise imaginable. They have strong ties to the Russian government, and many of them are former members of Russian police or intelligence organizations, making them practically untouchable in Russia—I've heard they pretty much do what they want there."

Gillian nodded as Gloria continued.

"Outside Russia, they operate through legal fronts where possible. They always engage the best lawyers, and if they can, they buy police or government officials—their businesses throw off a lot of cash."

"What about here?"

"Drugs, girls, loan-sharking—the usual." Gloria shrugged. "As far as bribes go, it's hard to say. Your guess is as good as mine, but given the money they have to throw about, I'll wager at least a few coppers are on the take."

"What makes them any more dangerous than any other criminals?"

Gloria shuddered. "Utter ruthlessness. They began to arrive in the UK in significant numbers eight or ten years ago, but the Armenian mob got here ahead of them and had established a foothold. Within a year of the Russians' arrival, all the leaders of the Armenian mob were either dead, along with their families, or working for the *Bratstvo*. If you cross the *Bratstvo*, they'll murder you and anyone close to you or, for that matter, anyone they even suspect is close to you, and they'll probably torture all their victims first. Coercing people by targeting innocent family members is their stock and trade, and everyone is vulnerable. Italian mobsters are gentlemen by comparison."

"If they have the girl here in London, any idea where they might be holding her?"

Gloria shook her head. "None of my contacts would be brave enough to poke their noses that deeply into *Bratstvo* business, and I wouldn't even consider asking them to." She stared hard at Gillian. "And you shouldn't pursue this either. These blokes are VERY dangerous."

"I'm only going to be passing the information along, so you needn't worry."

"You haven't been listening, Gillian. If you're involved in any way, you'll be in danger."

"Perhaps, but I have to pass this along nonetheless. It's all general anyway. I take it you were unable to find anything more specific?"

Gloria opened her mouth to speak, then seemed to think better of it and shook her head.

"Gloria? What aren't you telling me?"

"You don't want to pursue this. Nothing good will come of it."

"Gloria, if you don't tell me, I'll be forced to make inquiries elsewhere, and that might prove even more dangerous."

Gloria sighed. "You're not going to drop this, are you?"

"Not a chance."

"All right. I don't have much more, but I did find that the impression on the street is that most of the *Bratstvo*'s operations seem to be controlled from a single nightclub in Soho called Club *Pyatnitsa*. That apparently means Club Friday."

Gillian took a notepad from her purse and began to write. "Do you know the address?"

"It's in Berwick Street," Gloria said, "but don't even think of going there!"

CHAPTER THREE

Alex was still at work when Gillian reached home, but an anxious Cassie greeted her in the hallway, and Gillian's plans to phone Dugan and Anna were momentarily deferred.

"Did you tell him?" Cassie asked. "What did he say?"

Gillian considered her reply.

"Your father wasn't exactly thrilled about your relationship, but I suspect he'll come around eventually. I think we best give him time to come to terms with it."

"He's not going to do anything mean to Nigel, is he?" Cassie asked, then continued without waiting for an answer. "I knew I shouldn't have said anything. Papa will ruin everything!"

Gillian wrapped her arms around her stepdaughter and pulled her close. "Calm down, sweetheart. Your father isn't an ogre; he's just concerned about you, that's all. He'd do anything to keep you from being hurt."

"But Nigel would never hurt me, Mum. He's kind and wonderful! He doesn't care at all about… about a lot of things. Actually, he's a lot like Papa."

Gillian smiled. "Perhaps you should keep that observation to yourself for the moment. I'm not sure how your father would take it." She held Cassie at arm's length. "And where is young Nigel now, and what do you hear from him?"

"He was in Europe, and we've been emailing when he could get a connection. But his ship gets into Southampton late tonight, and I hope we'll be able to video chat via Skype. It's ever so much better when we can see each other," Cassie said.

"I'm sure. Hmm… Southampton. Perhaps it's time we renewed our acquaintance with young Mr. Havelock. I think we should invite him to dinner while his ship's in port."

Cassie looked terrified. "No! I mean, I don't know. He… he doesn't know I told you, so I don't know if he would want to come to dinner."

Gillian nodded. "I suspect facing your girlfriend's parents is intimidating enough. When the girl's father is also your employer, it would be more daunting still. That said, he's got to do it sooner or later, so there's no time like the present. I think I can give Mr. Havelock an assurance that I can keep your father on good behavior."

"Okay," Cassie said, doubt in her voice. "I just hope Nigel's not mad. I… I didn't tell him I was going to tell you about us."

Gillian hugged Cassie again. "I'm sure it will be fine, dear. Now off you go. Are you having dinner with us tonight?"

"If it's all right, Ingrid and I were meeting some friends for pizza."

"That's fine, but finish your schoolwork before you go, and let Mrs. Hogan know you won't be here for dinner."

"Thanks, Mum." Cassie returned Gillian's hug and flashed her a bright smile before rushing off to the kitchen.

Gillian watched her stepdaughter's retreating back, momentarily overwhelmed. She'd cared for Cassie almost since birth but had only become 'Mum' in the few years since she'd been married to Alex. At times when Cassie called her that, Gillian was almost overcome with emotion. She hoped for his own sake that Nigel Havelock was as wonderful as Cassie believed, because if he hurt the girl, Alex Kairouz would be the least of his worries.

Gillian composed herself and moved to the phone.

KAIROUZ RESIDENCE
LONDON, UK

Gillian arranged the meeting with a single phone call to the offices of Phoenix Shipping Ltd., where Alex Kairouz and Tom Dugan were equal partners and respectively the chairman of the board and the managing director. Dugan arranged to ride home from work with Alex and then called Anna at the MI5 offices in the nearby Thames House. She agreed to swing by their apartment and pick up the two Russians for a meeting at the

Kairouzes'. They were assembled around the dining room table within an hour of Gillian's call.

"That generally tracks what I learned from the Clubs and Vice Unit boys at the Met," Anna said, after Gillian had related what she'd learned from Gloria. "They mentioned this Club *Pyatnitsa*, though they didn't identify it as the nerve center. Either they don't know that or they were purposely a bit obtuse. They weren't particularly keen about me poking my nose into their playpen."

"Well, if they don't want us mucking about, did they present an alternative?" Alex asked. "Perhaps an offer to investigate themselves?"

Anna shook her head. "No, and I've no leverage. Clubs and Vice are a very specialized unit within the Metropolitan Police, and they normally have very little contact with MI5. No one owes me any favors there."

"Okay, I guess I need to go to this Club *Pyatnitsa* and see what I can find out," Dugan said.

"*Nyet, Dyed*," Borgdanov said. "I think it is better if Ilya and I go. As Gillian says, these are very dangerous people. I appreciate help with information, but Ilya and I should do this thing."

"Actually, Tom's right," Anna said. "No offense, but you two would stick out like sore thumbs. And it's unlikely that you'll just go in and spot Karina. A more likely scenario would be having to ask around discreetly."

"But most girls are Russian, and we speak Russian," Borgdanov reasoned.

"Which might do more harm than good," Anna said. "You told me yourself that some former *Spetsnaz* accept employment with the Russian mob, right? You lot may as well have 'military' tattooed on your foreheads. Don't you think it likely that if you show up and start asking questions, the girls will think you either work for their employer or a rival? Either way, they'll be reluctant to talk or at best will tell you what they think you want to hear."

Both the Russians nodded. "*Da*, I had not thought of this," Borgdanov admitted.

"Perhaps I should go," Alex said.

Dugan shook his head. "I think I'm a more convincing john, Alex. You're too obviously a local, and if you just show up out of the blue, the mob boys might get suspicious as to why they haven't seen you before. With my accent, I can come off as a horny middle-aged American, in town for business and looking for a good time."

"Accurate on several counts," Anna said with a smirk, "though I'll refrain from specifying just which ones."

Dugan shot her a dirty look while Alex and Gillian laughed and the Russians looked confused. As the laughter died, Ilya Denosovitch shook his head.

"I do not like it. Is my family, so I should take risks. These are very bad people, *Dyed*."

"I'm not keen on putting Tom in harm's way either," Anna said, "but we can work around that. We'll fit him with a wire so we can hear everything he says and you two"—she nodded towards the Russians—"can wait with me just outside the club. If he runs into trouble, you can go to his aid."

"*Da*," Borgdanov said as Ilya nodded. "This, I think, will work."

"When?" Dugan asked.

"I have to organize the wire and a van," Anna said, looking at her watch. "Obviously this will be an evening operation, and it's too late to get things going tonight. I'd say tomorrow evening."

BERWICK STREET, SOHO
LONDON, UK

Dugan looked out the window of the cab as it turned south onto Berwick Street. Soho had changed in the last decades, transforming from a seamy area of sex shops and adult entertainment to a district of theaters and an eclectic mix of upscale shops, restaurants, and offices. But here and there remnants of the sordid past remained, sex shops and adult entertainment venues scattered in the mix, now almost 'upscale' by association. It was no wonder the Russians had chosen this more prosperous location for Club *Pyatnitsa*, where the clientele was undoubtedly more prosperous. It was almost respectable.

Anna and the Russians were already in place in a van parked on a side street near the club, and Dugan was arriving by cab, a typical foreigner on the prowl in the big city. He saw the club just ahead, and the cabbie pulled to the curb.

"Here we are, guv," the cabbie said, looking at the meter. "That'll be sixteen quid."

Dugan passed the driver a twenty and waved away the change.

"Thanks, mate," the driver said as Dugan closed the door.

Dugan looked around and pulled his cell phone from his pocket. He held it to his ear as if he were talking to someone and then said, "I'm here. How do you copy?"

"I hear you fine, Tom," said Anna's voice in his ear. "But are you making a spectacle of yourself by standing on the street and talking to your invisible friend?"

"Sheesh, give me a little credit, will you. I'm talking into my cell phone."

He heard Anna's laugh in his ear. "Okay, Tarzan. Now that we've got our com check, you best lose the earbud before you go in. You remember the safe word?"

"No," Dugan said, "I've forgotten it completely in the thirty minutes since we last spoke. Of course I remember the safe word. It's *Stoli*."

"Good. Just don't forget and order vodka by mistake, or our two Russian friends will come crashing in to rescue you."

"I'll try to fend off senility long enough to remember that. I'm taking out the earbud now, so I don't have to listen to any more of this abuse." He cut off Anna's laughter as he discreetly plucked the small earbud from his right ear and pocketed it.

Dugan crossed the sidewalk towards the club, and as he approached, the doors opened and a large well-dressed man emerged, his arms around two attractive girls, one on each side. Pounding rock music blared from the door before it closed, and the man gave Dugan a drunken smile. "A wonderful place," he said in a thick German accent. "I've invited these two lovely ladies to dinner."

"Ah...well, good luck with that," Dugan replied.

"Ah, but that's the beauty of it," said the man, his smile broadening. "No luck required. Come, my lovelies, dinner awaits."

Dugan watched the trio lurch to the curb as the drunken German hailed a cab.

"Don't get your blood pressure medication mixed up with your Viagra, asshole," Dugan muttered under his breath.

He pushed through the door to be engulfed by music. Just inside, a man at a podium gave Dugan an appraising look. "Good evening, sir," he said, with the slightest trace of a Russian accent. "The cover charge is forty pounds, which includes two drinks. However I'm sure a prosperous-looking gent like yourself will want a stage-side table—only ten pounds extra."

Dugan nodded. "I always go top shelf," he said, pulling out a money clip prepared for his little excursion, holding a thick wad of fifty-pound notes. He peeled one off and passed it to the man.

The man nodded and pocketed the note. "I could tell you were a man of distinction." He motioned for Dugan to follow him.

The music was even louder in the club proper. A long, wide, horseshoe-shaped stage dominated the room, with brass poles at regular intervals, each occupied by a gyrating girl. All the dancers were nearly nude except for lingerie designed to highlight rather than conceal. The stage also served as the bar, and the barmaids behind it were equally scantily clad and attractive, smiling at the customers nonstop in hopes of receiving some of the notes that weren't being stuffed into the dancers' lingerie—or elsewhere.

Tiny tables crowded one side of the stage/bar, each with two chairs. The less affluent were seated at larger tables some distance back from the stage. Girls not onstage circulated through the crowded room, drinking and talking to customers. Occasionally a girl would take a customer by the hand and lead him to one of the booths that lined the back wall and then close the black velvet curtains behind them.

"Here you are, sir," the Russian shouted into Dugan's ear, motioning him to a small table. Dugan nodded and sat down just below an amazingly flexible girl as the man deposited two drink tickets on the small table and left.

He was staring up at the smiling girl and reevaluating his seating choice in light of his plan to remain low profile, when another girl sat down in the empty seat at his table. She looked to be somewhere between eighteen and twenty, with long dark hair pulled back in a ponytail that reached the middle of her back, and she was wearing the briefest of black bikinis. He felt a hand on his thigh as she leaned over, her smiling face only inches from his, her ample breasts barely contained by her halter.

"Hello, handsome," she cooed in accented English as she picked up the drink tickets. "Buy me a drink?"

"Ah. Sure," Dugan replied, and the girl held up the tickets and beckoned to another scantily clad girl nearby who was carrying a tray of assorted drinks.

Dugan's new companion took something in a champagne flute off the tray, and Dugan took a glass of what turned out to be lukewarm and watery beer.

The girl sipped the drink and then bent close again, her hand now on his inner thigh. "So tell me, handsome, what is your name? I am Tanya."

"I'm Tom."

The girl's smile widened. "Ah. You are American, I think. What brings you here, Tom?"

"Business." Dugan returned her smile. "And now pleasure."

"I know much about pleasure," Tanya said as she leaned closer still, slipping her hand between Dugan's legs to begin rubbing his crotch—with the inevitable result. "Would you like me to suck you?"

So much for small talk, thought Dugan, as he glanced around self-consciously to find no one was paying the slightest attention.

"Ah… here?"

The girl laughed. "Of course not. You must upgrade to a champagne booth." She nodded toward the curtained booths along the back wall. "Only fifty pounds for a bottle of fine champagne and a private drinking place." She smiled. "My tip we can discuss in booth."

"I'd like a little more privacy. I saw a guy leaving with a couple of girls when I came in. How about coming back to my hotel."

She shook her head. "*Nyet*. I am training. I cannot leave. But if you want more privacy, there are rooms in back but more expensive. One hundred pounds for thirty minutes. Room you must pay for before we go back."

Dugan nodded and reached into his pocket. He peeled two fifties off his roll and passed them to Tanya. She motioned him to keep his seat and moved to the front of the club, no doubt to give the money to the man at the podium, and returned a moment later with a key in hand. She led Dugan through a curtained doorway in the back wall and down a dimly lighted hallway with doors on either side. They stopped at the last door on the right, just short of an alarmed exit door, which Dugan presumed opened onto an alley.

"This hallway could use some more light," Dugan said, for the benefit of Anna in the van. "Does that door go outside into the alley? Maybe we could just slip out and go to my hotel."

"*Nyet*. I told you I cannot go out. And besides"—she smiled up at him —"you have already paid for room."

With that, she unlocked the door and led Dugan into an average-size and none-too-clean bedroom, with a door leading off it into an attached bath. She laid the key on a battered dresser and turned to Dugan, putting her arms around his neck and smiling up at him as she pressed her body against him.

"And now, Tom the American, we discuss what Tanya can do for you, *da*?"

Dugan gently disengaged the girl's arms before he stepped back and reached into his pocket. He pulled out his roll and peeled off a dozen bills and held them out.

He was surprised at the reaction. Tanya's eyes widened, and she looked apprehensive. Her body language telegraphed fear, and she took a half step back, her eyes on the money in his outstretched hand.

"Is a lot. Wh…what do you want me to do?"

"Nothing kinky. I just want some information."

The girl's face hardened.

"So you are police. I have nothing to tell you. Get out!"

"Take it easy. I'm not the police."

"Whoever you are, I don't want to talk to you. You must leave!"

"Okay, I'll leave." Dugan laid the money on the dresser and reached into his coat pocket. "But first just look at a picture and tell me if you recognize this girl."

Tanya turned her head, but Dugan moved the picture directly in front of her face so she had no choice but to look at it.

Blood drained from her face, but she shook her head.

"I have never seen her. I do not know her. Now get out!"

"You're getting awfully upset about a girl you don't know. C'mon, tell me what you know and the money's yours, and another five hundred along with it."

The girl looked about furtively, then lowered her voice and hissed at Dugan. "You are going to get us both killed, you fool! Take your money and go!"

***

In an office several doors away, Nazarov sat up straight at his desk, staring at the monitor. It was standard procedure to watch and listen when one of the girls took a john to the rooms. It was always much better to let the girls negotiate prices, because the johns were usually more generous if they thought the girl was getting the money. However, it was only good management to listen to the bargain and make sure the little bitches turned over all the money afterward. And besides, watching the sex was often amusing—he saved the funniest videos to watch again.

"Yuri," he said to a large man sitting on a nearby sofa perusing a girlie magazine, "Tanya is having some sort of problem with a john in room six. Bring him to me."

"*Da*," said the man as he stood up. He was at least six foot five and thick chested. Muscles bulged from the heavily veined arms protruding from the sleeves of his polo shirt, and he had all the telltales of steroid abuse. A tattoo on his neck peeked from beneath his shirt, barely concealed.

"Can I slap him around?"

Nazarov shrugged. "Just bring him here. Don't hurt him too bad unless he fights you, then do whatever is necessary."

Yuri nodded and started for the door.

"But don't kill him," Nazarov added. "He's up to something, and I need to know what."

CLUB *PYATNITSA*
LONDON, UK

There were heavy footfalls in the hall, and a surprised Dugan stepped back just as the door burst open to reveal a hulking Russian filling the doorway. Tanya fled to a far corner of the room and dropped to the floor, her arms wrapped above her head in a defensive position. Obviously she'd seen the man before. Dugan was rattled by the unexpected arrival, but tried to bluff it out.

"I paid for this room. Get the hell out!"

The Russian ignored Dugan and stepped into the room. "You must come with me." His English was heavily accented.

"I'm not going anywhere, pal," Dugan said as he took a step back, "unless it's back to the bar to get a shot of *Stoli*." He spoke the last sentence down at his chest, emphasizing *Stoli*.

"You come now." The Russian moved toward Dugan.

Dugan had circled around the bed now, to the opposite side, and the big Russian was at its foot, blocking the path to the door. Dugan wasn't a small guy himself, but there was no way he could stand toe to toe and trade punches with this guy. Where the hell were Borgdanov and Ilya?

"I sure could use some fucking *Stoli*!" he said again, almost shouting the last word.

The big Russian regarded him quizzically. "What is this talk of *Stoli*? Are you idiot? Now come before I hurt you." He punctuated the sentence by circling the bed, moving much faster than Dugan had thought possible.

Dugan leaped up on the bed, intent on crossing to the open door, but he felt the Russian's arms closing on his legs. Frantic, he turned in the man's grasp and hammered his right hand down hard on the top of the thug's bony skull, using the side of his fist to keep from breaking his knuckles. The Russian released Dugan and fell across the bed, and Dugan bolted.

But the Russian had other plans and managed to get a hand up, snagging a foot and pulling Dugan off balance. He fell off the bed and landed hard, flat on his back on the floor, the air rushing from his lungs. Then the Russian was towering above him with clenched fists—and an evil smile.

***

Anna sat in the driver's seat of the van and listened to Dugan's exchange through the speakers, privately amused at his imagined discomfort. The Russians were impassive and pointedly avoided Anna's gaze when the girl offered to perform oral sex on Dugan.

"He's letting us know he's on the move," she said, when Dugan mentioned the hallway lighting. "Sounds like he's near the rear exit. I'm going to pull around the corner to the entrance to the back alley, just in case."

The Russians nodded as she pulled the van away from the curve. Over the speakers, they heard Dugan cut to the chase and offer the girl money.

"A bit ham-handed," Ann muttered as she moved into light traffic. "He should have worked into that a bit more gradually."

She was pulling into a new parking place when through the speakers came the loud bang of the opening door, followed by Dugan's strange exchange with a male Russian.

"*Stoli*?...Bloody hell! He's in trouble," she said, tires squealing as she jack-rabbited from the curb and rocketed the fifty feet to the alley entrance. She slammed on the brakes and then threw the van in reverse and cut the wheel, rushing backwards down the narrow alley to come to a screeching stop near the rear entrance to the club. All three bolted from the van. Ilya reached the door first and tugged at the handle.

"Locked!" he said.

"Stand back." Anna drew her Glock from a belt holster and fired several rounds into the metal door by the lock.

Ilya jumped forward again and grabbed the handle with both hands. After a moment's resistance, the door opened with a metallic shriek followed immediately by the raucous clanging of an alarm.

Anna started in, but Borgdanov put a hand on her arm. "We will get *Dyed*. Better you have van ready to go immediately, so we waste no time."

She started to argue, thought better of it, and nodded. "Take this." She handed Borgdanov the Glock before rushing back to the driver's seat.

Borgdanov and Ilya rushed inside and found the open bedroom door only a few steps down the dimly lit hallway. Through the door they saw a big man crouched over Dugan, his fist drawn back as he prepared to land a blow.

"Stop!" Borgdanov yelled in Russian, and the big man's head snapped around just in time to receive a vicious front kick from Ilya that drove him over Dugan to land in a heap. Ilya was on the man in seconds, hammering his face with two more vicious haymakers.

"Enough, Ilya!" Borgdanov shouted in Russian. "He is finished. Help me get *Dyed* up."

Ilya turned back to see Borgdanov stuff the Glock in his belt and reach down to help Dugan. Dugan brushed off Borgdanov's hand and rose unsteadily on his own.

"I'm okay. I just got the wind knocked out of me."

"We must go!" Borgdanov said.

"Wait," Dugan said, looking at Tanya cowering in the corner. "She recognized the picture of Karina. She knows something. We have to question her."

Borgdanov stepped to the door and glanced down the long hallway. "There is no time, *Dyed*. I think we have company very soon."

Dugan looked from Borgdanov to the girl and back again, then motioned Ilya towards Tanya.

"Take her, and let's get out of here!" Dugan said, and Ilya rushed to the corner to scoop the girl up and flee the building on Dugan's and Borgdanov's heels.

They were nearly to the van before Tanya realized what was happening. She twisted in Ilya's arms and screamed curses in Russian as she struggled to escape. He clamped a hand across her mouth to silence her and got bitten for his efforts. At the van, Dugan waved the two Russians and their struggling captive through the cargo door and slid it shut behind them, then jumped into the front passenger seat.

"Go," Dugan said to Anna, as she looked back to see Borgdanov and Ilya struggling to restrain a half-naked girl who was fighting like a wildcat.

"Bloody hell!" Anna said.

"Go," Dugan repeated and was rewarded by the squeal of tires as Anna slammed the accelerator pedal to the floor.

KAIROUZ RESIDENCE
LONDON, UK

Anna paced the expensive oriental carpet and muttered under her breath, pausing occasionally to glare at Dugan and the two Russians seated on the sofa. Alex watched her from a chair across from the subdued trio.

"Bloody unbelievable," she said out loud at last, directing her ire at Dugan. "You've really topped yourself this time, Tom. How could you?"

"It seemed like a good idea at the time. Besides, we rescued her."

"Let's just recap, shall we. It's a 'rescue' when the person wants to come with you. When you take them against their will, it's called kidnapping. Do you see the difference?"

"She'll thank us when she understands," Dugan said.

"And how's that working out so far?"

"Anna, I know you're upset," Alex said, "and there's no doubt Thomas's action was impulsive, but what's done is done. And if anyone can reach the girl, it's Gillian."

"And what's the plan if Gillian can't 'reach' her? Do we drag her down to the basement and water-board her until she tells us what we want to know?"

"Please, Anna. Do not be angry at *Dyed*," Ilya said. "Is my fault. You are trying to help me, so problem is my responsibility, and I took the girl, not *Dyed*."

"After he told you to," Anna persisted.

"You're right," Dugan said. "I didn't think it through, but as Alex says, what's done is done. Let's just hope Gillian can get through to her. For sure she's not likely to trust any of us otherwise."

***

Gillian sat at the kitchen table across from Tanya. The girl still wore the scanty black bikini, but it was covered by an old bathrobe Gillian had scrounged from Cassie's closet. Tanya was trembling but no longer crying—her eye makeup ran in dark streaks down her cheeks. She stared down in silence at her hands folded on the table in front of her. She hadn't said a word since Gillian had shooed the others from the room and sat down with the girl, thirty minutes earlier.

"Would you like something to eat, dear, or a nice cup of tea?" Gillian asked.

Tanya shook her head, eyes downcast.

Gillian let the silence drag on a few minutes more and then reached across the table and took the girl's hand, holding it tight when she tried to pull it away.

"I know what you're going through," Gillian said softly.

Tanya's head flew up, and there was fire in her eyes. "You know nothing. You are fine lady in big house, probably with many servants. You go where you want and do what you want. You think world is safe and beautiful place and bad things only happen on TV. You think you can fix everything with 'nice cup of tea,' *da*? Well, you know nothing of MY life, fine English lady, so please, do not tell me you know ANYTHING."

She tried to pull her hand away again, but Gillian held on, gently but firmly. Finally Tanya gave up and resumed staring down at the table. Gillian said nothing for a long while and then began to speak, her voice low and gentle, completely at odds with the raw story behind the words.

"My mother was a drug addict and street prostitute, and my father was her pimp. She delivered me in a charity hospital after my 'dad' attempted to induce a late-term abortion by means of a savage beating." Gillian paused. "But I survived, so I guess you could say I was tough from the start."

Tanya raised her head, shocked.

"I never knew my mother," Gillian continued, "as she died a short time later from a drug overdose. I suppose I was born addicted, but no one would waste drugs on an infant, so fortunately I have no memories of that first withdrawal. I was passed around among the other girls of my father's stable, but my memories of that time are fairly dim." Gillian shuddered and seemed to steel herself before she continued.

"I do remember my eighth birthday, when my father told me we were going to have a party with a new friend. He stripped me naked and tied me to a dirty mattress, then proceeded to sell my virginity to a fat old man with rotten teeth and stinking breath." She paused, as if bracing herself to continue. "He bragged to me later that he made five hundred pounds off the transaction, and he bought me a bag of Jelly Babies as a reward. I've hated the vile things to this day.

"It got worse after that, as impossible as that may seem. There were many pedophiles, and dear old Dad made good money. When I got too old, he put me on the street. By that time I'd begun using drugs like the rest of the girls, just to escape the horrid reality of our lives. When the drugs and the life had ravaged me to the point I wasn't producing much income as a whore, he turned me to selling drugs on the street. In time, I was arrested. He visited me in jail just once to warn me to keep my mouth shut, then left without bothering to bail me out. I was sentenced to five years."

"You went to prison?"

Gillian nodded. "The best thing that could have happened to me. I got free of the drugs, healthy for the first time in my life, and a bit of education. I was terrified when I was released after serving my sentence, but I got a job as a waitress, and everything was looking up. Then he showed up again."

"Your father? What did you do?"

Gillian lowered her head for a moment to compose herself. When she faced Tanya again, the gentleness was gone, and there was steel in her eyes.

"I buried a kitchen knife in the bastard's black heart."

"Bu-but did you not go back to prison?"

Gillian smiled at her and spoke, her voice gentle again. "That's a rather long story for another time perhaps. But first I must know, do you believe me?"

Tanya reflected a moment and then nodded slowly. "*Da.*"

"Good. Then you should know that most of the people who helped me find this new and wonderful life are sitting in the next room. I trust them with my life, and you can as well. And if you will trust us all, we may be able to give you your own life back."

Gillian could almost feel Tanya's emotional turmoil as fear and disbelief contorted the girl's features, chased by a flicker of something else—hope. And she watched as hope emerged victorious and Tanya's chin began to quiver. Fresh tears wet the makeup stains on her face, and Gillian rose from her chair and rounded the table to pull Tanya upright and into her tight embrace. The girl's body shuddered with silent racking sobs as she clung to Gillian, and the older woman held her close and whispered reassurance that her nightmare might soon be over.

CHAPTER FOUR

KAIROUZ RESIDENCE
LONDON, UK

Tanya sat on the sofa beside Gillian, the robe wrapped tightly around her. The others surrounded them in the seating area of the comfortable living room. The girl was calmer now, but still clung to Gillian's hand. She'd hardly let go of the older woman since they'd come into the room, and every few moments she glanced over as if assuring herself that Gillian was still there. It had been quietly decided that Anna would do the questioning, given Tanya's recent experience with men.

"What can you tell us about Karina?" Anna asked gently. "Does she work at the club?"

Tanya shook her head. "I… I cannot speak. If they find out, they will hurt my family in Russia." She shuddered. "These are very bad men with powerful friends."

"Only if they know," Anna said, "and right now they think you were taken against your will. The room was obviously under surveillance, and the video will show you fighting Ilya. There will be no point in them harming your family."

The girl reflected a moment and slowly nodded.

"So please," Anna said, "tell us about Karina."

Tanya hesitated, then looked at Gillian, who gave a reassuring nod.

"I… I will try to help, but I do not know much."

"Good," Anna said. "Now, how do you know Karina? Does she work at the club?"

Tanya shook her head. "Not yet, but soon, I think. I met her at the boss's apartment."

"How long ago?" Anna asked.

"Three days," Tanya replied.

"Who is this man? What is his name? Where is apartment?" Ilya demanded.

Tanya flinched, earning Ilya a glare from Anna.

Gillian put a protective arm around Tanya's shoulders. "Gently, Sergeant, gently," she said to the big Russian.

Ilya nodded. "Forgive me, little Tanya. I did not mean to frighten you, but we are so close, and I must find my Karina."

Tanya relaxed and nodded. "He calls himself Sergei, but I don't know if that is true name. I know only that the others call him Boss. And I do not know where apartment is." She lowered her head. "I am in training. Not trusted to go outside yet. When they move us, we are in closed van or blindfolded, so we have no idea where we are. Until they put me in the club, I did not even know I was in London. This I learn from customers in club."

"Is the apartment where they hold all the girls?" Anna asked.

Tanya shook her head. "*Nyet*, not all. When we arrive, we go in place like warehouse. Is big room, but they put us each in small... small... I do not know English word. In Russian is *kletka*."

The others looked at Borgdanov. His face was a study in suppressed anger. "Cage," he translated between clenched teeth.

"*Da*, cage. But small, like for dog. They tell us we are all bitches, and we live naked in cages until we are properly trained."

No one spoke. "Bastards," muttered Alex after a long moment, but words failed the others, for no words could convey their building rage.

Anna recovered first. "So how did you end up in the apartment with Karina?"

"Each time there are new girls, Boss comes to look. They line girls up naked, and Boss picks one he likes to have for a while. He chose me, so they blindfold me and take me to his apartment. There I meet Veronika, who was Boss's choice from last group. Veronika told me she was there for ten days and told me before her there was Zoya. Zoya taught Veronika all the special sex things Boss likes, then she went back to club because Boss was bored with her. Veronika's job was to teach me all the things Boss likes then she goes back to club." Tanya hung her head and continued, her voice barely above a whisper. "Was my job to teach what Boss likes to Karina. But Karina was very... very..." She looked at Borgdanov. "I don't know English...*upornaya*."

"Stubborn," Borgdanov said.

"*Da*, stubborn. We must have sex together with boss, but Karina would not do some of the things Boss likes. Then she spit on him and called him pig." She lowered her head and shuddered. "It was very bad."

Gillian pulled the girl close and stroked her hair.

"Did he punish her?" Anna asked.

Tanya shook her head. "Not her. Me. And not the Boss. He does not get hands dirty. He just smiled and said, 'Why, Karina, you are being very unpleasant,' and then he leaves room. Three men come in and take us to kitchen. Then they… they…" She squeezed her eyes shut and shook her head again, pressing herself into Gillian.

"I think this is quite enough," Gillian said. "Let her rest."

"NO!" Tanya said, straightening in Gillian's embrace and looking the older woman in the eye. "You were strong. I will be strong. Like you,… and like Karina."

Tanya let go of Gillian and took a sip of tea from a cup on the coffee table in front of her. But she was still trembling, and the cup rattled on the saucer when she set it down.

"They do nothing to leave marks, because customers do not like to see bruises. But they shocked me with *elektricheskiy* wires here"—she motioned to her breasts—"and… and… between my legs. Then they held me down and put towel on my face and poured water on it until I cannot breathe and pass out. Then they wake me up and do again, many times."

"But why torture you to punish Karina?" Dugan asked.

"I think because they know she is very *upornaya*…stubborn, and will endure much herself. But they know also her heart is good, and to be the cause of pain to others is maybe worse for her than to take the pain herself. So while they do all these things to me, they make her watch and tell her to watch well, because this will soon happen to her sisters." Tanya paused and hung her head. "And the next day, Karina does everything the boss wants."

Ilya Denosovitch bolted upright and moved to the far side of the room, turning his face from the others. They watched his back in stunned silence as he clenched and unclenched his fists, struggling to control himself. When he turned, a single tear ran down his cheek, but his face was otherwise composed. His voice was full of quiet menace.

"When I catch these fuckers, they will beg for death."

Borgdanov rose and walked over to Denosovitch. He put his hands on his friend's shoulders and looked him in the eye. "*Da, tovarishch*. But you must not be greedy. There are enough of them for both of us, I think."

"Unfortunately, I think there are many more than enough," Anna said, "and they're now alerted to the fact that someone is watching them. We have to consider their probable reaction."

"Seems to me we still have the advantage," Dugan said. "They know some strange men abducted one of their girls, but they won't really know why. And even if they have me on the video asking about Karina, I never used her name, so there won't be any connec…"

Dugan trailed off mid-sentence to reach into his coat pocket. He blanched.

"What is it, Tom?" Anna asked.

"Karina's picture. I had it in my hand when the goon burst in the door. I thought I'd slipped it back into my pocket, but I must have dropped it."

ARSOV'S APARTMENT
LONDON, UK

Sergei Arsov stared at the picture, then tossed it on the coffee table in front of him.

"It's Karina. No doubt there. Now why do you suppose an American and two Russian military types are interested in our little Karina? And why would anyone be stupid enough to steal one of our girls?"

Across from him, Nazarov shrugged. "I don't know, Boss. Maybe someone is trying to move in on us. We are not the only organization."

Arsov shook his head. "I don't think any of our competitors would use an American, especially not an amateur like this fellow. The Russians are a different story. From the way the one held the gun and the way the other took care of Yuri, I think they are ex-*Spetsnaz* for sure." His face clouded. "Of course, if you hadn't let them waltz out of our club with the girl, we could question them directly."

"I… I had no choice. It happened very fast, and Yuri was the only one in the office with me. I called the boys from the front, but by the time they got back it was too late."

"And I don't suppose it ever occurred to you to defend our property? You were armed, were you not?" Arsov asked.

"Yes, but there were three of them and…"

"One of whom was lying on the floor, and the other two with apparently one gun between them. Hardly a formidable force, Nazarov."

Nazarov opened his mouth to protest further, but Arsov cut him off.

"Enough. Excuses get us nowhere. We must decide what to do about this."

"What if Tanya talks?" Nazarov asked.

Arsov shrugged. "To who will she talk? The men who took her are obviously not police, and even if they take her to the police, what can she say? The sex trade is not illegal in the UK. She is over eighteen, and we have a video tape of her describing how she loves being a whore and all the money she makes, and she hardly looks unwilling in the porn we shot. Her training is not complete, but I believe she understands what will happen to her family if she betrays us, but even if she does, it is her word against ours, and we have very good lawyers."

Nazarov nodded.

"No," Arsov said, "I'm not worried about the police. I want to find out about these stupid assholes who took our property. Go back to the club and check the security tapes again to try to figure out as much as you can about this American. Be sure to check the tapes for the street in front of the club, and see if you can determine how he arrived. If it was by car, perhaps we can get a license plate number and backtrack that."

Nazarov nodded but didn't move.

"Don't just sit there. Get moving."

"We have another problem," Nazarov said.

Arsov sighed—nothing but problems with this bastard. He silently vowed to bring Beria to London at the first opportunity.

"What is it now, Nazarov?"

"Our man in the US contacted me. His mole in ICE informed him that the US authorities know about the drug shipment on the *Igor Varaksin*. They plan to raid the vessel when she docks in Savannah."

Arsov glared. "Which means you may have a mole here as well."

"Not necessarily. The leak could have come from St. Petersburg. I cannot be held responsible for areas beyond my control."

Arsov just stared at his subordinate. Nazarov finally broke the uncomfortable silence.

"Wh… what do you want me to do?"

"What can we do? We have no choice but to jettison the container, and I assure you our superiors in St. Petersburg will not be pleased."

Nazarov rose. "I will notify the captain," he said and moved toward the door. Halfway there he turned back to Arsov.

"What about the security video?" He pointed to the open laptop on the coffee table.

"Leave that with me," Arsov said. "I'll share it with little Karina and see if she knows any of these men so eager to find her."

* * *

Arsov motioned Karina to the couch and patted the seat beside him.

"What is it?" Karina asked as she sat down beside him. There was a laptop open on the coffee table in front of them.

"I have a little video I'd like to watch, my dear." He reached over and clicked the mouse.

A poor-quality video appeared, showing Tanya in a room with an American. The American was trying to get her to look at something, but Tanya was resisting. Suddenly things began to move very fast, and Yuri burst into the room, and then two other large men and—Uncle Ilya! Karina gasped, and her hand flew to her mouth as she watched the remaining seconds before the screen blanked.

"Obviously you recognize one of our countrymen. Please tell me who he is and why these three men are looking for you."

"No, I was just startled and afraid they would hurt poor Tanya. Why do you suppose they took her? Did you get her back?"

Arsov smiled. This was a smart one, trying to deflect his question with a discussion of Tanya. He almost regretted what he had to do. Almost. He shrugged.

"I know you will never tell me voluntarily, and I admire you for it. But your obstinacy does become tedious at times."

At the snap of Arsov's fingers, two large men appeared in the doorway.

"Water-board her until she talks. Do it in the guest bathroom and try not to make too much of a mess this time."

CONTAINER SHIP IGOR VARAKSIN
EN ROUTE TO SAVANNAH, GEORGIA

The captain stood on the starboard bridge wing, peering out over the wind dodger at the sea ahead. The blue skies and moderate swells were hardly the weather associated with losing a container at sea, and he worried how he'd explain the loss when the authorities boarded in Savannah—a story of a 'rogue wave' perhaps?

The other officers would be no problem, of course. Like him, they were in on the plan. But he'd have to spread a great deal of money around to buy the unlicensed crew's silence and rehearse them thoroughly. Even then, he doubted he'd fool the authorities, but neither would there be proof to the contrary. He allowed himself a grim smile—innocent until proven guilty—a wonderful concept for those in his current profession.

None of the officers were smugglers by choice, and all had resisted initially, but when the third officer and his entire family were brutally murdered in St. Petersburg, the message was clear—cooperate or else. The captain sighed. They were all just unfortunate enough to be in the wrong place at the wrong time. The wrong place was a ship trading regularly into Savannah, Georgia, and the wrong time was when the *Bratstvo* was in need of 'mules' to bring their drugs into the lucrative US market. Savannah had been a natural choice—a smaller port with less enforcement presence than the much busier ports of the Northeast, and none of the extensive US Navy presence of Norfolk or Charleston. For even though the Cold War was long ended, Russian merchant vessels near US Navy facilities still received more than their fair share of scrutiny.

It had begun five long years ago, and accommodating the odd 'special cargo' was now routine, their consciences salved somewhat by large cash bonuses delivered personally to their homes by very dangerous-looking men—the very act of payment a tacit reminder of both the carrot and the stick. At least things had been routine, until this morning. The voice on the sat phone was emphatic, the container must be jettisoned, and the captain had set the long-planned but never executed operation in motion.

As usual, the 'special cargo' was in a twenty-foot container in the outermost top tier on the starboard side, near the flare of the bow—a spot chosen with care, where the containers were secured with twist locks and not tie rods. He watched as the first officer directed sailors releasing the twist locks and the chief engineer directed the placement of tough but thin rubber air bladders into the narrow space between the 'special cargo' container and the box below it. All the bladders were positioned on the inboard side of the container, so that when inflated, they would tip the container outboard, toward the side of the vessel.

The men finished their tasks and began to scramble out of harm's way, just as the radio on the captain's belt squawked.

"First officer to bridge."

"*Da*. This is bridge. Go ahead," the captain said.

"We are finished, and all men are clear."

"Good! *Spasibo*, Mr. Ivanov. Chief, do you copy?" the captain asked into the radio.

"*Da*, Captain. I am here," the chief engineer replied.

"Very well," the captain said. "Begin inflating."

He was answered by the hiss of air rushing through hoses, followed shortly thereafter by the distant sound of an air compressor cycling on. He watched in silence as the inside edge of the 'special cargo' container rose slowly into the air and the container tipped outward toward the starboard side. After a long ten minutes, progress stopped with the container at an odd angle. The captain keyed the mike on his radio.

"Chief, do you copy? What is the problem?"

"The bags will only lift seven hundred and fifty millimeters, Captain. I think we have hit the limit, and it is not enough to tip the container over. I can shore the container up with wood and reposition the bladders, but it will take some time."

The captain thought a moment and looked out at the sea around the ship.

"Let me try something first," the captain said into the radio as he moved into the wheelhouse. "It may take a moment. Make sure everyone stays well clear of the container."

"Understood," the chief replied.

"Put steering on hand," the captain ordered the helmsman, then glanced once again at the sea. A southerly wind was generating a moderate swell, striking the ship almost broad on the port beam, inducing a slight but gentle roll.

"Steering is on hand, Captain," the helmsman said.

"Very well. Five degrees right rudder," the captain said, and the helmsman confirmed the order and turned the wheel.

The captain moved to the wide windows at the front of the bridge and watched the sea with a practiced eye as the ship's bow swung northwest, and the swell began to strike the ship from astern and at an angle.

"Steady as she goes."

The helmsman repeated the captain's order and steadied the ship on her new course.

The captain nodded to himself at the anticipated effect as the ship began an increasingly violent corkscrew motion in the quartering seas, dipping further to starboard with each successive roll. On the fifth or sixth roll, the 'special container' reached the tipping point and rolled off the stack into the sea with a spectacular splash. He heard a cheer from the men assembled forward and allowed himself a small smile.

"Well done, Captain," said the chief over the radio.

"Come left to new course of two four zero," the captain said, waiting for the helmsman to confirm the order before moving back out on the starboard bridge wing to gaze over the side. In the ship's wake, the container was already sinking as it filled with water through holes pre-drilled near the bottom of the container for that very purpose. He lifted his own radio.

"And well done to you, gentlemen. Now, Chief, please take a sledgehammer to some spare twist locks so we have some evidence of the 'violent rogue wave' we encountered to present the authorities in Savannah."

The chief engineer acknowledged the order and the captain sighed. Now to craft some fairy tale for the logbook.

CHAPTER FIVE

"Sergei Arsov," Anna said, turning her laptop on the coffee table so the others could see the picture. "A lot of Russian nationals named 'Sergei' have entered the UK in the last year, but when we bumped the list against those with long stay or resident visas and with Tanya's description, the list got a lot shorter. This is our man; Tanya positively IDed him based on the photo."

"What else do you have on him?" Dugan asked.

Anna shook her head. "Not much. He entered the country with Indefinite Leave to Remain status, arranged very quickly, I might add. It looks like he has competent legal counsel or friends in high places. He listed his occupation as 'management consultant—self-employed.' He had to list a UK place of residence as part of the application, but that's a dead end. It's his solicitor's office. However, we'll find him now; it's just a matter of time."

"But time is what we do not have," Ilya said, rising to pace. "Already we have lost a day, and this Arsov now knows someone looks for Karina, so she is in more danger, I think. We must find this apartment and go there at once to save her."

"That might make things worse," Anna said. "The man's not stupid. I think we can assume he's already moved her somewhere. We know he's connected to Club *Pyatnitsa*, so we'll stake out the club until he shows up and then keep him under surveillance on the hope he leads us to Karina."

"I agree with Ilya," Borgdanov said. "I am not such big supporter of 'hope,' and we do not have time for this surveillance. If we catch this bastard, we will question him at once and make him tell us where he is keeping Karina. And HE can 'hope' we kill him quickly."

Anna stiffened. "Gentlemen, I'm prepared to do everything in my power to help you rescue Karina and turn this man over to the proper authorities. I understand and share your rage, and I've ignored your previous comments about killing this man, but I can't be a party to a murder, however justified."

Borgdanov glared. "And what will your authorities do to this bastard? You have already said that he has very smart lawyers, *da*? I think your authorities do nothing, just like in Russia."

Ilya muttered something in Russian, obviously in support of Borgdanov; then the room grew quiet, the tension palpable. Dugan moved to defuse it.

"Calm down, Andrei. Anna's sticking her neck way out here, and if this turns into a vigilante action, she could be in serious trouble."

Borgdanov glanced at Ilya, then turned back to Anna. "We had not thought of that, and we appreciate what you are doing. I promise we will not kill this bastard in the UK; beyond that I promise nothing."

Anna returned Borgdanov's gaze for a long moment before speaking. "We'll discuss that when the time comes. For the moment, let's concentrate on finding the elusive Mr. Arsov, shall we? Do I at least have your agreement that you won't rush in and beat him to a bloody pulp the moment we find him?"

Borgdanov looked at Ilya, who nodded.

"*Da*," Borgdanov said. "To this we will agree."

"It's settled then," Dugan turned to Gillian. "By the way, where is Tanya? I'm surprised she let you out of her sight."

Gillian smiled. "She's up in Cassie's room. Those two bonded immediately, and they're about the same size. Cassie is finding her something to wear."

In the chair beside Gillian, Alex stirred. "Do you think that's wise, my dear?"

"Well, I thought it preferable to having the poor girl run around half naked."

Alex scowled. "You know that's not what I meant. I just don't think Cassie should... should... associate too closely with this girl. One never knows... I mean..."

"Yes, I know exactly what you mean, Alex Kairouz!" Gillian's eyes flashed. "And you should bloody well be ashamed of yourself! Tanya is a victim, and I'll not have her treated like a leper because of what she was forced to do to survive and protect her family."

"I'm not suggesting she be treated like a leper, only that Cassie is innocent—still practically a child, for God's sake! I don't think she should be exposed to all this."

Gillian softened and leaned forward to lay her hand on Alex's cheek and look into his eyes. "The world is a dangerous place, Alex, and no one knows that better than I. I also knew from the beginning that Cassie could never protect herself from dangers she didn't understand, so I've taught her about 'all this,' as you call it, since puberty. She knows and understands what Tanya has endured, and wants to help her. I'm tremendously proud of our daughter, and you should be as well."

"Well, you could have told me."

Gillian smiled sweetly. "Yes, dear, but you would have objected, and I would have done it anyway, and we would likely have had a terrible and continuous argument. Isn't this much better?"

***

Tanya stood with Cassie in the walk-in closet and marveled at the racks of clothes.

"So many beautiful clothes. Is like Christmas. I do not know what to choose."

"You can have anything you like," Cassie said. "Mum said you can stay in the guest bedroom. Pick out what you want, and we'll move it in there. Except for underwear. I have some new stuff I haven't worn though so I'll give you that." Cassie made a face. "Wearing someone else's underwear is gross."

Tanya laughed. "I like you, Cassie. You make me laugh, and I have not laughed in very long time."

Cassie hugged her. "I like you too, and I'm glad you're staying with us. Mum says you can stay as long as you like."

They picked out a few outfits, and Tanya carried them to Cassie's bed. As she laid them down, Tanya noticed several pictures of a beautiful woman on Cassie's dresser. She had honey-blond hair and a peaches-and-cream complexion—she was the spitting image of Cassie.

"Who is this?"

"That's my birth mum. Her name was Kathleen, and she died when I was just a baby. But Mum Gillian told me all about her, and she gave me those pictures so I would never forget her. I think she loved my birth mum a lot."

"So Gillian is not your real mother?"

Cassie shook her head. "She was my nanny. My mum and dad hired her when I was a baby after I got real sick with a high fever. Then my mum got cancer and died, and Gillian stayed and took care of me and Dad. Then they fell in love and got married."

"Is like fairy tale." Tanya spied another picture at the back of the dresser.

"And so who is this handsome fellow that has you smiling so wide?" she asked, lifting a small photo of a beaming Cassie and a young man in uniform, obviously taken on a ship.

Cassie blushed. "That's Nigel. That was taken on his ship in Korea."

"So, your boyfriend is sailor man. Very nice!"

"He's not really my boyfriend," Cassie said, eyes downcast. "We only met in person one time. Mostly we text and email and video chat." She perked up. "But his ship got in to Southampton yesterday, and Mum is going to invite him to dinner."

"Trust me." Tanya looked at the picture. "I can tell by the way he is looking at you that he is your boyfriend."

"I really hope so. Do you have a boyfriend?"

Tanya looked away, tears welling up in her eyes.

"Oh, I'm sorry. That was really dumb! Please don't cry. I didn't mean to make you sad. I meant... you know... before. Oh, that's wrong too!"

Tanya turned back to face Cassie and wiped her eyes with the back of her hand. Then she put both her hands on Cassie's arms to calm her.

"Is okay, Cassie. Is just difficult to think of these things sometimes. And yes, I had boyfriend in St. Petersburg. His name is Ivan. He is very quiet but very nice. And very, very smart. He is computer programmer. We were going to marry."

"That's great!" Cassie got excited. "Maybe we can call him and let him know you're okay. Do you have his number?"

Tanya shook her head. "I think is dangerous for him if I call him now. And besides, I am not so sure that... after what has happened..." Tanya paused, once more on the verge of tears. "Maybe he doesn't feel the same way about me anymore."

Cassie looked perplexed. "What? Why?" she asked, then realization dawned. "You mean because of what you were forced to do? But that wasn't YOUR fault."

Tanya hung her head, her voice barely audible. "Perhaps his head will tell him this, but his heart may say something different. I am no longer the same person. Even I feel shamed and dirty. How can he feel any different?"

Cassie's temper flared. "That's terrible! If he stops loving you because of what someone else forced you to do, he's just a... just a..." Cassie groped for words. "Just a no-good wanker!"

Tanya looked up, shocked by Cassie's reaction, and her new friend's righteous indignation was so complete it struck Tanya as amusing. The corners of her mouth turned up in a smile, and though tears still ran down her cheeks, she burst out laughing and folded Cassie in a tight hug.

"I think you and I will become great friends," Tanya said, through the laughter and the tears.

CLUB PYATNITSA
LONDON, UK

"You're sure it's him?" Arsov asked.

Nazarov smiled. "Not just him. Them." He pulled a stack of photos out of his jacket pocket and tossed them on the desk.

"I found the cab," Nazarov said, "and the cabbie remembered the fare. He picked the guy up at a fancy house over near Kensington Square. I had Anatoli stake the place out, and he took those last night."

Arsov looked through the pictures. He recognized the American and both of the Russians. One photo showed the American exiting a large house in the company of a striking redhead. "Hmm. Kensington Square. That says money. Just who is this American?"

Nazavov's smile widened. "The Internet is a wonderful thing. His name is Thomas Dugan, and he is managing director of Phoenix Shipping Limited. The house belongs to an Alexander Kairouz, who is chairman of the board of the same company."

Arsov glanced back at the photo. "And the redhead?"

"Her name is Anna Walsh. She's this Dugan's live-in girlfriend. Other than that, I can find nothing on her, but we're still looking."

"And you saw no sign of Tanya?"

"Not so far. I slipped the doorman at this Dugan's flat a bribe, and according to him, he's seen no one resembling Tanya, so I think she must be at the Kairouz house. Anyway, we're covering Kairouz, Dugan, and the Russians around the clock. The Russians seem to be staying at Dugan's flat. Someone will lead us to Tanya sooner or later."

"You better make sure it's sooner," Arsov said. "We damn near had to kill Karina to get her to identify the *Spetsnaz* and admit the big blond fellow was her uncle, and I don't like unnecessary wear and tear on the merchandise. It's not good for business. We need to put an end to this."

"I don't understand why you just don't make a call to St. Petersburg. If they put pressure on the girl's family, this bastard Denosovitch and his old boss Borgdanov will get the message and back off. That's always worked before."

"Because, Nazarov, I am not eager to give our superiors in St. Petersburg the impression that we cannot handle one troublesome whore and her loving uncle. Must I remind you that our competence is already in question because of the loss of the drug shipment to Savannah?"

Nazarov bristled. "I told you, that was not our fault."

"And as I explained to you, it doesn't fucking matter. The leak was either here, in the US, or in St. Petersburg. We're responsible for the UK and the US, and do you really think our superiors in St. Petersburg will easily accept that the problem is on THEIR end? Perhaps I should send you to St. Petersburg so you can explain your theory to them in person, *da?*"

"I… I had not thought of that."

"Yes, well thinking does not seem to be a skill you've completely mastered." Arsov glanced at his watch. "It's almost noon. I want you to concentrate on finding Tanya, and then we'll take care of our *Spetsnaz* friends. They are the real threat. This American clown is just someone who is trying to help them. He will fade away without the Russians in the picture. I want you to locate Tanya by six o'clock. Use as many men as necessary, but get it done. Is that clear?"

Nazarov nodded and rose from his chair.

"Oh, and one other thing. Move Karina back to the holding warehouse, just to be on the safe side. I'm bored with the little bitch anyway. She's more trouble than she's worth."

NEAR KAIROUZ RESIDENCE
LONDON, UK

Nazarov slumped in the driver's seat of the car and took a sip of the cold, bitter coffee. He grimaced and set it back in the cup holder before glancing at his watch. He hated this surveillance and ordinarily would have delegated the task, but given Arsov's current mood, he couldn't afford a screw up. He'd decided to watch the Kairouz place himself. He had a man watching the back entrance as well, where the driveway led from a large garage on to a side street. So far, all they'd observed was Kairouz leaving for work, with his driver, and the arrival of a fat woman he assumed was a servant of some sort.

He had Yuri positioned outside Dugan's flat and Anatoli watching the Phoenix shipping offices, each with one man to help, but neither of the other two teams had reported anything of note. Bored, he dialed his cell phone.

"Yuri," he said when his man answered, "any activity there?"

"*Nyet*," Yuri replied. "The American and red-haired woman left earlier, and there was some activity as other people in building left for work. No sign of the *Spetsnaz*. I think they are still inside. Since then only minor foot traffic in and out of building, and one telephone repair truck goes into underground garage." Yuri paused. "We have been here long time. I am very sleepy and sick of pissing in bottle. When do we get relief?"

"You will get relieved when I say!" Nazarov snapped. "And I am pissing in bottle too, so quit whining. Call me if you see anything suspicious, and you better stay alert if you know what's good for you. Understand!"

Nazarov listened to the sullen "*da*," then hung up and called Anatoli.

"Anything new?"

"*Nyet*," Anatoli said. "Kairouz arrived, and his driver dropped him in front of building and then went into underground garage. The American and the woman arrived by taxi. She went into building with him and has not come out, so I think she must work here also. Everything else seems normal. Many people coming to work; no one leaving except some deliveries coming and going and one repair truck."

Nazarov sat up in his seat. "What kind of repair truck?"

"I'm not sure. Was a white van with design on the side. British Telecom, I think. Why?"

"Did it stay on the street? Can you still see it?"

"*Nyet*. It went into underground car park and left a few minutes later. Why? You think is problem?"

"I'm not sure," Nazarov said, "but stay alert, and call me if you notice anything at all."

Anatoli acknowledged the instruction, and Nazarov hung up and called Yuri back.

"Yuri, what did the telephone repair truck look like?"

"It was a white van," Yuri replied.

"Is it still there?"

"*Nyet*. It stayed only a few minutes and then left."

"Shit!" Nazarov hung up.

He tried to compose his thoughts. Something was up for sure. Having a telephone repair truck visit two of the locations they were staking out was just too much of a coincidence. Should he notify Arsov, or should he try to find out more first? He sat struggling with the decision when his phone chirped. The caller ID displayed the number of his man at the back entrance to the Kairouz house.

"What?"

"I spotted Tanya through the kitchen window," the man said.

"You're sure?"

"Absolutely. I had the binoculars on the window, watching the fat woman. Another woman came into the kitchen, Kairouz's wife I think from the way she was dressed. They were talking, but when they moved, I could see across the room, and I saw Tanya. I am sure."

"Did she look like she was a prisoner?"

"Not unless prisoners laugh and smile a lot."

"Okay, keep a close watch. I'll get back to you." Nazarov disconnected and dialed Arsov.

CHAPTER SIX

BERWICK STREET, SOHO
NEAR CLUB PYATNITSA
LONDON, UK

Anna watched from the back of the vehicle as Harry Albright, uniformed as a repairman, drove the British Telecom van slowly down Berwick Street and pulled to the curb near a utility manhole. He got out and quickly arranged a bright yellow plastic barricade in front of the manhole, stabbed a curved metal hook into a small opening in the heavy steel cover to drag it to one side, and placed a large 'Men at Work' sign in front of the barricade. He surveyed his work briefly and climbed into the back of the van.

"All set," he said to Anna Walsh.

"Thanks, Harry," Anna said. "And thanks again for doing this. I'd stand out as a repair person, and that lot in the club have all seen Tom and the others. We really appreciate the help." Beside her, Dugan and the Russians nodded in agreement.

"Glad to do it, Anna. But my chum in transport can only juggle things so long. The van is supposed to be in the shop for servicing."

Anna shrugged. "We can only use it for a while anyway. A BT van is a bit conspicuous for long-term surveillance. Hopefully we'll spot Arsov quickly and put a tail on him. Is Lou ready?"

"Parked around the corner in the chase car," Harry said, "ready to pick up the trail if Arsov starts moving."

"Brilliant." Anna's smile faded as she studied Harry's face.

"What is it, Harry? You look troubled."

"Nothing really, but are you sure you aren't attracting some attention of your own?"

"Why?"

"It's probably not related," Harry said, "but I did see a couple of blokes sitting in a parked car before I turned into the parking garage for your apartment."

"Did they seem overly interested in the building, or you?"

Harry shook his head. "Neither that I could tell, which is why I didn't mention it earlier. Nor did they look particularly observant, but I only got a quick look at them as I passed. It's more of a feeling, really. Quite frankly, I feel a bit foolish mentioning it now."

Anna was silent. Harry Albright was an experienced agent, and his 'feelings' were ignored at one's peril.

"What are you thinking, Anna?" Dugan asked from the seat beside her.

"I'm thinking if the bastards have identified us, we might have unknowingly led them to Alex's house, and Gillian is alone there with Tanya and Cassie."

"You think they've found us?" Dugan asked.

"No, I'm probably being paranoid. I guess I'm just overprotective of Tanya after all we know she went through. And I promised her we would keep her safe."

"Ilya or I will go there," Borgdanov said. "We do not need everyone to watch for this Arsov."

Anna shook her head. "You're both too conspicuous. If either of you leave the van here, someone from the club might spot you. Harry would be the logical choice, but we need him here to stay outside and fend off any police or anyone else that might show up. Tom's also a risk, because he's been seen, but at least he's a bit smaller and thus less conspicuous than you two, presuming we can disguise him somehow."

"I've got some spare BT repairman uniforms," Harry said. "They're part of the standard kit for the surveillance rig. One of them should fit our Yank friend here, and if he pulls the cap low on his face and walks directly away from the van and the club, he can be around the corner and out of sight in less than a minute. There's a taxi stand about four blocks away."

"Let's do it," Dugan said, and Anna nodded to Harry, who began pulling uniforms from a small cabinet mounted on the floor of the van and checking the labels for sizes.

"I'll ring Gillian," Anna said, reaching for her phone. "I don't want to alarm her, but she should know what's going on, and I'll tell her Tom is coming."

Five minutes later, Dugan was uniformed as a British Telecom repairman, pushing past the Russians to the rear door of the van when Harry stopped him.

"Are you armed, Yank?"

Dugan shook his head. "You folks aren't big on concealed carry permits."

"Permits be damned. These blokes are nasty bastards." He reached into another compartment and extracted a Glock and a spare loaded magazine. "The magazine in the gun is full," he said, handing both the Glock and the spare magazine to Dugan, "but there's not a round in the chamber."

Dugan nodded and slipped the spare magazine into his pants pocket and the Glock into his waistband. He adjusted his shirt to cover it and moved to the back of the van.

"Wish me luck," he said, hand on the door release.

"Let's wish you don't need it," Anna countered.

Dugan flashed her a hesitant smile, then crawled out of the van.

CLUB *PYATNITSA*
LONDON, UK

Arsov pulled his vibrating cell phone from his pocket and looked at the caller ID.

"Yes, Nazarov."

"We've spotted Tanya. She's in the Kairouz house."

"Is she being held?"

"No, she appears to be there willingly."

Arsov thought for a moment. "Too bad. That means we'll have to take her by force. Who else is there?"

"A woman I think is Kairouz's wife and a servant. A cook, I think. She seems to spend all her time in the kitchen."

"And no one else?"

"Not that we can see," Nazarov said. "Kairouz and his driver left this morning, and we followed him to his office."

"And the others?"

"The American and the Walsh women went to the office, and the two *Spetsnaz* stayed at the apartment. We did not see any of them leave either place," Nazarov hesitated. "But…"

"But what, Nazarov? Please do not tell me you couldn't even perform a simple surveillance."

"A… a British Telecom repair van, possibly the same one, entered and exited the underground garage of both buildings. I don't know for sure, but it seems too much of a coincidence…"

"So what is the problem? You have plenty of men. Surely you dispatched someone to follow this van."

"W-we did not realize it visited both places until it was out of sight. I do not know where the van went or if anyone was in it."

Arsov suppressed a sigh of exasperation and collected his thoughts. Now why would the American and the Russians conceal themselves in a repair van, assuming, of course, that this idiot Nazarov's suspicions were correct?

"Hold a moment," Arsov said into the phone as he moved from his office and into the club. The club wasn't open yet, and he motioned to a large man restocking the bar. "Victor, go out front and have a smoke. Look up and down the street casually, and see if you see a white British Telecom van anywhere, but don't be obvious."

The man nodded and moved from behind the bar and toward the door as Arsov reconnected with Nazarov.

"If they are moving around in a van," Arsov said, "perhaps they have decided to watch us. I sent Victor to check. However, it doesn't really matter where they are at the moment. In fact, whether they have obligingly gone to work as usual or collected in a van to try to watch us makes no difference. They are not around Tanya. Pull all the boys off the other surveillance and bring them to the Kairouz house. How long will it take them to get to you?"

"Not long. Both places are nearby. Ten minutes perhaps."

"Good. Leave two men watching the street outside the Kairouz place, and the rest of you go in and take Tanya. Understood?"

"*Da*," Nazarov said. "I will call the boys at once. Where do—"

"Hold a moment." Arsov looked up as Victor returned.

Victor nodded. "*Da*. There is this van as you said. It is far down the street out of the view of the security cameras, but I could see it. From the position of the van, I think they can see both the front entrance and the opening to the alley leading to the back door."

Arsov nodded, motioned Victor back to the bar, and spoke into the phone.

"The van is here, and since it stopped both places, we know both the *Spetsnaz* and their pet American are probably inside. Take the girl to the holding warehouse. I will join you shortly, and we can figure out what to do about our troublesome new friends." Arsov paused. "And Nazarov, listen carefully. We prosper here because we provide a needed service and we keep a low profile, so do not do anything stupid. Don't harm the cook or the Kairouz woman, but leave them tied up. The last thing we need is this escalating because of dead or injured British citizens, especially rich ones."

"*Da*," Nazarov replied, doubt in this voice, "but, Boss, surely when we take Tanya they will know it was us and report that to the police."

"Maybe not. We will have Tanya back under our control and will be able to remind her what will happen to her family. If they call the authorities at that point, the girl will say anything we want. They will know that, and they must also know, or at least suspect, that we have video from the club showing them kidnapping her. They will be the kidnappers, not us."

"But suppose a neighbor sees us or finds the women tied up before they free themselves?"

"Have the men wear ski masks, and no one is to speak Russian. In fact, have no one speak but yourself and then only two or three words at a time so your accent is not so obvious. And after you grab Tanya and tie up the women, ransack the house a bit and steal any valuables. That way, if it does get reported, it will look like a simple home invasion. The Kairouz woman and the others cannot say anything different without implicating themselves in Tanya's kidnapping."

"*Da*. But what about the American and the *Spetsnaz*?"

"One thing at a time, Nazarov. One thing at a time." Arsov disconnected.

He sat for a moment and considered his next move. It was very obliging of these fools to collect themselves in one spot where he could watch them, but what exactly did they expect to gain from watching the club? Surely they understood he knew they were after Karina and that he would never bring her near the club. Then it hit him—if little Tanya was now friendly with her kidnappers, she undoubtedly told them about him, and they probably expected him to lead them to Karina. His face clouded—he'd take care of Tanya later, but for the moment perhaps he should give his new fan club something to see. After all, he didn't want them to get too discouraged. If they kept watching him, he'd know exactly where to find them when the time came to deal with them.

Arsov sat for a moment and considered the possibilities. Tanya didn't know the location of his apartment, so these amateurs could only really know about the club. And since they had only just arrived, they couldn't know for sure he was inside. If he wanted to keep their interest focused on the club, he'd have to show himself. Should he take a stroll outside? Too obvious, especially after he'd just sent Victor out. Even amateurs wouldn't be that gullible. He dialed the number of a cab company and requested a pickup in ten minutes.

***

Arsov cracked the back door of the club and peered down the narrow alley through the slit. He couldn't see the surveillance van from the door, which meant that while the observers in the van could see the entrance to the alley, they couldn't see the club door itself. He smiled and opened the door wide to stroll across the alley to another door. He opened the door and stepped into the busy kitchen of an Italian restaurant preparing for the lunch rush. He was immediately confronted by a burly man in a once-white apron smeared with tomato sauce.

"You cannot come in this door—"

"Food Standards Agency. Surprise inspection." Arsov held up his open wallet as if it were credentials.

The surprised cook stepped back, and Arsov pushed past him, straight through the kitchen and into the dining room. He nodded at the servers setting up tables and continued out the front door without pausing. Five minutes and a block later, he climbed into a cab at the prearranged pickup point and gave the driver the address of the club.

"What?" said the angry cabbie. "My dispatcher said you was going to Heathrow. This bloody address is two streets away. You can walk it."

"Yes, but if you take me there, I'll pay the full fare to Heathrow with a nice tip besides."

The cabbie shrugged, mollified. "Your money, mate."

BERWICK STREET, SOHO
NEAR CLUB *PYATNITSA*
LONDON, UK

Harry Albright sat in the driver's seat of the van, pretending to study a clipboard as he conversed with Anna, unseen in the back of the van.

"You think they made us, Harry?"

"Hard to say. That was the world's fastest smoke break. The bloke only took a few puffs before he tossed the butt, and he did seem a bit too interested in what was up and down the street. Then again, they are a criminal enterprise, so I suppose it's only normal that they be cautious. It might just be routine. One thing's for sure though, whether they've twigged to us now or not, we can't be mucking about in this van too much longer without raising suspicions."

Anna sighed. "Agreed. However, I was hoping we'd at least spot Arsov before we had to come up with another means of surveillance. My inventory of favors subject to call is fairly limi—"

"Hello! What's this? You have that on your screen back there, Anna?" Harry asked.

"Affirmative." Anna watched on the monitor as a cab pulled up in front of Club *Pyatnitsa*. A tall man emerged from the cab, dressed impeccably in a suit that said Saville Row and wearing a snap-brim fedora set at a rakish angle. He stretched and checked the street in both directions, then strolled to the front door and entered the club."

"Well, well," Anna said. "Here's our guest of honor now. Now we just have to stay in touch."

"It shouldn't be too difficult, as long as he doesn't suspect we're onto him."

CHAPTER SEVEN

Kairouz Residence
London, UK

The smell of fresh-baked cookies filled the spacious kitchen, and Gillian watched as Tanya took two from the pile and then hesitated before placing a third on her plate. Mrs. Hogan beamed as she set a glass of cold milk beside Tanya's plate.

"Now that's what I like to see," the cook said. "A girl with a healthy appetite. A girl needs a few curves. None of this string bean stuff. It ain't healthy."

Tanya laughed around a mouthful of cookie and took a swallow of milk to wash it down. "If I keep eating your cooking, Mrs. Hogan, I think I have more than 'few' curves, *da*? Soon I look like beach ball."

"And a beautiful beach ball you'll be, dearie," Mrs. Hogan gave Tanya's back an affectionate pat.

Gillian smiled, amazed at the change in Tanya that even a short time in a safe environment had caused. The scars were deep, but Gillian knew they would heal, given time, and she wanted to keep the girl's life as stress free as possible.

Beside her on the counter, Gillian's cell phone chirped, and she recognized Anna's number on the caller ID.

"Yes, Anna," she said, and then listened a moment, tensing slightly.

"No, we're fine and enjoying some of Mrs. Hogan's delicious cookies. Thomas? He is? Well, we'll be sure to save him some cookies. Yes, dear, and thank you for calling." As Gillian disconnected, Mrs. Hogan gave her an inquisitive look.

"Mr. Dugan is coming over in a bit. Can you keep some of these cookies warm for him?"

"Aye," Mrs. Hogan said and began taking warm cookies from the plate and wrapping them in a tea towel.

Gillian strolled nonchalantly to the kitchen windows and gazed out into the backyard. "It's certainly a lovely day out." She locked the deadbolt on the back door as she passed.

"Why does Mr. Dugan come here?" Tanya asked, obviously still somewhat ill at ease in Dugan's presence.

"Oh, he's just coming to collect some papers Alex forgot on his desk this morning."

"And speaking of cookies gettin' cold," Mrs. Hogan said, "where is Cassie? She'll want some of these while they're nice and warm."

Tanya laughed. "I do not think she wants to be disturbed. She is in room, having video chat with Nigel. She is very nervous, I think, about asking him to dinner. I thought maybe better to give her some privacy. Do you think Nigel will come?"

Gillian paused, thoughts of Anna's call momentarily forgotten. With all that was going on, she'd contemplated postponing the dinner with Nigel, but his ship was only in port another two days, and Cassie had warmed to the idea of the dinner. At this point she couldn't postpone it without disappointing Cassie.

"He better, if he knows what's good for him," Mrs. Hogan said before Gillian could reply. "I need to get a look at him and decide whether or not he's suitable for our Cassie."

Gillian wondered, not for the first time, if young Nigel understood what he was in for.

OUTSIDE KAIROUZ RESIDENCE
LONDON, UK

Nazarov saw the Kairouz woman moving toward the kitchen window and ducked down behind the hedge. After a long moment he chanced another peek over the hedge and saw her back as she resumed her place near the center island. He nodded to himself. They were all in one place, and this should go quickly. He looked over at his men crouched beside him behind the hedge. He'd kept Yuri, Anatoli, and Dimitri with him and concealed the other two among the lush landscaping at the front and back of the stately home. He planned to be in and out in five minutes and doubted he'd need lookouts, but it was better safe than sorry.

"Remember," he whispered, "do not speak unless absolutely necessary, and then only in English and use few words. Yuri and I will grab the girl, and I want Anatoli and Dimitri to take care of the women. I don't think they will give us any trouble, but you are not to harm them. Keep your guns visible for intimidation, but do not draw them unless needed to enforce the point. I don't want one going off by mistake. We just tie them up, take the girl and leave. Understand?"

His men nodded.

"All right. Pull down your masks, and let's get this done."

His men did as instructed and followed him toward the kitchen door. He quietly tried the knob and, finding it locked, stepped back and nodded at Yuri. The massive Russian backed up half a dozen steps on the flagstone walk and launched his three hundred pounds pounds of muscle toward the door, striking it with his shoulder. It yielded with the sound of splintering wood, and Yuri crashed through with the others close behind.

Yuri and Nazarov wrestled Tanya off the stool, but to Nazarov's surprise, she was not the frightened girl of a few days before, and she fought like a tiger. As he struggled to hold the writhing girl, he glanced over to see Anatoli and Dimitri closing on the two women. The pair stood back to back and were obviously combative rather than intimidated. His men approached tentatively, mindful of orders not to harm the women. Anatoli shot Nazarov a questioning look.

"Take them! Now!" Nazarov barked, and his men rushed in. To unexpected results.

"Keep your bloody hands off me, you bastard!" shouted the older woman as she pulled a kitchen knife from the capacious pocket of her apron and slashed Anatoli's outstretched hand.

Anatoli cursed as he retreated, staring at the blood gushing through a cut in his glove.

His curses were soon joined by those of Dimitri, as his partner was on the receiving end of a savage kick to the groin from the Kairouz woman. Dimitri doubled over, and the woman shot past him toward the hallway.

"Cassie! Lock your door, and call the police!" the woman screamed as she ran toward the door.

"Shit," Nazarov said, as he struggled with the squirming Tanya. "Beat her down," he yelled at Yuri, and the big Russian nodded and delivered a massive blow to the side of the girl's head. She went limp, and Nazarov dumped her on the floor and took off after the Kairouz woman.

"Cassie! Lock your door," the woman screamed again, as he burst into a long hallway and spotted her at the far end, racing for an ornate staircase. Her toe caught on the edge of a carpet runner that stretched the length of the hall, and she sprawled on the hardwood stairs. As Nazarov rushed to her, she raised her head, intent on calling out again, and he silenced her with a vicious open-handed slap, Arsov's cautions forgotten in the crush of events.

He dragged the woman to her feet, savagely twisting her arm behind her and clamping his other hand over her mouth before pushing her toward the kitchen, controlling her with pressure on her arm. Christ, he couldn't believe things had gone completely to hell so quickly.

In the kitchen, he was greeted with the ludicrous sight of Tanya unconscious on the floor and his three underlings surrounding the fat cook. The woman was in a corner, holding them all at bay with her knife.

"Yuri, get over here and help me," Nazarov said, and Yuri left the cook to the others and rushed to Nazarov's side.

"Tape her mouth," Nazarov said, nodding at the woman squirming in his grasp. He twisted the woman's arm back further, and she gasped against his palm clamped over her mouth.

"I'm going to take my hand away while my friend tapes your mouth," Nazarov whispered in her ear. "And if you scream again, I'll break your bloody arm and then kill everyone in the house. Do you understand?"

The woman bobbed her head, and Nazarov checked to see that Yuri had a piece of duct tape ready before he moved his hand from the woman's mouth.

"Cassie! Call the police! Lock your doo—"

Nazarov gave the woman's arm a savage twist, but only Yuri mashing the tape across her mouth silenced her. It was an imperfect job with the woman's mouth open, and Yuri grabbed the roll and quickly wound a length of tape around her head several times, covering the bottom half of her face, as the woman fought.

"Tape her hands and feet, and cover her eyes! Quickly," Nazarov said. He restrained the woman, and Yuri rushed to comply, but no sooner than they had the Kairouz woman subdued, the fat cook took up the cry.

"Cassie! Call the police!" the cook shouted.

"God damn it! Shut that bitch up! Now!" Nazarov yelled at Anatoli and Dimitri as he pushed the bound Kairouz woman to the floor. "Go help those idiots," he said to Yuri before starting for the hallway.

"Where are you going?" Yuri asked.

"Obviously to find this Cassie. And I hope like hell she didn't hear any of this fiasco and call the police."

KAIROUZ RESIDENCE
LONDON, UK

Cassie laughed and shook her head at something Nigel said, and then winced as the headphones pinched her ear. As she reached up to adjust them, she saw a look of concern on Nigel's face as he stared up from the screen of her laptop.

"If the headphones are uncomfortable, why don't you take them off and just use the speakers?" he asked.

"Because," said Cassie, "there is NO privacy in this house. Everyone seems to think I'm two years old, and every time I close my door, I can just imagine them with their ears pressed against it."

Nigel laughed. "Surely it can't be that bad?"

"Well, I suppose not really, but sometimes it seems like it. I know they all love me, but it's really tiring to be treated like a child. It seems even worse after I told them about us, but maybe that's my imagination. Anyway, maybe it will be better after you come to dinner."

Nigel's face clouded. "About that, I really don't know—"

"Oh, Nigel, you ARE coming, aren't you? I couldn't bear it if you don't come after I've told everyone."

"Well, about that—"

"That's it isn't it? You're angry that I told about us without discussing it with you. I am SO sorry. Please don't be mad. I was just so happy, and it slipped out, and Mum pounced on it and wheedled the rest out of me—"

"Cassie, Cassie, calm down," Nigel said. "I'm not angry that you told. We had to tell them sooner or later. Perhaps it would have been better if we discussed it, but I understand how it happened, and I'm not the least bit angry. Okay?

"O-okay. But then why don't you want to come to dinner?"

"I WANT to come, but I have the watch. I know you think I'm the commodore of the fleet, but I'm a very, very junior officer who must do as he is told."

"But can't you talk to the captain or something? I know, I'll have Papa call him and tell him to let you—"

"Absolutely not," Nigel said. "None of my shipmates must know about us."

Cassie's face fell, and tears welled up in her eyes.

"Cassie, what is it?"

"Is it... is it because I'm... I'm... you know...Are you ashamed of me?"

"Cassie, oh God, no! Ashamed of you? Never EVER think that. I'd shout your name to the rooftops if I could. You're beautiful and caring, and I feel incredibly fortunate that you care for me."

Cassie blushed at Nigel's praise. "And just who are these women you're comparing me to, Mr. Havelock?"

Nigel smiled, relieved at her mock indignation. "No one you have to worry about, and that's a promise."

"Well, I still don't understand why you want to keep our relationship a secret from everyone. I could understand it when Mum and Papa didn't know, but what's the point now?"

"The point is, that you're the daughter of the chairman of the board of my employer, and some cheeky bastard is bound to make a snide remark about you or our relationship. At that point, I'd be compelled to punch him in the nose, and I don't think that would be very good for my career."

"It's bound to come out sooner or later. You'll just have to learn to control yourself."

"I'm not quite rational in regard to you, but I'll try to work on it." Nigel touched the computer screen, partially obscuring his face.

Cassie touched her own screen in return, as if they could share a tactile connection digitally. When she removed her hand, Nigel's face came back into view and took on a look of concern.

"Cassie, the door behind you is opening."

Cassie turned as she spoke. "Probably just Mum—"

A man in a black ski mask burst into the room, and Cassie leaped from her chair, the cord from her headphones to the laptop almost dragging the laptop off the desk before tearing the headphones from her ears. The intruder closed the short distance between them, trapping Cassie against the desk before she could move away.

"Who are you?" Cassie demanded as the intruder threw her over his shoulder, then started through the door toward the stairs.

She struggled at first, then let herself go limp, dead weight over the man's shoulder. She felt him relax, and as they started down the stairs, she struck, driving her right knee into his chest and hammering the side of his head with her elbow as she threw all her weight to one side, overbalancing him.

The man cursed in a foreign language as they collapsed on the stairs in a jumbled heap, and Cassie felt his grip lessen. She squirmed from his grasp and almost got away, crawling back up the stairs, but a strong hand closed on her ankle.

"Not so fast, you little bitch," he said and pulled her back down.

She twisted in his grasp and flipped over on her back to kick at him with her free leg, but he was too strong and too fast and was soon on top of her, grabbing at her flailing arms. Cassie clawed at his face, and her fingers closed on his ski mask and ripped it from his head. The man stopped, as if shocked, and then his face flushed red.

He drew back his arm, and Cassie felt his fist explode against her face.

***

The cook was still bellowing when Nazarov returned to the kitchen, his mask back in place and the girl over his shoulder. The cook's cry died on her lips at the sight of the girl.

"Cassie!" she said, her eyes on the girl as Nazarov lowered the girl to the floor and began to tape her hands and feet.

Yuri took advantage of the cook's momentary distraction to grab her right wrist, and with the threat of the knife neutralized, Anatoli and Dimitri closed in. They subdued her quickly, physically but not verbally, for she continued to scream abuse until they got tape over her mouth. Seconds later, she was trussed up on the floor beside the Kairouz woman.

"What now?" Yuri asked.

"Put those two in the pantry, out of sight," Nazarov said, nodding toward the Kairouz woman and the cook. "And tape Tanya up and carry her to the van."

He looked around at the blood on the floor.

"And get some tape on Anatoli's hand so he's not bleeding all over the place and then clean up this blood. Use some bleach; there must be some around here somewhere."

"What about her?" Yuri nodded at the blond girl they'd called Cassie.

Nazarov thought for a moment. Arsov had been clear; no one was to see their faces. He shook his head. "She saw my face. We'll take her with us."

CHAPTER EIGHT

Arsov sat and drummed his fingers against his desk. He'd expected to hear from Nazarov by now, but he didn't want to call him if he was still in the middle of the operation. The simpleton would probably find snatching Tanya challenging enough without a distraction. He comforted himself with the thought that even Nazarov couldn't screw up such a simple mission.

His thoughts turned to his friends outside. They would expect him to move at some point, and if he just slipped away and left them sitting there, they would figure things out sooner or later. Besides, even these amateurs couldn't be so inept as to think they could tail him in a BT van without being spotted. They must have a chase car somewhere nearby, and it would be good to smoke that out as well. Arsov punched the intercom and summoned Victor from the bar. Twenty seconds later, the bartender stuck his head into the door to find Arsov undressing.

"Yes, Boss," Victor said, obviously confused.

"Get in here and change clothes with me," Arsov said.

***

"We have movement," Harry said from the driver's seat.

"I have him." In the back of the van, Anna watched on her monitor as a cab pulled up in front of the club. Moments later Arsov walked out the front door and climbed into the cab.

"He's moving," Anna said. "Call Lou and give him the plate number. The cab should pass him in the next block."

"On it," Harry said.

***

Arsov climbed into a cab several blocks away. His exit through the kitchen of the Italian restaurant had gone more smoothly this time, after he apologized for his earlier deception and explained to the cook that it was all really a matter of the heart. His jealous wife had hired a private investigator to watch him, making it difficult for him to slip away from his club to meet his mistress, and so he needed a way to enter and exit the club unobserved. The cook had smiled and nodded at the story, his understanding and future help assured by the gift of a hundred pounds to compensate for his 'inconvenience.'

It was working out well. Victor had orders to have the cab drive about aimlessly for an hour or so and then to go to Arsov's apartment and stay there. The chase car would no doubt sit on the apartment, and the van would likely remain at the club. He'd hesitated at leading the pursuers back to his own apartment and briefly considered having Victor lead the pursuit to his own place, but quickly dismissed that idea. Victor likely lived in some shit hole, and he wanted the deception to be realistic. Besides, there was little of value in his own apartment he couldn't abandon if necessary, so the risk was minimal. And while his bumbling pursuers were chasing ghosts, he'd go deal with Tanya, find out who these people were and what she'd told them, and then return to take care of them as necessary. After all, he knew just where to find them.

OUTSIDE THE KAIROUZ RESIDENCE
LONDON, UK

Dugan ordered the cab to the curb and shoved money over the seat, exiting the cab without waiting for change. The taxi stand had been empty when he got there, and he'd had difficulty flagging down a cab. Evidently his British Telecom repairman's uniform didn't mark him as a prospective customer. A dozen cabs passed him before he caught one discharging a passenger and jumped into the back before the cab pulled away.

He'd had the cab stop at the entrance to the long drive leading to the back of the house, knowing that Gillian was likely in the kitchen with Mrs. Hogan. He rushed up the curving drive and stopped short at the sight of a black panel truck pulled up near the kitchen door. As he watched, the door opened and a large man in a ski mask walked out with a bundle over his shoulder. Then he saw the blond hair. Cassie!

Dugan slipped the Glock from his waistband just as another masked man emerged, speaking and pointing toward the panel truck. Dugan racked the slide on the Glock to chamber a round, and the men's heads jerked toward the sound in unison. They found Dugan in a shooter's crouch, the Glock steady on the center mass of the man giving the orders.

"Hold it right there, assholes," Dugan said. "Put the girl on the ground gently, and then both of you move away slowly and lay face down. Now!"

Dugan felt a tremendous jolt on the back of his skull, and his world went black.

***

Nazarov looked at Ivan, standing over the unconscious American, holding a bloody landscaping stone he'd obviously picked up from the flower bed.

His man shrugged. "I didn't know what else to do. You said no shooting."

"*Da.* You did the right thing," Nazarov said.

"Should I kill him?" His man gestured with the rock.

"No, my orders were clear. We weren't to kill anyone. Leave him. Let's just get the girls in the truck and get the hell out of here."

HOLDING WAREHOUSE
516 COPELAND ROAD
SOUTHWARK, LONDON, UK

Arsov sat at a battered desk in the office warehouse, seething as he stared across at Nazarov seated on a threadbare sofa. He suppressed an urge to scream. When he spoke, his voice was calm, almost conversational.

"You continually exceed my expectations, Nazarov. For instance, I knew you weren't the brightest fellow around, but I never expected that you were quite this stupid and so completely incompetent."

"It wasn't as easy as you think—"

"Yes, I'm eager to hear how six large men had difficulty subduing two middle-aged women? Go ahead, please. I'm all ears."

Nazarov glared. "We got Tanya back, didn't we?"

Arsov erupted. "You fucking idiot! Yes, you got Tanya back AND some girl who's likely Kairouz's daughter. And in the process, you assaulted two other British citizens. What part of 'low profile' don't you understand? A large part of our success here hinges on the fact that no one cares about these foreign girls. Even these people realize that, or they would have gone to the authorities by now. But things are a bit different now, aren't they? You've kidnapped a rich Brit, and I seriously doubt they'll hesitate to go to the police. This girl's face will probably be all over the media by this time tomorrow. How could you be so stupid?"

"I had to grab her. She saw my face."

"Which, from what you told me, would never have happened if you'd left her happily up in her room with her headphones clamped on her head. She'd have wandered down some time later and found the other two tied up, and that would have been the end of it. They couldn't report anything about Tanya, so at worst it would have been a home invasion by persons unknown."

Arsov sank back in his chair and glared at Nazarov, who wisely said nothing. After a long moment Arsov spoke.

"Well, I'll have to figure out something. We can't turn the girl loose, and she is a looker. Maybe we can get her out of the country and use her elsewhere. In the meantime, we have to take care of these damned *Spetsnaz* and the American. They seem to be the driving force, and with them out of the way, I suspect the authorities will give up in time, no matter how connected this Kairouz might be. We'll spread money around to hasten that result if need be."

Nazarov smirked.

"I don't think the American will be much of a problem for a while. I had Ivan brain him with a rock."

"What do you mean?"

"I was trying to tell you before. He showed up at the Kairouz place when we were loading the girls. I had Ivan on lookout, and he got behind him and smashed him with a rock."

"Where is he now?"

"W-we left him. He hadn't seen our faces, and you didn't say anything about snatching him. But we didn't kill anyone, just like you said."

Arsov buried his face in his hands and struggled to control himself.

CHAPTER NINE

Alex pressed the intercom button. "Yes, Mrs. Coutts."

"I'm sorry to disturb you, sir, but there's a Nigel Havelock on line one who insists he must speak to you. I wouldn't have bothered you, but he seems quite upset and says it's about Cassie."

"Very well. Thank you, Mrs. Coutts." Alex reached for his desk phone.

"This is Alex Kairouz. What can I do for yo—"

"Mr. Kairouz, thank God. Cassie's been attacked. We were—"

"Attacked? What the hell are you talking about, Havelock? If this is your idea of some sort of sick joke—"

"It's no joke, sir! We were video-chatting a few minutes ago, and a man in a black ski mask burst into her room and dragged her from her chair. The laptop was pulled out of position, and I couldn't see anything after that, but it sounded like he dragged her out the door."

Alex sat stunned.

"Mr. Kairouz, are you there?"

"Yes, yes, Havelock. The police—"

"I called them straightaway, sir. You were my second call."

"Good, good," Alex said absently. "Thank you. Now I must go."

"Of course, sir. If you could only—"

Alex hung up and started for the door. "Mrs. Coutts," he shouted, "have Daniel bring the car around straightaway."

M/V *Phoenix Lynx*
Port of Southampton, UK

Nigel Havelock heard the line go dead and resisted an urge to throw his cell phone over the side of the ship. Instead he put it in his pocket and tried to assess his options. He had none really; there was no way in hell he was going to sit here idly while Cassie was in danger. The train would get him to London faster than a car, and he didn't have the cash for an eighty mile cab ride in any event. He ran back into the deck house to have a word with the second officer, and then to his cabin to change. Five minutes later he rushed down the gangway and out to the street to flag down a cab for Southampton Central Station.

KAIROUZ RESIDENCE
LONDON, UK

Halfway down Alex's street, they encountered an ambulance speeding in the opposite direction, lights flashing. Alex swiveled in the back seat of the Bentley, momentarily torn between following the ambulance and continuing home. But no, he had no way of knowing if the ambulance was connected to events at his house, and he needed to find out what was going on. As they approached his house, there were several police cars parked on the street, colored lights flashing. Daniel pulled into the drive and was immediately confronted with yellow crime scene tape stretched across the drive between two trees. He brought the car to a stop, and Alex scrambled from the back.

"Hold it right there, sir," said a uniformed constable as Alex ducked under the tape. "No one's allowed beyond the tape."

"This is my house." Alex attempted to push past the policeman.

The policeman put a firm hand on Alex's chest. "Right, sir. That would make you Mr. Kairouz, then?"

"Of course I'm Kairouz. Now get out of my damned way. I want to see my family."

"Very good, sir," the policeman said, his hand still in place. "I'll just escort you to the house. Detective Sergeant Grimes will fill you in."

He removed his hand, and Alex shot toward the house, forcing the policeman to run beside him to keep up. As Alex rounded the turn of the drive, he saw Gillian outside the kitchen door, talking to a man in civilian clothes who was writing in a small notebook.

"Gillian!" Alex rushed to her and wrapped her in a hug.

"Alex, thank God you're here. They've taken Cassie and Tanya as well."

Alex released her and stepped back, his hand still on her arm. "Taken Cassie? Who?"

"That's what we're trying to determine, sir," the man in civilian clothes said. "I'm Detective Sergeant Grimes of the Metropolitan Police, and if you'll just step inside with Constable Hawkins here"—he nodded at the uniformed policeman—"I'll finish taking Mrs. Kairouz's statement, and we'll try to get this sorted."

"I'll do nothing of the sort." Alex put a protective arm around Gillian's shoulders. "I'm staying right here with my wife."

Gillian nodded, and Grimes started to protest but then seemed to think better of it. He looked at Constable Hawkins and jerked his head toward the drive, and Hawkins nodded and headed back down to the perimeter tape.

"Now, Mrs. Kairouz," Grimes began, "you say you'd never—"

Gillian faced the policeman and brushed back her hair, and Alex saw an ugly bruise below her ear along her jawline.

"My God, Gillian. You're injured."

"It's nothing," Gillian said. "The bastards slapped me and Mrs. Hogan around a bit, but nothing serious. Tom's injury was much more serious. He got a nasty crack on the head."

"Thomas? Here?" Then he remembered the ambulance. "Is he... is he... all right?"

"Mr. Dugan was apparently clubbed from behind with a rock," Grimes said. "He was groggy but conscious when we arrived, staggering around the back garden. The paramedics don't think it's too serious. However, they transported him to hospital for x-rays and scans. He may have a concussion."

Alex nodded, and Grimes waited a moment to see if he would continue; when he didn't, Grimes turned back to Gillian.

"Now, Mrs. Kairouz, this Russian girl..." He glanced at his notebook. "Tanya. You say she was taken along with your daughter. What was her relationship? Also, I'll need her address so we can notify her family."

Gillian hesitated for the slightest moment. "Tanya was Cassie's friend and our houseguest. To the best of my knowledge she has no family in this country."

Grimes nodded. "Fair enough, but I'll at least need her surname. Can you give me that?"

Gillian looked shaken. "Ah… no. I'm afraid I can't. She'd just been here for a day or so, you see. She told us, of course, but it was some unpronounceable Russian name that I didn't retain."

"Perfectly understandable," Grimes said. "Just how did Tanya and your daughter become friends?"

"Ah… well, they… ah—"

"What has all this got to do with anything?" Alex demanded. "This is a waste of time. We need to get on with finding them."

Grimes slowly closed his notebook and slipped it into his coat pocket, then cocked his head slightly as he stared at Alex.

"With all due respect, Mr. Kairouz, things aren't quite adding up here. Normally in a situation involving a family of obvious wealth, I'd treat this as a kidnap for ransom. However, we have this mysterious Russian girl no one seems to know much about, and the cook let something slip about 'bloody Russian bastards.' He paused. "And then there's this American Dugan found staggering around your back garden with an unregistered handgun. Fortunately he retained the presence of mind to drop it when ordered to, but that could have developed into a very bad situation."

Alex looked down and said nothing.

"If you expect our help, Mr. Kairouz, we have to know what's going on."

Alex looked at Gillian.

"Best call Anna," she said, and Alex nodded, pulling out his cell phone.

"I have to make a call, Detective Sergeant Grimes," Alex said. "Then I suggest we all go sit down in the house and wait. There's someone you need to meet."

St. Ignatius Hospital
London, UK

Dugan saw Cassie's inert body slung over a man's shoulder, moving through a fog. He tried to run toward them, but his legs wouldn't move.

"Cassie!" he cried, then jerked awake. He was in an unfamiliar bed in a dimly lighted room, and he saw a silhouette at a nearby window, framed against the night sky and lights of London.

"Easy," Anna said as she moved from the window to his bedside and took his hand.

"Where the hell am I?"

"St. Ignatius Hospital. You took a nasty blow to the back of your head, but you're going to be all right."

"Is Cassie okay? I saw—"

"Cassie and Tanya were both abducted. Obviously Arsov's work. We're —"

"Abducted? Shit. I have to get out of here." Dugan began to sit up.

"Easy, tiger," Anna said, hands on his chest pressing him back down on the bed. "You took quite a pounding. They've done all the scans, and you appear to be all right, but they've been waiting for you to wake up to do some follow-up. I'll pop out to the nurse's station and let them know. Do NOT get out of that bed while I'm gone. Is that clear?"

"Yes, ma'am," Dugan said, and Anna left the room and returned in less than a minute.

"How long have I been here? Was anyone else hurt?" Dugan asked when she returned.

"You've been here most of the day, and Gillian and Mrs. Hogan were knocked about a bit, but not seriously injured. Mrs. Hogan evidently got a piece of one of the kidnappers with a kitchen knife."

"Good for her." Dugan started to push himself up in the bed.

"Hold on." Anna reached for the bed control. There was a whirring sound as Dugan's head elevated.

"Better?"

"Much," Dugan said. "Now what's the situation?"

Anna sighed. "Evolving, I guess would be the best way to describe it. A Detective Sergeant Grimes was the officer at the scene, and he wasn't particularly happy with our freelance activities or with your possession of an unlicensed handgun. However, between my association with MI5 and Alex's contacts in government, there won't be any repercussions on either score. The Clubs and Vice Unit of the Metropolitan Police are now officially involved, though recent events haven't exactly enhanced my relationship with them either, I'm afraid. Gillian is in a state of depression and hardly talks. I've never seen her like this. She obviously blames herself for Cassie's abduction. Alex is at the other extreme. He alternates between black silence and rage, and he's calling in every favor anyone in government ever owed him. He must have contacted at least half a dozen MPs and senior government officials. He's succeeding in raising awareness, but is simultaneously stirring up quite a bit of resentment among the Metropolitan Police. In short, and to use one of your colorful American expressions, it's a complete cluster fuck."

"What about Borgdanov and Ilya?"

"I had Borgdanov with Lou watching Arsov's apartment, and Ilya stayed with Harry on the club. The one piece of positive news is that the police have taken over those stakeouts, so we're not spread as thin. That said, there's been absolutely no movement by Arsov, so I'm beginning to think he may have given us the slip. I sent Harry and Lou home to get some rest, and the Russians are doing the same in our apartment. We have a meeting with the Clubs and Vice Unit tomorrow to plan and coordinate a city-wide raid on suspected Russian mob operations."

"That's it?"

"For the moment. We've also got pictures of Cassie up all over the media and will soon have pictures of Tanya. We didn't have any of her, but Ilya remembered that Tanya said they had taken her passport. He suggested that if they had her here working 'legally,' that she had to have some sort of entry paperwork, and we found some. We figure they must have used one of their 'trained' girls who looks like Tanya to pose as her for entry purposes, using Tanya's real passport. We found an entry permit with a passport photo, and we've posted her picture on the media beside Cassie's. Ilya had another photo of Karina, and we're giving that to the media as well; by the late evening news, their pictures should be everywhere."

Dugan looked doubtful. "That might have unintended consequences."

"We thought of that, but Arsov already knows we're looking for all three girls, so we didn't think we had anything to lose. Going public doesn't change that, it just makes it more difficult for him to hide or transport them."

"That's the best option, I guess." Dugan glanced toward the door. "Why do I have to see the doctor, anyway? I feel fine."

"I suppose they want to make sure you know who you are and where you are and that you're not loopy." She smiled and squeezed his hand. "At least not any loopier than normal."

"Very funny," he said and returned her squeeze. "I'm overwhelmed by your sympathy."

"Well, the shaved patch and stitches might garner you sympathy in some quarters, I suppose."

Dugan reflexively put his free hand to the back of his head and probed at the bump. "I vaguely recall a little of that. I think they used staples, without any anesthesia I might add. You Brits don't seem to be much on painkillers."

"Stiff upper lip, Yank. It builds character."

"Yeah, well, my character's just fine, thanks. Now where the hell is that doctor? I want to get home, crowded though it is."

"Oh yes," she said. "There is something I forgot to mention. It will be a bit more crowded than you realize, I'm afraid. We've added a houseguest."

"What? Who?"

"Cassie's boyfriend, Nigel, showed up at Alex's house while the police were questioning everyone. Evidently he saw Cassie's abduction while they were video-chatting and phoned the police straightaway. He also called Alex."

"Smart boy. But why is he at our place?"

"Because it was patently obvious to anyone with eyes that he has no intention of leaving with Cassie still in danger. And it was equally obvious to me that the poor boy is extremely uncomfortable in Alex's presence, so I invited him to our place and put him on the couch. The major didn't fit on it very well anyway, and Ilya can't fit on it at all. He barely fits on the bed in the spare room. I moved the major into the spare room and bought an inflatable mattress for Ilya and put it in the living room. I think everyone will be more comfortable, but we won't have much privacy for a while."

"Sounds real friggin' cozy," Dugan said. "I can hardly wait to sit around in our jammies and tell ghost stories by candlelight."

CHAPTER TEN

Arsov glared at the collage of photos on the screen of the small TV in the shabby office and thumbed the remote to raise the volume.

"...*believed to be victims of a kidnapping ring engaged in human trafficking. The suspected kidnappers are thought to be Russian or Eastern European, but that has yet to be confirmed. Anyone seeing these girls is requested to call the number on your screen. The Metropolitan Police have emphasized that the kidnappers are armed and dangerous, and no one should attempt to intervene. Again, if you see anything or have any information, you should call the number on—*"

"Shit!" Arsov screamed and hurled the remote across the room at Nazarov sitting on the couch. His underling ducked, and the remote slammed against the cinder-block wall and popped open, raining batteries down on Nazarov as the TV screen blinked off.

"I hope you're happy, you idiot! Our very low profile and profitable business is now going to get a lot of attention. This is on every fucking station!"

"So what?" Nazarov said. "They couldn't prove anything before, and they can't prove anything now. We have the girls, and there are no witnesses. We keep the girls who aren't fully trained out of sight and threaten their families for good measure. The trained girls will support us as usual." He shrugged. "Nothing has changed."

"Can you really be this fucking obtuse? Of course things have changed. How much juice and influence do you think it takes to get these pictures all over the media this quickly? And the lead story on every single channel? The shit is about to hit the fan, Nazarov, and we're going to be splattered."

"But they know nothing—"

"They know about the connection to Club *Pyatnitsa*, or at least the American and the *Spetsnaz* do, so we can assume the police know now as well. And besides, do you think our little pleasure operations are a secret? Our methods make it impossible for them to get a conviction, and we don't get our girls from the local population, so they've learned that prosecuting us has a low political priority. We are out of sight and out of mind, at worst the public perception is that we are facilitators of a 'victimless crime.' In one afternoon you've managed to make us kidnappers and the subject of a media campaign. The authorities have no choice now. Even if they know it will be difficult to get convictions, they have to be seen as trying, and that will have a major impact on our operations."

Arsov could see from the expression on Nazarov's face that it was finally sinking in.

"Wh-what should we do?"

"Partially what you already suggested," Arsov said. "They already know about Club *Pyatnitsa*, so there's no point in shutting that down. However, make sure to leave no girls there except the most trustworthy. The same for the other clubs. They won't necessarily know of our ownership, but in this shit storm you've stirred up, they will likely be hitting any adult business with suspected Russian involvement. Bring any girls you have the slightest doubt about back here to the warehouse. And shut down all of the brothels for the time being. Close the ones with the kids first. Bring everyone here. Stop all drug operations as well—"

"The street distributors won't like that. The junkies will be howling, and the distributors may try to find other sources."

"The junkies can howl for a month or so. They'll come back when we're ready," Arsov said. "Brand loyalty is not exactly something junkies care about. And if the distributors desert us temporarily, it won't be a problem. If they won't come back when we're ready, we'll just kill a few and their families as well. Understood?"

"But where am I going to put all the whores? We don't have enough cages here to hold them all."

"There are plenty of empty containers in the warehouse. Lock them in those. Now get moving."

Nazarov nodded and rose. He stopped halfway to the door. "What about Tanya and the other two, should I put them with the rest of the whores?"

Arsov considered that for a moment. "No. They're troublemakers and would likely infect the others. We won't be able to use them in the UK any time soon. Export them."

"How? Their pictures are all over the place, and all the normal routes will be closely watched."

Arsov thought a moment. "Do we have any of the 'special cargo' boxes we can modify?"

"The only time we tried shipping whores by container, they were dead on arrival."

Arsov shrugged. "Then disposing of the bodies will be someone else's problem. Put Yuri and Anatoli on modifying a container while you attend to the other business."

Nazarov nodded and left the room, and Arsov sat staring down at his cell phone on the desk. He sighed and picked it up to dial St. Petersburg.

SPECIALIST CRIMES DIRECTORATE 9 (SCD9)
HUMAN EXPLOITATION/ORGANIZED CRIME
VICTORIA BLOCK, NEW SCOTLAND YARD
BOADWAY
LONDON, UK

"We're not the Clubs and Vice Unit any longer, Agent Walsh, and we haven't been for some time, though I expect you lot in the exalted halls of Thames House don't keep up with such mundane matters. However, I'd appreciate it if you'd use the correct unit designation."

Anna returned the man's gaze across the conference table and bit back a sharp retort. The meeting had started badly when the police inspector insisted on excluding Alex, Dugan, and the Russians. In fact, he made clear that the involvement of Anna and her MI5 colleagues was only tolerated on orders from above, a tolerance that did not extend to civilians. Alex had been near apoplectic at his exile to a waiting room along with Dugan and the others, and Anna was struggling to salvage the meeting. She gave the inspector her most winning smile.

"Apologies, Detective Inspector McKinnon," Anna said. "It's been 'Clubs and Vice' for so long I suppose it's just a habit to refer to it that way. However, I'll make a point to use the proper unit designation and make sure everyone else does as well."

Flanking her on either side, Lou and Harry nodded their assent, and McKinnon's glare softened—barely.

"That would be appreciated, Agent Walsh. As you're no doubt aware, the old Clubs and Vice Unit had a long history, not all of it positive. Most of us are now new to the unit, and we've done our best in the last eighteen months to distance SCD9 from that legacy." McKinnon sighed. "We've made some headway, but we're still very much a work in progress."

Anna nodded. The Clubs and Vice Unit had always been the backwater of the London Metropolitan Police and long considered a career-ending assignment. From its establishment in the 1930s, it had a checkered past, reaching its low ebb in the 1970s when chronic allegations of corruption were proven true and over twenty detectives were sacked. Since then, there had been periodic and to date unsuccessful attempts to upgrade the unit. The recent name change and infusion of new personnel was only the latest of those attempts.

"Understood," Anna said, "and I assure you will have MI5's support in that effort."

McKinnon cocked an eye. "Which brings me to my first question. How does any of this concern the Intelligence Service? This is clearly a police matter, and I can see no rhyme or reason for MI5 involvement. What am I missing?"

Anna hesitated. "Alexander Kairouz, Thomas Dugan, and their company have provided exemplary service to the Crown on prior occasions. Because of that, and Mr. Kairouz's political connections, they enjoy the favor of Her Majesty's government, so it's only natural that in a situation like this Mr. Kairouz would seek the government's help." She paused. "And as a word to the wise, Inspector, I'm not sure it's a good idea to exclude Mr. Kairouz from these discussions."

"Yes, well, I think there's rather more to it than that, Agent Walsh—I sense a personal connection, but I'll leave that for the moment. As far as this operation goes, I will deal with YOU with complete transparency, and what you tell Mr. Kairouz and his entourage or how you choose to involve them is entirely your concern. However, I also expect them to stay completely out of our way; is that clear enough?"

"Completely," Anna said. "Where do we begin?"

McKinnon opened a thick file folder in front of him and passed Anna a stapled packet of papers.

"Lacking detailed intelligence and with time an issue, with brute force," McKinnon said. "That's a list of every known or suspected Russian-operated illicit business in London and its environs. We're gearing up to raid all these locations simultaneously. No matter where the girls are, we should find them, and perhaps a lot of other things as well."

Anna paged through the list. "There must be over fifty locations here. How are you going to pull this off? It will require massive manpower."

"Fifty-seven, to be exact, and I suppose I have your Mr. Kairouz to thank for the manpower. People who would never give me the time of day are now calling to offer me resources, and magistrates who previously made us jump through hoops are now signing off search warrants with a minimum of hassle." He smiled for the first time. "Actually, it feels a bit like Christmas."

"Brilliant!" Anna said.

"When do you start?" Lou asked.

"In forty-eight hours, or maybe a bit longer," McKinnon replied.

"So long?" Anna asked.

"We have to make sure we get as many as we can, and that takes coordination. When we start the operation, word will spread quickly to any locations we miss. Understand that if we don't turn up the girls on this sweep, they'll likely get much more difficult to find."

"Maybe we should hold off a bit and try to pinpoint the girls first," Harry said.

McKinnon looked at Anna. "Do you think we have time for that, Agent Walsh?"

Anna looked down at the list and back up at McKinnon before slowly shaking her head. "No, unfortunately I don't. I think your massive quick sweep is our best shot, but God help us if we're wrong."

CHAPTER ELEVEN

HOLDING WAREHOUSE
516 COPELAND ROAD
SOUTHWARK, LONDON, UK

Arsov stepped into the empty container with Nazarov close behind. Nazarov let out a relieved sigh as Arsov looked around and nodded. A rack along one wall of the container held a long row of one-gallon bottles of water, and a few cases of 'Meals, Ready-to-Eat' were lashed in a corner. Three bare mattresses lay on the deck in the far end of the container.

"Looks like you have enough water," Arsov said, "but are you sure there are enough MREs? We don't want them looking like survivors of the Gulag. It will make them less marketable until we can put some weight back on them."

"But we don't want them fat either," Nazarov replied. "Americans seem to like them skinny. Anyway, they have enough for one meal per day—it is enough, I think. But I don't know about these." He pointed to a row of empty twenty-liter plastic paint buckets with tight-fitting lids lashed to the opposite wall. "I think a chemical toilet would have been easier."

Arsov shook his head. "It would fill up too fast and slosh around when the ship rolls, splashing all over the place and stinking. If they do their business in the buckets, they can seal them tight and prevent that. Just make sure they have enough buckets."

Nazarov shrugged. "Who the fuck cares? So the whores arrive stinking— we give them a wash."

"I don't care about them, you idiot! I don't want to draw any attention to the container. It's not airtight, and don't you think a container reeking of shit and piss might draw more than a casual inspection from a boarding inspector?"

"I hadn't thought of that."

"Why doesn't that surprise me?"

Arsov ignored Nazarov's glare and continued. "Make sure they have a flashlight and some spare batteries. They'll need light to open the food and go to the toilet, but make them understand they are to use it sparingly—and put the fear of God in them about remaining quiet."

"*Da*," Nazarov said. "I will handle it."

"When will they leave?"

"A drug shipment was scheduled to leave Felixstowe tonight for Jacksonville, Florida, but I'm substituting this container. There should be no problem. Containers originating in the UK receive less scrutiny these days; that's why we've begun the drug transshipments through here."

"The crew is reliable?"

"*Da*. Mostly Ukrainians and Croatians," Nazarov said. "As usual, we first had to make a few examples to ensure their complete cooperation, but they've handled three 'special cargoes' for us so far. They know what to do, I don't foresee any problems."

"You'd best make sure there aren't any. St. Petersburg is far from pleased, so we can't afford any more screwups."

HOLDING WAREHOUSE
516 COPELAND ROAD
SOUTHWARK, LONDON, UK

Arsov looked around the seedy office and grimaced—it was a far cry from his well-appointed office at the club, and he was already sick of this dump. He cursed Nazarov's ineptitude and stood up from the squeaking office chair to stretch his aching back, a by-product of his night on the threadbare dilapidated sofa. He thought of the nights he had yet to spend here and regretted his own lack of forethought in establishing a more comfortable hideaway. Still, the warehouse was their most secure location, known only to a handful of his underlings, and he could manage here until the worst blew over. He'd send Nazarov to run things at Club *Pyatnitsa* and to take whatever heat might be generated there. It would serve him right, and a night in jail might teach the stupid bastard a lesson, presuming their solicitors couldn't free him within a few hours of any arrest.

He thought back over the day's events—he was as prepared as possible. All of the questionable whores and the children had been brought to the warehouse and locked in the cages or containers, and Yuri and Anatoli were here to watch and feed and water them. Drug operations had been temporarily suspended, and as Nazarov predicted, the distributors had started to moan, but that was a minor problem. And most importantly, the container with the troublemaking whores had left earlier this afternoon and should be at sea and out of reach by tonight. He was ready.

The big question was, ready for what? Security surrounding the anticipated police operation was tight—much tighter than usual. His informant could only tell him the planned operation was 'big' and that it would happen 'soon.' With preparations complete, the timing of the attack no longer concerned him as much as the scope. He'd downplayed the situation to his superiors in St. Petersburg, hoping he'd be able to contain things and ride out the storm. He could probably survive if the pending operation shut them down for a week or ten days—he'd skimmed enough cash to make up the shortfall—but beyond that there would be a serious cash-flow problem. Then he'd be faced not only with admitting his 'error,' but also explaining why it had taken so long for profits to dry up. A visit from an 'auditor' from St. Petersburg wasn't an event he'd likely survive.

All because that buffoon Nazarov couldn't obey a simple order. And that being the case, it was only right that Nazarov take the fall should things go badly. Arsov sat back down, ignoring the tortured squeal from the office chair as he swiveled back to the battered desk and opened his laptop.

DUGAN AND ANNA'S APARTMENT
LONDON, UK

Anna stood in front of the bathroom mirror, fresh from the shower and wrapped in a towel. She was reaching for her toothbrush when Dugan stepped in from the bedroom, clad only in a pair of boxers. He stepped close behind her and wrapped her in his arms as he smiled at their reflections in the mirror.

"Alone at last," he said as he pressed his body against hers. "All our houseguests are bedded down for the night."

Anna returned his smile and pressed back against him. "And why do I have the feeling that you have further plans for the evening, Mr. Dugan? I see the crack on the noggin had no impact on your libido."

"What can I say? I could never resist a woman in a towel."

"Yes, well, if you don't let me finish brushing my teeth, we'll see how you feel about a woman in a towel with the breath of a camel." She reached behind her with her free hand and placed it on his cheek. "Off with you now. I'll be in bed straightaway."

Dugan leaned down and kissed her neck. "See that you are." He caressed her bottom before moving away.

Five minutes later, Anna slipped naked between the sheets, to find Dugan lying on his back with his arms behind his head, staring up at the ceiling with a scowl on his face. She moved to his side, and she saw him smile in the dim half-light leaking from the partially closed bathroom door.

"All right, Dugan, what were you lying here thinking about? I could tell by the scowl it wasn't sex."

"Nothing that won't keep." He pulled her close and nuzzled her neck.

She pushed herself back from him and looked him in the eye. "Sorry, not good enough. I want your undivided attention. Now what's troubling you?"

Dugan sighed. "Nothing we can do anything about. I was talking to Borgdanov while you were in the shower. He and Ilya are very concerned with the impact all of this may have in Russia."

"You mean repercussions against their families?"

Dugan nodded. "Borgdanov's parents are dead, and he has no close relatives, but Ilya's concerned about his sister's family. He called them as soon as we figured out this asshole Arsov knew we were looking for Karina, and they went into hiding. But they can't hide forever, at least not in Russia."

"Have they had any indication anyone is looking for them?"

"That's the strange part. These Russian mob types don't normally screw around, but some of Borgdanov's old *Spetsnaz* buddies are keeping an eye on the house, and they've seen no indications anyone is after Karina's family. It's almost like what's happening here isn't being reported back to Russia. That doesn't add up."

"What do Borgdanov and Ilya think?"

Dugan shrugged. "They're clueless but don't think it will last indefinitely. They're working on some sort of plan for dealing with things in Russia, but they won't elaborate, at least not yet."

Anna looked concerned. "They're not going to go 'cowboy' on us, are they? Now that the Met is officially involved, I won't be able to protect them if they try to take things into their own hands."

"They understand the situation. I don't think they plan anything here in the UK."

"Well, that's good to know, if somewhat tentative. Let's just hope we get the girls back on the sweep tomorrow night."

Dugan nodded in the dim light. "Amen to that." He looked into Anna's eyes. "Are we done now?"

She pressed her body against him and ran a hand down his bare belly. "Not by half, Mr. Dugan. Not by half."

CHAPTER TWELVE

BERWICK STREET, SOHO
NEAR CLUB *PYATNITSA*
LONDON, UK

Dugan sat in the back seat and fidgeted as he looked out at the night lights of Soho, concentrating on the neon marquee above Club *Pyatnitsa*. Beside him he heard the low squawk of Anna's tactical radio, the volume lowered. He looked at his watch.

"How much longer?" he asked, not for the first time.

"From the sounds of the radio traffic, not long," Anna said from the front passenger seat. "But remember Detective Inspector McKinnon is coordinating a citywide strike, so he's got to ensure all the pieces are in place before he gives the go-ahead."

"I know, I know," Dugan said, "but it seems like we've been here all night."

"Two hours, actually," Harry said from behind the wheel. "Hardly any time at all as these things go, so don't get your knickers in a twist, Yank." Harry smiled at Anna. "He's an impatient sod, isn't he? I wonder if Lou is having to put up with this from the Russkis and the kid?"

"I suspect our Russian friends' military background has made them a bit more accustomed to lengthy waits," Anna said, "but I expect young Nigel is fit to be tied. He's been beside himself ever since the kidnapping." She looked over the seat back. "By the way, Tom, that was nice of you to square things for Nigel with the captain."

Dugan shrugged. "It was pretty obvious he wasn't going back to the ship, no matter what anyone said, and I didn't want the ship to sail shorthanded. He's just lucky personnel was able to find a replacement for a pier-head jump. Anyway, I figured I better do something, because Nigel's obviously not Alex's favorite person."

"I don't quite understand that," Anna said.

"I suspect it's a 'dad' thing," Dugan replied. "Remember Alex had just learned about Nigel and wasn't too happy about it to begin with, and then in the space of forty-eight hours, Cassie was taken and Nigel was the one who delivered the bad news. I'm sure Alex realizes it's unfair to associate that with Nigel, but on a gut level it's probably something he can't control. I think it's best just to keep them apart."

"Which reminds me, Yank," Harry said, "just how did you keep Kairouz away from our little party tonight?"

"With great difficulty, but ultimately with the truth. I pointed out that Gillian's at her wit's end, and he shouldn't leave her to wait for word alone. He was obviously torn but had to concede the point."

"Yeah, well, he's probably just as well off at home," Harry said. "It's not like any of us are anything more than spectators at McKinnon's show. We just have a bit better seats."

Anna and Dugan nodded agreement. Detective Inspector McKinnon had made it abundantly clear they were to take no part in the raids. Dugan and the other 'civilians' were allowed to observe only if accompanied by an MI5 agent. He did provide them radios to follow the progress and agreed that when the girls were located they would be informed and could go straight to them. He also allowed them to choose their vantage points, and they'd elected to split up into two cars and position themselves outside Club *Pyatnitsa* and Arsov's apartment building.

The radio squawked again, and Harry looked at Anna. "That sounds like it might be it. Turn up the volume."

Anna did so just in time to hear, "—ecute. Repeat. Execute."

Down the street, they watched as three uniformed constables exited an unmarked car and raced up the alley to seal the rear door of the club just as two patrol cars careened around the corner from a side street and skidded to a halt in front of the club. Six policemen boiled out of the cars and made a bee line for the front entrance of the club and pushed their way inside, followed shortly by the two policemen driving the cars, who stationed themselves at the front door to ensure no one entered or left.

"If all goes well, this is happening all over London," Harry said. "Now it's just a matter of sorting through the catch. That might take a while."

SPECIALIST CRIMES DIRECTORATE 9 (SCD9)
HUMAN EXPLOITATION/ORGANIZED CRIME
VICTORIA BLOCK, NEW SCOTLAND YARD
BOADWAY
LONDON, UK

The gray light of dawn leaked between the slats of the blinds into the Spartan conference room, competing with the harsh glow of the fluorescent fixtures. One tube in a fixture in the far corner blinked on and off sporadically and emitted a barely audible but annoying buzz, a fitting complement to the sullen mood that permeated the room.

"Bloody fuck all," McKinnon said. "Not only did we fail to find any of the girls, we uncovered nothing else of substance. One of the biggest operations in the history of the Metropolitan Police and we turn up nothing except a handful of immigration violations and a few minor offenses. I was sure if we hit them hard from every quarter, we'd turn up something to nail them with, at least." He slumped in his chair and shook his head. "I'm not likely to ever be able to marshal this much support again."

Across from him, Anna nodded sympathetically while Dugan and the Russians said nothing. It had been agreed that since they were there under sufferance, Anna would do all the talking. For that same reason, they'd excluded a quite agitated Nigel, but Lou and Harry were keeping him company elsewhere so the exclusion wouldn't seem so obvious.

"What do you think happened, Inspector?" Anna asked.

"It's clear as the nose on my face, isn't it? Though thank you for not pointing out the obvious. Someone tipped the bastards off, didn't they?"

"Perhaps it was the media campaign over the missing girls," Anna said. "I'm sure they may have been expecting something."

"Something, yes," McKinnon said, "but they were far too well prepared. We hit them simultaneously at eleven in the evening, and two hours later when we started hauling people in for questioning, there were already lawyers here waiting for them. And we found almost nothing—a bit of marijuana, some Russians that had overstayed their visas and the like, but no hard drugs, no guns, no girls that will admit to being anything but thrilled with their employers, and this bugger Arsov's a bloody ghost. Not only has no one seen him, no one even admits to knowing him."

"What are you going to do?" Anna asked.

McKinnon ran both his hands through his thinning hair and then clasped them behind his neck while he stared down at the table as if considering his reply. Finally he lifted his head.

"Whatever I can, which admittedly isn't much. We'll detain everyone guilty of any offense as long as legally possible. We caught a number of the girls engaged in sex in the back rooms, and for those clubs we can charge the managers with 'keeping a brothel.' We probably can't make those charges stick in the long run, because the johns will have to admit to paying for sex, and that's unlikely to happen. We may get the visas revoked for the girls that are supposed to be students or nannies, which only means they'll move them elsewhere." He shrugged. "I can tie a knot in their knickers for a few days or perhaps a week, but after that it will be back to business as usual."

"You said there was no sign of Arsov," Anna said, "even at his flat or Club *Pyatnitsa*?"

"There were clothes at his flat and toiletries, that sort of thing. Nothing at all in the way of papers or anything to indicate he'd lived there. The place was leased by a shell company that's another dead end. These buggers are smart."

"Then who was running the club?" Dugan asked, earning him a look from Anna.

"A bloke named Nazarov," McKinnon said. "He's been in the country a couple of years and is generally known by some of our undercovers as the man in charge. This Arsov is a relatively unknown quantity. If he is pulling the strings, he is doing so through Nazarov."

"Then we must question this Nazarov, *da*?" Borgdanov said. "If you have him, we must make him talk."

McKinnon stiffened. "We don't do things that way here, Mr. Borgda—"

"It is Major Borgdanov, Inspector," Borgdanov said.

"Very well, 'Major' Borgdanov. We can't very well just beat the information out of him, now can we?"

"Of course not," Borgdanov said. "I know many other ways that do not leave marks. We could—"

"Your point is well taken, Inspector," Anna said, cutting Borgdanov off. "I think perhaps you and I should continue this discussion in your office." She shot a pointed look at Dugan and the Russians. "Alone."

McKinnon nodded and rose without a word. He walked to the door and held it open for Anna and then followed her out into the corridor.

As the door closed, Dugan looked at Borgdanov. "Not too subtle, Andrei."

Borgdanov shrugged. "I do not know what means 'subtle,' *Dyed*. But I do know you will make no progress with *Bratstvo* bastards with nice questions and lawyers. I think we tried Anna's way and did not work. I think now we try our way."

Beside him, Ilya nodded.

"Aren't you forgetting your promise to Anna?"

"*Nyet*," Borgdanov said. "I promised I would not kill Arsov in UK, and Nazarov is not Arsov. And besides, we do not plan to kill Nazarov."

"And if we do, we take him outside UK," Ilya said. "We would never break promise to Anna."

CHAPTER THIRTEEN

Cassie sat on the floor with her back against the steel side of the container, bracing herself against the constant roll of the ship and clutching a large plastic bucket as she fought down the gorge rising in her throat once again. She lost the battle and hung her head over the bucket as her stomach spasmed, but there was little left to eject, and she endured yet another round of painful, mostly dry heaves. The episode passed, and she slumped back against the wall and closed her eyes, hoping that when she opened them, she would find it had all been a bad dream. But that didn't happen.

The others slumped beside her, each girl clutching her own bucket, the odors rising from the open pails combining to produce an oppressive miasma in the dead air of the container. Cassie judged it was near midday, because the temperature in the container had risen steadily since the first bit of light began leaking through the holes high up on the container walls. It wasn't much light, barely enough for her to make out the other girls only a few feet away from her. Tanya was the worst off—the seasickness had hit her almost immediately, and she'd vomited on the container floor before she could make it to one of the buckets. The blond girl, Karina, seemed least effected, and as Cassie looked at her, Karina nodded and produced a wan smile.

"I think we will survive, *da*?"

"I…I guess so," Cassie said, "but where are they taking us?"

Karina shrugged. "It makes no difference. Everyplace is the same. Only the accents of the bastards they sell us to changes."

Cassie's lower lip started to tremble, and Karina reached across Tanya and gave Cassie's leg a reassuring pat. "But for now we cannot think of that. We must try to figure out how long we will be in this box." Karina passed her bucket over Tanya's legs. "Here. Hold my bucket so it does not turn over. I want to check something."

Cassie took the bucket and held it on the floor beside her own with her free hand, and watched Karina pull herself up and turn on the flashlight she had jammed in the pocket of her jeans.

"Wh-what are you going to do?" Cassie asked.

"I go to count the food they give us. Nazarov said to eat only one box each every day. It means if I count meals, I know how long they think to keep us here. If we know this, we can count water and see how much we have for each day. Maybe if there is little extra, we can wash a bit, *da*?"

Cassie nodded, encouraged, and followed the light as Karina's figure faded into the gloom toward the far end of the container. She saw the light moving around the boxes lashed in the corner and then saw it illuminate Karina's hand as she tore open one of the cartons. Then the light played over the water jugs in a rack along one wall and bobbed back through the darkness toward her.

"Is enough food for maybe ten days," Karina said as she resumed her place on the floor. "Assuming they would only put in whole cases, I think maybe our trip is seven or eight days. There is plenty of water—fifteen jugs." Karina held the flashlight out to Cassie. "Here, Cassie, hold light for me."

"Just a minute," Cassie said and transferred one of the cumbersome buckets to between her knees so she could hold it with her legs against the ship's motion. "Okay," she said and took the light.

"Hold it on my hands," Karina said, and Cassie watched as the Russian girl opened a package marked MEAL - READY TO EAT.

"How can you eat?" Cassie asked, surprise in her voice.

The mention of food propelled Tanya away from the wall and over her bucket in an episode of dry heaves. Karina reached out with her free hand and patted Tanya's back until her friend finished retching and slumped back against the wall.

"I am searching for crackers or biscuits," Karina said. "Something light to start. And we must drink water, or we will become dehydrated."

Tanya groaned. "What does it matter? It is hopeless."

Cassie saw Karina shake her head as she continued to rummage through the contents of the MRE. "There is always hope, no matter how dim. And we must keep ourselves strong to take advantage of any opportun—Aha!"

"Did you find biscuits?" Cassie asked.

"No, but I have the solution to something else that has been concerning me." Karina held up a packet of toilet paper.

HOLDING WAREHOUSE
516 COPELAND ROAD
SOUTHWARK, LONDON, UK

Arsov held the phone to his ear and listened to the attorney with a growing sense of relief.

"… and six girls have immigration violations—two Russians and four Ukrainians. They're subject to deportation, but I can file appeals—"

He cut the lawyer off. "On the contrary. Use all your contacts to expedite their deportations; then get me their names and flight information. I'll take it from there. Understood?"

The lawyer confirmed his understanding, and Arsov scribbled a note on the pad in front of him. The girls would be met by *Bratstvo* soldiers when they arrived in their homelands and shuttled right back into the system, after any refresher training needed. It was the quickest way to get them back to income-producing status. They could no longer sell the girls in the UK, but the world was a big place, and the *Bratstvo* served many markets.

"What of the club managers?"

"As I told you previously, Mr. Nazarov and three others are being charged with 'operating a brothel,' but the charges are unlikely to hold up unless the clients are willing to testify they exchanged money for sex. However, the authorities are holding the managers pending a bail hearing, stipulating that as foreign nationals they represent a flight risk. I'm pressing for a hearing this afternoon, so we should have them out by this evening at the latest."

Arsov was silent a moment. "Don't press so hard. Tomorrow afternoon will be fine."

"Yes… but don't you want me to get them out as soon as—"

"Do we have a bad connection, or are you just slow?"

"Ah… no… no, I understand," the lawyer said. "Tomorrow, then?"

"Or the next day. Whatever is convenient. Is there anything more?"

"No, not unless you—"

"Goodbye." Arsov hung up.

He sat back in the squeaking chair and put his feet on the battered desk. All in all, things were going much better than he had hoped. The raid would impact revenue, of course, but not as badly as he feared. It would slow, but not stop for a week or two, and then he could start ramping things up again. Better still, with Nazarov out of the way for a couple of days, he could continue his plan. He had already set up the Cayman Islands bank account in Nazarov's name, and he just had to plant a bit more evidence before he alerted St. Petersburg as to the full extent of the problem and his suspicions about Nazarov. Perhaps he would pick the least competent of the other club managers presently in custody as well. After all, Nazarov would undoubtedly have had an accomplice. He smiled. The bosses in St. Petersburg would be pleased that he'd come to London and uncovered these irregularities so quickly. Perhaps he would be in line for yet another promotion?

CHAPTER FOURTEEN

"Absolutely not!" Anna said. "I made this clear from the beginning. We have to be careful, and now that the Met is involved, we have even less room to maneuver. You can't just snatch Nazarov as he leaves New Scotland Yard and beat a confession out of him."

Borgdanov shrugged. "Actually, Anna, I think you mean the POLICE cannot do this. I think we can do what we want as long as we do not get caught. After all, is what the *mafiya* does, *da*? So we must, as you say in English, fight the fire with the fire. Is this not logical?"

"Andrei is right, Anna," Dugan said. "The police gave it their best shot and got nowhere. If we don't take matters into our own hands, what's Plan B?"

Anna opened her mouth to respond, but Alex cut her off.

"I concur with Thomas and Major Borgdanov." Beside Alex on the sofa, both Gillian and Ilya nodded.

Anna looked around the room. "I wasn't aware we were voting, but if you're all quite done, I'd like to make something clear. I love Cassie as much as anyone here, and I'm not about to abandon the effort to get her and the other girls back. What I said was that we had to be CAREFUL or the police will shut us down in a heartbeat." She looked at Borgdanov. "That means you can't just snatch Nazarov as he exits the police station. He'll undoubtedly be met by other mobsters, and that might result in a confrontation that draws attention. You must have a plan—where to grab him quickly and quietly, where to take him for interrogation, etc."

"You are right," Borgdanov said. "I am sorry, Anna. We must discuss these things."

"Yeah, but maybe Anna shouldn't be involved from here," Dugan said. "She's already pushed the envelope, and if things go south, it may be better if she has some plausible deniability."

Anna shook her head. "No, I'm in, but I'll keep my distance from the interrogation. If you turn up anything of use, I'll need to feed it back to the police and attribute it to a 'confidential source.' Given his desire to wipe out the Russian mob, I don't think McKinnon will ask too many questions. But I'm only speaking for myself—Lou and Harry can't be involved. They're both near retirement, and this could be costly for them if it goes badly."

"As far as a place for the interrogation," Alex offered, "we have some surplus warehouse space that's up for sale. It's empty and relatively isolated. I'll call the real estate agent tomorrow and tell him we're thinking about keeping it and not to show it to anyone for a few days."

"Good idea," Dugan said, "but you'd better let me do that, Alex. You probably need to keep your distance too. The police already know my face and my relationship with Andrei and Ilya, and if this goes badly, one of us needs to stay out of jail to keep the company going."

"Now see here, Thomas—"

Gillian reached over and took Alex's hand. "Tom is right, dear. I know you want to do more to save Cassie, but if something goes awry you have to be available to carry on the effort. We can't let our emotions overrule our intellect."

Alex gave a reluctant nod, and Gillian patted his hand.

"So," Ilya said, his impatience evident, "we will have place to question this bastard, but when do we take him?"

"He has a bail hearing tomorrow afternoon, and there's little doubt he'll be released," Anna said. "We'll shadow him from that point and figure out the best time and place to grab him. I don't think it will take very long."

"What about McKinnon?" Dugan asked. "Won't he have a tail on Nazarov and the others?"

"Maybe," Anna said, "but after the failure of the raid, he'll be back to limited resources, so he'll be a bit thin on the ground. We'll just have to cross that bridge when we come to it."

CLUB PYATNITSA
LONDON, UK

Nazarov sat behind Arsov's desk in the office, looking over the receipts from the previous evening. They were down, of course, given the raid, but even the threat of arrest couldn't dampen the allure of what they provided for long, and business was rebounding. With the 'trainees' out of action for a while, he'd have to work the remaining whores that much harder. He'd have Ivan gather them together before business picked up this evening and inform them they had to get more aggressive. Maybe he'd start opening earlier in the day and see if he could draw in a matinee crowd. He'd feed the whores uppers if he had to, Arsov's prohibition on drugging the bitches be damned.

Arsov! He knew that asshole would leave him to take the fall, but he hadn't expected to spend two nights as a guest of the government. He suspected that was Arsov's doing. To be sure, the UK jails were a paradise compared to some of the Russian jails he'd been in as a boy, before he smartened up and joined the *Bratstvo*, but that didn't mean he enjoyed spending time there. Just another thing he'd chalk up on the ledger. Arsov wasn't the only one who had a few friends in St. Petersburg.

Nazarov stretched and yawned; he hadn't slept well in jail. Everything seemed in order here, so he decided to go home and get some sleep. He let Ivan know he was leaving, then walked down the corridor to the rear exit. He cracked the door to verify it was all clear before he rushed across the alley to the back door of the Italian restaurant. He had to give Arsov credit for establishing this discreet access. The Italian chef no longer needed a cover story, and Nazarov didn't even slow down as he stuffed a fifty-pound note in the big man's hand and kept walking. Seconds later he was headed for the cab stand two blocks away.

BERWICK STREET, SOHO
NEAR CLUB *PYATNITSA*
LONDON, UK

"This could get a bit tricky," Dugan said, watching the two plain clothes cops in the car parked fifty feet away. "What if they follow us if we leave?"

"They won't," Anna said from the driver's seat. "And if they do, so much the better. We'll lead them away from Borgdanov and Ilya."

"You're sure this is gonna work?"

"It's the only thing that makes sense. We know Arsov successfully gave us the slip before, and we were watching both the front entrance and the opening to the alley. He never came out of either place. Therefore, he must have gone through one of the businesses facing onto the next street. If Nazarov leaves, he'll likely do the same, and our Russian friends can pick him up while we stay here and keep the constables company."

"Yeah, well, maybe the cops are doing the same thing?"

"I don't think so," Anna said, smiling sweetly, "because I never shared my conclusions with Detective Inspector McKinnon. Also, we're watching one location, but McKinnon's likely still trying to cover several, and he's back to being short on manpower."

"Let's hope you're right."

HOPKINS STREET CAR PARK
LONDON, UK

Ilya Denosovitch sat behind the wheel of the rental car, with binoculars pressed to his eyes, peering over the waist high side wall of the open-air car park into the street below. He'd been fortunate to find a vantage point on the third level of the facility that allowed him to look directly into the alley behind Club *Pyatnitsa*, two blocks away. He smiled as he saw the back door of the club open a crack and then fully, as Nazarov exited and scurried across the narrow alley and into another door. He picked up his radio and keyed the mike.

"Chase One, this is Eagle Eye. Do you copy, over?"

One block away on Wardour Street, Borgdanov responded from the driver's seat of his own rental car. "Eagle Eye, this is Chase One. I copy, over."

"Chase One, suspect should exit somewhere in your vicinity at any time. Be prepared. Over," Ilya said.

"Eagle Eye. I have him. Repeat. I have him. Over," Borgdanov said.

"Affirmative, Chase One. I am leaving my position to join you. Keep me advised as to your location, and I will catch up."

"Affirmative, Eagle Eye. Babysitter, this is Chase One. Did you copy last transmissions? Over."

Anna's voice came over the radio. "Chase One, this is Babysitter. We copied all transmissions. We will stay in place and watch our friends. Good hunting, and please advise when you are well out of area. We will disengage here and join hunt if possible."

"Affirmative, Babysitter. This is Chase One out."

Thirty minutes later, Anna's radio squawked. "Babysitter, this is Chase One. Do you copy? Over."

"This is Babysitter. Go ahead, Chase One. Over."

"We are well away from you. Target exited taxi and entered apartment building on Chesham Place. I think is his place. Over."

"We copy, Chase One. We are in transit to your location. Babysitter out." Anna started the car.

"Fancy. The Belgrave Square area," Anna said as she pulled away from the curb.

"Won't the cops think it strange if we leave?" Dugan asked.

"Not likely. They've only seen the two of us, and they know we can't stay here round the clock. They'll probably just attribute it to lack of resources and figure we'll rely on them. After all, they know half the team is amateur." Anna smiled. "Be sure to wave at them as we pass, so we can cement that impression."

CHAPTER FIFTEEN

Dugan stood in the beam of the car's headlights and unlocked the padlock before leaning his weight into the edge of the large sliding door. After a moment's resistance, the big door started to move, slowly at first and then faster as it built up momentum, the disused metal wheels on the track above squealing a lament. When it was halfway open, Dugan released the door and stepped back, and inertia carried it another few feet before it rumbled to a stop. He waved the car through the gap and took a quick, furtive look up and down the street before he stepped inside and tugged the door closed after him.

The car's headlights cut a bright tunnel through the pitch-black interior of the warehouse, illuminating a section of the back wall. Dugan pulled a flashlight from his pocket.

"Stay there a minute," he called out toward the car as he made his way to a breaker box near the door. "I'm going to get us some light."

Seconds later the interior of the warehouse was bathed in light, and Dugan watched as Borgdanov and Ilya climbed out of the vehicle and looked around. Dugan followed the Russians' gaze. It was a cavernous space, mostly empty, and the sound of the closing car doors was returned from the bare walls in a metallic echo. Here and there coils of old mooring lines and empty oil drums were stacked in disarray, the detritus of a successful shipping operation left behind when the expanding operations had necessitated a larger warehouse. They'd have to get this place cleaned up a bit before they sold it, Dugan thought, momentarily distracted. He looked back at Borgdanov as the Russian approached, shaking his head.

"I think we need quieter place, *Dyed*. In here the sound will be, how you say, amplified, and we do not want to attract attention."

Dugan pointed to a door in a cubic structure built into the far corner of the warehouse.

"That's the office. It's insulated and soundproofed, and there's probably some old furniture left. That should do."

Borgdanov nodded. "Ilya," he called to Denosovitch, who was dragging a bound and gagged Nazarov out of the trunk. "Take him to the door in the far corner."

Ilya nodded and tossed Nazarov over his shoulder, none too gently. He started for the door.

"Did you have any trouble?" Dugan asked.

"*Nyet*. The only real problem is keeping Ilya from killing him."

"You promised—"

"I know, *Dyed*. We promised Anna, and we keep promise. We kill no one in the UK." His face hardened. "But I assure you, very soon our friend Nazarov may wish he is dead. I think also, it may be better if you leave, *da*? We call you when we finish."

Dugan shook his head. "There are private security patrols on several of the nearby warehouses. If they see or hear anything, they may phone it in to the police. I have identification and work for Phoenix, so if they come, I can assure them everything is okay. Besides, maybe I can help out. I'm sure Nazarov is terrified of you guys, but maybe I can be the alternative. You know—bad cop, good cop."

Borgdanov shook his head. "I am afraid 'bad cop, good cop' does not work so well with Russian *mafiya*. For them we must use 'bad cop, worse cop,' *da*?"

PHOENIX SHIPPING WAREHOUSE B
EAST LONDON, UK

Dugan watched as Ilya tipped the chair and dumped Nazarov on his back on the tile floor, still bound to the chair hand and foot. Nazarov screamed what Dugan assumed was abuse in Russian until Ilya placed a thick towel over his face and slowly began to saturate the towel with water from a plastic jug. Nazarov grew silent as he held his breath for what seemed like forever, and then the silence was replaced by the sound of Nazarov's strangled attempts at breathing.

Ilya glanced at his watch, timing the man's struggles, and then hoisted the chair back upright to allow the sodden towel to fall away. Nazarov bent at the waist and alternated between wet, racking coughs and gasps. Dugan shook his head and moved toward the door into the warehouse, motioning for Borgdanov to join him. Once they were outside the office and in the warehouse proper, he turned to Borgdanov.

"This isn't working," Dugan said. "I don't know what the hell he's saying, but you've water-boarded him five times now, and it looks to me like he just gets more defiant each time."

Borgdanov shrugged. "We had to try easy way first, *Dyed*, but I did not really expect this to work. Also, he is *Bratstvo*, and these scum think they are very tough guys. Now he is congratulating himself that he has endured our punishment and is big tough guy. So. When we start more aggressive methods, he will have big surprise. Is how you say 'psychological.' *Da?*" Borgdanov patted Dugan's shoulder. "Do not worry so. We know what we are doing."

"I sure as hell hope so," Dugan muttered as he followed Borgdanov back into the office.

They found a silent Nazarov glaring defiantly at an impassive Ilya, and Dugan held back as Borgdanov approached, smiling before addressing Nazarov in Russian.

***

"So, Nazarov," Borgdanov said cheerfully, "did you enjoy your last little swim?"

Nazarov spit and screwed his head around to look at Borgdanov. "Is that the best you have, *Spetsnaz*? I am *Bratstvo*. You will never break me."

Borgdanov shrugged. "Well, we will in time, but I would prefer for you to cooperate with no more little unpleasant things, *da*? We are not savages. So, I ask you again, please tell me where you are keeping the girls and also where Arsov is hiding."

Nazarov sneered. "Fuck you, soldier boy. You want girls? Then come to club, I fix you up with many girls." Nazarov looked up at Ilya and grinned. "But too bad you missed one of the best ones. Her name is Karina, and she loved to suck my cock. Also she was crazy about taking it up the ass. We have some nice videos of her satisfying five big guys at once. Maybe I can get you two a copy. You can use it to jerk off."

Nazarov threw his head back and laughed, and Borgdanov watched Ilya, half-expecting him to kill the man immediately, but the big Russian remained outwardly calm; the only indication of his rage a red flush creeping up the back of his neck and into his-close cropped blond hair. Borgdanov shook his head and addressed Dugan in English.

"I see we must change methods, *Dyed*. Can I count on you to assure Anna we did at least try to do things nicely?"

Dugan nodded, and Borgdanov pulled a syringe from his pocket, uncapped it, and ejected a bit of fluid before sinking the needle into Nazarov's neck. The man jerked a few seconds and then slumped in the chair against his bonds.

"Come," Borgdanov said to Dugan as he recapped the syringe and tossed it in the corner. "Please help me carry in the rest of the supplies while Ilya prepares our friend."

Ten minutes and several trips to the car later, Borgdanov and Dugan stood watching Ilya cut Nazarov's clothes off. Borgdanov followed Dugan's gaze as the American looked at the floor and studied the collection they'd carried in.

"Christ, Andrei!" Dugan said. "Where the hell did you get all this stuff?"

Borgdanov smiled. "Harry and Lou are a little less concerned about methods than Anna. I gave them my shopping list. They got me the tranquilizer too."

***

Nazarov floated on the edge of consciousness, fighting unsuccessfully to open his eyes. Something was tickling his nose, and he tried to scratch it, but his limbs wouldn't respond. Then the acrid smell of ammonia filled his nostrils, burning the inside of his nose as he gasped for a breath. His eyes flew open in time to see a retreating pair of hands holding the crushed remains of an ammonia popper, and he gazed up the arms attached to those hands into the smiling face of Borgdanov.

"Very good, Nazarov. You've decided to rejoin us. Apologies for waking you so abruptly, but we are a bit pressed for time. I'm sure you understand."

"Fuck you." Nazarov studied his surroundings.

He was stark naked, seated semi-reclined on the floor, the cracked tile cool against his bare ass. He was leaned back against some sort of support, his arms stretched out to his sides and duct-taped at the wrist to a board stretched across his back to keep them that way. He tried to sit up but couldn't. The board was obviously securely fastened to something. His legs were also stretched wide and-duct taped at the ankles to another board. B-t most worrying were his balls. His genitals rested slightly elevated on a flat triangular piece of concrete that had been shoved between his legs. He felt the rough point against his anus and tried to shift his weight away from it, but he was totally immobile. He fought down his terror and grinned up at Borgdanov.

"You think you can scare me, soldier boy? You can't do this shit in the UK. This is all a bluff."

Borgdanov shrugged. "I think perhaps you should consider this warehouse to be a little piece of Mother Russia for the moment. That may help you focus your thoughts, *da*?"

"I will tell you nothing."

"On the contrary. You have already confessed to doing very bad things to my friend Ilya's favorite niece, so he very much wants to kill you. Fortunately for you"—Borgdanov shrugged—"or perhaps unfortunately— you have information we need. But I will not bother to ask you again, because I know you will only resist. Instead we will have to do things the hard way." Borgdanov stepped aside, and Nazarov lifted his head to see the one called Ilya standing nearby. At the big blond's feet lay an assortment of pliers, various sharp instruments and other tools, and a propane torch. Ilya smiled down at him.

"Fuck you too," Nazarov said again, but there was fear in his voice.

"I admire your courage," Borgdanov said. "And Ilya and I agree it may take some time for you to agree to cooperate. So we've decided to save all these little toys for later and to use them only if necessary. Instead we have decided to go to the most extreme measures immediately so you will understand we are very serious." Borgdanov shrugged. "Then, if you are still not convinced, we can always resort to the tedious cutting and burning."

Nazarov swallowed, his mouth dry. He tried to speak but didn't trust his voice.

"After some consideration," Borgdanov said, "we decided the worst thing we could do to a big stud like you was to remove your genitals. We considered various methods—you know, like dull knife or maybe burning them off with the propane torch. But my Ilya is a man of action. He said to me, 'We should not pull the wings off the fly like some cruel child. *Nyet*. We are not barbarians. We should be humane and crush the fly quickly.'"

Nazarov cut his eyes back to Ilya as the big blond reached down and rose with a long handled sledgehammer. It was a massive thing, with a flat face on one side of the head tapering to a rounded point on the opposite end. Nazarov watched with horror as Ilya stepped around the table, raised the hammer over his head, and charged forward, with the obvious intent of flattening Nazarov's genitals. The huge hammer descended in an arc, and Nazarov closed his eyes and screamed as he felt the hammer impact.

"Ilya, dammit, I told you to be careful. You missed completely."

Nazarov opened his eyes and moaned, his balls aching from the impact of the hammer on the concrete only millimeters away.

"It is not my fault," Ilya said. "I told you we needed to center his balls on the stone. Now look what you made me do. Put his balls back in the center, and I'll try again."

"I'm not going to touch his balls," Borgdanov said. "Use the pliers and… oh shit, Ilya. You cracked the stone. Now we'll have to get another one."

"All right, I'll talk," Nazarov whimpered.

"We don't need another stone," Ilya said, ignoring Nazarov. "This one is perfectly fine. It's only a small crack."

"I'LL TALK!"

Borgdanov looked down at Nazarov and then back at Ilya. "He wants to talk."

Ilya shook his head. "I don't care. He hurt Karina, and you promised me I could smash his balls. Besides, he talks with his tongue not his balls, and we have plenty of ways left to make him talk." Ilya stepped back and raised the hammer again.

"No… no, it wasn't me! I never touched Karina. Arsov wouldn't let me. He kept her for himself."

Ilya hesitated, the hammer raised.

"And where is Karina now?" Borgdanov asked.

"In a container on a ship bound for the US. All the girls are… that is the three troublemakers. They left port three days ago."

"And what is the name of this ship, and what is its exact destination?"

Nazarov looked from Borgdanov to the hammer raised above Ilya's head. "If I tell you, will you promise not to smash my balls?"

Borgdanov shook his head. "No. But I do promise you that if you don't tell me in five seconds, your balls will be looking very different."

Nazarov said nothing, and Borgdanov shrugged and nodded to Ilya, who grinned and repositioned the hammer for another swing.

"Wait! It's the *Kapitan Godina* bound for Jacksonville, Florida. That's all I know. I swear."

"I think you are far too modest my friend," Borgdanov said. "I think you also know where our friend Arsov is hiding, *da*?"

"I… I cannot. He… he will kill me if I tell."

"Then I think you are in a very bad situation, Nazarov, because we will kill you if you don't tell. After, of course… well, you know…"

"You must give me something."

Borgdanov sighed. "All right, all right. If you give us Arsov and then behave yourself, we will not smash your balls and we will not kill you. Okay?"

Nazarov looked at Ilya, who was still standing with the hammer in his hand. "What about him?"

Borgdanov looked over at his subordinate. "Ilya?"

Ilya scowled and lowered the hammer. "*Da*. But I am going to smash this Arsov's balls for sure."

"We'll see," Borgdanov said, turning back to Nazarov. "Now where is Arsov?"

"In our secret warehouse on Copeland Road in Southwark. Number 516."

"And who is there with him?"

"Just two men to take care of the unreliable whor— the girls."

"And no one else?"

"Just the kids," Nazarov said, then flinched as he saw Borgdanov's jaw tighten and Ilya tighten his grip on the hammer. "I have nothing to do with the children," he blurted. "That was all Arsov's doing. The perverts pay a fortune."

"What else is in this warehouse?"

"Just the drugs. It is our distribution center. Heroin, cocaine, Ecstasy, that sort of thing."

"All right." Borgdanov wrinkled his nose and turned to Ilya. "I think our tough guy shit himself. Cut the bastard loose and take him to the toilet to clean himself up. If he makes one wrong move, kill him."

***

"Brutal but effective," Dugan said to Borgdanov as they waited for Ilya to return with Nazarov. "If Anna feeds this warehouse location to McKinnon, the cops can free the captives and scoop up Arsov and a couple of his men at the same time."

Borgdanov hesitated. "We want this Arsov, *Dyed*. I think the police do nothing."

"They can do plenty if they catch him with captives and drugs."

Borgdanov's skepticism was apparent. "I think with smart lawyers is never a sure thing. This Arsov is very clever."

"And if he turns up dead, the police are going to be looking for us, and that's not a distraction we need while we're still trying to get the girls back. Thanks to you, we know where they are, and we should be concentrating on freeing them and leave Arsov to the police. Besides, if we take out Arsov and his thugs by ourselves, what are we going to do with his captives? They'll need more help and support than we'll be able to provide. And just taking out Arsov won't solve the larger problem, because some other London-based thug will just step into his role. But if the police scoop up Arsov with a bunch of drugs and witnesses, they have at least a fighting chance of wiping out the whole *Bratstvo* operation, at least here in the UK. If, as you fear, he manages to escape or beat the charges, you can hunt him down later."

Borgdanov gave a reluctant nod. "*Da*, everything you say makes sense. I will think about it. Ilya will not be happy, but I know he will agree that nothing should interfere with our ability to rescue Karina and the others."

Dugan let out a relieved sigh. "Good. Now, what are you going to do with Nazarov."

"Perhaps you should not concern yourself with this, *Dyed*. In fact, is maybe better you wait for us outside in the warehouse, *da*?"

"Just a damn minute, Andrei! You promised Anna you wouldn't kill—"

Borgdanov held up his hands. "Calm yourself. We will not kill this scum, though you know he deserves it. But we cannot let him go or turn him over to the police either. If the police know we got information by force, I think your stupid law maybe will prevent them from raiding this warehouse, *da*? So we cannot give him to police, and we cannot let him go. We do not have enough people to keep him prisoner, and even if we did keep him prisoner, sooner or later we must either give him to police or release him, and either way he will eventually go free, I think." Borgdanov's face hardened. "And to this, I cannot agree. He deserves some punishment. He was here long time before Arsov, so I do not believe that he has nothing to do with selling children and these other things. You do not rise to a position in the *Bratstvo* without killing many people along the way."

"I can't argue with that, but what's left?"

"As I said, we have a plan. Now if you just go into the warehou—"

Borgdanov looked up as the toilet door opened, and a naked Nazarov re-entered the large office, trailed by Ilya still carrying the sledgehammer.

"I'll stay," Dugan said.

Borgdanov shrugged. "As you wish." He turned to face Nazarov.

"Nazarov! Take three steps forward and stand at attention!"

Obviously puzzled, Nazarov took three slouching steps toward Borgdanov and stood up marginally straighter, shooting a nervous glance over his shoulder at Ilya.

"Eyes on me," Borgdanov yelled, and when Nazarov hastened to comply, Borgdanov nodded to Ilya.

Without hesitation, Ilya stepped to one side and drew the hammer back to take a side arm swing as if he was chopping a tree. He landed a crushing blow to Nazarov's back, expertly centering the rounded point of the hammer on the man's spine just below the shoulder blades. And like a tree, Nazarov went down, collapsed in a heap on the floor.

For a long moment the quiet was broken only by Nazarov's strangled sobs.

"Jesus Christ!" Dugan moved back a step.

"I-I can't feel my legs," Nazarov sobbed as Borgdanov knelt beside him, speaking English now.

"And you will never feel them again, you worthless piece of shit. And in the future, while you're sitting in a wheel chair, wallowing in your own filth in some shit hole of a government nursing home, I want you to think about all the people you hurt and the lives you destroyed, *da*? Now we are going to dump you naked in the street beside the nearest charity hospital. I suggest that you tell the authorities that you have amnesia and that you never regain your memory. Because there will be a big raid on the warehouse, and we're going to make sure that the *Bratstvo* know that you were the informant. So you see, my friend, they will be looking for you, and you will not be able to run and hide. So it is best you remain anonymous, *da*? Then you can live out the rest of your miserable life begging God for forgiveness. I suspect He is more charitable than Ilya and I."

"You promised!"

"I promised not to kill you, and you are still alive. I promised not to crush your balls, and they are still there. The fact that you will never feel them again is not my problem. Oh, I keep my promises, Nazarov, and I will make you another one. If you ever open your fucking mouth, I will have Ilya visit you again and apply his hammer a bit further up your spine and remove the use of your arms. Understood?"

"You bastard!"

"I assume that means yes." Borgdanov turned to Ilya. "Put some tape over this asshole's mouth and help me get him to the car."

Dugan watched as Ilya complied, and the ex-*Spetsnaz* men each hooked a hand into an armpit and began dragging Nazarov toward the door. He wasn't sure what he'd expected, but it certainly wasn't what had just transpired. He trailed the Russians, trying to figure out how much of this to share with Anna.

CHAPTER SIXTEEN

Dugan watched Alex pace the room, wringing his hands. "How long before we can mount a rescue, Thomas?"

Dugan shook his head. "The *Kapitan Godina*is in the middle of the Atlantic. They're already out of reach from this side, and according to their AIS signal, it looks like three days minimum before they're in chopper range of the US coast. I've called Jesse Ward, and we're working on a plan, but we have to be discreet. Like Anna, Jesse's helping us off the books. By the time he got official approval for an op like this, presuming that's even possible, it would be too late."

"Yes, of course." Alex continued to pace. "But assure Ward we'll fund whatever resources are needed—"

"Alex! You're wearing a hole in the rug," Gillian said. "Come sit down and finish listening to what Tom has to say. This is all stressful enough without you dashing back and forth like a bear in a shooting gallery."

Alex bristled, then seemed to compose himself. He sat down beside Gillian on the sofa and she took his hand. "I'm sorry to be cross, dear. But we're all overwrought, and we can't let our emotions rule us, especially at this point." She turned to Dugan. "Finding the girls' location was brilliant, Tom. We can't thank you enough."

"You can thank the Russians."

"And speaking of our Russian friends, where are they?" Anna asked, then narrowed her eyes. "And just exactly how did they get this out of Nazarov?"

"I dropped them off at our apartment," Dugan said, ignoring the second part of the question. "Nigel has been there unsupervised, and I didn't want to leave him alone too long in case he might decide to do something stupid like storming into one of the clubs by himself."

"Answer the question, Tom."

"Borgdanov and Ilya can be quite convincing."

Anna sat quietly for a moment. "Is Nazarov still alive?"

"He's definitely alive and enjoying the finest care the National Health Service can provide," Dugan said, then added, "Under an assumed name. He's disappeared, and it's better for all concerned if he doesn't reappear, so you should really let it rest. You've often pointed out to me that MI5 is intelligence, not law enforcement, so it seems to me if you get the intelligence, how it was collected should make no difference as long as you personally didn't violate any laws."

"Still, how do you suggest that I present this to McKinnon, who DOES have legal restrictions on how information can be obtained?"

"Say you obtained it from a confidential informant whose identity you can't disclose for reasons of national security. Trot out the Official Secrets Act. You folks seem to use that as much as the US uses the Patriot Act."

Anna nodded. "I suppose that might work. McKinnon wants the bastards so badly I'm sure he won't look a gift horse in the mouth. If we act fast, we might be able to roll them up before you leave."

"That fast?" Dugan said. "I'm sure our Russian friends would be relieved to see Arsov behind bars before we head to the US to prepare our little arrival party for the *Kapitan Godina*."

"When do you plan to leave?" Alex asked.

"We can leave anytime within the next thirty-six hours and still make it," Dugan said. "So I figure we'll take off as soon as Arsov's behind bars."

"Hear, hear," Alex said. "I'll call and have the Gulfstream serviced. Gillian?"

"I'll have our bags packed within the hour. We'll be ready."

Dugan looked back and forth between the pair. "Just a minute, you two. You're not—"

"We most certainly ARE," Gillian said. "Surely you didn't think we were going to sit here by the phone when Cassie's in danger? We're going, and that's final, Tom."

SPECIALIST CRIMES DIRECTORATE 9 (SCD9)
HUMAN EXPLOITATION/ORGANIZED CRIME
VICTORIA BLOCK, NEW SCOTLAND YARD
BOADWAY
LONDON, UK

"I'm not even going to ask where you got this information, Agent Walsh," Detective Inspector McKinnon said. "I'm only going to ask if you're confident of its accuracy?"

"I am," Anna said.

McKinnon grinned. "Well, then it's bloody perfect. A single location with only three Russians and a large number of captives and illegal drugs—we may be able to sweep up enough evidence and testimony to smash their entire UK operation."

Anna hesitated. "About... before..."

McKinnon held up a hand. "You don't have to remind me, Agent Walsh. It was obvious we had a leak on the last operation. They have someone on the inside, and I don't know who." He sighed. "Given the amount of money they have to throw around, it's not surprising. And the last operation was so large that keeping it quiet was all but impossible. You can't run an operation of that size without involving a lot of people." He smiled again. "But that's what's so perfect about this setup you've given me. They have all their eggs in one basket, and I can mount this op with a half-dozen men. And I'm not taking any chances on a leak. I'm not even using my own men. A mate of mine in CO19 owes me a favor and got me authorization to use five of his SFOs. Trust me; I'm keeping security very, very tight on this one. I'm not even logging the paperwork until immediately before the strike."

Anna raised her eyebrows at the mention of CO19, the London Metropolitan Police Firearms Unit, made up of highly trained Specialist Firearms Officers or SFOs, the elite of the London Police.

"CO19 lads. Impressive. It would seem you still have some support from on high."

McKinnon shook his head. "I fear I'm rapidly running out of favors to call in, Agent Walsh, so I hope this works. At any rate, we can't afford to pass up this opportunity. I intend to hit them hard and fast."

"Fast means when?"

"How's tonight sound?" McKinnon asked, then added, "Would you like to ride along? After all, we wouldn't be there without you."

"Absolutely," Anna replied. "And about that, I was wondering if—"

McKinnon's face clouded. "No way. Your civilian colleagues will have to sit this one out. And you're to keep this absolutely confidential. I'm not taking a chance on a leak from ANY source. Is that clear."

"Perfectly."

"What do you mean we cannot be there?" Borgdanov demanded. "If not for Ilya and me, this policeman McKinnon would still be standing around with thumb up ass!"

"*DA!*" Ilya said, nodding his head in angry agreement.

"And you both know quite well that McKinnon can't officially KNOW that you two got the information or how you got it," Anna said. "And unless you want to taint the case completely, the best thing you can do is stay as far away as possible. McKinnon's right about that. He's not trying to slight you; he's trying to make sure some slick slimy solicitor doesn't get these bastards off on some technicality."

"Ms. Walsh is right," Nigel said. "We shouldn't waste time with this warehouse anyway. Leave it to the police."

Nigel flushed as all eyes turned to him, the Russians obviously angry at his interruption.

"I-I mean, it's a distraction, isn't it?" he stammered. "We should be concentrating on Cassie and the others, not wasting time trying to do the police's work."

Dugan laid a hand on Nigel's arm. "We're doing both, Nigel. I've already made some calls to get the ball rolling on the US side, but we can't overtake the ship quickly by any surface craft, and just flying over her in a plane won't do any good. We have to get to her by chopper, and she won't be in chopper range of the US coast for at least a couple of days. If I thought it would do Cassie any good, we'd be in the air right now. But since it won't, it makes sense to try to make sure this Arsov character is behind bars first."

"And besides," Borgdanov said to Nigel, "do you think Ilya and I would do anything to jeopardize rescue of Karina and the others?" Borgdanov's eyes narrowed, and he looked at Dugan. "I think maybe is better if you send little boy back to his ship. We have too much at stake and too few resources to waste time as babysitters, *da*?"

Nigel clenched his fists and started to stand, but Dugan grabbed his forearm and restrained him.

"Sit!" Dugan said to Nigel, then turned to Borgdanov. "Nigel's got a stake in this too, Andrei, so he has a right to be here. And you," he said, turning back to Nigel, "try to remember that you're here on sufferance, and that you have the least experience of anyone in this room. Behave accordingly."

Nigel stiffened and glared at Dugan a moment, then relaxed a bit and nodded.

"Good," Dugan said. "Now where were we?"

"I believe Major Borgdanov was berating me for incompetence, based on my demonstrated inability to have foreign national civilians included in an ongoing Metropolitan Police operation." Anna smiled sweetly.

Borgdanov flushed. "I do not know what means 'berating,' and I did not say you are incompetent. But I do not think it is right that we cannot at least observe the operation. Maybe we can help, *da*?"

Anna shook her head. "I'm sorry, Andrei, but that's not happening. McKinnon was firm on that and I'm already on shaky ground there. We have to play by his rules on this one."

Borgdanov said nothing for a long moment, and then nodded. "Okay, but we still have tactical radios from first raid, *da*? So if we are nearby listening in, I think this McKinnon will not know, and we will be there if needed. We do not want to sit here in apartment wondering what is going on."

"McKinnon's a bit sharper than that, I'm afraid," Anna said. "The Met has specially assigned frequencies for their tactical radios, and they rotate them between operations as a routine security precaution."

"But he will give you these new frequencies, *da*?"

"I asked, of course, but he refused."

Borgdanov looked confused. "But why?"

Anna said nothing, but Dugan read the look on her face.

"Son of a bitch!" Dugan said, and Borgdanov turned to face him.

"What do you mean, *Dyed*?"

"Think about it, Andrei. There was a leak on the last operation from an unknown source. You're Russian. Arsov and company are Russian. There are plenty of ex-*Spetsnaz* working for the Russian mob. McKinnon's not taking any chances."

Beside Borgdanov, Ilya exploded. "*yob tvoyu mat', ublyudok!*" he cursed. "So this policeman thinks we are *Bratstvo* scum!"

Borgdanov only nodded thoughtfully and rested his hand on Ilya's forearm. "Calm yourself, my friend. Is only logical for McKinnon to think this. In his position, we would think the same, *da*? I should have thought of this myself." He looked at Anna. "The question is, what do we do now?"

Anna looked at the Russians' faces and knew she was fighting a losing battle. Dugan had managed to convince them to let the police handle Arsov, but they obviously had limited confidence in the Met's ability to capture Arsov, and were equally skeptical the legal system could contain him if captured. Their forbearance was tenuous at best, and if they were shut out of the operation, she had little doubt they'd launch their own preemptive strike. She sighed and moved to the 'Plan B' she'd already put together in anticipation of their objections.

"The Met's tactical frequencies are limited by bandwidth, so they don't have that many options," Anna said. "They defeat most commercially available scanners or other equipment to which the criminal element might have access, but they're nothing our technical boys at MI5 can't easily defeat. I can get a scanner to monitor the tactical bandwidths. You won't be able to transmit, but that's all the better, because I definitely DO NOT want McKinnon to know you're listening. Is that clear?"

Borgdanov smiled, and Ilya nodded in agreement. "*Da*," Borgdanov said. "Thank you, Anna."

"Don't thank me yet. There's a condition."

"What is condition?"

"Under absolutely no circumstances are you to come within a mile of the warehouse. McKinnon cannot see you. And just to make sure you don't get 'confused,' I'll get you a map and draw a circle around the forbidden area. Agreed?"

Borgdanov stroked his chin. "Okay. *Da*. I agree."

Anna nodded and stood, obviously relieved at his agreement.

"I'm going back down to New Scotland Yard to go over some details with McKinnon. I'll have Harry or Lou bring you back the scanner." She paused for emphasis. "And a map."

"Good," Borgdanov said. "Ilya and I will stay here with *Dyed*. We must discuss how to approach the *Kapitan Godina*."

Dugan rose and followed Anna to the door. She pecked his cheek before leaving, and Dugan locked the door behind her. As he walked back into the living room, Borgdanov caught his eye and jerked his head toward the master bedroom. Dugan nodded and moved into the bedroom. Seconds later Borgdanov entered the room and closed the door.

Dugan sighed. "What is it now, Andrei?"

"I am concerned about the rescue operation. First I hear Alex is coming to US with us, and I cannot say no because, after all, is his jet. Now also I learn not only Gillian is coming but the little boy is coming. This will not work. I think we need only me, Ilya and you." Borgdanov flashed a fleeting smile. "After all, you I have pushed out of chopper before. You are not so useful in gunfight, but you know all things about ship if we should need expert, *da*?"

"I understand, but Alex and Gillian don't plan on coming on the rescue. They just want to be in the US so when we rescue the girls, they're close to provide what comfort or support they can."

"Okay, but what about this kid Nigel? He is nice kid, and I think he loves Cassie, but if we have to watch him, it will distract us from mission. Is not good idea."

"I agree, but perhaps you've noticed he's stubborn as hell. If we exclude him, he's not going to just go away, and I'm concerned he might do something stupid. I figure it's best to keep him with us for now, where we can keep an eye on him. We'll leave him ashore in the US."

"Okay. Is good. I should have known you would be thinking of this," Borgdanov replied, moving back toward the door to the living room.

"Andrei, one more thing. Thank you for agreeing to Anna's conditions. This is a difficult situation for her."

Borgdanov nodded. "I understand, and we will stay outside of her circle. And who knows? This Arsov is a crafty fox I think, and maybe the fox will run out of the circle, and they will need someone to chase him, *da*."

Christ, I hope not, thought Dugan.

CHAPTER SEVENTEEN

Container Ship *Kapitan Godina*
En route to Jacksonville, Florida

Cassie sat on the mattress, breathing through her mouth, her back resting against the corrugated steel wall of the container. Like her two companions, she was stripped to her bra and panties, and the bare steel was hot on her back. Tanya's head rested in her lap, and Cassie tried to shift her weight without disturbing the other girl—a low moan signaled the failure of that effort. In an hour or so, the steel would be too hot to lean against, and she'd be faced with the unpleasant choice of sitting upright and bracing herself against the continual slow roll of the ship or lying on the fetid smelly mattress. The first choice was exhausting, the second vomit-inducing. Tanya moaned again, and Cassie mopped the girl's head with a precious piece of clean cloth torn from her skirt and soaked in water from their dwindling reserve.

"I think she's hotter, Karina. The fever is getting worse."

Beside her, Karina stirred and reached out to pat Cassie's arm. "Tanya will be fine. She is tough. All four of her grandparents survived the Battle of Stalingrad. Survival is in her genes, *da*?"

But her optimism seemed forced, and Cassie sensed the fear behind the words.

Cassie shook her head. "It's all just so horrible…" Her voice trailed off as she looked around in the dim light of the container.

It had been tolerable enough at first, when their seasickness had finally abated, but then the seas got really bad, and even stretching out on the mattresses gave no relief from the constant movement. Rest seemed impossible, and even when fatigue overcame them and they fell into exhausted sleep, they soon found themselves thrown off onto the hard floor of the container. Cassie remembered Nigel's tale of sleeping in rough seas by shoving his life jacket under the outer edge of his bunk to form a V-shaped trough along his cabin bulkhead, and they emulated the trick, shoving all three mattresses against the long wall of the container and then elevating the outside edges of the mattresses with the boxes of MREs. They'd slept secure for one night at least, resting in the notch they created, with gravity holding them in place and their backs against the steel wall.

Then the rolling got worse—far worse—and the second night one of the toilet buckets came loose from its lashing and slammed against the far wall of the container, losing its lid to dump its vile contents on the container floor. The girls' fumbling efforts to re-lash the bucket by flashlight had ended in failure when a huge roll caused Tanya to slip in the mess and go down hard, smashing the flashlight and cutting her hand on the broken lens. The girls had groped their way back to their mattresses, to huddle in the pitching dark, listening as one by one, other buckets and water bottles broke free to career through the container.

Gradually the seas abated, and when dawn began to leak through the small holes near the top of the container, daylight found them clinging to their little mattress islands, awash in a half inch of unspeakable filth that sloshed back and forth with the roll of the ship. Over half their thin-walled plastic water jugs had burst and added their contents to the stew of vomit and body wastes disgorged from the toilet buckets, and the intact bottles rolled around in the filth, as the mattresses and the cardboard of the MRE boxes wicked up the sewage.

Karina had taken charge, wading through the sloshing filth to pull undamaged bottles of water onto her mattress. Then she'd retrieved the three empty and unused toilet buckets that hadn't broken free and brought them to the mattresses. She'd ordered everyone out of their clothes and sealed the relatively clean garments in one of the buckets, retaining her own dress, which she immediately began tearing into rags. Then she used one of the rags to wipe an intact water bottle as clean as possible before she opened it. While Cassie and Tanya held the other unopened jugs out off the mattresses, Karina sacrificed water from her open jug to frugally, but thoroughly, flush the exterior of the other bottles.

When she'd flushed the bottles, she had the other girls dry them with rags and resecure them in the wall rack, while she dug the MREs from the wet cardboard boxes and pushed all the sodden packing material to one side. Finally, she'd flushed the exterior of all the food packages, dried them, and packed and sealed them in the remaining two clean buckets. At last all three girls braved the ankle-deep mess one last time to stack the three mattresses on top of each other and crawl on top of the stack, discarding their sodden shoes and sacrificing another bit of precious water to rinse their feet.

They'd survived since crammed on their tiny mattress island, hoping against hope the rough seas would not return and destroy what they'd managed to salvage. The remaining food and water was lashed to the near wall within easy reach, along with a single toilet bucket. The bottom mattress had wicked up much of the effluvia from the floor of the container, leaving a slick sheen through which ever-smaller waves rippled with the roll of the ship. The second mattress was sodden as well, as it wicked up fluid from the bottom mattress and the remaining liquid from the top mattress drained into it. Only their small sanctuary was dry, but the mattresses seemed to concentrate the smell.

The discomfort of the hot steel on Cassie's back returned her to the present, and she shifted again. Tanya moaned in her sleep, moving her right hand as she did so. She cried out and came half awake. Cassie held her tight.

"Shhh... Tanya. It's okay. I have you. Go back to sleep. Rest is good for you," Cassie whispered, and Tanya whimpered and closed her eyes again.

When Tanya's breathing indicated she'd fallen back into a troubled sleep, Cassie studied Tanya's right hand in the dim light. It was swollen to almost twice its normal size, the skin stretched tight and shiny. The edges of the cut from the flashlight lens were red and angry, and the discoloration had begun to creep up her arm.

"It's getting worse, Karina," Cassie whispered.

"*Da*," Karina agreed. "No doubt some shit got into the cut. There is nothing we can do now but try to keep her comfortable and hope the ship arrives somewhere soon. I think is good thing she sleeps."

"Wh-what if we don't get there before... before... you know..."

"We will, Cassie," Karina said through clenched teeth. "We will all survive. It is the way we will beat these bastards, *da*?"

HOLDING WAREHOUSE
516 COPELAND ROAD
SOUTHWARK, LONDON, UK

"...and you haven't seen him at all?" Arsov asked into the phone.

"*Nyet*," said the voice, "not since we were released. We dropped him at Club *Pyatnitsa*. He said he was going to check a few things there and then go home to sleep."

"Okay. If you hear from him, tell him to call me."

"*Da*," the man responded and hung up.

Arsov laid the phone down and drummed his fingers on the battered desk. Where the hell was Nazarov? He hadn't showed up back at the club, and no one had heard from him for a full day. What was the idiot up to now? He wasn't in police custody—his informant had been sure about that—but he was nowhere to be found. Had Karina's uncle and that other ex-*Spetsnaz* asshole grabbed him? It seemed unlikely, but that was really the only explanation.

What were the possible implications? He wasn't worried that Nazarov would talk—no one was more aware of what the *Bratstvo* did to informers than other members of the *Bratstvo*. No, Nazarov would keep quiet even if it killed him. Arsov smiled—and it probably had. And what could be more perfect? He was on track to resume operations in a week or ten days, and Nazarov was no longer here to defend himself. His narrative was complete. He had come here from Prague and discovered irregularities. Nazarov was not only skimming money into an offshore account, but was also playing both ends against the middle as a paid police informant. The treacherous bastard had set up a massive police raid, and when he, Arsov, had discovered the offshore account and foiled the raid, Nazarov had disappeared.

Arsov hummed a little tune and considered his next move. He still needed to set up one of his other underlings as Nazarov's accomplice, but that could wait. In fact, hinting to St. Petersburg that he was still struggling valiantly to root out all the problems would make him seem even more indispensable.

He picked up his phone and speed-dialed St. Petersburg.

Specialist Crimes Directorate 9 (SCD9)
Human Exploitation/Organized Crime
Victoria Block, New Scotland Yard
Boadway
London, UK

Detective Constable Cecil Peterson sat at his desk, mouse in hand. He liked his desk position in the bullpen, with his back to the far wall and with the others able to see only the back of his monitor. He could pass his time playing computer solitaire without anyone sneaking up on him, and he had a good view of the whole squad room as well. He liked the late night shift too, without so many prying eyes. Not that he'd had any choice in the matter. No one else wanted it, and it had been 'offered' to him on a take-it-or-leave-it basis when they 'reinvented' his unit. They'd acted like he should bow down and kiss their bloody arses for the right to stay on a few more years until his full pension kicked in, rather than being sacked or pensioned off early at reduced pay like the rest of his mates.

Twenty-five years in Vice and that's what he got as a thank you. Twenty-five years of having Barbara's snooty family say things like, "Oh yes, Cecil's with the Met, but he's not a proper copper, is he? He's in Vice, you know, mucking about arresting whores and breaking up poker games. I don't see why he doesn't request a transfer to a real unit, but he seems to like it."

If only they knew. It wasn't like that at first—new men joined the unit intent on making a difference. But then they learned they couldn't, because no one really wanted things to change, did they? If they cracked down on prostitution, there were the inevitable campaigns ranting about the focus on 'victimless crime' while 'real' crimes went unsolved. And when they eased off, there were the equally strident news stories of the Vice cops 'allowing' pimps and other low-life scum to victimize innocent girls.' Damned if you did, damned if you didn't.

But you didn't know that at first, did you? And by the time you wised up a few years in, you were irrevocably tainted. Other departments shied away from accepting transfers from Vice, so you stuck it out and grew more cynical year after year. So what if a few of the lads took a few quid here or did a favor there? It's not like any of it made a difference. Everyone just wanted to eke it out to full pension, and crawl out of the cesspool. And then along comes Detective Inspector Colin bloody McKinnon, with his high and mighty attitude and new names, sacking good lads left and right. Peterson sneered. Specialist Crimes Directorate 9—Unit SCD9. It sounded like something in a damned James Bond movie.

He straightened at his desk as the object of his ire walked out of his office and into the squad room, trailed by the redheaded bitch from MI5. What the hell were they doing here at this hour? They both had on tactical vests and were armed, and as he watched, they hurried across the nearly deserted squad room and into the corridor. Through the open door, Peterson heard the chime as the lift arrived.

Peterson's mind raced. The MI5 bitch had been part of the big operation against the Russians, so it didn't take a genius to figure out something was up. He closed his game of solitaire and accessed the department server to check new warrants. And there it was—a search warrant for 516 Copeland Road, Southwark, filed less than thirty minutes earlier. McKinnon, you sneaky bastard.

This was bad. The money from Arsov was good, but penalties for failure didn't bear thinking about. If the Russkies went down to a raid and he hadn't at least tried to warn them, he doubted he'd survive the week. And they wouldn't stop with him—Barbara and the kids would be at risk too. But what the hell was McKinnon's game? He obviously wasn't planning on raiding Arsov with just himself and the woman, and he hadn't used any SCD9 assets. And giving Arsov sketchy information was almost as likely to incur his wrath as giving him none. He needed to find out more, and fast.

He stood up and stretched. "Christ, I'm knackered," he said to his nearest colleague a few desks away. "I'm going out for a smoke. Cover my phone for me while I'm gone, would you, mate? I'll be back straightaway."

The man shrugged. "Sure. Take your time. I doubt anything exciting is likely to happen anytime soon."

Peterson smiled and tried to appear nonchalant as he walked toward the door. *If you only knew mate*, he thought.

Once in the corridor, he raced straight to the stairwell and flew down the two flights to the ground floor. He cracked open the stairwell door and confirmed the corridor was empty before exiting and walking toward the car park at the back of the building. He slowed as he neared the glass door and exited quietly, ducking down behind the nearest patrol car to scan the car park. He spotted them in the far corner.

Bloody Hell! He spotted McKinnon's car parked behind a 'Trojan,' one of the ARVs, or Armed Response Vehicles, of Unit CO19. McKinnon and the Walsh woman were standing near his car, and McKinnon was obviously introducing the woman to a group of black-clad Specialist Firearms Officers. They were all well-equipped and all wearing tactical vests. Peterson spotted assault rifles, and at least one had night-vision glasses hanging from his web gear—likely they all did. This was bad!

Peterson slipped back through the door and raced down the corridor to the toilet. He did a quick check of the stalls to ensure he was alone and then pulled the burner phone from his pocket.

CHAPTER EIGHTEEN

"I think you can get a little closer, *Dyed*," Borgdanov said from the front passenger seat.

Behind the wheel, Dugan pointed to the GPS display mounted on the console. "We're already well inside the agreed one-mile radius. And besides, this is as good a spot as any. We're inconspicuous here, and the last thing we want is to be spotted and screw up the op."

They were parked on Talfourd Road, facing north toward the intersection of Peckham Road, just one car of many parked along the curb.

"Of course we are inconspicuous," Borgdanov grumbled. "We are so far away Arsov would need spy satellite to find us. It will not hurt to get a little closer. If nothing happens, Anna will never know, and if there is problem and we help, we will be forgiven, *da*?"

"*Da*," Ilya agreed from the seat behind Dugan.

Dugan twisted in his seat to look at Ilya and Nigel sitting beside him. Nigel remained silent, but his expression spoke volumes. It was clear he agreed with the two Russians.

"That's a big *nyet*," Dugan said. "Besides, exactly where else would you like me to go? In the unlikely event this operation fails, the bad guys could run in any direction, and we can't be everywhere. I think we can count on them having other safe houses, and they'll likely stay in the city center where they don't stand out as much, and Peckham Road is the fastest way back to the city. If that happens, we'll hear it on the scanner and be in a position to maybe cut them off."

"Okay, okay," Borgdanov said. "So we stay on this road, but maybe just a bit closer?"

"Absolutely not. Anna's got her neck stuck out on this as it is, and we promised her that McKinnon wouldn't even know we were nearby, so here we stay unless something goes amiss."

Borgdanov glared at him a long moment just as McKinnon's voice erupted from the scanner.

"Unit Two, this is Unit One. Do you copy? Over."

"Unit One, this is Unit Two. We copy," came the reply.

"Two, what is your status? Over," McKinnon asked.

"We are in position near the loading dock. All the large roller doors are closed. There is one man-door, a heavy metal industrial job. Suggest we use breaching charges on the masonry surround. Over."

"Affirmative, Two," McKinnon said. "Are there security cameras or vehicles? Over."

"Negative on cameras. There are two cars in the yard near the far end of the loading dock. We have eyes on the inside of the warehouse. Ramsey snaked fiber optics under one of the roller doors. There is movement in an area on the south wall. We can see the head and shoulders of two men over the back of a sofa. Some sort of makeshift living area. Third target is not visible, but there is what looks like a door to an office area on your side." He paused. "And there are cages and containers on the north end of the warehouse. The cages are full of... people."

The scanner fell silent, and Dugan looked at the Russians, his jaw clenched.

"Bastards," Nigel muttered, but the Russians sat in stoic silence, their expressions saying everything that needed saying.

"I copy, Two," McKinnon said. "Are the hostages in the line of fire? Over?"

"Negative, One. If you take the target in the office area and we enter simultaneously from both doors, we'll catch the other two in a cross fire. Over."

"Okay, Two. Disable the vehicles and set the breaching charges on the door. How long before you're ready? Over."

"Estimate five minutes. Should I keep Ramsey on the fiber optics?"

There was another pause, as if McKinnon was considering the question, then he responded. "Negative, Two. We're shorthanded as it is. I need all three of you to crash the door, and I want Ramsey to insert himself between the hostages and the targets. Advise when you have the charges set and are ready to breach. Over."

"Affirmative. Unit Two out."

Borgdanov nodded. "Okay, *Dyed*, we stay. I think we soon find out if McKinnon captures the fox, *da*?"

HOLDING WAREHOUSE
516 COPELAND ROAD
SOUTHWARK, LONDON, UK

Arsov answered his phone.

"It's me," a voice said. "You're about to be raided."

"What? When? By who?"

"McKinnon and that MI5 bitch," Peterson said. "NOW!"

"MI5? What the hell are you talking about? What's MI5 got to do with any of this?"

"That redhead bitch, Anna Walsh. I was wondering how she seemed so thick with McKinnon, and I sniffed around a bit and found out she's with British Intelligence," Peterson said.

"And you're just telling me now?"

"I-I just found out earlier today, and the big raid was already a bust, so I didn't think it was urgent. But when I saw her sniffing around tonight, I put it together and figured—"

"Or maybe you figured I might pay a little more for that information and were saving it for later, eh? Let me assure you, you'll be paid, but maybe not as you intended."

"No… really…I had no clue. I mean, I found out about the woman, but I just found out about the next raid by accident. That bastard McKinnon didn't even log the warrant until a half hour ago. I called you as soon as I found out. I swear."

Arsov's mind raced. There would be time enough to deal with Peterson later—assuming there was a later. Now he needed information.

"How many and when?" he demanded.

"Seven, including McKinnon and the bitch, at least as far as I could tell. But they're not from our unit. At least five are CO19 lads, full tactical gear, night-vision kit, the works. And if they're not outside your location now, they soon will be."

"All right. We'll talk later." Arsov hung up.

He took a deep breath and struggled to calm himself. He thought of the captives and the drugs in the warehouse—so much for staying under the radar. No lawyer could get him out of this, no matter how good he was. And MI5? What the hell could that mean? He pulled his laptop over and clicked on the feed from the security cameras concealed around the perimeter of the building. Other warehouses made sure the cameras were visible to discourage robberies, but the *Bratstvo*'s security needs were a bit different. They didn't need to discourage thieves; everyone in the underworld knew you didn't touch certain warehouses and you didn't talk about them—ever. He pulled up the feeds from the front of the building first and saw nothing within the range of the cameras, but the loading dock was a different story. Two black-clad figures worked around the back door, and when he zoomed in, he saw they were setting breaching charges. He zoomed out and panned the camera to see another man puncturing the tires on Yuri's Mercedes. He assumed his own car would be next.

Not much time, but he did have the element of surprise. He moved to a metal storage cabinet and pulled a canvas duffel bag from a lower shelf and quickly stuffed it with items from the cabinet. He slung the bag over his shoulder and raced out into the warehouse.

His underlings were in the makeshift living quarters along the south wall of the warehouse. There were two old sofas on either side of a card table where they ate their meals. A large refrigerator, a microwave on a stand, and a big-screen TV completed the furnishings. The two men spent their time eating, playing video games, or enjoying the pleasures of the whores they released from the cages when they felt the need. Yuri sat on a sofa with his pants around his ankles as he forced a naked teenage girl's face into his crotch. Anatoli was sitting at the other end of the sofa, laughing and making critical comments on the girl's performance.

Arsov heaved the duffel bag on to the card table and unzipped it as he gave orders with quiet urgency. "Pull your fucking pants up, and put her back in her cage," he said to Yuri. "We're about to be raided."

"What?" Anatoli asked as Yuri pushed the girl away roughly and stood to fumble with his pants. Arsov glared at him again, and he quickly zipped his pants and dragged the girl upright by her hair to push her in the direction of the cages across the cavernous warehouse.

"They'll be coming in the front and back doors any minute," Arsov said to Anatoli, as he laid out weapons in a line on the table, three compact Kedr submachine guns with extra box magazines, with a flashlight next to each. He flinched slightly as a cage door slammed, and looked up to see Yuri returning. He motioned him to hurry, and when Yuri got close, Arsov continued his instructions in a rush.

"They'll probably be three or four through each door, and we'll be waiting. Yuri, I want you to cover the door from the office area. Anatoli, take the back door, but be careful. They'll blow the door with explosives, so stay behind cover until they detonate. They'll be wearing vests, so take their legs out from under them first. I'll kill the interior lights, so each of you take a flashlight. You may need—"

Yuri looked confused. "But wha—"

"Shut the fuck up! I don't have time to explain."

Both men bobbed their heads and began to arm themselves, and Arsov continued as he donned the single pair of night-vision goggles and flipped them up out of his line of vision. "They'll probably use flash bangs from both doors, so be ready to shut your eyes and cover your ears."

"But how did they find us?" Anatoli asked, risking Arsov's wrath.

"That bastard Nazarov must have talked. But there aren't many of them, so we should be able to take them down. Now get in position."

Yuri nodded and rushed to cover the front entrance, but Anatoli hesitated.

"What are you going to do?"

"I'll stay mobile and arrange a little surprise and then support either you or Yuri, depending on circumstances. We have to kill all these bastards quickly and then take one of the cars and get the hell out. We're done in the UK for now, but if we can make it to a safe house, we can hole up a while and then get out of the country. Now quit asking questions and get to your god damned station."

Anatoli nodded and rushed to cover the rear door.

Copeland Road
Near Holding Warehouse
Southwark, London, UK

"Unit One, do you copy? Over," the radio squawked.

McKinnon looked at Anna and spoke into his shoulder-mounted mike. "Two, this is One. I copy. Are you ready? Over."

"Affirmative, One. Over," came the reply.

"Good, Two. Prepare to breach on my order. Over," McKinnon said.

"This is Two standing by for your order. Be advised the bit of light leaking under the big roller doors just went out. It looks like they may be bedding down for the night. Over."

McKinnon frowned. "Do you think they've moved? Over."

"Possibly," Two replied, "but they'll either be on the sofas or somewhere in the office area. We didn't see anywhere else to sleep. Either way, the plan should work. Over."

"Affirmative. Stand by."

McKinnon turned and nodded at Anna as he opened the car door. "Well, wish us luck, Agent Walsh."

"I do indeed." Anna opened her own door.

"Just a minute. Where do you think you're going?"

"With you, obviously. You did invite me to ride along."

"Correct," McKinnon said. "As in 'ride,' which implies you're to stay in the car. Need I remind you that this isn't exactly a matter for MI5 and that I invited you to OBSERVE as a courtesy."

"Not likely," Anna said sweetly. "And besides, there are only six of you. That's not exactly an overwhelming force now, is it?"

"Six of us and complete surprise. This should be a fast and easy take down."

"In which case there's no harm in me OBSERVING from a closer vantage point than the car, is there? The word does mean 'to see,' you know, and I won't be able to see bloody fuck all from the car, now will I?"

McKinnon shook his head. "All right, damn it! But stay well behind us. If this doesn't go as planned, I'll have a hard enough time explaining your presence, and all the more so if you get shot in the bargain."

Anna smiled. "Your solicitude is touching, Inspector."

McKinnon muttered something under his breath and got out of the car, striding toward his two constables on the sidewalk without looking back. Both constables had their assault rifles slung, and one was carrying a crowbar and the other a short but obviously heavy breaching ram. McKinnon nodded as he reached them, and they all started for the front door of the warehouse in a crouching run, with Anna close behind.

The front of the warehouse appeared to be office space, with a vacant reception area opening on to the street. Large floor-to-ceiling windows dominated the front of the reception area, and the entrance was a glass door set in a heavy aluminum frame. McKinnon nodded to the constable with the crowbar, and the man inserted the flat end of the bar into the crack between the door and the frame just above the lock and leaned into the bar. The metal frame of the door resisted and then began to distort, as the heavy glass gave a soft pop and cracks spider-webbed across the door. The constable pushed harder, and the door came open.

McKinnon rushed inside, his two constables and Anna on his heels, as he whispered into his shoulder mike.

"Two, this is One. We're in the reception area. Blow your door and prepare to deploy flash bangs."

The words had hardly left his mouth when they heard a rumbling roar from the back of the building, followed immediately by the screams of terrified women, muffled slightly by the thin interior walls of the office area.

"Go! Go! Go!" McKinnon said, and the man with the ram ran forward and slammed the heavy weight against the door leading to the interior office area. The flimsy door frame shattered in an explosion of splinters as the door flew open and slammed against the wall. McKinnon and the two constables entered the short dark hallway, flipping down their night-vision glasses as they entered. Anna, with no NV equipment, trailed cautiously, her Glock in a two-handed grip, as the three policemen leapfrogged each other down the hallway, clearing the two empty offices. They stopped at another flimsy wooden door. The screams from the warehouse interior were deafening now.

"Flash bangs! Now!" McKinnon said into his mike as he nodded to his own men. Anna holstered her weapon as one man smashed the door open with a well-placed foot near the doorknob, and the second lobbed a flash-bang grenade into the black interior. All three policemen slung their weapons, and Anna followed their cue as they turned away with their eyes closed tight and palms pressed over their ears. Even then, Anna saw the lights from the twin explosions flash through her closed eyelids, and the concussions felt almost like physical blows.

She staggered a bit and opened her eyes as she groped for her Glock. After an instantaneous lull, the screaming started again, even louder.

"Go!" McKinnon said, and his constables rushed through the open door and deployed to either side. McKinnon followed and cleared the door just as the interior of the warehouse was bathed in bright light and the roar of automatic weapons fire drowned out the screams of the terrified women. Anna watched, paralyzed, as the three police men jerked from the impact of multiple rounds and collapsed.

She spotted the shooter through the open door, some distance into the warehouse, crouching near an oil drum. She raised her Glock and opened fire, trying to relieve the pressure on the three wounded cops lying in the open. A round hit the drum with a metallic clang, and the shooter turned his attention to her. She dived to the floor as concentrated automatic fire shredded the thin walls of the office area around her.

CHAPTER NINETEEN

Arsov waited among the caged whores on the north wall of the warehouse, his flashlight illuminating an electrical panel. He had his eyes averted from the door in the east wall, almost fifty meters away. His wait was finally rewarded by an explosion that sent masonry rubble sailing across the darkened warehouse, to pepper the floor like falling hail. He smiled as all around him the whores began to screech in terror. He hadn't thought of that—what a wonderful little addition to the confusion he wished to generate.

Anticipating what was to come, he held his small flashlight between his teeth, cupped his palms over his ears and faced the wall, presenting his back to the interior of the warehouse, his eyes tightly shut. Moments later, he felt the twin concussions of the flash bangs and held his position a second longer to make sure there wouldn't be a third. When he took his hands from his ears, the terrified wails of the whores were even louder. Even better! The cops should be coming in just about... now! He turned his flashlight on the electrical panel and threw the main breaker.

The interior of the warehouse was flooded with light, and the black-clad policemen stood in the open, stunned as their NV glasses made it seem as if the sun itself had gone supernova in their faces. Arsov nodded in satisfaction as Yuri stitched the three policemen charging in from the office area across their lower bodies, and they went down together. Someone returned fire from the office area—the MI5 bitch, no doubt—and he again nodded approval as Anatoli began shredding the office area on full auto, attempting to silence his unseen adversary.

Arsov turned to the rear door and shook his head. Anatoli had obviously not listened as well as Yuri. Two of the policemen were down, but the third had taken most of Anatoli's fire in the vest, though he was limping badly as he staggered towards the hole in the wall where the door had been. Arsov unfolded the stock of his Kedr, raised it to his shoulder, and took careful aim. He pulled the trigger and watched as the limping cop's head exploded, washing the masonry wall with a swath of blood and brains.

Anatoli redeemed himself in the next moments by killing the other two downed cops, and then Arsov turned back to check on Yuri's progress. Just in time. Yuri still hadn't silenced the woman and seemed oblivious to the fact that one of the wounded cops on the floor had his hand to his shoulder mike, attempting a distress call. Arsov cursed under his breath, the last thing he needed was more cops riding to the rescue before he got far enough away. He pressed the gun to his shoulder and aimed at the struggling cop.

***

Blinding light flashed in McKinnon's eyes, stunning him. *Ambush*, he thought, just as three hammer blows hit him mid-thigh, knocking his legs from under him. He hit the floor face first, the concrete driving the useless NV glasses into his face, and he felt them gouge into his forehead. He lay there a second, blinking beneath the now useless goggles, as something wet flooded his eyes and the air above his head filled with the cacophony of terrified screams and full automatic rifle fire.

He moved in slow motion and, with great effort, flipped up his damaged NV goggles, but he still could see nothing. He turned his head and willed his hand to key his shoulder mike. It came up gradually, almost as if it wasn't attached to his arm.

"All units near... near... 516 Cope... land... Road. Offi... officers down... ambush... auto..."

***

Blood sprayed from the back of the cop's head onto the shattered wall of the office area, and his ruined face rolled to one side, away from the shoulder mike. Almost done. Arsov jerked as a bullet ricocheted off the wall beside him into the caged whores, eliciting an even louder round of screams. One of the two wounded cops had his night-vision glasses flipped up and had recovered sufficiently to return fire, and the second was attempting to do so as well.

He couldn't have that, now could he. Arsov reached over and threw the breaker again, plunging the warehouse into darkness just before he flipped down his own NV glasses.

"Hold your fire," he bellowed in Russian, loud enough to be heard above the screams, just as Yuri stopped to change magazines. It wouldn't do if one of these idiots shot him by mistake.

He ran across the warehouse, watching as the two wounded policemen struggled with their NV glasses. But they were blind fish in a barrel, and Arsov killed them both before they got off another shot. He turned without breaking stride and ran back through the dark, flipping his NV glasses up just before he turned the lights back on. He glanced down at his watch—less than two minutes since the cops had blown the rear door—but he still had to hurry.

"Anatoli! Come to this side and help us finish off the woman. Hurry!"

Seconds later, the Russians were lined up in front of the office area, with fresh magazines in place. Arsov glanced over at the cages where the whores cowered, quiet now, as if afraid to attract attention.

"I think I hit her earlier, before you finished off the cops," Yuri said, as Arsov looked back. "I heard her yell. She's on the right side of the door."

Arsov nodded. "Keep your fire low. She will be on the floor."

All three men sprayed the base of the wall to the right of the door with automatic fire.

***

Anna flattened herself against the floor and gazed at her useless Glock. She'd expended both her first magazine and her spare and was out of ammunition. The walls were rapidly being blown away to nothing, and light shined through the ragged holes, suffusing the previously dark space with a dull glow that threatened to steal her invisibility. She hadn't caught a bullet, but the furious fire had turned the office walls into shrapnel, and blood puddled around her, leaking from a half-dozen wounds where ragged splinters had driven into the flesh of her unprotected limbs. She fumbled with her phone and had just pressed Dugan's preset when another burst of fire shredded the cheap carpet in front of her and ricocheted off the concrete floor beneath, sending her smashed phone flying out of her hand along with the tip of her right index finger.

"Shit!" Anna said before she could stop herself, and then she scrambled to her left and under an old metal desk just as a fresh burst ripped through the place she'd occupied seconds before. She was unarmed and helpless, and apparently the sole survivor. She was pondering surrender when hope surged as different guns joined the battle to the left of what remained of the door. There were others still fighting back! Then the lights went out again. Someone yelled in Russian, and hope died as she heard unanswered automatic fire from where she knew the cops had fallen. They were being executed. There would be no surrender to these bastards.

Moments later, the lights came back on, and there was more shouting in Russian before the fire directed at her increased in intensity, all of it ricocheting off the floor now at a shallow angle, walking toward her. She rolled over quickly and turned her back to the gunmen, ducking her head and drawing her legs up to her chest, presenting as little unprotected flesh to the unseen gunman as possible, and gasping as multiple rounds bounced off the floor and slammed into her protected back, hammering the breath from her. Then she felt a jolt and a searing pain in her left hip below the vest, and something warm and wet flowing down her legs. She thought she'd wet herself until she smelled the coppery odor of fresh blood and knew she was badly hurt.

Suddenly she just felt tired. Very tired. How very nice it would be to take a bit of a nap. If only they would stop making all that noise. She closed her eyes and was at the edge of consciousness before something slammed into the desk above her with a tremendous crash. *Bloody noise makers,* she thought again and then slipped away.

***

Arsov watched as the shattered remains of the office wall folded over and the suspended ceiling crashed down into the ruined office area in a great cloud of drywall dust.

"Hold your fire," he yelled and moved toward the rubble.

"Should we dig her out and make sure she's dead, Boss?" Yuri asked.

Arsov watched a growing puddle of blood leak out from under the wreckage, mixing with white drywall dust to form a pink sludge.

He shook his head. "No time. Look at the blood. She's either dead or soon will be. Besides, if she's still alive when help arrives, they'll waste a bit of time trying to save her."

"So we go?"

Arsov nodded. "Go gather up your stuff, and let's get out of here."

He watched as Anatoli and Yuri pushed past him, and when they were a few feet away, he shot them both in the back. Just on the off chance he did get captured, he needed someone to blame all the dead policemen on now, didn't he? He was congratulating himself on his cleverness when he looked up and saw the whores staring at him through the wire of the cages.

"Fuck!" He was so accustomed to thinking of them as furniture he'd totally forgotten about them as potential witnesses. He glanced at his watch again—five minutes since it had all started, though it seemed like an hour. He had no way of knowing if the cop got a call off before he killed him, but he had to assume he did. So first things first—he needed transportation.

He first searched the cop that tried to call and got lucky, pulling a set of car keys with an electronic key fob from the man's pants pocket. He wiped the blood off on a dry section of the cop's pants and looked over at the collapsed rubble of the office area. The collapsing walls had exposed a section of the glassed front of the reception area. He moved to the glass and pressed his face against it as he thumbed the button on the key fob and smiled as lights blinked in the distance up Copeland Road. Now to tidy up and leave.

He put a fresh magazine in his Kder and started toward the cages.

PECKHAM ROAD AND TALFOURD ROAD
LONDON, UK

Dugan sat with the others in tense anticipation as they listened to McKinnon's orders to breach the warehouse door and deploy the flash bangs. Then came the order to rush the warehouse, followed by—nothing.

He looked at Borgdanov. "Shouldn't we be hearing someth—"

Dugan's phone buzzed, and he fished it from his pocket and checked the caller ID before answering. "Yes, Anna?"

"Anna, are you there?" he asked into the phone as Borgdanov glanced over, a puzzled look on his face.

Dugan disconnected and stared at the phone.

"What is it, *Dyed*?"

"A call from Anna's phone," Dugan replied, still staring at the phone. "But I hardly think she'd call me in the middle of an operation, especially since we're not supposed to know it's going down. Maybe she just pocket dialed me by mistake." He looked up at Borgdanov. "Do you think I should try to call her back?"

Borgdanov shrugged. "I do not know, *Dyed*. Perhaps it is as you say, a mista—"

The scanner squawked, "All units near... near... 516 Cope... land... Road. Offi... officers down... ambush... auto..."

Dugan's blood ran cold.

"Go, *Dyed*!" Borgdanov yelled.

But Dugan was already starting the car. Tires squealed as they rocketed from the curb and careened around the corner onto Peckham Road.

CHAPTER TWENTY

INSIDE HOLDING WAREHOUSE
516 COPELAND ROAD
SOUTHWARK, LONDON, UK

Arsov glanced at his watch again as he hurried back from the cages, his mind working overtime as he strode across the warehouse. If anyone was coming, he needed to buy some time, just in case, and the best diversions were always the unexpected.

He saw the answer from across the warehouse, provided courtesy of MI5. One of the drums Anatoli had ducked behind was punctured by the woman's fire, a single round just below the liquid level. A pungent smell assailed Arsov's nostrils, and he saw clear liquid leaking down the side of the drum and puddling around it. A rivulet crept across the concrete floor toward a floor drain ten meters away. He drew close to read the labels on the drum and a dozen others around it. Nitroethane—raw material to feed multiple methamphetamine labs the *Bratstvo* was establishing across the UK. He nodded to himself and hurried over to Yuri's body and searched the dead man's pockets.

Moments later Arsov moved across the warehouse, unwrapping one of Yuri's vile little cigars as he walked. He sniffed the air to make sure he no longer smelled the fruity odor of the nitroethane. He didn't want an open flame near the chemical—not yet. Satisfied, he lit the cigar with a book of matches from Club *Pyatnitsa* and drew on the disgusting thing until the end glowed red. He then placed the butt of the burning cigarillo next to the matches in the open book and closed the cover, pinning the butt of the little cigar in the match book before he moved back to where the stream of chemical inched its way toward the floor drain. He set the matchbook down on edge in the stream's path, two meters away, the matchbook forming a tiny stand to hold the burning end of the little cigar up in the air—an improvised, but effective fuse.

He took a last look around. Unlike the cages he'd been able to fire through, he'd no time to open each container and deal with the occupants, but the whores inside the containers hadn't seen anything, and the fire should take care of them. And if help arrived while they were still alive, their rescue would provide yet another time-consuming diversion. Then he remembered the caged whores screaming during his ambush and had a flash of inspiration. He rushed back and picked up Yuri's Sedr and opened fire, the bullets ricocheting noisily off the heavy metal containers. He ceased fire as screams rose from the terrified women and children trapped inside the boxes—he obviously had their attention. He moved closer, shouting, "Run! The whole place is about to explode! Forget the whores! Leave them, and let's get out of here!"

Arsov nodded, as the screams from the containers rose to a satisfying din—that should be enough to occupy any first responders. With any luck, everyone would die together.

He jogged toward the section of exposed reception area glass at the front of the warehouse, blasting it apart with Yuri's Sedr as he approached. The last bit of glass fell from the window just as he reached it, and he tossed the now empty automatic to the side and stepped lightly through the ruined window, fishing the cop's keys from his pocket as he did so. He pressed the key fob, and car lights blinked down the street. He set off toward it at a jog.

CLAYTON AND CONSORT ROADS
LONDON, UK

Dugan gripped the wheel tightly as he whipped around the roundabout and raced due south on Consort Road. He searched above him for the point where the London Overground tracks passed over the road, the landmark for a hard right on to Copeland Road.

"Hurry, *Dyed*," urged Borgdanov, but Dugan already had the accelerator floorboarded.

Then the tracks were overhead, and Dugan barely slowed as he braced for the right turn. He blew through the traffic signal on screaming tires in a barely controlled skid, only to encounter the headlights of another car coming in the opposite direction.

"Watch out, *Dyed!*" Borgdanov screamed, but Dugan was already cutting the wheel, avoiding a head-on collision by inches. He clipped the back of the other car and sent both cars spinning away from each other to lurch to a halt against the curbs at opposite corners of the intersection.

"Is everyone all right?" Dugan asked.

"Arsov!" Ilya yelled from the back seat, and Dugan looked across to see Arsov behind the wheel of the other car. The mobster obviously recognized them as well, and the tires of his car squealed as he fled north up Consort Road.

"After him, *Dyed*," Borgdanov shouted, but Dugan hesitated only an instant before he roared down Copeland Road toward the warehouse.

"What are you doing?" Borgdanov demanded.

"If Arsov's hauling ass and McKinnon called for help, things went to hell at the warehouse." Dugan handed Borgdanov his cell phone. "I doubt the cops will listen to us, so get Lou or Harry on the phone and tell them which way Arsov is headed so they can alert the cops. And tell them to get all the help they can over here. I have a feeling we're going to need it."

Borgdanov swallowed his frustration and nodded as he took the phone. Dugan accelerated toward the warehouse—and Anna.

A minute later, the car skidded to a halt, bucking as the front wheel rode up on the curb. Light leaked through a smashed floor-to-ceiling window at one end of the warehouse reception area, dimly illuminating the wreckage of the remainder of the office area visible through the intact panes. The car was still rocking on its suspension as Dugan threw open his door and tumbled out to race toward the shattered window.

"*Dyed*, wait!" Borgdanov cried. "It could be a trap."

Dugan ignored him and ran toward the warehouse, with Nigel close behind. The Russians had no choice but to follow.

As he approached, Dugan heard muffled screams, but nothing prepared him for the scene inside the warehouse. Bodies lay scattered, and the pools of blood glistening in the harsh lights left little hope anyone was still alive. Heart in his throat, he scanned the bodies, momentarily relieved that he didn't see Anna, then fearful at her absence. He scanned the walls, and fear turned to rage when he saw more inert and bloody forms on the floor inside the cages.

He stood trembling as Borgdanov walked through the blood and stooped at each inert policeman's body to check for a pulse. Then he saw Ilya rush to the steel containers, obviously drawn by the screams. Ilya ran down the line, disengaging the locking dogs on each set of container doors and throwing them open. The screams died, and women and children rushed out of each container, to stop and gaze at their rescuers, confusion and fear in their eyes.

"Is Anna there?" Dugan called.

Ilya surveyed the small crowd of milling hostages. "*Nyet*," he called back. Dugan heard a gasp behind him.

He turned to see Nigel pointing at a flame racing across the floor towards a collection of drums stacked near the wall of the warehouse. The small flame reached the drums and ignited a larger puddle around them, engulfing all the drums.

"What the hell is that?" Nigel asked.

"Nothing good," Dugan said and screamed at the Russians, but they were already herding the hostages toward the hole in the back wall of the warehouse where the door had been.

"Go help them. I've got to find Anna," Dugan said to Nigel, then turned without waiting for a reply. He rushed toward the wreckage of the offices, the only place that might conceal her.

"Anna!" he called, wading into the debris. "If you can hear me, make a noise."

He stopped and listened, straining to hear over the growing roar of the fire behind him and feeling the heat on the back of his neck. Whatever was in the drums was burning hotly, and it was only a matter of time before the barrels ruptured and engulfed the whole building in flames. He pushed that from his mind and moved through the rubble calling Anna's name. Please God, let him find her in time.

Then he was deep into the wreckage, his movement raising thick, swirling clouds of drywall dust to mix with the acrid smoke of the chemical fire, stinging his nose and eyes and obscuring his vision. A section of shredded wall loomed out of the haze, blocking his path, and as he wrestled it aside, his foot slipped on something slick. He went down hard and cursed as his left knee slammed painfully into the concrete floor, and when he dropped his hand to steady himself, he felt something wet and slimy. He lifted his hand and squinted through stinging eyes.

Blood!

"Anna!" he screamed at the top of his lungs and was rewarded by a low moan from beneath a huge debris pile.

"I'm here! Hang on, Anna! I'll get you out of there."

It was becoming difficult to breathe in the increasingly toxic atmosphere, and Dugan succumbed to a bout of violent coughing. He struggled to his feet. Saving Anna was all that was important now.

What looked like half the suspended ceiling had collapsed upon the debris pile in front of him, the metal supports and acoustical tile twisted into a solid mass. The loose end of the obstruction rested on top of the pile of wreckage, and the other end was still connected overhead some distance away. Dugan squatted and put his shoulder under the free edge of the mass and lifted with a desperate, adrenaline-fueled strength. The load stubbornly resisted, and he redoubled his efforts until the whole mass began to creep upward, inch by inch. Dugan's straining hamstrings and butt muscles were on fire, but then he was upright, and he locked his knees, transferring part of the load to his skeletal structure. But what now? He heard a cough, and then someone shouted behind him.

"Mr. Dugan! Where are you? We have to get out. The whole place is going up!"

"Here, Nigel," Dugan yelled back over his shoulder, and Nigel scrambled through the rubble toward him, the sounds of his passage barely discernible over the increasing roar of the conflagration.

"Mr. Dugan. We hav—"

"Negative," Dugan shouted. "I found Anna. We've got to get her out!"

"Yes… yes, sir," Nigel said, moving to help Dugan shoulder the load.

"No," Dugan said. "I've got this. She's under the desk. Get that piece of wall out of the way and then slide the desk over so we can get at her."

Nigel set to work, his slight figure straining as the heavy wall section rose slowly and then crashed back onto the desk as his strength failed.

"It's too much for one man," Dugan yelled. "Go get the others!"

Nigel peered through the thick smoke and shook his head.

"It's too late. The fire's blocking the way. I came back just as they got the last of the hostages out the back, and I barely made it. I'm sure they're coming around the outside, but it's a long way, and there may be fences to deal with."

Dugan coughed and struggled for a breath.

"O-okay, then find something we can use to prop this ceiling up, then we can—"

"I understand," Nigel said, scanning the wreckage. He disappeared into the smoke and returned in seconds with a broken piece of wood slightly longer than Dugan was tall.

"This will have to do," Nigel said, tipping the wood at an angle and placing one end under the end of the collapsed ceiling near Dugan's shoulder and the other end on the floor. "If you can lift the ceiling a few more inches, I'll push the bottom of this board in along the floor until it's taking the weight."

"Let's do it," Dugan gasped, twisting to get the heel of his hands beneath the ceiling panel—and failing.

"What's the matter?"

"I-I've got to get out from under the load to reposition myself," Dugan said, "and as soon as I let go, this panel's coming down unless your little stick can hold the weight, so make damn sure the bottom of that thing doesn't slide out. Got it?"

"Just a minute," Nigel said, and Dugan felt the ceiling panel vibrate as Nigel kicked at the bottom of the board, trying to force it more vertical under the load. "Okay. I'm going to drop down and brace the bottom. Lower the load onto the board whenever you're ready."

Dugan nodded. "We'll go on three. One, two, THREE."

He twisted quickly and repositioned the heels of both palms under the edge of the ceiling panel. He'd barely gotten into position as the load began to increase.

"God damn it, Nigel! Hold it, I'm not ready! I can't hold it with my arms alone."

"The floor's... slick... with... blood. It's... sliding," Nigel gasped between grunts. "I can't... hold it... much longer. Get... clear!"

Dugan cursed and stepped back, releasing the load to sink on to the pile of debris, as the increased weight on the board pushed Nigel back a foot or so before the board came loose and clattered to the floor. Dugan stripped off his shirt and dropped to all fours to mop the blood off the floor.

"Take off your shirt and help me," Dugan yelled, and Nigel rushed to comply. In seconds they had cleared a small area of the floor of the sludge of blood and drywall dust.

Dugan squatted under the edge of the ceiling panel and extended his arms straight above his head, his palms resting on the load. Catching on immediately, Nigel worked the board back under the edge of the ceiling panel at an angle, pressing the bottom of the board to the newly cleaned floor to hold it in place.

"Okay," Dugan shouted above the fire. "At every count of three, I'll push up as hard as I can, and you push the bottom of the board in and let me know when you've stopped. You'll have to keep the bottom of the board in place while I'll rest for a second or so, and then we'll repeat. Start whenever you're ready. Got it?"

"Go," Nigel said, and Dugan began to take a deep breath and stopped as the smoke burned his throat. He coughed and steadied himself for the effort.

"One. Two. THREEEE…" Dugan clenched his teeth and pushed up with all his might.

"Stopped!" Nigel shouted.

Dugan relaxed a split second and squatted back down a bit to take advantage of the space his last push had gained him and began the count again. "One. Two. THREEE…" he called and fired upward on burning legs, gaining a bit of momentum before he shouldered the weight.

"Stopped," Nigel yelled. "That was a good one. A few more and we'll be done."

If I have 'a few more' in me, thought Dugan, as he dropped back down.

"Let's go for broke, junior. Just keep pushing and call out progress. Got it?"

"Ready when you are," Nigel replied.

"One. Two. THREEE…" Dugan fired upward, straining for all he was worth.

"Stopped," Nigel shouted, "just a bit more."

Dugan fought the urge to suck in a lungful of the smoke-filled air and tried to ignore his burning muscles. He closed his eyes and thought of Anna's face and strained harder still, oblivious to the pain.

"That's it! That's it! The board's vertical and taking the weight."

Dugan stumbled out from beneath the load, barely able to keep his feet, then gasped for breath and sucked in smoke instead. A coughing fit drove him to his knees, and as he struggled back to his feet, he squinted through the smoke toward the approaching inferno. The flames had reached the outer edges of the destroyed office area, and the heat was intense.

He stumbled toward the debris pile, and Nigel leaped to his side to help him wrestle the heavy section of destroyed wall off the desk. Seconds later they pulled the desk aside to reveal Anna's inert form lying in a pool of blood. Dugan's heart was in his throat as he dropped to her side and felt her carotid artery. Her pulse was weak but discernible, and Dugan gathered her in his arms and attempted to stand, but his exhausted legs betrayed him.

Nigel dropped down on Anna's opposite side, and between them, they lifted her and stumbled through the wreckage, breathing near impossible and their vision obscured as dense smoke burned their eyes. Bits of debris burst into flame, and they coughed as they staggered on, barely able to breathe.

"Wh-where's the window?" croaked Nigel. "Ca-can't see…"

"Just mo-move away from… fire. Hi-hit front wall and fo-follow it left t-to window," Dugan replied, with more certainty than he felt. Nigel stifled a cough, and they stumbled on, blind men in a maze.

"*Dyed*! Are you there?" came a voice.

"Here," Dugan croaked, and relief washed over him as two hulking figures appeared through the smoke. Ilya plucked Anna from their grasp and disappeared back the way he came. Borgdanov inserted himself between Dugan and Nigel and pulled them along in Ilya's wake.

"This way. Hold your breath," Borgdanov gasped through the thickening smoke as he dragged them through the wreckage.

Dugan slipped on a loose board and went down, rising with difficulty as Borgdanov tugged him to his feet. His lungs screamed for oxygen, but he dare not take a breath. Smoke burned his eyes, and he could see nothing, so he squeezed his eyes shut and stumbled on, relying on the big Russian to lead them to safety. Then he felt cool air on his face and sucked in a lungful of air tinged with the acrid stench of smoke. He blinked away the tears and rushed toward the blurry vision of the window, a rectangular outline in the glow of the streetlights.

"We are at the window," he heard Borgdanov say. "Watch your step—"

Dugan's toe caught on the low windowsill, and he pitched forward, landing hard on the sidewalk among the shards of broken window glass.

***

He came to sometime later, lying on a gurney as the flashing lights atop various emergency vehicles washed over him. He blinked and tried to sit up, but hands gently restrained him.

"Easy, sir," said a voice he didn't recognize. "You've had a nasty spill and inhaled quite a lot of smoke."

Dugan tried to speak, but there was something on his face. He tugged the oxygen mask free before the paramedic could stop him, and tried to sit up again.

"Anna," he said. "You need to be helping her! I'm—"

"Easy, *Dyed*," said Borgdanov's voice from the other side of him. "Ilya put Anna directly in first ambulance. She is already at hospital, I think. This ambulance will take you and Nigel to hospital."

The paramedic tried to put the oxygen mask back on, but Dugan pushed him away.

"How… how is she?" Dugan asked Borgdanov.

Borgdanov paused before answering. "Honestly, I do not know, *Dyed*. But she is alive, and she is strong woman, *da*?"

CHAPTER TWENTY-ONE

Dugan stole another glance at the clock on the wall and willed the time to pass, infuriated at the asinine hospital rules that allowed him only ten minutes at Anna's side every hour. He rose from the uncomfortable chair and began to pace just as Borgdanov and Ilya entered the tiny waiting room.

"How is she?" Borgdanov asked.

"She lost a lot of blood, but we got her here in time," Dugan said. "They repaired the damaged vein, and there was some muscle damage, but the doctor said she'll make a full recovery. The doc also said she was very lucky. The bullet barely missed the femoral artery. An inch lower and she'd have bled out for sure." Dugan paused and closed his eyes a moment, overcome by the thought of how close he'd come to losing her. Borgdanov rested a reassuring hand on his shoulder, and Dugan shook off the morbid thought and continued. "Anyway, she's still heavily sedated. I haven't had a chance to talk to her."

Both the Russians gave relieved nods. "Is good," Borgdanov said. "I told you she is strong woman, *da*? But what about you, *Dyed*? We went by your room first, but you were not there. Nurse did not seem so happy that you left against doctor's advice."

Dugan shrugged. "They were surprised to see me again after just releasing me from the crack on the head, so I think they're just being overly cautious. But I've got a pretty thick skull, and I don't have time to lie around in the hospital. As soon as I'm absolutely sure Anna's going to be okay, we have to get across to the US and get Cassie and the others back."

The Russians looked skeptical but said nothing, and Dugan changed the subject.

"How many did you save from the containers?"

Borgdanov's face darkened. "Twenty-three," he said through clenched teeth. "Eighteen women and five children. Three boys and two girls."

No one spoke for a long moment. Finally Dugan broke the silence.

"How many..." he hesitated, "... didn't make it?"

"All six policemen died, along with two of the *mafiya* bastards," Borgdanov replied. "And they found the charred remains of eleven women—girls, really—in the cages. Obviously Arsov's plan was for everyone to die."

"Son of a bitch!"

Borgdanov shook his head. "No, *Dyed*, son of a bitch is too kind for this scum. I think there is no word for him, but there is one I would like very much to apply to him. Ilya and I will not rest until he is *dokhlyy*—dead."

Ilya nodded, and Borgdanov lapsed into pensive silence for a moment before continuing.

"But we are few, and our priority is to rescue Karina, Cassie, and Tanya, but we cannot allow the trail of Arsov to grow cold either. We must be smart and careful."

"How are we going to do both? Lou and Harry told me the police lost Arsov. I figure he's out of the country by now."

"I am working on plan," Borgdanov said, "but for now we must—"

"Mr. Dugan?" said a nurse from the door of the waiting room.

Dugan turned to her. "Yes? Is Anna okay?"

The nurse smiled. "More than okay, Mr. Dugan. She's fully awake and asking for you." She glanced at the clock. "And I think under the circumstances we can relax the rules a bit."

INTENSIVE CARE UNIT
ST. IGNATIUS HOSPITAL
LONDON, UK

Anna looked up and gave Dugan a wan smile as he slipped through the curtains surrounding the bed.

"This place is rather like being in a fishbowl," she said, "but I did prevail upon the nurse to draw the curtains."

Dugan moved to the left side of her bed. An IV tube sprouted from Anna's right forearm, and on one finger of her right hand she wore a pulse monitor. Dugan took her left hand in both of his own and squeezed it gently.

"I'm told you're my savior."

"Well, I found you first, but if not for Nigel's help and then Borgdanov and Ilya getting us out, it would've been over for all of us."

Anna smiled. "Modest as always, I see." Her smile faded. "Ho…how are McKinnon and his men? No one will tell me anything."

Dugan was silent a long moment. "I'm sorry, Anna."

"All of them?"

Dugan nodded, then squeezed her hand.

"Bloody hell!" She turned her head away as a tear coursed down her cheek.

She struggled to compose herself and turned back to Dugan.

"The hostages?"

"The Russians managed to save over half of them." Dugan tried to soften the blow, but Anna wasn't deceived by semantics.

"Which means almost half of them are dead. How many, Tom?"

"Don't think about that now. Just worry about getting well."

"How many?"

"Eleven," Dugan replied softly and felt her flinch as if he'd struck her.

"What a complete fiasco."

Dugan felt the deaths all over again, Anna's pain combining with his own. He trembled when he thought how fragile life was and how close he'd come to losing her. He felt the ring box in his pocket and hesitated, but now was not the time. Not like this.

Suddenly the curtain parted, and the nurse appeared.

"I'm sorry, Mr. Dugan, but time's up," she said, not unkindly. "She needs her rest."

Dugan bent down and kissed Anna's lips, then pulled his face back a few inches.

"Rest now, and don't think of anything but getting better."

"I'll concentrate on recovering, right enough, but don't think I won't be thinking of Arsov." Her voice hardened. "Revenge is a powerful motivator."

Dugan nodded, and Anna continued. "What are you going to do?"

"We have to go after Cassie and the others. Now that you're out of immediate danger, we'll leave tonight."

Anna put her free hand behind his neck and pulled his face down to her. She kissed him tenderly, oblivious to the nurse clearing her throat at the curtain. She released him, and Dugan lifted his head to stare into her eyes.

"Do be careful, Tom," she said softly.

KAIROUZ RESIDENCE
LONDON, UK

Dugan shook his head. "I don't like it, Andrei," he said again. "You shouldn't go back to Russia alone. Come with us on the rescue, and we'll deal with Arsov after we've freed the girls."

"I don't like it either, *Dyed*, but we have no choice. I am sure Arsov is back with his superiors now, or soon will be, and the *Bratstvo* will know who we are. They will not take this lying down, and you can be sure they will retaliate. We must now, as you say, fight the war on two fronts, *da*?"

"Which is exactly why you going back to Russia alone makes no sense. If you insist on going, at least take Ilya to watch your back."

Borgdanov shook his head. "You do not know what resistance you will meet on ship, and while Agent Ward can maybe get you transport and logistical support, this is still an 'unofficial' matter as far as the US is concerned, and I don't think he can provide manpower. That leaves only you and young Nigel here to go on ship. Maybe you need help, and maybe not, but I do not think people on ship will just nicely deliver the girls to you. And if you must 'persuade' them…" he paused and nodded at Ilya, "I think Ilya is handy fellow to have around. And besides, I cannot ask Ilya to abandon the rescue of Karina and the others. Is primary mission, *da*?"

Beside Borgdanov, Ilya nodded his agreement.

"Still, I don't see what you can accomplish in Russia alone, other than get yourself killed."

"I think Mr. Dugan is right," Nigel added. "I can't see what you can accomplish alone in Russia either, but you would be an obvious asset on the rescue mission."

Dugan saw Borgdanov stiffen a bit at Nigel's implied criticism, and then visibly relax. Nigel's role in Anna's rescue had done much to raise the others' opinion of his usefulness, and he was now accepted as a member—though very much a junior one—of the team.

"Thank you for your high regard for my usefulness, Nigel," Borgdanov said, "but you and *Dyed* should not worry so about me. I am not so easy to kill, and Russia is my home. If all goes as planned, the *Bratstvo* bastards will not even know I'm there until I want them to know."

"But still, what can you do alone?" Nigel pressed.

"That is just the point. I do not plan on being alone. There are plenty of Russians who are sickened by what the *mafiya* and the corrupt politicians who protect them are doing to our country. Good people, many ex-*Spetsnaz* among them, who would like to do something about it."

"I don't doubt that," Dugan said, "but even if you recruit a few, I don't see you making much of an impact. This is a huge problem."

"But I am not trying to solve the whole problem, *Dyed*. The *mafiya* is too entrenched, and nothing will happen to them unless and until the government moves against them, and this will not happen. I also understand that even if I succeed in hurting this branch—this *Bratstvo*, another group of scum will arise to begin trading girls, drugs, and all the rest. My goal is not to solve the problem, because that is impossible, rather I only seek to make them leave us in peace."

"That's still a pretty tall order," Dugan said.

"True, but I know they will attempt to retaliate, and our choice is to sit here and wait for them to do so at the time and place of their own choosing, or to surprise them by striking first. You must understand that everything these bastards do is by calculation, and their brutality is by design, to intimidate their rivals. But we are not their rivals. They will only attack us now because we have annoyed them and they think we are weak, so punishing us will be easy. However, if we succeed in hitting them first, they will understand that retaliation against us will not be so easy. If they also realize we are not potential rivals attempting to take over their territories, the profit motive will be missing, and they will not be so eager to continue the attack. They are both bullies and businessmen. When faced with resistance, bullies turn away, and businessmen will not invest time and resources if there is no profit at the end of the operation."

"So essentially, your plan is to sucker punch them and hope it makes them go away," Dugan said.

Borgdanov nodded. "If 'sucker punch' means what I think it does, then *da*—that is my plan."

"And what if they don't stop coming?"

Borgdanov shrugged. "For sure, they will stop temporarily, to figure out what is happening. Then if they come after us again, I think they will concentrate on those of us who have hurt them. You who have helped us here in UK will be a minor concern, quickly forgotten." Borgdanov nodded both at Dugan and also Alex and Gillian, who had been sitting quietly, watching the exchange. "We will, as they say, draw their fire."

"Now see here, Andrei," Alex said, "we can't let you do that. Surely the authorities—"

Borgdanov held up his hand. "Alex, my friend, your authorities must play by certain rules, while the *Bratstvo* bastards have none. And how can they protect you, really? One lone assassin can come into the country, kill you all, and escape. Do you want to spend the rest of your life living in fear for Gillian and Cassie?" Borgdanov shook his head. "No. We brought these people to your door, and we will lead them away." He turned and looked at Ilya. "*Da?*"

"*Da,*" Ilya agreed.

"Lead them away where?" Dugan asked. "Aren't you forgetting something? What about Ilya and Karina's family, and the people you recruit to help you and all of their families? Surely nowhere in Russia, or even Europe will be safe for them."

Borgdanov nodded. "Is for this, I will need a bit more help."

CHAPTER TWENTY-TWO

MARITIME THREAT ASSESSMENT SECTION
CENTRAL INTELLIGENCE HEADQUARTERS
LANGLEY, VIRGINIA, USA

Jesse Ward slouched at his desk. A blue sports coat hung over the back of his chair, and the knot of his loosened tie hung at half mast, three inches below the open collar of his rumpled white shirt. His sleeves were rolled up, exposing corded muscles beneath the dark skin of his forearms, but here too he could see the beginnings of age-related decline. He sighed. It was inevitable he supposed, but things had only gotten worse since he took the job as section chief and no longer got into the field much. He'd have to start finding time to go to the gym or he'd turn into a complete marshmallow.

He abandoned thoughts of encroaching decrepitude and turned his attention back to the computer screen. These little 'unofficial favors' for Dugan and the Brits were always a challenge, and he studied the monitor again, trying to gauge just how far he could push the envelope without getting his ass in a crack. Or another crack, that is—dealing with Dugan always seemed to involve sticking his neck out.

His desk phone rang, and he looked over at the caller ID. Speak of the Devil.

"I hope you haven't called to ask me for another favor. I'm still working on the first one."

"And hello to you too," Dugan replied. "Are we in a bad mood, Jesse?"

"Well, I don't know about we, but I've been better. Do you have any idea how difficult it is to marshal government resources to interdict a foreign vessel in international waters when US security interests aren't at stake and I have absolutely no official justification for doing so?"

"I'm sure it's quite a challenge. How are you doing?"

"I'm still trying to figure out how to spin it," Ward said. "I thought about saying I had intel it was a big drug shipment, but then I'm sure everyone will want to let the ship actually dock. Then I thought about saying I'd received a tip the ship had a WMD aboard so that interdiction at sea was the safest option, but if I go that route, we'll attract a LOT of attention we probably don't want." He paused. "Are you sure we need to intercept them at sea?"

"Absolutely, Jesse. We don't know what condition the girls are in, and I want to get to them as soon as possible. We'd have tried to reach them from here in the UK if they hadn't already been out of chopper range. Even if a chopper only saves us a day, we need to do it."

Ward sighed. "Okay. I hear you. I'll make something work. Is there anything else?"

"Well, since you asked—"

"Shit. When will I learn to keep my mouth shut?"

"I need you to get some people into the US."

"What people?"

"Borgdanov and Denosovitch and some people they're recruiting in Russia."

"How many?"

"Maybe a dozen. Maybe fifteen."

"Just like that, huh?" Ward said. "I snap my fingers and produce fifteen visas?"

"Actually, I think they'll need green cards."

"Oh, really? Is that all, Mr. Dugan? I'll get right on it. Will there be anything else? We try to be a full service agency."

"Uh… yeah, well, they'll also have their families with them, and they'll all probably need new identities."

"Christ on a crutch, Tom! Let me get this straight. You're asking me to commit to getting permanent residence status for a large—but currently unknown—number of foreign nationals, none of whom have anything whatsoever to do with US national security. You then expect me to get them in some witness protection program—"

"I never said anything about a witness protection program. They'll take care of their own protection. I just need to get them in with new ID to help cover their tracks."

"You're really pushing the limits here, buddy. Maybe you better start at the beginning. If I'm gonna sell this to anyone, I need at least some way to connect this to a national security concern, however tenuously."

Dugan sighed and recounted Borgdanov's idea. Five minutes later, he finished and waited in silence for Ward to respond.

"Why do they want to come here? Why not stay close to home somewhere in Eastern Europe where they could blend in a bit better?"

"Because they'll be too many of them to hide in plain sight," Dugan said. "And any Russian mobsters searching for them in Europe will blend in well too. If they go to a rural area of the US, they may be conspicuous but they should be able to concoct at least a somewhat plausible cover story, and anyone searching for them will be equally conspicuous. Also, in the rural US they'll be able to arm themselves without constantly worrying about violating gun laws."

"And who's going to pay for all this?"

"Alex and I are kicking in, and I called Ray Hanley down in Houston. He still owes Borgdanov and Denosovitch for helping to get his crew back from the Somali pirates. He grumbled a bit but agreed to kick in. It won't cost the US taxpayers a cent."

Ward sighed. "All right. I still have access to some of the black op resources, so I may be able to swing the green cards and new IDs—but it can't be a 'favor'—not something this big. I report to people too, and I have to have some justification for this, and you better be sure the Russians understand what will be expected in return."

"Let's hear it."

DUGAN AND ANNA'S APARTMENT
LONDON, UK

"I will do anything Ward requires of me unless it involves acting against Russia," Borgdanov said. "Russia is our *Rodina*, our homeland, regardless of the bastards who are in power at the moment. I will never betray her."

Beside him, Ilya nodded agreement.

Dugan said nothing for a long moment.

"I think that's Ward's concern," Dugan said at last. "He was insistent I made that point clear to you. If he gets you the new identities and green cards, his expectation is complete loyalty in return. He has the ability to fast-track you all to citizenship, but he expects you all to commit to the US completely and unconditionally. He'll use you and whoever you recruit when needed as private contractors in future CIA operations and will pay you all well. He'll also try to make sure you're never forced to operate against Russia, but we have to face the facts. In situations where Russia and the US are at odds, there may be times when native Russian speakers are an asset, and I think you can count on being called upon to act against Russian interests. That's just a fact of life. If you can't do that, you should decline this deal and we'll have to work out something else."

"There IS nothing else, *Dyed*. We have no other connections, and we are not safe in Russia, even now."

"But I do not want to be a traitor to the *Rodina*," Ilya said, morosely. "Things are not so good there now, but it is my home."

"I understand," Dugan said, "but you have to decide, and also make sure that anyone you recruit understands the commitment. And I know it's a hard decision, but ask yourselves if you see any possible scenario in which the situation in Russia improves."

The Russians said nothing, and Dugan rose from the sofa.

"I'm going to the hospital to check on Anna before we take off. You guys think it over. I hate to rush you, but we need to leave for the US in a couple of hours, and if Ilya is coming with us and you're heading back to Russia, you need to make a decision before we leave so Ward can set things in motion."

Borgdanov merely nodded and continued to stare down at the coffee table. Dugan briefly laid a hand on the man's shoulder, then moved toward the apartment door. "I'll be back in an hour."

***

Borgdanov looked up when Dugan entered the apartment an hour later. The two Russians sat on opposite sides of the coffee table, a shot glass in front of each, and a much depleted bottle of vodka on the table between them.

"We did not think you would mind, *Dyed*," Borgdanov said. "We helped ourselves to your vodka."

"No problem." Dugan sat down on the sofa beside Borgdanov. "Did... did you make a decision?"

"We did." Borgdanov pushed his empty shot glass in front of Dugan and poured it full before refilling Ilya's glass. "But first, a toast."

Ilya picked up his glass and raised it in the air, and Borgdanov motioned for Dugan to take his glass as he raised the bottle.

"To Mother Russia, the *Rodina*," Borgdanov said, and Ilya raised the glass to his lips and threw back the shot as Borgdanov took a healthy pull from the bottle. Dugan's heart sank, but he courteously followed suit. The vodka burned his throat.

Not a good sign, thought Dugan, as he set the glass back down on the table and waited for the bad news. Borgdanov poured both glasses full again.

"A final toast." He looked at Dugan. "You know *Dyed*, once Ilya and I made you an honorary Russian, but now it seems we are to be countrymen for real." He raised the bottle, and Ilya raised his glass.

"To the USA, our new *Rodina*, and to a safer and better life for our families!"

ST. PETERSBURG
RUSSIAN FEDERATION

Arsov sat reviewing his story, struggling to hide his unease as he sat in the well-appointed outer office, a task made considerably more difficult by the presence of the two muscle-bound thugs flanking the ornate double door to the inner office beyond. The pair radiated malevolence, their ill-fitting suits stretched tight across steroid-enhanced musculatures, and they studied him with undisguised interest, sensing he might soon be the subject of interesting diversions. Arsov pretended to ignore them as he paged through a magazine he'd picked up from the end table beside his chair.

His reception so far had been chilly to say the least. London was a significant and growing market for the *Bratstvo* and, more importantly, was considered a training ground for seasoning the whores for the planned expansion of the US market. The near total collapse of the UK operation was not playing well here in St. Petersburg. His immediate superiors had been openly skeptical of his version of events, but with the death of his underlings and Nazarov's convenient disappearance, there was no one to dispute his story. And like all good fabrications, Arsov's tale contained elements of the truth. The police could only have learned of the warehouse from Nazarov, that much seemed apparent and added credibility to Arsov's claims. Ironically, Nazarov's obvious perfidy was the principal obstacle between Arsov and immediate execution and that, along with Arsov's voluntary return to Russia, had earned him a reprieve and led to his case being kicked up the chain of command. Far up the chain of command.

Arsov stiffened as one of the thugs guarding the door put his hand to his earbud, obviously listening to someone.

"*Da*," the thug said and then reached behind him and opened one side of the double door before pointing at Arsov.

"You," the guard said, "inside."

Arsov ignored the man's rudeness and casually tossed the magazine on the coffee table. He stood and moved toward the door with feigned confidence. Unimpressed, the guards smirked as he moved between them into the office beyond. It was much darker in the inner office and as Arsov stopped to let his eyes adjust, he heard the soft click of the closing door behind him and felt a momentary surge of fear.

"Do you intend to stand there all day like a statue, Arsov?" asked a disembodied voice from the far end of the palatial office, and Arsov moved toward a circle of light.

The man sat behind an ornately carved oak desk, lighted by a single desk lamp. The light was pointed down at the desk, and he sat in the shadows, a dim silhouette on the edge of the light. He was known only as *Glavnyy*—the Chief—and few people outside of his small circle of trusted associates had ever seen his face—and those who had never lived long enough to be a concern. Even in circumstances such as these, he was known to alter his voice and appearance in subtle ways, more to preclude the necessary elimination of the interviewee than out of any concern for his own safety. Arsov kept his eyes on the desk, encouraged. If the Chief intended to kill him, he had no doubt the meeting would have been face to face.

The Chief's right hand reached for a glass of tea on the desk and moved it into the shadows. Arsov heard a noisy slurp, and suddenly his own throat felt very dry. He watched as the hand moved back into the light and set the empty glass on the desk, and stood silently, waiting for the Chief to open the discussion. Seconds turned to minutes, and the minutes seemed like hours. Arsov felt sweat running down his cheeks.

The Chief slapped the desk with his open hand, upsetting the empty glass and producing a loud bang that caused Arsov to flinch.

"Tell me what happened in London, and don't give me that ridiculous fairy tale," the Chief said.

"I-I caught Nazarov skimming and—"

"Bullshit! Why is this the first we've heard of it?"

"I wasn't sure. I wanted to get evidence before I reported him. Bu-but he must have found out I was on to him and became a police informant."

"So let me see. Nazarov is stealing from us and then decided to become an informer. So that means we make no more money, so he has nothing to skim. Does that make sense to you, Arsov? Surely you can come up with something better than that?"

"But I explained! He must have figured out I was on to him and knew the money would dry up. Then he set us all up with the cops. I think his plan was that none of us would survive, and that he paid the cops to make sure that happened. I think the plan was to burn the building so the bodies would be unidentifiable; then he would disappear with his money. And it would have worked if I hadn't escaped. Besides, I have proof. The offshore accounts—"

"Yes, yes, the offshore accounts. And how convenient that you discovered those and so thoughtfully provided them to us. But I am a little confused, Arsov. First, you tell me you did not inform us because you were waiting to get proof, and in the very next breath you tell me you HAVE proof. I am sure you can see my problem, *da*?"

Arsov took a deep breath and struggled to calm himself.

"I discovered the accounts only shortly before Nazarov set us up and disappeared. So I DID get the proof, but I didn't have time to let you know before Nazarov sprang his trap. I came here as soon as possible after I escaped."

Arsov saw the head of the silhouette nod and relaxed a bit. Perhaps he could sell his story after all.

"That sounds… possible," the Chief said, "but there are still many little 'loose ends,' as the Americans say. For example, Nazarov has been in London for over four years, mostly as number two in that operation, but these offshore accounts you've discovered were opened only two months ago, and the balances are really quite small. If our Nazarov is an embezzler as you say, he must be quite incompetent or very patient."

"It makes perfect sense if you think about it," Arsov countered, warming to the discussion. "Nazarov was put in charge of the London operation for two months when Tsarko rotated back here to St. Petersburg and I had not yet arrived from Prague to replace him. I think Nazarov seized that opportunity to set up his skimming operations, assuming he could steal enough to escape before I discovered the problem. I just caught him sooner than he anticipated, that's all."

Again the silhouette nodded, and Arsov relaxed a bit, his hopes growing, only to be dashed.

"That is one explanation," the Chief said. "Nazarov is not a particularly clever fellow. But then again, I think he understands his own limitations. So, you will perhaps understand why I find it difficult to believe that he had the *yaytsa*—the balls—to steal from the Brotherhood."

The Chief paused, and even though Arsov could not see his face clearly, he felt the man's eyes boring into him.

"But you, Arsov. You are quite clever. Perhaps even as clever as you THINK you are. I can easily envision a scenario in which you convinced yourself that appropriating a little of the *Bratstvo*'s money as your own was

163

a good idea. And it hasn't escaped me that these offshore accounts were opened AFTER your arrival in London. Perhaps YOU were the one skimming the money and our now absent friend Nazarov caught you? An interesting theory, is it not?"

"Never! I assure you, sir, that I—"

"Calm yourself, Arsov. Your assurances, however passionate, are meaningless, so don't bore me. Be content to know that with Nazarov missing, I will accept your story for the time being, but know also that your loyalty is now suspect. Because of your previous outstanding performance, you will be given a very rare second chance, but do not disappoint me again. Is that clear?"

"Perfectly, sir! I will do everything in my—"

"Save your assurances, Arsov. The only acceptable assurances are your actions. You will perform or you will die a slow and painful death. It is that simple, and no flowery speech will change it. Now. Tell me how you managed to attract such intense scrutiny from the police."

"I… I'm sorry if it seems like I'm repeating myself, but it was Nazarov."

The Chief sighed. "The absent are always guilty, it seems. So how did the conveniently absent Mr. Nazarov bring the police down upon us in such force?"

"We had a girl from Volgograd named Karina Bakhvalova. We seasoned her in Prague, but she was a real spitfire and needed additional work in London. Two ex-*Spetsnaz* showed up looking for her—one of them was her uncle—and evidently, and unbeknown to us, they had influential friends in London. They kidnapped Tanya—"

"I thought you said the girl's name was Karina?"

"I did. Tanya is a different girl they were questioning in the club. When Nazarov sent in a man to break it up, the *Spetsnaz* overpowered our guy and kidnapped Tanya. When I sent Nazarov and some men to get Tanya back, he also kidnapped another girl at the house where Tanya was staying. It turns out she was the daughter of a very influential and well-connected Brit, and the shit hit the fan."

"Am I to understand that after years of low-profile operations, you and Nazarov thrust us into the limelight with one incredibly stupid move?"

"Not me. Nazarov."

"And just who did Nazarov work for?"

Arsov said nothing, and the silence grew to the point that he feared the Chief might have a change of heart about giving him a second chance.

"We'll be toxic in the UK for months, if not years," the Chief muttered before addressing Arsov again. "Very well. What happened to this Tanya, or Karina, or whatever her name is, and this British girl? I trust you at least took care of them in a way that will not lead the police back to our door?"

Arsov's mind raced. He hadn't spared a thought for the troublemaking little bitches since he'd shoved them in the container. However, now was not the best time to appear uncertain and indecisive in front of the Chief.

"Absolutely. Dead and buried where they won't be found."

The silhouette nodded. "Well, at least you didn't screw that up."

Arsov hesitated a long moment and then ventured the question he'd been holding back.

"Where will I go next?"

"We'll put you back in your old position in Prague. You seemed to do well there, at least. But before you go, we have a few loose ends to clear up. Give me what you have on the whore that started all this trouble and the *Spetsnaz* idiots."

"The girl was Karina Bakhvalova from Volgograd. One of the *Spetsnaz* was her uncle, Ilya Denosovitch. He was formerly a sergeant, I believe, but I'm not sure what unit. The other was his commanding officer, a man named Borgdanov, first name unknown. However, I'm sure he won't be difficult to find."

"And the Brits?"

"Actually one was an American, Thomas Dugan. He's a business partner with a Brit named Alex Kairouz. It was Kairouz's daughter that Nazarov kidnapped."

"Anyone else involved?"

Arsov hesitated and briefly considered telling the Chief about the dead MI5 bitch, but was pretty sure that would be the straw that broke the camel's back. He was apparently getting out of this interview alive, and he didn't want to do anything to change that. Besides, he was the only one who knew she'd been MI5, and if that fact turned up later, he could just pretend he hadn't known.

"No. That's it. Are you going to retaliate?"

"Of course we're going to retaliate. We can't have people thinking they can fuck with the *Bratstvo*, now can we? But we have to consider how to go about it. We need to send a clear message, without making the situation worse. We'll have a difficult time getting reestablished in the UK as it is."

"I'd like to participate in the strike," Arsov said, the first honest statement he'd made since he walked in the door.

"Oh, you've done quite enough, Arsov. Now get out of here and get your ass on a plane to Prague. And remember. We're watching you."

Arsov nodded and turned for the door, hurrying before the Chief changed his mind. The guard thugs turned and scowled as he opened the door, then moved to block his exit.

"Let him go," said the Chief's voice in the gloom behind him, and the two men parted, their disappointment obvious. Arsov gave them a smirk. Who was laughing now?

His brief elation died in the elevator as his thoughts turned to the troublesome bitches en route to the US. Had Nazarov informed the receivers in the US of the girls' names? He doubted it. The receivers probably had no clue who the girls were, just another shipment of whores as far as they were concerned. The unorthodox method of delivery might generate some local curiosity, but other than that, his secret was probably safe. Or was it? None of the girls were stupid, and if they somehow escaped, it might come to the Chief's attention that Arsov had been less than forthcoming. And both the Russian girls could identify him to the authorities if it came to that. No, he had to make sure the shipment never arrived.

***

Vladimir Glazkov, Chief of the St. Petersburg and Leningrad Oblast Directorate of the Federal Security Service of the Russian Federation, AKA "the Chief," watched Arsov's retreating back as the fool fled. Meeting with the idiot was perhaps unwise, but he really needed a better sense of the London debacle, and some things could not be communicated via underlings or even video. Sometimes you needed to be in the same room with a man, to sense his tension, to smell his fear. And besides, he had been juggling his dual identities as St. Petersburg's chief policeman and head criminal for so long, the deception was second nature to him.

One thing was clear—nothing was quite as this fool Arsov related it. While there was no doubt that Nazarov had somehow been compromised, the circumstances of that treachery were very much in question, and Arsov had likely played a role. He would have to be killed in time, but he was good at training the whores, and the Brotherhood might as well get as much use out of him as possible for the time being. It wasn't good business to squander resources, and Glazkov was nothing if not an astute businessman.

Which brought him back to this UK disaster. That there had to be retaliation was clear, but the scope and targets were problematic. These *Spetsnaz* bastards and their families would die, of course, but beyond that, things became more difficult. The *Bratstvo* operated with impunity throughout Russia and many of the former Soviet satellites, on the back of generous 'gifts' to politically connected 'friends.' But in those countries where bribery was not an accepted way of doing business, the model (which he had developed) always involved flying well below the radar. The sex trade was staffed by foreign talent acquired outside of the country being served, and drugs were sold primarily to the bottom tier of society, in both cases the 'victims' being persons held in low regard by the general population. It boggled the imagination that Arsov and Nazarov had managed to violate the most basic tenet of their operation.

And not just by targeting some common Brit—oh no—they had to kidnap the daughter of this Kairouz, who was obviously not only wealthy, but politically connected as well. The sheer idiocy of it made his head hurt.

Well, at least the girl was no longer a problem, and if Arsov was to be believed—a somewhat doubtful assumption—there was nothing left to lead the authorities back to the *Bratstvo*, except, of course, unprovable suspicion. But therein lay the rub. If everyone suspected that this Kairouz and his American partner had brought ruination down on the *Bratstvo*, their apparent weakness would encourage rivals to muscle in on the UK business. Viewed from that angle, retaliation against this Kairouz and Dugan seemed mandatory. However, if they DID retaliate, would that not raise their profile with the authorities even more and make reestablishment of their UK operations that much more difficult? He cursed Arsov once again for putting the Brotherhood in this difficult position.

Then again, things were going to be hot in the UK for some time anyway, so if they intended to eliminate the Kairouz family and this Dugan, there was no time like the present. The sooner things heated up, the more quickly they would cool down. He picked up the phone and pressed a preset. Halfway across the city, a voice answered.

"Arkady," Glazkov said, "get me everything you can find on an Alex Kairouz and Thomas Dugan in London. They're partners in a shipping company, I believe. I want everything on them and their families. Is that clear?"

"Yes, Boss. Since it's outside Russia it may take a bit longer, but I should have you a full report by tonight. Anything else?"

"Yes. Do a similar search for Ilya Denosovitch, who was previously a sergeant in some sort of *Spetsnaz* unit. He's from Volgograd, I think. And also check for a Borgdanov, first name and hometown unknown. However, he is also ex-*Spetsnaz*, and I believe he was Denosovitch's commanding officer, so you should find him in the records for the same unit. He was likely a field grade officer, a major or a lieutenant colonel."

"Much easier. I should have those within the hour."

***

Arkady Baikov, Chief Data Analyst for the Federal Security Service for St. Petersburg and Leningrad Oblast, looked down at the name on his scratch pad. Borgdanov. He didn't have to look up the name. He knew it. Andrei Nikolaevich Borgdanov, Major Andrei Nikolaevich Borgdanov.

"Whatever you're doing, Dyusha," he said softly, "you're making a big mistake."

Arkady sighed and turned to his computer.

CHAPTER TWENTY-THREE

CONTAINER SHIP *KAPITAN GODINA*
EN ROUTE TO JACKSONVILLE, FLORIDA

Tanya's hand was dark bluish black, the discoloration visible well up the inside of her right arm, almost to the elbow, and the festering wound leaked thick foul-smelling pus into the makeshift bandage they'd tied around her hand. The girl burned with fever and lapsed in and out of consciousness, rousing only enough to swallow small sips of water Cassie gently trickled into her mouth from one of the few remaining bottles of clean water. She slept now with her head in Cassie's lap, a troubled sleep punctuated by whimpers between labored breaths, and Cassie gently stroked her forehead with a wet rag, attempting to soothe her fevered brow.

"She's getting worse, I think," Cassie whispered.

In the dim light leaking through the holes near the top of the container, she saw Karina nod agreement.

"*Da*," Karina said. "The infection has spread, and there is nothing more we can do. Without treatment soon she will not survive."

"But she CAN'T die. Not like this. Not from a little cut!"

Karina shook her head sadly and laid a hand on Cassie's arm. "I don't want her to die either, Cassie, but you must be prepared. If we do not reach port today, I think she will not last the night, and even if we do, I think she will lose at least her hand and maybe part of her arm."

"But we're not even close. Look at the food, we have four or five days left," Cassie said.

"I honestly don't know, Cassie. We weren't eating much when we were seasick, and Tanya has hardly been able to eat at all. The days have run together, and I've lost track. I don't even know how long we've been in this damn box."

"We'll get there soon. We HAVE to. And then they'll treat Tanya. I mean if they intended to kill us, they wouldn't have bothered to put us on a ship, would they?"

Karina nodded, more to placate Cassie than because she believed it.

AIRBORNE
EN ROUTE TO JACKSONVILLE, FLORIDA

Dugan fidgeted in the leather seat of the Gulfstream and considered having a drink from the bar, then decided against it. His stomach already boiled from too much coffee, and he was wired on a potent combination of adrenaline, caffeine, and anxiety. Alcohol would hardly improve things.

He worried for the hundredth time if he'd done the right thing leaving Anna in the hospital, even though she'd insisted he do so. Then he suppressed a pang of guilt at his insistence that Alex and Gillian stay behind to watch over Anna, arguing that they could do nothing ashore in the US. It was a totally logical argument, and they reluctantly agreed, even though they clearly wanted to come on the flight.

Dugan looked over at Nigel and Ilya, both apparently lost in their own thoughts. Leave-taking had been an emotional affair all the way around, with the two Russians embracing before Ilya climbed aboard the plane ahead of Dugan.

"Do you think Andrei will have any trouble in Russia? I'll bet these mafia bastards have eyes and ears everywhere."

Ilya looked up and shook his head. "*Nyet*. Part of the time the major and I were on counter terrorism assignments, we worked undercover. He has many contacts where he can get new identity papers, and with your generous support, he has all the money he needs. Is no problem, I think."

"Still, with automated video surveillance at all the international airports, I think it's dangerous. He can't change his appearance that much."

Ilya laughed. "More than you think, *Dyed*. But the major will not use any primary entry point. Since the end of Cold War and breakup of Soviet Union, our border is not so secure anymore. There are hundreds of possible overland entry points, and after he gets inside, traveling on domestic transportation with false papers is not big problem, especially if he keeps changing identities."

"I'm still worried. He's completely on his own."

Ilya shook his head again. "No, *Dyed*. We have many *tovarishchi*—comrades—there. Some will help him, some will not because of concern for families or similar things, but none will betray him, I think, especially not to *mafiya* scum."

"Do you know his plan?"

"He has no clear plan—yet," Ilya said. "First he must do reconnaissance. Then he can form plan and figure out resources he needs to proceed. He will contact us when he is ready, not before. Then we strike, *da?*"

"We?"

"Of course, I will be there. This rescue operation will be over in a day or two at most, one way or another. Then I go to Russia as soon as the major needs me."

Dugan scowled at the Russian fatalism inherent in the 'one way or another' but ignored it. He was much more irritated by what Ilya had just revealed.

"Christ! If that's the case, why the hell didn't he wait until we finished up here like I suggested? Then we could have all gone together?"

"Because we would have to separate anyway. The major and I can move about Russia independently with false papers, but together we would be very obvious, *da*? So—if we must separate anyway, is better the major goes ahead and gets things started." Ilya paused. "And besides, *Dyed*, you are not coming to Russia."

"What the hell do you mean I'm not coming? I want this asshole Arsov as much as you do."

"Forgive me, *Dyed*, but you are not Russian. The major and I can sneak across border and move freely in disguise, especially if we separate, but you, I think, will stick out like sore finger."

"I think you mean sore thumb."

Ilya shrugged. "Whatever. You are not going. The major was clear on this."

"I guess he forgot to tell me that part."

Ilya shrugged again, but said nothing.

We'll see about that, thought Dugan, but he didn't press the point with Ilya.

∗∗∗

An hour later, Dugan dialed the satellite phone.

"Maritime Threat Assessment," Ward answered.

"Jesse, where do we stand?"

"You've got clearance to land at Cecil Field, which is a joint civil-military airport on the west side of Jacksonville. It's also the home base for the Coast Guard's HITRON, so that worked out well."

"Hit what?"

Ward chuckled. "HITRON. It's an acronym for Helicopter Interdiction Tactical Squadron. They're the Coasties that support ops against drug trafficking and that sort of thing. I have some contacts there because they also support the USCG Maritime Security Response Team. I ran a few drills with them right after we set up the Maritime Threat Assessment group here at Langley."

"Any problems arranging it?"

"Yes and no."

"That's not very illuminating, Jesse."

"No, it wasn't difficult to get you a chopper. These guys jump at any excuse to get some air time, especially if it can be back charged to some other agency's budget. And by the way, you're welcome. I was able to sneak this little joy ride on to what remains of my rapidly dwindling black budget."

"And that's much appreciated," Dugan said, "but what about the 'yes' part?"

"Yes, it was tough to figure out a plausible cover story, but I managed. This is being billed as an AOR—and before you ask, that's 'Area of Responsibility'—familiarization flight. In other words, an excuse to go up and fly around somewhere they might reasonably be expected to conduct operations someday. You guys are members of a 'multinational task force' going along as observers."

"How's that work?"

"There's an ongoing cooperation between our guys and the Royal Bahamian Defense Force called Operations Bahamas, Turks and Caicos or OPBAT. Since the Turks and Caicos Islands are still a British Overseas Territory, it's not too much of a stretch to think the Brits might send some observers to the operation from time to time."

"So we're all supposed to be Brits?"

"No, you're billed as a company man, working for me—which is partially true since you do that on occasion. The others are British intelligence. Lou and Harry are going to backstop us and confirm that if necessary," Ward said.

"That might work for Nigel, but what about Ilya. He's carrying a Russian Federation passport."

"Don't worry about it. I called in another favor. An immigration officer will board the plane on landing and take care of everything. After that, just tell Ilya to keep his mouth shut and nod a lot around the Coasties."

"Okay. I follow. And the Coasties know we're going after the *Kapitan Godina*?"

"Uhh... no."

"What do you mean, no? How the hell are we supposed to get to the ship if these guys don't know the target."

"I mean my imagination is tapped out, and I've stretched this about as far as I can. You have the AIS number for the ship, so after you get airborne, you'll have to use your boyish charm to convince the pilot to take you there. I can get you in the room, Tom, but you have to close the deal yourself. I'm sure you're up to it. By the way, are you armed?"

"Harry got us an assault rifle, which I gave to Ilya so I don't shoot myself in the foot. He also got us a couple of Glocks, but I'm not too worried about that. This is a merchant ship, and I doubt they're armed, or heavily armed anyway. I'm more concerned with what I'm going to tell the Coasties. What do they think they're supposed to be doing, anyway?"

"Right now they think they're just going to fly around offshore and pretend to be intercepting drug-traffickers for the edification of a group of their British cousins. If I push any harder, this whole thing could fall apart in a hurry."

Dugan was quiet a moment before responding.

"I understand. Thanks, Jesse," he said at last.

"Look Tom, these are good guys. I suspect that after you're in the air and all the bureaucrats are out of the way, you won't have any problem. Use your own judgment, but I suspect if you level with them, they'll find a way to help you."

"Your lips to God's ears, pal. And however it turns out, I appreciate the help."

"No problem. What's your ETA?"

Dugan looked at his watch, suddenly worried. "About 2100, I think. Listen, since the Coasties think this is a bullshit show-and-tell operation, do you think they'll be ready to deploy tonight? They may want to wait until daylight since they don't know it's urgent.'

"Damn, I didn't think of that. Do you want me to try and push from here?"

Dugan thought a moment. "No, you can't really push without setting off alarms, and like you said, it might all unravel. It's 1900 now, so we'll be on the ground in a couple of hours, and I'll see what I can do face to face."

"Okay. Call me if you need me to run interference."

"Will do," Dugan said and hung up.

He unfastened his seat belt and headed for the cockpit to tell the pilot to change his flight plan to Cecil Field.

CHAPTER TWENTY-FOUR

Arsov sat at his old desk and looked around. In a way, it was good to be back in Prague, especially considering the alternatives. True, Beria hadn't been particularly pleased at his return and only grudgingly vacated the office. However, Arsov had been able to placate his underling with the assurances that it was only a temporary situation.

But he had to take care of loose ends to keep it that way. He picked up his phone and dialed the sat phone on the *Kapitan Godina*, listening as the buzzes and clicks ended in the strange ring tone.

"*Kapitan Godina*, captain speaking," said a voice in English.

"Good evening, Captain," Arsov replied in Russian. "I trust you're taking very good care of our shipment?"

After a long pause, the man replied in Ukrainian-accented Russian. "Yes, sir, all is in order. We should dock in Jacksonville late tomorrow evening or early the following morning depending on the availability of a pilot."

"There has been a change of plans. I believe you will encounter a storm and lose the container overboard. Most regrettable."

"Bu-but we cannot! We are too close to port, and the weather is fine. And there are many ships in this area, converging on the US coast. No one will believe we encountered heavy weather. If you wanted to dump the shipment, you should have informed me when we were in mid-ocean with less traffic."

"I'm telling you now, and I won't tell you again."

"But what will I tell the insurers and the customs inspectors?"

"I'm sure you'll think of something, and while you're considering that, I suggest you think of your lovely wife and beautiful daughters for inspiration. Your wife is a bit old to be of any use, so regrettably, we'll have to dispose of her. Your daughters, however, are promising, and I'm sure we could find places for them in our operation."

"No. No. I'll take care of it. Don't worry."

"Oh, I never doubted it for a moment, Captain," Arsov said. "And if you have any trouble with the other officers, please remind them we have all of their loved ones under our protection."

"I… I will. It will be done. Don't worry."

"Thank you. Call me when it's done. And, Captain, do have a pleasant evening."

Arsov hung up and leaned back in his chair with his fingers laced behind his head, satisfied he was getting things back on track. As soon as the captain reported the death of the troublesome whores, there was absolutely nothing more that could connect him to the unfortunate events in London. He could forget about Karina and her little friends and go about rebuilding his reputation in the organization here in Prague. He regretted his missteps, but one always learned more from mistakes than successes. Next time, he'd be a bit more careful.

KAPITAN GODINA
AT SEA EAST OF JACKSONVILLE, FLORIDA

"Have you ever done it before," the captain asked the chief engineer.

"No, but it should not be too difficult, I think. The container is well positioned, and we have the air bladders they gave us aboard." He glanced out the porthole of the captain's office. "But I don't think we should do it at night."

"We must. Every hour we get closer to shore. And if we dump it at night, no one can see."

The chief shook his head. "On the contrary, everyone can see. We can't work in the dark, especially doing something we've never done before. You'll have to put on the deck lights, which will look strange and attract the attention of any passing ship. I think it's actually better to do it in the day time. The activity on deck won't attract any interest, and we can flip the container overboard when there are no ships nearby. You're sure the container has holes top and bottom, to flood and sink quickly?"

The captain nodded. "They told me that is standard for their 'special shipment' containers."

"So if we time it right, it will be over the side and gone before anyone sees. Right?"

"Very well, there is something to what you say. But we have to slow down. The closer we get to port, the more traffic, and I don't want anyone to see us dumping the container. Its disappearance will be hard enough to explain as it is."

The chief stood. "Okay. I'll go down to the engine room and prepare to reduce speed. Give the order whenever you're ready. I'll also have the first engineer gather all the tools and equipment. We'll be ready to start on the container at first light. It shouldn't take long."

The captain nodded and the chief started out the door, but turned back in the doorway.

"What do you think is in the damn thing, anyway?" the chief asked.

The captain shrugged. "Drugs or guns, I suppose. I don't know, and I don't really want to know. I just want my family safe."

CECIL FIELD
JACKSONVILLE, FLORIDA

Ward was as good as his word. An immigration officer boarded the plane as soon as they rolled to a stop beside a nondescript building. He took their passports and stamped them without saying a word, then returned them and shook hands all around.

"Gentlemen," he said, "welcome to the United States."

Then he left, hurrying down the short stairs without looking back.

"Very efficient," Ilya said, and Dugan nodded and looked at his watch.

"Well, boys, let's go see if we have a welcoming committee." Dugan started for the hatch. His feet had barely hit the tarmac when he heard his name being called, and looked up to see a man walking toward him. The newcomer was of medium height with sandy hair, and he wore the uniform of the US Coast Guard with lieutenant's bars on his shoulders.

"Mr. Dugan?" the man said again as he approached.

Dugan nodded, and the man smiled and extended his hand. "Joe Mason. I'm going to be your taxi driver tomorrow."

"Nice to meet you, Lieutenant Mason. But please, call me Tom."

"Only if you call me Joe."

Dugan grinned. "That's a deal, Joe. And these guys are Nigel Havelock and Ilya Denosovitch."

Mason shook Nigel's hand, and as he shook Ilya's, he regarded the big Russian with interest.

"*Dobro pozhalovat' v Ameriku*," Mason said.

Ilya struggled to hide his surprise. "*Spasibo*," he replied.

Mason studied Denosovitch a bit more closely.

"*Spetsnaz?*"

Ilya's discomfort was obvious. "*Da*," he said after a moment's hesitation.

Mason grinned. "I can always spot a snake eater, no matter what the nationality."

Well, there goes that plan, thought Dugan. Mason laughed at the group's obvious unease.

"My brother's a SEAL and two of my cousins are Army Special Forces, so I've been around a lot of special ops guys. They just carry themselves a little differently from most people. And my family is Russian. Our name was Kamenshchik, which translated—obviously—to Mason. I'm second generation, but my parents spoke Russian at home to my grandparents, so I sorta picked it up. Don't get to practice much, though."

"Sounds pretty good to me," Dugan said.

Ilya nodded. "*Da*, his pronunciation is perfect, *Dyed*."

Mason grinned. "*Dyed*? You don't look quite old enough to be this guy's grandpa, and you don't look Russian at all. What's with the *Dyed*?"

"It's a long story." Dugan glared at Ilya, who was struggling to suppress a grin.

Mason looked back and forth between the two. "Sounds interesting."

"Maybe later," Dugan said. "What's the plan?"

"Well, I apologize, but we don't have suitable quarters here at HITRON. Cecil Field isn't strictly speaking a full Coast Guard facility—we share it with the Florida Air National Guard support folks and some commercial operators. However, I booked you rooms in a Hampton Inn about six miles down I-10. I can take you there now, or if you're hungry, we can stop somewhere and get some chow first. I've got the boys coming in to preflight the chopper at oh five hundred, so we'll be ready anytime you folks are. Just let me know when you'd like a pickup in the morning."

"Ah... could we get started a little sooner?"

Mason looked puzzled. "Sooner? You mean, like... tonight?"

"Yeah, if that's possible."

"Well, sure, it's possible. We're equipped with night vision for twenty-four-hour ops, but I guess I'm a bit confused as to the point. My briefing said this was a routine familiarization and training flight for drug interdiction."

"That's right," Dugan said quickly.

Mason gave Dugan a strange look. "Mr. Dugan, do you mind if I ask you all for some identification. I was told to expect three intelligence agents, an American and two Brits, but Mr. Denosovitch doesn't look very British to me. I'd really like to know what's going on here."

Dugan noticed the use of the title and felt the situation slipping away. He knew he'd blown it somehow but decided to try to bluff it out. He smiled at Mason.

"If I told you, I'd have to kill you."

Mason said nothing and waited. The silence grew.

"Okay. I see you're uneasy," Dugan said. "Why don't you tell me what's bothering you?"

"What's bothering me is that for guys that are coming as observers on a drug interdiction exercise, you seem to know jack shit about the procedure. Our role is normally to scout for and intercept the drug-traffickers' small 'go fast' boats and force them to stop and remain in place while we vector surface vessels to their position. We're all about intimidation. If they refuse to stop, we either put a shot across their bow with our machine gun or try to take out their engines with a fifty-caliber sniper rifle. The point is, intimidation works best when your target can SEE you, so while we're capable of night operations, that isn't a standard training op. Besides which, night ops involve the crew using night-vision equipment and as 'observers,' you wouldn't have much to observe except the backs of our heads. All of which leads me to believe something isn't quite right here. This has all been a very low-key 'do me a favor' op, but I'm getting a real bad vibe. So, absent a direct order from my chain of command, I'm not risking my bird or my crew unless and until I know what the hell is going on. How about I take you to the hotel, and tomorrow at oh eight hundred we'll meet with my superiors and we can sort this all out?"

Dugan sighed. "Okay. I guess we need to start over. It's a long story, so why don't we go somewhere we can all sit down, and I'll tell you the deal over a cup of coffee. After that, we'll do it any way you want."

***

179

An hour later, they sat crowded into a corner booth in a near-deserted Denny's, well away from the few other customers, speaking in low tones. The waitress started toward them, coffee carafe in hand, but Dugan waved her away. She shrugged and turned toward the counter as Mason glanced over his shoulder to make sure she was out of earshot before continuing.

"So these girls are being held captive on the ship," Mason said. "I get that. But why not wait until the ship docks in a day or so and hit them then. I mean, they've been on the ship a week as it is, and a shore-based op would be way easier."

Dugan shook his head. "We have no idea what shape the girls are in, and we don't know that they'll even be on board when the ship docks. And there's all sorts of scrutiny when the ship reaches port. It's not like guns or drugs, people make noise, so for all we know, they intend to take them off at sea just before they make port. That's why I want to hit them as soon as they get into chopper range and before they can connect with anyone."

Mason still looked skeptical. "Well, maybe, but I still don't buy it. I mean, I'm sympathetic, but this looks very much like something for law enforcement, and for the life of me I can't understand why the CIA and British intelligence—assuming you guys actually are who you claim to be, which I doubt—has any skin in the game here. I don't see any national security issues involved at all, so what AREN'T you telling me, Dugan?"

Dugan wasn't sure whether the transition from 'Tom' to 'Mr. Dugan' and back to simply 'Dugan' marked progress in his relationship with Mason, but at least the Coastie was still listening. He decided he had nothing to lose by coming clean, and Mason wasn't anyone likely to be conned.

He sighed. "I work for the CIA part time, and I also have connections with British intelligence. However, these gentlemen are not affiliated with either organization. It's a very personal matter for us all, I'm afraid."

"I'm listening."

"One of the kidnapped girls, Cassie Kairouz, is my goddaughter. Another is Ilya's niece."

"What about Havelock here?" Mason inclined his head toward Nigel.

"Nigel is Cassie's…" Dugan hesitated; 'boyfriend' seemed diminishing somehow, but he didn't know what else to call him. "Nigel cares a great deal about Cassie," he said simply.

Mason shook his head. "Okay. That makes more sense. But this is WAY outside the lines. I really think we need to discuss this with the unit commander—"

"There's no TIME, Joe. Do you really think that discussion would end before the ship got to the pilot station? I mean, you're cleared for the flight, right? PLEASE, let's just make the flight as planned and adapt to circumstances as we find them. If we miss this chance, they might either be dead or out of our reach!"

Mason shook his head again, but didn't respond, and Dugan felt the opportunity slipping away. Then Ilya began to speak to Mason in Russian, his voice barely above a whisper.

***

Ilya watched with growing concern as Dugan's attempts to convince the Coast Guard pilot seemed to be failing. He couldn't follow all the nuances of the conversation, but there was no mistaking the pilot's body language, and the head shakes were growing more emphatic as the conversation progressed. When both men lapsed into what seemed a final silence, he could contain himself no longer.

"I am sorry, Joe Mason," Ilya said in Russian, "but I do not have the English words to say to you what I must. But I beg you to listen to *Dyed* and take us in your helicopter without delay. I suppose all families everywhere have a great bond, but I KNOW I feel these things, and if your family is Russian, I suspect you do as well. I think your parents and grandparents and brothers and sisters and cousins and nephews and nieces meet several times each year to eat and drink and laugh and dance and fight and argue. I think you have family members you love without limit and others that piss you off every time you think of them. But I think that when one is in trouble, no matter which one, you will help with your last ruble or ounce of strength if necessary, because this is family, *da*?"

Mason nodded, and Ilya continued.

"I was a teenager when little Karina was born, and I bounced her on my knee and took her to the park and the zoo and all the places children like. When I became a soldier, I knew it was not such a good life for family, and so I have never married, but my sister's children are like my own. And these scum, these *mafiya* bastards have taken my little Karina and done unspeakable things to her." The big Russian's look hardened. "And for this, they will pay, of that I assure you. But first, we must save Karina and the others. So before you say no or take the easy road of referring the matter to your superiors, I ask you to think of your OWN family and what you would do if one of them was in the clutches of these monsters. So the decision is yours Joe Mason, and I have nothing to give you but my gratitude, but I swear to you that if you do this thing, you will be my *tovarishch*—my comrade—for life."

***

Dugan watched the exchange, clueless as to the meaning of the words, though he sensed it was an appeal. Ilya leaned forward as he spoke, his intensity obvious, and when he finished, he leaned back in the booth as if the speech exhausted him. Dugan watched Mason. The silence grew.

"Okay," Mason said at last.

"Okay, what?" asked Dugan.

"Okay, I'll take you maniacs up, though I'm about ninety-nine percent sure I'm going to end up with my ass in a crack."

"*Spasibo*," Ilya said.

"*Vsegda pozhaluysta*," Mason replied. You're welcome.

"Great," Dugan said. "Let's get going."

"Not so fast. I'm STILL not taking you up tonight. There are way too many variables to attempt a landing or insertion on a hostile ship in the dark without recon. They could have wires strung up to foul us, or if we go in with NV, they could switch on all their lights at the last minute and blind us, and there are about a dozen other reasons a night approach is a bad idea. And apart from Ilya here, I'm guessing none of you have any experience fast-roping out of a chopper, so I may have to land, or at least hover, on top of the containers."

Ilya was nodding. "Joe is right, *Dyed*. I am eager to get to ship too, but these things he says are true."

"Besides," Mason added, "we need to figure out where the hell the ship is first. Do you have her Automatic Identification System number?"

"I do," Dugan said. "It's on my laptop in my bag in the car."

"I'll go get it," Nigel said, obviously eager to make a contribution.

Mason nodded and fished his car keys out of his pocket as Nigel stood up. Mason handed the keys to Nigel, and he hurried for the door.

"Any chance the bad guys have disabled their AIS?" Mason asked.

"I doubt it," Dugan replied. "She'll still show up on the Vessel Tracking System as an 'unknown' when she gets close enough to shore, and disabling the AIS would just be calling attention to herself."

Mason nodded, and they lapsed into silence until Nigel returned moments later and passed the laptop across the table to Dugan.

"This place got Wi-Fi?" asked Dugan as he booted the computer.

Mason shrugged. "Probably. Just about every place has nowadays."

The computer whirred to life and went through the boot routine, and Dugan heaved a little sigh of relief as he saw the icon at the bottom of the screen indicating a wireless connection was available. He connected to the internet and logged on to the subscription tracking service, where he'd already entered the *Kapitan Godina*'s AIS number.

"Right there," he said and centered the cursor over the icon for the *Kapitan Godina* before sliding the open laptop over in front of Mason.

Mason shook his head. "She's about a hundred miles beyond our maximum range anyway, so we have to wait until she gets closer." He studied the screen a moment. "Are these course and speed numbers accurate."

Dugan shrugged. "Mostly, I think. I believe they're projections calculated from the ship's previous positions over time, so I suspect they're always a bit behind. I'm not sure how often they refresh. What's her course and speed," he asked, leaning over to have a look himself.

"She's headed due west, right toward us. And this shows a speed of eighteen knots."

Mason looked at his watch. "It's almost eleven now. At her current speed, she'll be at the extreme edge of our range about daylight. If we leave at six or so, that should be about right."

"Why not earlier?" Dugan said. "Let's hit her at first light."

"Because I'm assuming that you'd like us to have enough fuel to stay over her long enough to do some good. Unless you just want to get close and wave at her in the distance before we turn back. One way trips in multimillion dollar helicopters are not exactly career-enhancing events."

"Can we, I don't know, get another chopper with longer range... or something," Dugan offered, knowing it sounded somewhat lame as soon as he said it.

Mason shook his head. "Not at this point and not with me. We fly the MH-65C at HITRON, and that's what you've got. Understand, Dugan, we normally operate as one element of a team and in concert with one of the flight-deck-equipped cutters. In fact, USCGC *Legare* was supposed to be our launch platform and home base for this little 'training exercise,' but then no one knew you had a specific target in mind."

"Can't she head in the direction of our target?" Dugan asked.

"Sure, but not on MY say so, and not without a good reason. I suppose I can say that our British guests have requested a change to the planned area of operations. Her skipper will be pissed, but he'll probably comply. After all, this is all supposed to be a dog and pony show for you 'Brits' anyway."

Dugan nodded. "Good idea. Put it on us. Tell'em we're pushy assholes that threatened to create all sorts of waves, and you were just trying to satisfy us."

Mason grinned. "Well, you are sort of a pushy asshole now that you mention it. And I hope you and Ilya here can perfect your British accents before you have to talk to anyone above me. Otherwise you'll have to let Havelock do all the talking."

"Don't worry. We appreciate what you're doing, and we'll back you 100%."

"Okay," Mason said. "I'll get on the horn to *Legare* with the change of plan, but understand it probably won't do any good anyway. I think she's a bit too far south to do us much good on this accelerated timetable."

CECIL FIELD
JACKSONVILLE, FLORIDA

Dugan sat in the chopper and struggled to conceal his impatience as he looked out over the tarmac, watching in the predawn light as helicopters and fixed-wing aircraft took shape around him. He glanced over at Ilya seated in the web seat across from him, the borrowed assault rifle across his lap and the coveralls Mason had provided stretched tight across the big Russian's massive chest and bulging biceps. The Coasties inventory of flight coveralls for visitors seemed to be very much based on a 'one size fits all policy,' and sitting beside Ilya, Nigel was swallowed in his, the slight Brit looking for all the world like a kid in his father's clothing—except for the grip of the Glock protruding from his pocket. Only Dugan's coveralls fit reasonably well, as he was apparently what the US Coast Guard considered average.

The other three Coasties in the crew displayed no overt curiosity about the strangely armed multinational trio of 'observers,' leading Dugan to surmise that Mason had briefed them on the somewhat extralegal nature of their mission. If they had any qualms, they hid them well, and each had shaken hands and seemed friendly enough when Mason made the introductions. After settling their visitors as far out of the way as possible, they'd methodically worked their way through the preflight checklists.

When the checks seemed complete and nothing happened, Dugan risked breaking the silence.

"Uh… what are we waiting for?" he asked into his mike.

Ahead of him, he saw Mason swivel a bit in his seat and tilt his head back toward him.

"AIS shows the target still at 225 miles out, a bit beyond the edge of our range."

"Yeah, but she's closing on us," Dugan said, "and it'll take us time to get to her, so by that time she'll be within range, right?"

"Negative. Looks like she's slowed down considerably. She may have increased speed again, but we can't tell exactly how much until the next time the satellite data refreshes. If we leave now, we might not be able to stay over her very long—or maybe at all. I figure we sit tight another half hour to be on the safe side."

Dugan thought about that a minute. "Why the hell would she slow down that far from shore? You think maybe she's meeting another vessel? Christ, if that happens we could lose the girls completely."

"I hadn't thought of that," Mason said. "I guess we better get into the air." And with that he called the control tower and requested immediate clearance.

Ten minutes later, Dugan looked down through the open door as Jacksonville flashed by below them.

CHAPTER TWENTY-FIVE

KAPITAN GODINA
DUE EAST OF JACKSONVILLE, FLORIDA

The chief engineer grunted as he helped the first engineer drag the heavy rubber bladder up the deck. The damn things were cumbersome, even uninflated, and he didn't look forward to wrestling two of them into the small gap between the 'special container' and the one below it. As the two engineers approached, they saw the chief mate in the early morning light, directing sailors releasing the twist locks at each corner of the container. Soon only the weight of the container itself held it in place.

The sky was clear and the sea calm, with only a slight following wind that matched the speed of the ship, with the result that there seemed to be no wind at all over the deck. The chief engineer wondered again how in hell the Old Man was going to convince anyone they'd encountered heavy weather, and was glad it wasn't his problem.

As they neared the container, the chief engineer wrinkled his nose in disgust.

"Christ! What's that smell? It's like a mixture of rotten meat and shit."

The chief mate shrugged. "I don't know, but I think it's coming from this container. Some of the guys mentioned it a few days ago, but with the wind, it was only an occasional whiff, and we couldn't tell for sure where it was coming from."

"What do you think it is?" the chief engineer asked, his unease obvious.

"None of your business or mine," the chief mate growled. "Now let's get this fucking thing over the side, and we won't have to worry about it."

He turned from the engineers and barked orders to the sailors, who grabbed some loose staging planks and set about rigging a scaffold on each end of the short container stack.

***

"She's gone, Cassie," Karina said as she reached down into Cassie's lap and closed Tanya's sightless eyes. "We did all we could, but she's gone."

Cassie said nothing, but in the dim morning light leaking through the holes in the container, Karina saw her shake her head in wordless denial as she reached down and hugged Tanya's lifeless body.

"Sh...she can't be dead. It was only a tiny cut."

"But it got infected," Karina said as she eased Tanya's head off Cassie's lap and pulled Cassie to her in a comforting embrace. "We did all we could, but she's gone," Karina said again, and this time she felt Cassie nod against her chest, and she stroked the girl's hair and pulled her closer.

They both jumped as something struck the outside of the container with a metallic clang, and then they heard more thumps and muted voices. They had heard an occasional voice before, but always at a distance—and though they couldn't quite make out what was being said, these voices seemed to be right outside the container.

"Wh-what should we do?" Cassie asked.

"I'm not sure. Nothing for the moment, I think," Karina said. "Let's see what happens."

***

The two engineers connected the air hose to the second bladder and climbed down from the scaffold at the aft end of the container. The chief engineer surveyed their work and nodded to the chief mate.

"Both bladders are positioned and the air hoses are connected. Tell the Old Man we're ready," the chief engineer said. The chief mate, nodded and relayed the news to the bridge via his walkie-talkie.

"Go," came the captain's voice over the radio, and the chief engineer nodded to the first engineer to open the air valve.

Air hissed through the hoses, and the group watched as the bladders swelled, slowly at first, then faster. The container shuddered, and the inboard edge began to rise, lifted by the bladders and tilting the steel box toward the side of the ship—and the ocean beyond.

Then they heard muted thumps and the sound of movement inside the container, and the sailors looked at each other as the edge of the box continued to rise.

"What the hell is that?" the chief engineer asked.

"Nothing. Just something shifting in the box. Keep going," said the chief mate, just as an unmistakable human cry sounded above the air hissing through the hose.

"Help us! Please!"

The first engineer closed the air valve without asking permission.

"There's someone in there!" he said, and the chief mate raised the walkie-talkie.

"Captain," he said, "I think you should join us on deck."

***

The captain stood looking up at the tilted container, then shifted his gaze to the men grouped around him. He did his best to ignore the stench, and thankfully, the muted cries from within the container had stopped, its occupant or occupants apparently mollified by the fact the container was no longer moving. But those were minor concerns at the moment, as he studied the uneasy faces of his officers.

"What should we do?" the chief mate asked.

"What the hell do you mean, 'what should we do?' There's someone in there. A woman by the sound of it, maybe more than one. We must let them out," the first engineer said.

"How many voices did you hear?" the captain asked.

No one spoke at first. "Only one that I could tell," the chief engineer said at last.

The Captain nodded, as if considering that, and the silence grew.

"What does it matter if there is one or ten or a hundred?" the first engineer said. "We must help them, no matter how many there are."

"To what end?" the captain asked. "All of us have families. Even you, Ivan," he said, looking at the first engineer. "You are young and do not have a wife and kids, but what of your parents and grandparents? What if we save whoever is in the container? What do you think will become of us and our families? Do you have any doubt that we would pay dearly? It is a case of a life, or maybe a few lives, against many, and the many lives in question are those of our loved ones."

"We can go to the authorities when we dock in Jacksonville."

"And tell them what, exactly? Here are some people we rescued from a container? We think the Russian mob put them there, and oh, by the way, we know that because we are smugglers for the Russian *mafiya*, but never mind because we are all really good fellows. And, because we are all really good fellows, perhaps you could protect our families, who are thousands of miles away in Russia and Ukraine. Oh, I almost forgot to tell you, please do not notify the Russian authorities because they have ties to the *mafiya* and will most assuredly inform the mob and then look the other way while the bastards murder our families." The captain paused. "Is that what you would like us to do, Ivan?"

The first engineer shook his head. "If it were your wife or daughter in that fucking box, you would feel differently."

"Sadly, Ivan," the captain said, "if we don't finish this terrible business, it likely will be my wife and daughter in a box like that, perhaps with the rest of our loved ones with them, while we all rot in unmarked graves."

The captain turned to the chief engineer. "Finish the job. How long before you get it over the side."

The chief engineer swallowed. "I can get it a bit higher, but I don't think I can tip it with one inflation. We'll have to shore it up and reposition the bladders for another lift. Maybe another thirty minutes."

The captain nodded. "Get busy. The more quickly this is finished, the better for everyone."

"Okay," the chief engineer said, and as the captain walked back toward the deck house, he turned to the first engineer.

"Turn the air back on, Ivan," the chief engineer said.

"Fuck you. Do it yourself," the first engineer said, and stomped off after the captain.

USCG MH-65C Helicopter
75 miles due west of *Kapitan Godina*

"We've got a problem," said Mason's voice in Dugan's headphones. "I just got an update from the VTS guys ashore. We'll be over the target in less than thirty minutes, but she's still at the very edge of our range."

"Why is that a problem? We can reach her, right?"

"Yeah, just in time to maybe circle her twice and head for the barn."

Dugan was quiet a moment. "Okay, what's your plan?"

"What's MY plan? Christ, Dugan, I'm the taxi driver here! I don't HAVE a plan. I agreed to HELP, but none of this is by the book."

"How about the cutter, is she close enough for you to hang around a bit and still make it back to her?"

"Negative. When we reach the target we'll be about equidistant from both Cecil Field and the *Legare*, and both will be on the hairy edge of our range. She's closing on us, and another hour might make a difference, but we don't have an hour."

"But you CAN get us aboard?"

"Probably, one way or another," Mason said. "But that's what I'm trying to tell you. We normally stop the bad guys, then circle and wait for the fast-pursuit boat. But I can't do that, and I can't just set down on a potentially hostile vessel. That violates so many rules I couldn't even list them all. I assumed I was going to drop you aboard and hover to support you and intimidate the bad guys, but if I drop you at this range, I'll have to haul ass. And I'm sure as hell not leaving any of my guys in that situation. You'll be totally on your own for at least three hours."

Dugan glanced over at Ilya and Nigel, both of whom had been listening on their headphones. Both nodded.

"Let's do it," Dugan said.

USCG MH-65C HELICOPTER
IN SIGHT OF *KAPITAN GODINA*

"Got her," Mason said, and Dugan craned his neck to peer forward through the windshield at a ship in the far distance.

"I'm going to circle wide and high and slow, so as not to alarm them. We'll look them over from a distance as we pass, and then I'll fall in behind them and overtake her fast from dead astern. I'll flare and drop straight down in front of the bridge onto the top of the container stack. Everyone copy?"

Through the headset, Dugan listened as each crewman confirmed their understanding and Mason continued.

"Landry," he said to the gunner, "I want you in the open door facing the bridge windows with the M240. Don't fire, but try to look threatening as hell. Sinclair," he said to the fourth crewman, "I want you at the other open door, ready to help our guests disembark. I'll have the skids within a foot of the containers, so they won't have to fast rope. Just get 'em out the door so we can get out of here. Got it?"

Again the crew acknowledged the orders.

"Dugan," Mason said, "Landry and his machine gun will probably be all the intimidation you need, but we can't hang around long. You guys have to bail out, go around the chopper and haul ass for the bridge. From what I see from here there's some sort of platform running across the front of the bridge you can climb up on from the top of the container stack. As soon as you reach the bridge, you're on your own. Got it?"

"Affirmative. Anything else?"

"Yeah," Mason said. "Make sure you keep your heads down and circle around in front of the bird so I can be sure none of you run into the tail rotor."

"Thanks for the tip."

"Think nothing of it," Mason said. "It's hard to take off with a fucked-up tail rotor. You guys go ahead and move over by the door. This is going to happen fast."

Dugan and his companions complied, crouching near the door as the chopper veered starboard as it approached the ship, passing down the vessel's port side at a distance.

"There looks like there's some activity over on the starboard side near the bow," Dugan said, "but I can't make out what it is."

"We'll probably get a better look from astern," Mason said. "I'll drift out a bit to starboard and give you a look through the side door before I start to close."

Dugan said nothing as the chopper completed its run and circled to steady up on the same heading as the *Kapitan Godina*. He waited impatiently, unable to see anything from his position until Mason changed the orientation of the chopper to give Dugan a view through the side door.

"What the hell are they doing?" Dugan asked aloud, as he saw a container on the short stack near the starboard bow tilted at a crazy angle. Then as he watched, the container began to move almost in slow motion as it tipped over the side and tumbled into the water with a great splash.

"Mason! They must be onto us, and they're dumping the girls. Forget the ship and get us over that container. Now!" Dugan screamed.

Seconds later the chopper hovered over the floating container, the downdraft from the rotor sending ripples across the water in all directions as Dugan and the others peered down at it through the open door.

"How long will it float?" Mason asked in Dugan's ear.

"How the hell should I know? A while at least, assuming the door seals are tight. But I'm not worried about that as much as what shape the girls are in. That wasn't any gentle drop, more like a car crash. If they're alive in there, they're probably injured. How long before that cutter can get here?"

"Five or six hours at least. I'll get on the horn and…"

"I think it's sinking!" Nigel said, and Dugan saw he was right. The container was sitting deeper in the water than it was when they arrived moments before.

"Shit! The bastards must have drilled—"

Nigel was out the open door and falling feet first toward the water twenty feet below, and before Dugan could stop him, Ilya stripped off his own headset and was out the door after Nigel.

Dugan watched helplessly as his friends swam toward the container, knowing there was no way they could open it in its present condition.

"Do you have any duct tape?" he asked into the mike.

"What the hell are..." Mason began and then stopped himself. "Actually we may have something better. Landry, you got any of that 100-mile-an-hour tape around?"

"Never leave home without it," replied the gunner, as he dug around in a bag at his feet and emerged with a roll of what looked like black duct tape. "This is the best shit I ever used. It'll stick to anything, wet, dry, oily—"

Dugan snatched the tape and slipped his hand through the roll, pushing it tight on his left wrist like a bracelet. Without another word, he ripped off his headset and jumped out of the chopper feet first.

CHAPTER TWENTY-SIX

Dugan splashed into the water beside the container and surfaced to find Nigel and Ilya clinging to the front of the steel box. His first sensation wasn't visual but olfactory—a putrid stench that seemed to engulf him. A fine mist of water whipped up by the chopper's rotor wash obscured his vision, and he wiped his eyes to clear them. Nigel was hammering the door of the container with his closed fist, and Dugan could just make out his shouted words over the roar of the chopper.

"Cassie! We're here! Hang on, we're going to get you out."

Dugan swam the few strokes to the container, and Ilya turned as he swam up. The look on the Russian's face belied the promise of Nigel's shout. The twenty-foot container was floating at a crazy angle, cocked with one long edge submerged perhaps two or three feet deep and the opposite bottom edge just under the surface of the water—Ilya pointed to the bottom of the doors.

"The bottom of both halves of the door are below water, *Dyed*," Ilya screamed to be heard over the chopper. "If we open them, water will pour in and fill box in seconds. We will have no chance to get them out."

Dugan nodded. "We have to stop the water going in now, and then figure out how to deal with the doors."

Without waiting for an acknowledgment, Dugan swam around to the high side of the container. The bottom edge was just below the water line, and he started at the near corner and found what he was looking for immediately—water was pouring through a two-inch hole drilled in the side wall just above the bottom of the container. Ilya and Nigel splashed up on either side of him.

"What are you doing?" Ilya shouted.

"Looking for the holes," Dugan shouted back. "If we can find them and plug them, we can keep the box afloat long enough to figure out how to get the girls out. You and Nigel go along this edge and see how many more there are while I try to plug this one. Whatever we find along this edge will probably be duplicated along the deeper side, but if we can plug these first we'll have an idea of what we're dealing with. Hurry!"

As the pair nodded and started to pull themselves down the length of the container, Dugan steadied himself on the container with his left hand, positioning the roll of tape around his left forearm directly in front of him. He picked at the edge of the tape with the fingers of his right hand, fumbling as he tried to tease the edge of the tape up, and hoping this stuff would stick as well to other things as it did to itself. He finally got it started and pulled off a foot-long strip before reaching down and taking the edge of the tape in his teeth so he could tear it with his free hand. As he finished, his companions were back beside him, Nigel in the lead.

"Two more holes," Nigel shouted, "one about halfway down and the other at the far corner."

Dugan nodded and turned back to his hole. He had no illusions he'd get a complete seal, but he hoped he could slap enough of the heavy tape across the hole to slow down the water and buy a little time. IF Landry's magic 'stick to anything tape' worked as advertised. It didn't. Apparently he'd never tried it under salt water.

"It's not working," Nigel said, panic in his voice. "Ball it up and try to make a plug."

"Worth a shot," Dugan agreed, wadding the tape. It still stuck to itself, at least. He studied the tiny ball and shook his head.

"Nice theory, but it will take a helluva lot more tape than we have to make six plugs," Dugan said. Then it hit him.

"Quick. Take off your socks and give me one," Dugan shouted.

"But what—"

"Just lose your shoes and give me a fucking sock! No time to explain!"

Nigel ducked his head under the water, and Dugan started to pull a strip of tape off the roll. Nigel surfaced a moment later, socks in hand.

"Okay," Dugan shouted. "Roll one of them into a ball, tight as you can get it, then hand it over."

Nigel nodded, holding the sodden sock up to let the water drain from it as he rolled it tight.

"That's good," Dugan said. "Now hold it tight while I wrap it."

Seconds later Dugan had a black ball, perhaps three inches in diameter, pliable but not overly so.

"Cross your fingers, junior." Dugan took the ball from Nigel and began to compress it and twist it into the hole. It worked.

"Brilliant," Nigel said, as he began to roll his second sock.

"*Dyed*, I think water is coming in lower holes faster, *da*? If you and Nigel make plugs, I will dive down and plug bottom holes first."

"Good point." Dugan pulled the first plug from the hole and passed it to Ilya. "Start with this one. We'll have another one ready by the time you get back."

USCG MH-65C HELICOPTER

"How much time?" Mason asked.

"None," his co-pilot replied. "We should have started back five minutes ago. Even now it'll be close, and the winds are shifting. Any sort of head wind at all, and we're getting our feet wet."

The 'and losing a twenty-million-dollar helicopter' went unspoken.

"Well, I can't just fucking leave them bobbing around a sinking container in the mid-ocean."

"Drop them the raft and locater beacon," the co-pilot suggested. "In this weather, *Legare* can be here in twelve hours at flank speed. For that matter, we can probably make it to her, refuel, and be back in three."

"And what if they get the girls out of the container? They're bound to need medical attention, and Sinclair has EMT training. Three hours could make a big difference."

"So could going in to the drink because we don't have enough fuel," the co-pilot said.

"Shit!" Mason said and shook his head. "Okay. Landry, you and Sinclair deploy the raft."

"What about the ship?" the co-pilot asked.

"What about her?" Mason replied. "She'll either continue for Jacksonville or she won't, but even at top speed, she's not getting away from us, not this close to home. We can have *Legare* send a boarding team or vector another chopper in on her anytime we want."

ATLANTIC OCEAN
EAST OF JACKSONVILLE, FLORIDA

Ilya pulled himself into the inflatable raft and then helped Nigel and Dugan in after him, as the thump of the chopper's blades faded to the west. Dugan spared a quick glance at the receding speck in the western sky and turned back to the container. He could hardly fault Mason, and right now he had other priorities. He grabbed a paddle and shot a quick glance at the reference marks he'd scratched on the side of the container with his pocket knife. They were still right at the waterline.

"She's tight, for now at least," Dugan said as he propelled the raft around to the door end of the container. "Now let's see what we can do about those doors."

"Is still no good, *Dyed*," Ilya said. "If we break door seal, the container will sink like stone."

"Maybe not. From the force of the water flowing into the holes, I don't think the water inside had equalized with the outside water level yet. That means the water level inside the box is below the outside waterline. If we can tilt it down on the far end, even a little, the water inside should run to that end, causing it to sink and lifting the door end a bit. Maybe."

"But how?" Ilya asked, but Nigel was already nodding and studying the end of the container.

"We'll have to climb up this end," Nigel said, "using the door locking bars as hand and footholds. But if we put more weight on this end, it might have the opposite effect."

"Which is why you'll go first," Dugan said, "since you're the lightest. Work your way down to the far end and then shout out. I'll go next, and when I get down there, our combined weight should more than compensate for Ilya."

Nigel nodded again and reached up for a hand hold, but Dugan put a hand on his arm.

"I don't have a clue how much weight it will take to shift this thing or how quickly it will happen, so get your ass to the far end as fast as you can. Got it?"

Nigel nodded and swallowed hard before grabbing one of the locking bars to steady himself and then standing up in the raft. He reached as high as he could for another handhold and then placed his foot on one of the tilted locking bars and launched himself up. The free-floating container rocked slightly under his weight as he struggled upward, and his foot began to slip down the bar. Ilya shot his hand out, grasping the bar just below Nigel's foot, forming a step with his wrist and forearm. Steadied, Nigel got a fresh grip and pulled himself up onto the top of the rocking container and disappeared.

"I'm here," he shouted a moment later from the far end of the container.

Dugan tied the raft off to one of the locking bars and looked up. He was thirty years older—and considerably less nimble—than the young Brit.

"*Dyed*, I have idea," Ilya said, rising to his knees and facing the end of the container. He reached up and grabbed a locking bar as far up as he could, then turned his head and spoke over his shoulder. "Use me like ladder, *da*? First my shoulder, then my wrist on bar. Will get you high enough very quickly, I think. And part of your weight will be on me in raft."

"Good idea, but try to keep all your weight on your knees. The way that thing rocked with Nigel's weight, it's tender as hell."

"*Da*. Now go."

Dugan put his hand on the side of the container to steady himself and stood in one swift motion, putting a foot on Ilya's shoulder and reaching as high as he could for a handhold. He heard the big Russian grunt as he pulled himself up and put his other foot on Ilya's wrist. In seconds, he was on the upraised top edge of the container, as if he were straddling the top ridge of a roof. He placed his hands and knees on either side of the raised corner and quickly worked his way down to Nigel. The container rocked even more violently from the shifting weight of his transit.

"I'm here, Ilya. Go," Dugan shouted.

Ilya was over the end of the container in a flash, moving toward them standing up in a strange crablike run, his bare feet splayed on either side of the upraised corner of the container. Dugan marveled at his ability to maintain his balance as Ilya settled down beside him.

The container rocked a bit more, then slowly subsided. For a long moment, nothing happened.

"Is not working," Ilya said.

"Give it a second." Dugan hid his fear the Russian was right. Then, almost imperceptibly, the high side of the container began to fall as the container turned on its axis, and just as gradually, their end of the container began to sink lower. Then it happened in a rush, the movement increasingly rapid as the water inside the box rushed to the lower end, driving it even lower, and the opposite end of the box began to elevate. In moments the box had reached a new equilibrium, and Dugan looked down the side of the box, toward the door end.

"Is it up, Mr. Dugan? Is it out of the water?" Nigel asked.

"It's close, but I can't tell for sure. Nigel, you're the lightest. Ilya and I will stay here to keep our weight in the equation. You swim around to the door end and have a look."

Nigel dove overboard before Dugan even finished his sentence. The container rocked violently from his sudden departure, causing his companions to clutch at the steel beneath them to maintain their balance. Nigel stroked furiously for the door end of the container and Dugan heard him splashing as he dragged himself up into the raft.

"What do you see, Nigel?"

"We did it! We bloody well did it," Nigel screamed. "It's only by an inch or so when the container isn't rocking, but the bottoms of the doors are above the water."

Dugan's mind raced. An inch wasn't much. If either he or Ilya left this end of the container, the door end might very well drop back below the waterline, and even a quarter inch would be deadly.

"Okay, Nigel. Ilya and I have to stay back here, so this is all on you. Do you think you can get both of the doors open so we can see what the situation is? We'll play it by ear from there."

"I'm on it," Nigel shouted, and Dugan whispered a prayer beneath his breath. *Please Lord, let them be alive.*

ATLANTIC OCEAN
EAST OF JACKSONVILLE, FLORIDA

Nigel untied the raft from the container so he could maneuver around the doors. He rotated the dogs on the four locking bars, disengaging them one by one, breaking the seal around the doors. The stench intensified, and he suppressed consideration of what that might portend.

The steel doors were heavy, tilted as they were, with gravity holding them closed. Nigel struggled to get a purchase, floating in the raft, but dare not climb on the container lest he tip the opening below the water level. Finally, through force of will and adrenaline-fueled strength, he succeeded in lifting the left door open ninety degrees. From that point gravity took over, pulling the door from his grasp as it fell open on its hinges with a crash, once again rocking the container violently.

***

Dugan and Ilya perched precariously on the far end of the container, and the stench wafted over them when Nigel broke the seal on the container door. Ilya turned to Dugan, his eyes wet.

"I know this smell, *Dyed*. Before I was not so sure, and I wanted to be wrong. But I have smelled it many times. Too often. It is death. We are too late, I think."

Dugan nodded, a lump in his throat, but as he reached over to lay a comforting hand on Ilya's shoulder, the box rocked violently. He tried to steady himself against the unexpected movement, but he lost his balance and went over backward. Ilya moved quickly, clutching at Dugan's leg as he went over, but the Russian was off balance himself, and both men tumbled into the water.

***

Nigel watched in horror as the now open end of the container sank toward the raft and water poured over the door sill into the dark maw of the container. Inside in the roiling water, he saw a flash of white flesh and glimpsed an arm, and acted instinctively, diving through the open door without thought or hesitation, a scant second before the box slid beneath the surface. He swam blindly through the filthy water inside the container, groping down the hard steel walls, and through a clutter of what felt like buckets or pails rising around him. And then flesh, a wrist. Let it be Cassie!

He was disoriented now, clueless as to up or down, his lungs near bursting. He followed the wall, ever faster as his lungs screamed for air, kicking and pulling himself along the corrugated steel with one hand, the other clamped tight around the wrist. He reached for another handhold and pulled with all his might, propelling himself upward in a rush—and smashed head first into unyielding steel—the still-closed right half of the container double door.

Stunned, he instinctively released the wrist to use both hands to claw his way around the unexpected obstacle. Then he was out of the container and sunlight filtering down from the surface far above showed the container plunging downward, already far below him. Cassie! He dove and was kicking for the container when he felt rather than saw a presence beside him, and then felt a jolt to the side of his head and... blackness.

***

Nigel blinked, then opened his eyes. His head ached, and orange filled his vision. The raft. He was on the raft. He tried to lift his head and was unable to suppress a moan as he felt a stabbing pain on the side of his face.

"Easy," said Dugan's voice. "You took a pretty good hit."

Nigel stayed down but rolled toward Dugan's voice to find both his companions staring at him with concern in their eyes.

"Wh...what happened?"

"I am sorry, Nigel," Ilya said, "but I had to knock you unconscious. Even for strong swimmer is not possible to bring struggling man to surface from many meters below, and I knew you would fight me."

"Cassie!" Nigel said, sitting up this time, despite the pain.

"Gone," Dugan said. "I'm sure they were gone long before we opened the container. I suspect that's why the bastards dumped them. They were getting rid of the evidence."

"But I saw... I had someone," Nigel said.

"Alive?" Dugan asked gently.

"I... I don't know. I couldn't see. But they were very cold."

Nigel lay there, tears running down his cheeks, and nothing broke the silence for a long while. Finally Ilya spoke quietly to Dugan.

"*Dyed*, when we get ashore, we should have Nigel checked by doctor. I think the water in the container was very contaminated, and for sure he took some in."

Nigel overheard and responded. "What does it bloody matter?"

CHAPTER TWENTY-SEVEN

The captain peered far astern through the binoculars, tensing as he watched the orange helicopter leave the jettisoned container and fly straight toward his ship. It overtook the ship rapidly, passing just above bridge level on the starboard side, the door gunner tracking the ship with his machine gun, his clearly visible face a mix of anger and eagerness. The captain heaved a relieved sigh when the chopper continued westward without firing.

"They're leaving," the chief mate said, his relief obvious.

"They will be back. Or someone will, in any event," the captain said, turning to the chief mate. "Mr. Luchenko, you have the bridge. Notify me at once if we are approached by any aircraft or ships."

"Yes, Captain."

"Chief," the captain said to the chief engineer who had also been on the bridge watching the chopper, "let's go down to my office and get this over with, shall we."

The chief engineer nodded and followed the captain into the central stairwell and down to his office on the deck below. The captain motioned the chief to his sofa as he moved to his desk and picked up the sat phone. He dialed a number from memory.

"Is it done?" asked a voice on the other end.

"*Da.* The container is over the side and was sinking as we sailed away."

"Any problems?"

"*Nyet,*" the captain said.

"Good," said the voice and hung up without another word.

The captain hung up the phone and pursed his lips to blow out a relieved sigh.

"What will he do if he finds out you were lying?" the chief asked.

The captain shrugged. "If I told him the truth, he would likely harm my family because I failed, even though I tried. So what can he do, kill my family twice? This way at least, we have a little time. Anyway, we did what he said. If it comes to that, we merely say that the helicopter was unseen in the distance and apparently saw us dump the container, and that we were not aware of that until later, when they boarded us to investigate. After all, I did warn him we were too close to the coast to jettison the container."

"So you think the authorities will come?"

"Most assuredly, either at sea or when we reach Jacksonville. And we will be arrested, or at least I will, if everything goes well."

"You WANT to be arrested? Why?"

"Because I am much more afraid of these *mafiya* bastards than anything the US authorities can do to me, and being arrested will demonstrate to the *mafiya* that I followed instructions to the letter. And what can the Americans charge me with, exactly? They saw a container go over the side, and it sank, so they have no physical evidence. And it was in international waters, and we are a foreign flag ship, so I actually don't think we have broken any US laws. They can SUSPECT that there is some sort of insurance fraud going on, but unless the company files a claim, there is no fraud. They can suspect we are smugglers, but what are they going to use for evidence?"

"I hadn't thought of that," the chief admitted.

"Furthermore, I am sure that the *mafiya* has clever and expensive American lawyers, and they will want to make sure this goes away. So I doubt I will be spending much time in jail."

"Aren't you forgetting something?" the chief asked. "What about our other problem?"

"I'm forgetting nothing," the captain said. "We did what we had to do, and may God help us if we were wrong."

ATLANTIC OCEAN
EAST OF JACKSONVILLE, FLORIDA

Dugan sat in the raft with Ilya, his eyes half-closed against the mist of salt water being whipped up by the chopper's propeller wash as he watched Nigel being winched aboard the chopper. Moments later the empty harness came back down, and Dugan grabbed it and offered it to Ilya, who shook his head and indicated Dugan should go first. Dugan shrugged and slipped into the harness, then looked up and motioned for the chopper crew to take him up.

Five minutes later, he was strapped into a web seat beside a dejected Nigel, and he watched the two chopper crewman haul Ilya through the door. Ilya took a seat across from Dugan and put on the headset before he even strapped himself in.

"Where is ship?" Ilya demanded.

"About fifty or sixty miles due west," Dugan heard Mason reply in his headphones. "We passed her on the way here. She's evidently continuing to Jacksonville as if nothing happened."

"Good," Ilya said. "Take me to ship."

Dugan felt Nigel stir in the seat beside him, and a glance at his face showed his approval of the Russian's demand.

There was nothing but silence from the headsets.

"I said take me to ship. Now," Ilya said. "These bastards killed Karina and the others, and they must pay."

"I'm sorry, Ilya, but that's not happening. We've already dispatched another chopper with a boarding party. They should be getting aboard any time. They'll take it from here."

The Glock came out of Ilya's pocket and he half-turned to level it at Mason over his shoulder. Dugan saw the other crewmen tense, unsure what to do at the unexpected development.

"I am sorry, Joe Mason. But you must take me to ship. I do not want to kill you, but I will wound you, then co-pilot can take us to ship."

"So. Is this the way you treat a '*tovarishch* for life'?"

"No... I mean..." Ilya's momentary indecision faded, and his voice hardened. "I must avenge Karina. You are Russian. You understand this."

"I understand I agreed to risk my career and my life and these men's lives to SAVE the lives of your Karina and the others, not for your revenge. And you know that's true. If you are a man of honor, you will respect that agreement. And besides, the boarding party will reach the ship long before we do. What do you plan to do, leap aboard and single-handedly fight your way through a heavily armed and well-trained team in order to kill their prisoners? You know that as soon as you leave the chopper, we'll warn them you're coming. We must—unless, of course, you plan to kill us all first. Is that your plan, *tovarishch*?"

Dugan sat silently and watched the emotions play across Ilya's face—anger warred with resolve, and then uncertainty, and finally, anguish and defeat. The big Russian seemed almost to deflate, and he flung the Glock out of the open door of the chopper and buried his face in his hands.

"*Yob tvoyu mat', lokhi*," he said, between clenched teeth. "As God is my witness, someday I will kill them all."

"STOP!" said Mason into the headphones as Landry and Sinclair moved to restrain Ilya. "Leave him alone," Mason said more quietly. "Just leave him alone. He'll be okay."

Dugan looked at Ilya and Nigel slumped in their seats. Would any of them ever really be okay again? His thoughts turned to Cassie, and he tried to swallow the lump in his throat—and wondered what he would say to Alex and Gillian.

CHAPTER TWENTY-EIGHT

ST. IGNATIUS HOSPITAL
LONDON, UK

Anna sat on the side of the bed, fully clothed, and glared at Dugan.

"I'm perfectly capable of walking," she said. "I DO NOT need a wheelchair."

"Hey, don't get mad at me. I'm just telling you what they told me. Hospital rules. All released patients get a wheelchair ride to the exit. No wheelchair, no release."

"Well, in that case they should be a bit more efficient. I've been ready to go for an hour."

As if on cue, an orderly rolled a wheelchair into the room. "Who's ready to go home?" he asked with a bright smile, and Dugan saw Anna bite back a sharp response.

"That would be me," she said, and despite her previous attestation of fitness, she grimaced a bit as she stood, holding the bed for balance as she turned to allow the orderly to wheel the chair up behind her. Dugan jumped up from his own seat and steadied her arm as she sat down in the chair. She still had a bit of healing to do.

The orderly looked at Dugan. "Your car?"

"I have a taxi standing by at the front entrance," Dugan said, and the man nodded and rolled the chair out into the corridor with Dugan at his side. A few minutes later, after an elevator ride, the orderly rolled Anna across the expansive main lobby and out to the waiting cab.

Dugan helped Anna settle into the back seat of the taxi, and then ran around and climbed into the other side. He leaned forward and gave the driver the address of their apartment and then sat back as the car began to move. Anna reached over and took his hand.

"How are they?" she asked.

Dugan looked over and shrugged. "They were a bit numb at first, like us all, I think. But it's started to sink in over the last few days. I don't know who's more devastated, Alex or Gillian. The house is like a tomb. Mrs. Hogan is looking after them, but she can't get either of them to eat. Alex has taken to sitting alone in his study, staring at the empty fireplace. She tells me he's hitting the brandy pretty hard, very much like when Kathleen died, except that this time, Gillian is equally distraught and dealing with demons of her own."

"And how about you?"

Dugan shrugged again. "I… I guess I'm all right. I just can't help but feel if I'd done things differently—if we'd somehow gotten there even an hour earlier—"

"Tom, you can't blame yourself. You did everything in your power to save them. You all did. I'm sure Alex and Gillian know that."

"Maybe, but when they look at me—when they look at any of us—I can't help but feel they blame us on some level, whether it's conscious or not."

"You know that's ridiculous. Alex and Gillian know how much you loved Cassie, and Ilya lost his own niece."

Dugan nodded. "On an intellectual level, I know you're right, but there's just something about it that makes it hard to be around them now. It's like we're not sharing our grief, but somehow when we're all together it's compounded. I can't explain it, but the others feel it too."

"And how ARE Nigel and Ilya?"

"Nigel's nearly a basket case. I know he's having nightmares because he cries out in his sleep. Ilya's like a ticking time bomb. He doesn't talk much, and when he does speak, it's in monosyllables. You can almost feel the hatred and rage, no small part of it directed at me."

"YOU? Whatever for?"

"He really wanted the guys on the ship that dumped the container—we all did—but the Coast Guard pilot wouldn't land us on the ship. And the pilot apparently sent word up the line about the volatility of the situation, because before we even landed back at Cecil Field, I got a call from Ward. He told me that if we even tried to get near the ship and crew that the deal he'd cut for Borgdanov's 'recruits' was off. I can see his point. I'm sure selling the idea was difficult enough without one of the potential new permanent residents shooting up a ship full of foreign nationals in the Port of Jacksonville before the program even gets off the ground."

"How did Ilya take that?"

"Badly, but what could he do? Borgdanov's incommunicado at the moment, recruiting people on the strength of Ward's assurances. Ilya would never do anything to compromise Andrei, no matter how enraged he gets. But he's chomping at the bit for word from Borgdanov summoning him to go to Russia. I pity the bastards when he gets there."

"How did you leave things with Ward?"

"Not good. We hung around a day trying to find out what was happening with the crew of the Kapitan Godina—nothing much as it turns out. I mean, I was willing to let the authorities handle it, but I thought SOMETHING would happen to them. Ward told me the captain lawyered up, and with a very pricey shyster at that, and that it's likely nothing will stick at all."

"I can see why Ilya is upset. How did he take THAT?"

Dugan shook his head. "He was upset enough; I didn't dare share that with him. Christ, if he finds out the truth, there's no telling what he might do. Anyway, Ward and I had words, not nice ones. Let's just say he's not on my Christmas card list anymore, at least for the moment."

"You and Jesse Ward have been friends for a long time."

"And we still are, I suppose. And we'll continue to work together on the deal he promised Borgdanov. But for the moment, or the next few days anyway, I don't want to get into it again with him. He's actually called a few times, but what is there to say? I let it go to voice mail."

"Did you listen to the messages?"

"Nope, and I don't intend to for a while."

Anna nodded. "You're upset, I get that. But perhaps the memorial service will give everyone a bit of closure. Have Alex and Gillian decided on a time?"

"No. It's like if they plan a memorial service they're giving up on Cassie. I know Mrs. Hogan has been gently pushing them in that direction, but without result. She's set up a visit with Father O'Malley first thing tomorrow morning and asked me to come. I don't look forward to it."

"Would you like me to come?"

Dugan shook his head. "No. The doctor released you on the condition that you take it slow. I think the deal was no more than an hour or so on the crutches at a time for the first week. I intend to hold you to that." He put his face close to hers and looked into her eyes. "I've lost enough people in my life, Anna, and I intend to take good care of you, whether you want me to or not."

ST. PETERSBURG
RUSSIAN FEDERATION

Vladimir Glazkov held the phone to his ear, shaking his head in silent exasperation. He sighed. There was no professionalism anymore it seemed, only a dwindling pool of spoiled and whining practitioners of a dying art. Sometimes he missed the old days.

"… and you know multiple hits are difficult. As soon as I hit one of the targets, I'll no doubt spook the others. They may go into hiding and delay completion of the job, and you were emphatic that you wanted this finished quickly."

"Obviously you hit them all at the same time and place," Glazkov said. "A bomb or car crash when they're all in the same car perhaps."

"What about collateral damage? Are additional casualties acceptable?"

Glazkov sighed again. "Well, obviously we don't want to slaughter a dozen innocent school children or random tourists in a public place. That would elevate it to the level of terrorism and make matters even worse in regard to raising our profile with the authorities. However, so long as casualties are confined to these Kairouz people, their American friend, and close associates, I think that would be acceptable. My experience is that the general public doesn't react too strongly to the killing of wealthy people; I think there's even a certain subliminal sense of satisfaction. In a few months, it will all be pushed from the headlines by another sensational news event of some kind, and we can go quietly about rebuilding our UK operations."

"Getting them all in the same place at the same time may prove difficult. I can't guarantee a time frame. But I have them all under surveillance now, and I'll probably be able to move soon."

"Are you monitoring their communications?" Glazkov asked.

"Not so far. I haven't been able—"

"So let me understand, Fedosov. Your plan is to follow them around until they just happen to get together in one place and then kill them?"

"No, of course not, but we only just began discussing hitting them at the same time—"

Glazkov erupted. "We only just began discussing it because it was such an obvious requirement that only a simpleton such as yourself would have failed to grasp it. Now monitor their communications, find out when they'll be together, and TAKE THEM OUT! Is that sufficiently clear, or must I email you a diagram?"

"No, Boss. I'll get on it at once."

"You'd better. And keep me informed."

He slammed the receiver into the cradle, rested his elbows on the desk, and put his face in his hands. He definitely missed the old days.

CHAPTER TWENTY-NINE

The back garden was awash in the light of a full moon, augmented by nearby streetlights, and Fedosov cursed the time table that forced him to take risks he would normally avoid. But then any risk, no matter how high, was preferable to the certain danger if he disappointed the Chief. He shuddered at the possibility and tried to concentrate on the task at hand.

He was well concealed in the shrubbery and had been since he'd arrived at two in the morning to find lights still burning throughout the stately home. An hour later, the lights began to wink out, indicating the residents were retiring—all except one—which was still burning now almost an hour later. He glanced toward the east—it would be getting light soon—and other than the single light, he'd no other indications that anyone was still awake in the house. Common sense told him to abort, but the memory of the last conversation with the Chief was a strong motivator. He crept close to the window of the room still showing a light, keeping his head well below the sill.

Fedosov rose slowly, not wanting sudden movement to draw the gaze of anyone inside, and as his eyes rose above the windowsill, he looked through the open blinds. The light was coming from a shaded desk lamp on an ornately carved wooden desk. No one sat at the desk, but slumped in an overstuffed leather chair in the corner he saw Kairouz, obviously unconscious. He wore a dressing gown, sagging open at the waist to reveal a hairy chest. His bare feet were on a footstool, slippers lying below them on the floor at odd angles, as if they'd fallen off. His head had fallen to one side, and his mouth was slack in sleep, a tendril of drool leaking out of one corner and down his unshaven chin. Beside him on a side table was an empty brandy snifter and a decanter with perhaps a half inch of amber liquid left in the bottom. Out like a light, no problem there. That left only the woman, and based on the timing of the lights being extinguished, she'd been asleep for over an hour.

He glided around the house to the back door into the kitchen, keeping in the shadows. He picked the lock without difficulty, entered the kitchen, and moved quickly to the security panel. The technician from the security company had been reluctant at first and, to his credit, unpersuaded by any amount of money offered. However, in the end, the graphic videos of what might happen to his family had convinced him, along with the promise that the information would only be used to relieve an obviously wealthy man of some of his possessions. By the time the technician figured out differently, he would already be implicated in the crime.

Fedosov covered the small speaker on the panel with his right hand to muffle the chirps, and tapped in the security code with his left, nodding as the lights on the panel flashed to 'unarmed.' He crept to the basement doorway off the kitchen and descended, lighting his way with a small headlamp rather than risking turning on a light. The utility closet was in a far corner of the basement, and in minutes he'd wired a voice-activated transmitting device into the phone circuit, rearranging the wiring to conceal it. There were still the Kairouzes' mobile phones, of course, but since they seemed to be staying close to home, he reckoned they might be using their landline for the majority of calls. He quickly checked his work. Satisfied, he crept back up the stairs.

It was a moment's work to conceal tiny listening devices throughout the ground floor in locations likely to yield interesting conversations. He considered planting some in the upstairs bedrooms, but he had no idea how soundly the woman was sleeping. No point in pressing his luck. Stopping in the doorway to the study, he spotted Kairouz's mobile phone lying in plain sight on the desk just beyond the sleeping man. As he stood trying to decide whether to go for the phone, Kairouz moaned in his sleep and began to wave his arms as if he were struggling with some unseen assailant. His arm flew out to the side, and Fedosov jumped out of sight to the side of the door a scant second before he heard the sound of the brandy snifter smashing on the hardwood floor. He stood deathly still, his heart pounding.

"Alex? Are you all right?" came the woman's voice from up the stairs, followed by the sounds of someone rising and then footsteps across the floor above. "Alex?" the woman said again.

Fedosov willed himself calm and faded quietly down the hall and around the corner into the living room as the woman's footsteps sounded on the stairs. He fingered the silenced pistol in his pocket and considered killing them both now. But no. The Chief wanted them all killed together and quickly. If he snuffed these two now, an alerted Dugan would be an exponentially more difficult target. He waited.

He heard shuffling and muttered curses from the direction of the study, and then a moment later the woman's voice from the direction of the study door.

"For God's sake, Alex, put your slippers on. There's glass all over the floor and—oh, sit back down, you've cut your foot."

"Fuck offf," came the slurred reply. "… i's my bloody foot, isn't it?"

Fedosov heard noises as if someone was stumbling into furniture, followed by more muttered curses and then a bitter mocking laugh.

"And it IS a bloody foot, isn't it?"

"Alex, SIT DOWN and let me look at it."

"Oh? Givin' bloody orders are we, dear? You're good at that, aren't you? Always has to be YOUR way, doesn't it? You and Thomas bloody Dugan and those fuckin' Russkis. I told you to leave it alone. I told you they were dangerous. But no, everyone knows better than old Alex, don't they? She drowned in a box like a fucking rat! And where was I? Tending the bloody home fires while our little girl died. And what did Thomas and those fucking Russkis do? Bloody fuck all!"

"Alex, you don't mean that," the woman said. "You know Tom did everything—"

"THE HELL HE DID," screamed Kairouz, and Fedosov heard the crash of what he assumed was the brandy decanter smashing against a wall. "THE HELL HE DID! IF HE'D DONE ALL HE COULD, CASSIE WOULD BE ALIVE!"

The outburst was followed by an unintelligible cry of anguish and then dissolved into the sounds of wracking sobs mixed with cooing sounds, as if the woman was comforting an infant.

"Come along, dear," the woman's voice said. "Let's sit you down here on the sofa and have a look at that foot." There was a pause. "It doesn't look too bad, and the bleeding's mostly stopped. Let's get you up to bed. I have some plasters in our bathroom."

Fedosov heard them making their way up the stairs, the man's steps halting and stumbling, and he imagined Kairouz leaning on the woman. The sounds moved to the bedroom above, and he waited a moment, considering the risks. He had to reset the security system when he left, and with the woman fully awake, she might hear the chirps. Then the decision was made for him. He heard the woman coming down the stairs.

She seemed to stop at the bottom, and he heard muffled sobs. Slowly he peeked around the door, and in the light leaking into the hallway from the open door of the study, he saw the woman sitting on the bottom step, her face buried in her hands and her shoulders shaking.

He began to panic. It was close to sunrise, and the stupid bitch was between him and his planned exit point, and she had a clear view of the front door as well. If she sat there and bawled until daylight, he may have to take her out anyway, regardless of what the Chief preferred. She began to wipe her eyes with the back of her hand, and Fedosov ducked back into the living room.

Panic rose again as he heard her coming down the hall in his direction, and he put his hand on his gun. Then she stopped, and he heard her lift the receiver of the hall telephone.

"Tom," the woman said, "I'm sorry to wake you at this hour—"

"Oh, you weren't? Well, I guess none of us are sleeping too well these days," she said, then responded to another unheard question.

"Me? Oh, I'm fine, or as well as can be expected, I suppose, given the circumstances. It's Alex I'm concerned about. I'm going to cancel the meeting with Father O'Malley this morning, and I didn't want you to come over for nothing."

"I appreciate that Tom, but I really think it's better if you don't come over just now. Alex is in no state to see anyone, much less discuss the memorial service. I'm just going to tell Father O'Malley to schedule it for the day after tomorrow—well, I guess that's actually tomorrow now, given that it's almost morning—just after midday. We can all meet here at the house after the service. Just family and close friends."

The woman was silent, as if she was considering the answer to a difficult question.

"Of course you're welcome, Tom. But I can't pretend this isn't difficult for Alex. In truth I think he blames us all, myself included. They say that time heals all wounds, but…well, it's possible that some wounds are just too deep. Time will tell, I suppose."

"Thank you, Tom. I will. Best to Anna." She hung up.

Fedosov tensed, anxious about the woman's next move, then heaved an inward sigh of relief when he heard her footsteps on the stairs. He waited a moment and then slipped down the basement stairs and moved to one of the two small basement windows set high in the exterior wall and examined it critically. It would be tight, but he could make it. He pulled an all-purpose tool from his pocket and quickly wired around the security system sensor, so that the system would always show 'closed' regardless of the position of the window. He then unlocked it and made sure it would open easily before pulling it closed and gliding back up the stairs to exit through the kitchen, muffling the alarm and resetting the security system on his way out.

He tried to appear casual as he strolled through the predawn light to where his car was parked several blocks away. It had been a productive evening despite a rocky start. He had the place and time of the hit nailed down and had arranged access to the site. All he needed now was a little time and a lot of plastic explosive. And from the sound of things, he'd be putting them all out of their misery. It was practically an act of mercy.

DUGAN AND ANNA'S APARTMENT
LONDON, UK

Dugan disconnected from Gillian and sat down in the wrought-iron chair on the small balcony of the apartment. He'd being lying awake when she called, watching Anna sleep, and going over the events of the last few days in his mind. The phone vibrated on the night table before it rang, and he had snatched it up before it disturbed Anna, and retreated to the balcony.

He looked through the closed glass door into the living room and saw Nigel sprawled on the couch. With Ilya in the spare bedroom, there was literally no place in the small apartment other than the bathroom where Dugan wouldn't disturb someone. He considered going back to bed, but knew he'd only toss and turn and probably disturb Anna, and she needed her rest. He decided to stay out and watch the sunrise, so he set the phone on the table beside him, leaned back in the chair and put his feet up on the rail of the balcony.

He jumped as the phone vibrated on the table beside him and picked it up, thinking Gillian had forgotten something and was calling back, but he didn't recognize the number on the caller ID.

"Dugan."

"I was beginning to think you were dead," Ward said. "Don't you check your voice mail?"

Dugan felt a flash of guilt, followed immediately by irritation.

"Yeah, well, I've been kind of busy. Where are you calling from, anyway? I didn't recognize the number."

"I was counting on that. I'm calling on the plane's satellite phone. I'm over the Atlantic, and we should be landing in London in an hour. I need you to meet me."

"For Christ's sake. It's five o'clock in the morning—"

214

"So if you leave soon, you can beat the traffic."

"This isn't the best time, Jesse. Care to tell me what this is all about?"

"I can't, not over the phone. Just meet me there, okay? You won't be sorry."

"Yeah, well, I've heard that before." Dugan sighed. "All right. I'll meet you. The private terminal at Heathrow, I presume?"

"Negative. Meet us at London RAF Northolt. Do you know it?"

"I know of it, but I've never been there. I can get there all right."

"Great! I'll wait for you on board. There are some things we need to discuss before we disembark. I'll arrange clearance for you straight to the plane. The stairs will be down, just come aboard when you get there."

RAF NORTHOLT JET CENTER
LONDON, UK

Dugan rolled to a stop at the gate and lowered his window as the uniformed guard approached.

"My name is Tom Dugan." He offered his passport. "I'm supposed to meet Mr. Jesse Ward, who's arriving by private jet."

The guard took Dugan's passport and scrutinized it closely before looking back at him with the same intensity. He then turned to a companion in the small guard shack and nodded, and the man walked out of the shack and got into a golf cart parked just inside the open gate.

"Yes, Mr. Dugan," the guard said. "Mr. Ward touched down a few minutes ago. If you would be kind enough to follow my colleague, he'll escort you to the plane."

"Thanks." Dugan accepted his passport back from the guard and put the car in gear.

He followed the golf cart down a perimeter road and around the end of what appeared to be a terminal building. Arrayed along the back side of the building were a number of executive jets of various sizes, but they bypassed them all and went to the last parking place some distance from the others, to a large Gulfstream sitting alone. The guard motioned for him to stop and then circled the golf cart around beside the car.

"Park your car there near the fence, if you will, sir. You'll see some spaces marked as you get nearer. Then board the aircraft. I understand they're expecting you."

"Thank you," Dugan said, and the guard touched his finger to his cap and sped away.

Dugan parked the car and walked across the tarmac, puzzled at the unusual manner of Ward's arrival. On those rare occasions when he traveled on the CIA's private jet rather than the more customary trips by commercial carrier, Ward normally landed at the private terminal at Heathrow. Thoroughly confused, Dugan mounted the short flight of steps up into the plane.

He turned to his right as he entered the small but luxurious cabin of the executive jet, and saw Ward facing him at the far end, sitting across a coffee table from two dark-haired men, both with their backs to the door of the plane. Ward smiled as he saw Dugan and began to stand.

"Okay, Jesse," Dugan said. "Care to tell me what all the cloak and dagger shit is—"

"UNCLE THOMAS!"

Dugan froze, confused, as both dark heads turned in unison, and one man leaped from his seat and moved toward him, wearing Cassie's smiling face topped with a short mop of black hair.

"UNCLE THOMAS!" the figure cried again, and there was no mistaking the voice. It was Cassie, however impossible that seemed, and she flew into his arms. He hugged her tight, unable to speak as tears flowed down his cheeks and his shoulders shook.

"Oh, Uncle Thomas, I'm so glad to see you!" Cassie was crying herself now as she returned his hug, and they both lapsed into silence, clinging together and unable to speak. Time seemed to stand still, and they stood there motionless, as a thousand questions crowded Dugan's mind and he was unable to articulate any of them. He just stood in joyful acceptance of the miracle, indifferent for the time being as to how it came about.

Dugan looked over Cassie's head to see Jesse Ward standing a few feet away, beaming.

"Can I assume," Ward asked, "that you're no longer pissed off at me?"

Dugan blinked back tears and returned Ward's smile, still unable to speak. He nodded.

"Good," Ward said, "and I don't want to rush your reunion, but we have a lot to talk about. But first, I don't think you've met Karina."

Dugan looked at the other person he'd assumed was a man, to see a beautiful young woman perhaps an inch taller than Cassie. There was no mistaking the family resemblance.

"Yo-you're Ilya's niece."

Karina nodded. "*Da*, but I am not so sure he will recognize me with new hairstyle."

Dugan returned her smile. "Trust me. He won't care if you're bald. I can't wait to see his face when I tell him—"

"About that," Ward said, "you can't tell him, at least not yet. But that's going to take some explaining, so take a seat."

Dugan raised his eyebrows but allowed Cassie to lead him to a seat by the coffee table. He settled in the seat as Ward sat down across from him.

"So when did you find them?" Dugan asked.

"Yesterday. I was goin—"

"YESTERDAY! Why the hell didn't you call…"

Dugan shut his mouth and stared down at the coffee table.

"That's right," Ward said, "not exactly the kind of information I'd leave in a voice mail, is it? So why the hell didn't YOU return my calls?"

Dugan nodded. "You're right. I'm sorry. I'll shut up and let you bring me up to speed."

"Can I get you something to drink first? This may take a while."

"Well, the sun's hardly up, but I think I could use a drink. Bourbon if you got it. Neat."

∗∗∗

Half an hour later, Dugan drained his glass, then looked at the two girls and shook his head. "Well, the hair makes a huge difference, but these two still don't look like Filipino seamen to me. I'm amazed they were able to sneak past the authorities and get ashore."

"The crew hid us when the authorities were searching the ship," Cassie said. "We only pretended to be seamen to get out the port gate, and it was at night."

"*Da*," Karina added, "and we did not try to pass the guards at the gangway, because they were checking very carefully. We went by rope ladder down the side of ship away from dock and swam further down the wharf. Then, out of sight of ship's gangway guards, we met with a group of the Filipino seamen who went down the gangway in normal manner. They wore extra dry clothes under their own clothes and also had identification cards for two of their shipmates who remained on board. We all walked out the port gate together, holding up identification cards. Port guards don't pay so much attention to seaman leaving; they seem more interested in people coming into the terminal. When we got away from the port, we gave

217

them the identification cards back, and they gave us some money the ship's officers had collected for us."

"I didn't know what else to do," Cassie said, "so I called Agent Ward."

Dugan nodded. "Well, I think you both did great." He turned to Ward. "But what are we supposed to do now, Jesse? Are they supposed to disappear forever and live under assumed names? That doesn't sound too workable."

"Truthfully, I don't know," Ward said. "But I do know that we need to keep them under wraps for the next few weeks at least until we can figure out what to do. I mean you may be able to protect THEM here in the UK, but there are all sorts of vulnerable targets you can't protect, like Karina's family, and now the families of the guys on the Kapitan Godina. Hitting the soft targets is the way these Russian mobsters work."

Dugan nodded. "Well, hopefully Borgdanov will have some ideas along those lines. Just because we've gotten the girls back, I don't think he's going to cancel his plans. If anything, I expect he may see them as even more of a necessity to keep these bastards at bay. That's probably the solution to everything anyway, just making the Russian mob guys understand that their least damaging option is just to leave us all the hell alone."

"Have you heard from him?"

Dugan shook his head. "No, and that's a bit troubling. Ilya's chomping at the bit to get to Russia and getting nervous, but he promised Borgdanov he'd wait for word. Borgdanov's playing it by ear, and he didn't want Ilya to show up until he'd established a firm cover."

"Well, I hope he knows what he's doing. This could backfire big time."

"We'll cross that bridge when we come to it. Right now, I'd like to take these young ladies for a little visit and make some people I know very happy."

"Ahh, at the risk of pissing you off again, I don't think you should do that just yet. That's the main reason I contacted you alone."

"I understand. We'll continue to play along. We'll go ahead with the memorial service and—"

"That's my point. The Kairouzes have many friends as well as business colleagues and associates, and I'm presuming the service is going to be well attended?"

Dugan shrugged. "I'm sure it will be. What of it?"

"And just how do you think Alex and Gillian will behave if they see Cassie before the service? They'll be a lot of eyes on them, perhaps even from our Russian friends. They have to be convincing as grieving parents."

"I'm sure they can handle it."

"Really? Like you? Whether you know it or not, you've had a shit-eating grin plastered all over your face from the moment you realized Cassie was alive. Relief and elation are hard to disguise, especially to trained observers."

"Then we'll cancel the service."

"You're not thinking straight. How would that look? You'd likely draw even more attention to the situation." He shook his head. "No, best have the service with the Kairouzes and Ilya genuinely distraught in plain sight. Then we can secretly reunite them with the girls."

"I'm not putting those people through another twenty-four hours of hell just as window dressing," Dugan said through clenched teeth. "Alex and Gillian are already—"

"Mr. Dugan," Karina said, "I am sorry to interrupt, but I think Agent Ward is right. I do not want to see Uncle Ilya suffer more, and I think Cassie also feels pain for the additional suffering of her poor parents, but it is MY family that may be in danger if we are somehow discovered, so I would beg you to listen to Agent Ward. Also, I am not sure what means 'shit-eating grin' or why anyone would smile while eating that, but he is right that you have been very happy since you saw Cassie. I think it will be even more difficult for her parents to hide their joy."

Dugan looked at Karina and then turned to Cassie, who nodded.

"I don't want Mum and Papa to suffer anymore either, Uncle Thomas, bu-but they're right, I think," Cassie said.

Dugan sighed. "Shit! All right. So how do we do this?"

"Good," Ward said. "What I figure is that I'll bring the girls to Alex's house during the memorial service. If you can get the Kairouzes and Ilya there, with maybe Anna and Mrs. Hogan, we can tell them all at once right after the service. Will that work?"

"I'm not sure. When Mrs. Hogan was first talking about the service yesterday, I believe the plan was for people to come back to the house afterwards. I think people have already begun dropping off food."

"Can you kill that? Maybe have the minister announce that the family's too distraught to receive visitors?"

"I can try, and that's not far from the truth. But things are a bit strained at the moment, and I'm not sure I can just go in rearrange whatever they've already set up."

"The quicker we can get everyone together without an audience, the quicker we can end their anguish."

"I'll try."

"Do you think there's any safe way to get word to Nigel on his ship?" Cassie asked, obviously hesitant. "I don't want to put anyone in danger, but I'm sure he's worried. We were video-chatting when I was taken and—"

"Nigel hasn't left our sides since you were taken, Cassie. In fact, he alerted the police and left his ship right away to search for you."

"He did?" Cassie beamed.

Dugan nodded. "Yes, he's quite a resourceful and determined young man. I'll make sure he's there along with everyone else. He certainly deserves to be included."

"All right then, it's settled," Ward said. "I have a place here to stash the young ladies. I'll take them there, and you try to get the after-service gathering canceled. We'll play it by ear from there. And Tom"—Ward laid a hand on Dugan's shoulder,—"when the others see the girls alive, they'll forget all about being mad at you."

"Yeah, until they realize I could have told them about it twenty-four hours earlier. Then they'll get really pissed."

Ward grinned. "Well, concentrate on that. It'll help you keep a grief-stricken look on your face for the next day or so."

"You know, Jesse, sometimes you're an asshole."

"You know, Tom, sometimes I have to be. It comes with the territory."

ST. PETERSBURG
RUSSIAN FEDERATION

Borgdanov sat at a corner table in the Starbucks, still crowded at late morning, sipping a double espresso. He would have preferred a local place, but anything Western was popular in Russia, and crowds were his friend. Even so, it didn't pay to get too comfortable, and he studied the patrons around him over a folded newspaper as he reflected on his progress. Crowds might be his friend, but situational awareness was his best friend.

He wasn't overly concerned with being spotted. Russia was the last place the *Bratstvo* would expect him to be, and his disguise was complete. His week-old beard was dyed jet black, a bit in contrast to his now salt-and-pepper hair—just another aging man vainly trying to hold time at bay. The oral prostheses in his cheeks made them look puffy and bloated, and a bit of padding under his loose and somewhat shapeless clothing spoke of a man attempting to disguise a thickening waistline rather than conceal a rock-hard body. A pair of horn-rim glasses completed the disguise, and he looked threatening to no one or nothing, except perhaps the half-eaten pastry that sat on a plate on the table in front of him.

In his pocket was a passport and wallet full of credit cards, a driver's license, and other documentation identifying him as Vasily Gagarin, a Ukrainian of ethnic Russian descent who was in town to purchase textiles. His ethnicity accounted for his flawless Russian, and now that Ukraine was a separate country, the foreign passport made things a bit more difficult for local law enforcement to verify his identity should he be stopped for any reason. Most police wouldn't bother to follow up if there was too much work involved.

Despite his ability to move freely, things had been more difficult than he'd imagined. Corporal Anisimov had been a willing recruit, even before Borgdanov had described his need, but the others had been less enthusiastic. While some warmed to the idea of a fresh start with new names in America, they balked at doing so as fugitives from the *Bratstvo*, especially since Borgdanov could not yet clearly define the mission. So far, he had Anisimov and two other former comrades, but he was nearing the end of the short list of people he felt safe contacting, and rapidly coming to the conclusion that he would have to organize the men he had and summon Ilya. Then they would do the most damage they could with the manpower available.

He raised his cup and took a sip of the now lukewarm coffee, the bitter dregs a suitable companion to his growing disappointment.

CHAPTER THIRTY

OFFICES OF PHOENIX SHIPPING LTD.
LONDON, UK

Dugan sat at his desk, reviewing vessel position reports and making a few notes to email to his subordinates. After returning to the flat to check on Anna, he'd decided to come into the office for a few hours, if only to escape the funereal gloom that permeated the apartment. With nothing to occupy their time or thoughts, both Nigel and Ilya merely sat listlessly staring at the television, present but disengaged, no doubt reliving the events of the past few days.

The atmosphere in the office was only marginally better, but there was some mindless comfort to be found in familiar tasks, and before he knew it, Mrs. Coutts walked in and set a bottle of water and a sandwich from the corner deli on his desk. Dugan looked up, surprised.

"Is it lunch time already?"

She nodded. "I just assumed you'd want your usual."

"I'm really not hungry, Mrs. Coutts. But thank you."

"That's what I thought you'd say, which is why I didn't ask. Did you have breakfast?"

Dugan thought back to the bourbon he'd had on Ward's plane.

"Ah… sort of."

"Which means no. So you can either promise to eat that sandwich, or I'm going to sit here and stare at you until you do." As if to back up her words, she sat down in the chair across from Dugan's desk and fixed him with a disapproving stare.

Dugan smiled. "All right, you win. But why is it I'm often unsure exactly which of us is the managing director around here?"

"I'm sure I don't know what you're talking about, sir. And talk is cheap. I haven't yet seen any action to back up your promise."

Dugan sighed and reached down for the sandwich. He took a big bite.

"Sah-dis-vied?" he asked, around a mouthful of food.

"Yes." she stood up, "But don't talk with your mouth full. And don't think you can get away with throwing half of it in the rubbish bin, because I intend to check."

Dugan watched her retreating back and shook his head. For all, or perhaps because of, Alicia Coutts's peremptory ways, she was hands down the best secretary he'd ever had, and seldom wrong. A fact he was rediscovering once again, as he realized he really was famished and wolfed down the rest of the sandwich. He washed it down with the water, feeling a great deal better than when he'd arrived at the office. The feeling quickly evaporated when he turned to the next task at hand.

He'd given it a lot of thought and decided the best approach was through Father O'Malley. He looked the priest's number up and dialed.

"Saint Mary's. Father O'Malley speaking."

"Father, Tom Dugan. How are you?"

"I'm fine, Tom, though it's me that should be asking you that. How're you holding up, lad?"

"As well as can be expected, I guess, Father."

"Things will heal in God's own time and not our own, though it's a bitter pill to swallow. Now how can I help you?"

"It's about the memorial service tomorrow, or more specifically, the gathering after. I just... I just don't think either Alex or Gillian are up for it."

"Aye, you might be right. I have spoken to Gillian, and though she seems understandably distraught, I'm more concerned about Alex. Mrs. Hogan has made a couple of attempts to get us together, but they've come to naught. I understand Alex isn't handling it well."

"That's an understatement, I think. My understanding is that he's neither dressed nor bathed nor shaved since he heard the news, and mainly crawled inside a brandy bottle."

"Your understanding? So you've not seen him, then?"

Dugan hesitated. "He... he hasn't wanted to see me, Father. I think he blames me for what happened to Cassie, and to be honest, he's probably right."

"It's a black day that causes us to harden our hearts against those that love us and mean us no harm. I'm sure it's just his grief talking, Tom. When he can see clearly again, he'll be sorry for his actions now, I've no doubt."

"I hope you're right, Father, but Alex is pretty much a basket case right now. I'm sure he can probably sit through a short service, but I don't know if he'll be able to handle a houseful of people attempting to comfort and console him. He just doesn't seem ready to interact with anyone right now—like you said, it will require God's own time, and we're not even close yet."

There was silence on the line, as if the priest was mulling over what he'd just heard.

"All right, Tom. I'll discuss it with Gillian and suggest canceling the post-service gathering. If she agrees, I'll make an announcement at the end of the service to the effect that the family is too distraught at the moment to receive visitors, and ask all gathered to keep you all in their thoughts and prayers. I'll suggest to Gillian that perhaps we can have a celebration of Cassie's life in a few weeks, when the wounds aren't quite so fresh. Of course, you know it will be up to her?"

"Of course. Thank you, Father."

"And Tom, though this is Gillian's decision, if she decides to cancel the post-service gathering be aware it might upset Mrs. Hogan. I just thought you should know that."

"Ahh Okay. But why?"

"Well, I can't be sure, of course, but Mrs. Hogan's a bit traditional. I'm not trying to borrow trouble, mind you, but I thought I'd mention it."

"Okay, thanks."

"You're welcome. And while I have you on the phone, why don't you come round in a few days? It sounds like you might need a sympathetic ear yourself."

"Ahh... thanks for the offer, Father. I'll keep it in mind."

O'Malley sensed the hesitation.

"Sure and that sympathetic ear is nondenominational, lad," O'Malley said, a smile in his voice, "available even to unchurched heathens such as yourself. My door is always open."

Dugan smiled. "Thank you, Father. I'll remember that."

***

Three hours later, Dugan powered down his laptop and slipped it in his bag. He hadn't accomplished much, but his short foray into the office had been a welcome respite from the apartment. He considered calling either Gillian or Father O'Malley to see how things had gone. If the gathering was still on, he and Ward were going to have to revise their timing for bringing Cassie and

Karina to the Kairouz house. He was reaching for the phone when the intercom buzzed.

"Yes, Mrs. Coutts?"

"Mrs. Hogan is holding on line one, sir, and she doesn't sound too happy. Should I tell her you've gone for the day?"

Dugan sighed. "I wish it were that easy, Mrs. Coutts, but she has my mobile number, and if she thinks I'm avoiding her, I expect that may upset her even more."

Dugan pressed the flashing button on the desk phone.

"Yes, Mrs. Hogan, what can I do for you?"

"Well now, you can start by telling me why you're puttin' your oar in the water and preventing us from givin' our Cassie a proper farewell?"

"I'm not sure I'm following you."

"Oh, so it wasn't you that called Father O'Malley and suggested we cancel the gathering after poor Cassie's service?"

"I suggested that neither Gillian nor Alex was up to it and that perhaps he might discuss it with Gillian to find out what she preferred. Until this moment, I didn't know myself what decision she made."

"And how would you be knowin' what state they're in, since you've not bothered to bring yourself round to the house, now have ya'?"

"Mrs. Hogan, you know that's not fair—"

"Fair? Fair, is it? Is it fair our beautiful Cassie's gone and we've not even a body to put in the ground? And who's to blame for that, I ask you? And now we're to say farewell without even the dignity of a funeral feast. Just a few words in a church and no gatherin' to share tales, no relivin' of her life? It's neither fittin' nor proper, I tell you. Even if himself can't bear it, he could be sat in the study with his brandy to help him dull the pain, and there's none that could begrudge him that solace. But what of the rest of us, I ask you. Did you think of that when you decided to go sticking your Yank nose in things that don't concern you?"

"Mrs. Hogan, I know you're upset but—"

"Upset? Oh, aye, I'm upset all right. And know this, Mr. Thomas Dugan, it'll be a cold day in Hell before you set your feet under my table again."

The line went dead, and Dugan sat holding the receiver a moment, then slowly returned it to its cradle. Feelings were obviously running high all around, and after everyone started coming down from the euphoria of Cassie and Karina's survival, he was quite sure the realization that he'd kept the news from them all wasn't going to endear him to anyone, regardless of the justification. The clear implication was that none of them were to be trusted with the secret.

Perhaps things might go better in his absence, but how would he explain that? He hesitated a moment and picked up the phone again, dialing Gillian's mobile phone and hoping she wasn't with Mrs. Hogan when she answered.

"Hello," Gillian said.

"Gillian, this is Tom. Ahh... I just had a call from Mrs. Hogan and—"

"And it didn't go well, I presume? That would account for all the muttered curses and slamming cabinet doors I hear coming from the kitchen."

"Yeah, that's what I'm calling about. I really didn't mean to upset anyone when I called Father O'Malley—"

"No, actually you were right to do that. To be honest, I was already thinking along those lines. I wouldn't have agreed to cancel the gathering otherwise."

"About that. I assumed that even though the larger gathering was canceled that we could come over to the house after the service, but maybe that's not such a good idea."

"Don't be silly, Tom. Of course, you and Anna must come, and Ilya and young Nigel as well. I just assumed that would be the case. Don't even think about not coming. And by the way, since we're forgoing the post-service gathering, I've moved the service to late morning. It will be at ten thirty."

Try as he might, Dugan couldn't think of a way to refuse gracefully.

"Okay. We'll be there."

ST. PETERSBURG
RUSSIAN FEDERATION

Borgdanov was once again sitting in Starbucks, consistency being part and parcel of his cover identity. While a man on the run might skulk in the shadows, Ukrainian textile buyer Vasily Gagarin was conspicuous by his mundane daily routine. In truth, there was little to hide, as he was having less than stellar success with his recruitment mission. He'd already lowered his expectations and begun to consider how best to use his limited resources.

He caught movement from the corner of his eye and glanced casually to the right. It was the man he'd seen come in a bit earlier, expensively dressed and carrying a leather briefcase, but it was his face rather than his clothing that caught the eye. He was horribly disfigured, thick ropes of burn scar extending up out of his collar and across the right side of his face. His body was twisted, one shoulder and hip higher than the other, and his ruined face bore the lines of constant pain as he shuffled toward the exit, dragging his right leg. Poor bastard. Borgdanov looked away, fighting the urge to stare.

As the man passed Borgdanov's table, he stumbled and grabbed the back of an empty chair and the edge of the table for support, dropping his briefcase in the process.

"Oh! Excuse me," the man said as he regained his balance.

"No problem." Borgdanov stood and reached down to retrieve the briefcase. "Here, let me help."

"Most kind of you." The man took the case from Borgdanov and gave him a twisted smile. "Most kind of you, indeed. Thank you very much."

Borgdanov nodded. There was something familiar about the man. The voice perhaps.

"You're welcome," he said to the man's back as the stranger shuffled for the door, faster now, with an obvious sense of urgency.

Very strange. Borgdanov sat back down and picked up his newspaper. Something fluttered out of it to the floor, and he glanced down to see a folded square of white paper. On the front of it in block letters was printed BORGDANOV.

He stared down at the paper a long moment, willing his heart rate back to normal, then reached down casually, picked it up, and unfolded it.

YOU ARE NOT AS INVISIBLE AS YOU THINK. MEET ME AT 2AM. WHERE YOU FIRST TRIUMPHED. COME ALONE. A FRIEND.

1 AM
KAIROUZ RESIDENCE
LONDON, UK

Fedosov crouched in the shrubbery watching the house, a suitcase on either side of him, eager to get to the task at hand. He'd been nervous when he'd monitored the bugs throughout the day, unsure how the cancellation of the gathering impacted his plan. The last call from the American confirming the presence of all three targets had come as a great relief. The entire thing was working out well, actually much better than he could ever have hoped. He'd been a bit nervous about targeting a gathering where he was unsure about the guest list—it would be just his luck to blow up a Member of Parliament or some other important personage—and identifying the potential victims specifically and reducing the collateral damage was an unexpected boon. The only question now was when the occupants of the house would go to bed.

Finally the lights on the ground floor began to wink out until only the study window showed a light. He heard raised voices muffled by the closed window and saw shadows on the glass indicating movement within, but finally that light was extinguished as well. Twenty minutes later, the lights on the second story went dark, and Fedosov let out a relieved sigh. He waited an additional half hour to allow the occupants time to fall asleep and then crept through the darkness to the small basement window, a suitcase in each hand.

VAVILOVICH STREET
ST. PETERSBURG
RUSSIAN FEDERATION

Borgdanov stood well back in the shadows of a narrow alley, watching the front of the abandoned school building across the street. He'd arrived two hours earlier, casually strolling down the near deserted streets surrounding the old school, walking at least two blocks in every direction. Satisfied, he'd come back to wait in the shadows of the alley, shifting his weight from foot to foot and reliving all of his actions since he'd arrived in the country, racking his brain for what he'd done wrong.

He heard a faint noise and moved cautiously to the entrance to the alley to peer around the corner of the building. Far up the empty street at the edge of one of the few working streetlights, a figure approached, dragging his right foot. Borgdanov reached into his coat pocket and wrapped his hand around the grip of his pistol, then faded back into the alley to wait.

Long minutes later, his quarry limped into view, stopping at the gate in a tall chain-link fence beside the school building. Borgdanov saw the man reach into his pocket and extract something, then heard the metallic rattle of a chain on metal—he had a key and was unlocking the gate.

The man disappeared into the darkened schoolyard, leaving the gate standing open—an invitation. Borgdanov stared at the open gate a long moment, then hurried across the street and into the school yard, his hand still gripping the gun in his pocket. He moved through the darkness of the narrow side yard from memory, sensing rather than seeing when it opened onto the spacious school yard behind the building. He yearned to use the small flashlight in his other pocket, but feared making himself an even better target than he already was. He jumped at a sound to his right and spun in that direction, gun in hand.

"Good evening, Dyusha," said a voice from the darkness. "Thank you for coming. I can't see well, but I assume you are pointing a gun in my direction. If so, please put it away. You have nothing to fear from me, and I doubt you could hit me in the dark anyway."

"Ar-Arkady...Arkady Baikov?"

"Very good, Dyusha, but I am surprised you recognized me. I've changed a bit since last we saw each other as schoolboys."

"It was your voice and the fact that you wanted to meet here. Though I wasn't really sure until you spoke again just now. But wh-what happened to you? Was it an accident?"

The man laughed, but there was no humor in it. "An accident? Hardly. As you may recall, most people here are not so accepting of those of us who are different. Those that view us as anything more than freakish curiosities seem to feel somehow threatened by us. One evening after a drinking session, some of our more intellectually challenged countrymen decided it would be good fun to set a freak on fire. They caught me coming out of a restaurant, dragged me into a nearby alley, then tied me up. Then they poured petrol all over me and lit it. I still remember their drunken laughter before I lost consciousness."

"My God! How could you survive?"

"My screams attracted a crowd, who chased the bastards away and doused me with rain water that had collected in a bunch of discarded buckets in the alley." He paused. "Apparently they didn't know I was a freak."

"But how did the bastards even know about... you know?"

"How does anyone know anything? They observe, they suspect, they guess. How long can one avoid sports and locker room showers with medical excuses? Doctors' offices have nurses, and secretaries, and file clerks, and my condition is just too interesting not to discuss. People always find out somehow. How did you find out about me when we were schoolmates?"

Borgdanov didn't answer right away. "I overheard my aunt tell my mother and warn her not to let me associate with you."

Borgdanov heard the pain in Arkady's laugh. "You never were very obedient, but you see my point, *da*? Gossip is a most efficient means of communication. But I've always been curious. Even after you knew, you were the only one who didn't shun me. Who would have thought, Andrei Nikolaevich Borgdanov, the most popular fellow in school, captain of the wrestling team and city champion, would maintain a friendship with the hermaphrodite freak, the 'he-she.' Why, Dyusha?"

"As you said, Arkady, we were friends. One does not abandon a friend because he has a medical condition beyond his control. I… I was sorry when we lost touch with each other after you moved and changed schools."

"Sorry, Dyusha? Or relieved? I tried to contact you several times, but you never returned my phone calls or answered my letters."

Borgdanov said nothing, and after a long silence Arkady sighed in the darkness.

"It's all right, Dyusha. I know it was difficult to stand by me, and you stood firmly when I most needed you. I cannot fault you if you tired of being my sole support. To be honest, I was a bit tired of myself, and I'm sure my being out of sight made it quite easy for me to be out of mind as well," Arkady said. "But enough of that, I didn't meet you to discuss old times. You are in great danger."

Borgdanov stiffened. "What? How can you know—"

"What you're doing? Quite easily, my old friend. I am the chief of data analysis for the Federal Security Service for St. Petersburg and Leningrad Oblast, and you've apparently made enemies in very high places. I was tasked with finding out everything about you and your friend Sergeant Denosovitch. I have been following your activities for the last two days."

Borgdanov tightened his grip on the gun. "So you intend to denounce me?"

Arkady chuckled. "Hardly. If that was my intent, I would not meet with a fellow your size in a deserted school yard, now would I? No, I came to warn you—and to help you."

Borgdanov weighed the gun in his hand but said nothing. He hadn't seen Arkady in over twenty years. Could he be trusted?

"Some days ago," Arkady continued, "I got a call from Vladimir Glazkov, the Chief of the FSB here in St. Petersburg. He gave me Denosovitch's name, which meant nothing to me, and then added yours as Denosovitch's former commander and known associate. I was to provide him background information on you both—which I did, of course—and also to attempt to track your movements. Of course, I recognized your name, and rather than assign the task to one of my subordinates, I kept it for myself."

"How did you find me? I thought I was being quite careful."

"Remarkably so. I couldn't really watch you out of the country, and since I wasn't sure when, or even if you'd return, I initiated surveillance on all your old comrades. When a rather slovenly Ukrainian textile buyer visited three or four of your ex-*Spetsnaz* comrades in a forty-eight-hour period, that was a bit suspicious. And as clever as your disguise is, it could not fool the facial recognition software."

"Who else knows?"

"No one, Dyusha. Kill me now and your secret is safe. I know that's what you're thinking, old times notwithstanding. But I think you should hear me out first."

Borgdanov considered the alternatives. Nothing pointed to treachery on Arkady's part. He had so far done nothing illegal in Russia, so the FSB had no grounds to pick him up, and if Arkady was supplying intelligence to the *Bratstvo*, the mob would have surely attacked him by now. Whatever the threat, it wasn't Arkady. He slipped the gun into his pocket.

"Go on, then."

"I don't know exactly what you're doing, but my research showed that Denosovitch's niece disappeared some months ago. Also Glazkov directed me to look into a British couple named Kairouz and an American named Dugan, all in London. That led me to news reports of the recent police activities against the Russian mob in the UK." Arkady paused. "My conclusion is that the *Bratstvo* is heavily involved, and that you are somehow attempting to mount some sort of action against them. How am I doing so far?"

Borgdanov said nothing, then flinched as ten feet away, Arkady struck a match, bathing them both momentarily in a circle of light as the flame flared. The flare died to a small flame, illuminating Arkady's twisted face as he held the match between cupped hands to light a cigarette. Borgdanov studied the face, not worried about staring now. Beneath the scars, the face looked drawn and jaundiced.

Arkady shook out the match and took a long drag on the cigarette, causing the tip to burn brightly, and Borgdanov heard him exhale audibly into the night air and smelled the cigarette smoke.

"You're playing a dangerous game, Dyusha," Arkady said. "You probably know the *Bratstvo* has powerful connections to the police and the FSB, but what you may fail to understand is that, here in St. Petersburg at least, the *Bratstvo* IS the FSB. You've no chance against them without my help."

"Forgive me, Arkady, but how can you help me?"

"I already have, because you're not being beaten in some squalid dungeon, nor do you have a bullet in your head. But I can do much more. Hold out your hand."

Borgdanov did as requested, and he saw Arkady dimly, as the man approached out of the deeper shadows. He felt something hit his palm.

"That is a flash drive," Arkady said. "On it you will find complete information on the leadership of the FSB and their complementary ranks in the *Bratstvo*. There are also other things—very powerful things. With this information, who knows, you may even survive."

Borgdanov felt the hair rising on the back of his neck. Things that seemed too good to be true usually were.

"How did you get this information?"

"Is it not obvious? In addition to my FSB duties, I am a member of the *Bratstvo*. They do not like 'freaks' any better than anyone else, but my skills as a data analyst are unsurpassed, and because of this, they tolerate me."

"Arkady, how could you join these murderous pigs? Do you know what they have done? What they continue to do to innocent people?"

"I suppose that's a rhetorical question, Dyusha, since it is obvious I know what they do. As far as how I could join, everyone has their price, and the *Bratstvo* met mine. The four bastards that set me on fire died horrible deaths, and this time I got to light the match."

Borgdanov said nothing for a long time, trying to process what he'd just heard.

"So why give this to me? And why now?"

"I'm giving it to you because you will obviously need it, and other than my parents you are the only human being on the face of the earth who has ever treated me decently. And I'm giving it to you now because it no longer makes any difference to me."

"What do you mean? If I use this information against the *Bratstvo*, it may harm you as well. Or worse, they will suspect you gave it to me. I cannot imagine what they will do to you."

Arkady's laughter seemed genuine this time. "I am afraid God, if he exists, has beaten them to it, old friend. Six months ago I was diagnosed with pancreatic cancer. The doctors give me six weeks to live. But don't worry. The pain is already quite exquisite, and I suspect it will feel like much, much longer." He laughed again. "In any event, I don't intend to wait around and find out. In a few days, I will enjoy a fine meal, drink a toast to my one and only true friend Andrei Nikolaevich Borgdanov, and eat the barrel of my pistol for dessert."

"I... I have some contacts in the West. They have advanced treatments for—"

Borgdanov heard another chuckle, then watched the bright tip of the cigarette fall to the ground and disappear as Arkady crushed it underfoot. He sensed his old friend moving even closer and flinched in surprise as he felt hands on his shoulders, and smoker's breath washed over him.

"Dyusha, do not worry so. I have no place in this world. I never have. My parents are dead, and I have no other family. My life has been nothing but pain with promises of more to come. I joined the *Bratstvo* for revenge, and for a while took some perverse satisfaction in inflicting pain on others. But there was no real solace there—I know that now. I've done much harm, and my soul is as twisted and tortured as this body. But if life was once unfair, it is no longer, for now I have earned this fate." Borgdanov saw him smile in the dim light. "Besides, we are Russian! Tragedy is in our genes, is it not? And you always were one to hog the spotlight. Let me be center stage for once, old friend. Take this gift I give you, and let me die the flawed and tragic hero/villain." Arkady laughed again.

Borgdanov nodded, unable to speak, and Arkady pulled the big man into his embrace and then stood on tiptoe to kiss both his cheeks. Then he pushed Borgdanov away.

"We don't have much time, and I want to make sure you fully appreciate the power of this gift. The *Bratstvo* is a huge organization, and like all such entities, now runs on computers. I was instrumental in managing the development of the systems they use and included on the flash drive is a file with the source code for many of their most critical applications. Buried in the code are multiple 'back doors' to allow undetected access to the systems. There are my notes there as well. This will likely all be gibberish to you, my friend, but I assure you that in skilled hands there is no end to the damage this can do. Wield the weapon sparingly and well. Do you understand?"

Borgdanov bobbed his head in an unseen nod, then muttered a soft, "*Da.*"

"Go then. I will wait half an hour before I leave."

"*Do svidaniya*, little brother," Borgdanov said softly. "*Stupay s Bogom.*" Go with God.

Arkady's teeth flashed in a smile through the dim light. "*Spasibo*, Dyusha, but I suspect that God would prefer that I travel alone. I haven't done much to please Him of late."

Borgdanov smiled sadly and turned toward the gate.

"Oh, and Dyusha, I don't know how well you know these people in the UK, but if they are friends, you should warn them. The *Bratstvo* plans to kill all three of them. Everything I was able to find out is in a file on the flash drive labeled UK."

CHAPTER THIRTY-ONE

Dugan sat next to Anna and glanced down the pew to his left at Alex and Gillian. Gillian was sobbing softly into a handkerchief as on her opposite side Mrs. Hogan was gently rubbing Gillian's back in a vain attempt at consolation. Alex was suitably dressed and shaved for the first time in several days, but he seemed unfocused and near catatonic, staring straight ahead as a single tear leaked down his pallid cheek. Mrs. Hogan peered past the grieving couple at Dugan, and her face turned dark. He quickly looked away.

Gillian had given him a sad smile when they'd arrived, and Alex had offered his hand perfunctorily, his handshake like holding a dead fish, and Dugan caught a whiff of brandy. Ilya and Nigel sat to Dugan's right, on the other side of Anna, the big Russian stone-faced and stoic, while Nigel was visibly struggling to keep it together. But Dugan's discomfort was greater still, knowing that he could have relieved his friends' suffering with a word, and he was struggling with strong second thoughts about having subjected them to this ordeal. This was shaping up to be the longest hour of his life.

The service was not only for Cassie, but also the two Russian women, and Father O'Malley had graciously invited the priest from the nearby Russian Orthodox church to assist him in the service. Dugan was impressed by O'Malley's sensitivity and kindness, but under the circumstances, his greatest concern was that the gesture might double the length of the service and thus his discomfort.

Father O'Malley walked to the pulpit and began to speak.

OUTSIDE THE KAIROUZ RESIDENCE
LONDON, UK

Unsure as to the exact timing of the day's events, Fedosov decided to take up a position early, to be prepared for any last minute complications. Thus he'd arrived and parked the van on the street in good time to watch the departure of both the Kairouzes, in the company of their driver and the Irish cook. He sat in the back of the van now, with a good view of the driveway through a concealed viewing port. He would be able to observe both the Kairouzes' and Dugan's return, to confirm they were all in place before he detonated the bomb. He was waiting patiently when he got some unexpected visitors.

A taxi pulled to the curb beside the drive, and a rumpled-looking black man got out. He stood a moment, glancing casually around himself. He peered at the van for a long minute and then seemed to mark it in his memory and move on, slowly making an arc as his gaze traversed a full circle around the taxi. Fedosov's sixth sense started sounding an alarm. The man was obviously aware of his surroundings, but what was he doing here. Private security? For who?

He got his answer a short time later, and the man lowered his head and spoke into the taxi. Two dark-haired women exited the cab, and the man motioned them up the drive as he fell in behind them, his head on a swivel. They moved out of sight around the curve in the drive, and Fedosov tensed, trying to assess what impact this latest development might have on his plan. He kept his eye on the house and slipped on the headphones. A short while later, he heard the kitchen door open, and a woman's British-accented voice.

"I'll shut off the alarm."

"Okay," replied a man's voice, undoubtedly the black man, an American by the sound of it. "Then I need to get you two upstairs and out of sight."

"Why?" the woman asked.

"Because I think it would be too much of a shock for your folks to just walk in and find you sitting here. I need to prepare them a bit before I spring you on them," the American said.

"I think for Uncle Ilya it will be no problem," said a second woman, the accent Russian this time.

"Well, maybe," the American said, "but humor me. Let's get you both upstairs for the time being. I'll call up when you can come down."

Fedosov heard murmurs of agreement and then, a moment later, the sound of footsteps on the stairway and cursed the fact that he had no listening devices upstairs. Who were these people, and what were they doing in the house? Should he abort? No, the Chief had already given the green light to some collateral damage as inevitable, and besides, Fedosov had never expected that this Dugan and the Kairouz people would be completely alone.

He sat back in his chair and waited, his patience wearing thin now. He just wanted to finish the job and get the hell away.

St. Petersburg
Russian Federation

Borgdanov tried Ilya's cell phone again, muttering a curse when the call went to voice mail. He left another message.

"Ilya, I have been trying to reach you. Call me at this number immediately."

He didn't want to communicate in the open, and by doing so he was compromising the strict communication protocol he'd established with Ilya. There were just too many ways communications could be compromised, especially if one end of the call was in Russia, even though both he and Ilya were using burner phones.

The agreed procedure was to leave a draft email message in a dummy Gmail account, to which both men had the user ID and password. Each would log into the account twice a day—Ilya at eleven AM and PM and Borgdanov at noon and midnight—and read any draft message left. Additionally, either could log on at any time with an urgent message, though the sender would know it was unlikely to be received until his correspondent's regular check-in time. Since the messages were never actually sent, they were less likely to attract scrutiny. But despite the low probability of being compromised, the Russians were still circumspect regarding message frequency and content. The only message from Ilya to date, which Borgdanov assumed was sent after the rescue mission, was as heartrending as it was brief. "Regret we failed."

Borgdanov's only message was sent at one in the morning London time, as soon as he'd been able to get to a computer and check the content of the UK file on Arkady's flash drive. His message was equally concise. "Imperative you call me. No. 4." The number four indicated Ilya was to call the fourth number on a list of a dozen numbers Borgdanov had given him, each to a different burner phone that would be discarded immediately after the call.

Ilya should have gotten the message a half hour earlier, and the lack of a call indicated something was seriously wrong, prompting Borgdanov to abandon communications protocol in favor of a direct approach. When Ilya hadn't answered, he'd tried Dugan and then Anna, but both calls went to voice mail. He didn't have numbers for the Kairouzes;, but as a last resort he'd tried Anna's colleagues Lou and Harry, with similar results. Where the hell was everyone?

Borgdanov stood and paced the worn carpet of the shabby hotel room and prayed for Ilya to return his call.

CHAPTER THIRTY-TWO

If anything, the conclusion of the service was the most stressful part. Father O'Malley gave a benediction and, along with the Russian Orthodox priest, moved down the aisle to bid the mourners farewell as they exited the church. The rest of the attendees waited respectfully for the family to file out first, but when they all stood, Alex collapsed. He sank back into the pew, tears streaming down his cheeks and shoulders heaving, as if physically unable to stand. Dugan and Ilya helped him to his feet and along the aisle to the waiting car.

With the family so obviously indisposed, it had fallen to Dugan to return to accept the condolences and well wishes from the exiting mourners—a feat made considerably easier by the presence of both Father O'Malley and the Russian Orthodox priest (whose name he couldn't remember or pronounce) at his side, gently hurrying folks along if they lingered. When the last attendee had shaken hands and moved on, Dugan hurried away before either of the priests could suggest visiting the house to comfort the grieving family.

He glanced at his watch as he rushed to the car park, where Anna waited with Ilya and Nigel. Gillian and Alex would undoubtedly be home by now, and he didn't have a clue as to what was transpiring. Other than bringing the girls to the house, he and Ward didn't have a plan, and Dugan was starting to realize they should have given it a great deal more thought. What exactly were they going to do, say, "Surprise! Your daughter's not dead!" and have her jump out of a fucking cake?

Anna and the others saw him coming and were already sitting in the car by the time he slid behind the wheel, Anna in the front passenger seat, and the two men in the back. Dugan reached for the ignition, then stopped and sat back in his seat. Maybe it was better to break the news to everyone separately. Then maybe Anna could help him figure out the best way to tell

Gillian and Alex. Presuming, of course, Ilya and Nigel didn't beat him to death here in the church car park.

"Tom?" Anna asked. "Is something wrong?"

Dugan shook his head and half-turned in his seat so he could see all of them.

"No. But I have something to tell you all. It's going to sound crazy, but I need you to trust me, and you'll understand in a very few minutes." He paused. "Cassie and Karina aren't dead."

No one said anything for a long moment; then Ilya broke the silence.

"*Da, Dyed.* I know. I listened to the sermon. They are with God in Heaven. And maybe is true, and maybe is not. I do not know, but I am not such a strong believer. But… but I like to think the priest is right."

"That's not what I mean. I mean they're both ALIVE. Not in Heaven, but right here in London. I saw them myself yesterday morning, and right now they should be at Alex and Gillian's house."

"What sort of rubbish is that?" Nigel demanded. "We all saw them die. I… I touched her, or one of them, anyway. If this is some sort of cruel Yank funeral humor, it's not amusing."

Dugan shook his head. "The guys on the ship opened the container before they dumped it and rescued Cassie and Karina. Tanya was already dead, and they left her body in the container—that's who you saw, Nigel."

"Why are we just finding this out," Ilya demanded. "Why did the girls not come forward when ship docked?"

"Because they were protecting the guys who saved them. They had no clue we were close by, and the guys on the ship were ordered to dump the container, so the Russian mob would have probably killed their families if they knew any of the girls were rescued—"

"Dugan!" Anna said. "Just drive! You can give us the details on the way."

"*Da,*" Ilya said, followed by a 'bloody right' from Nigel.

"I guess that makes it unanimous." Dugan started the car.

OUTSIDE THE KAIROUZ RESIDENCE
LONDON, UK

Fedosov watched the car turn up the drive with the cook and chauffeur in front and the Kairouz couple in the back. So far, so good. Now if this Dugan would just show up, he could finish the job and get out of here—presuming the arrival of the black American and the women didn't complicate matters. He slipped the headphones back on to check out the action inside the house. He heard the back door open and then a surprised gasp.

"Jesse?" he heard the Kairouz woman say. "You startled me. What are you doing here?"

Fedosov heard the hesitation in the man's voice.

"I… I just came to pay my respects," the man said. "I'm so sorry for your loss."

"Thank you," the woman said, "but why didn't you come to the church… and how did you get in? The door was locked and the alarm set."

"I… I just arrived and knew I'd be too late for the service. I called Tom earlier and he told me where the spare key was and gave me the alarm code—"

"I NEED A BLOODY DRINK," said a male British voice, the speech slurred and accompanied by the abrupt sound of chair legs sliding across a tile floor.

"ALEX! Careful! You'll fall," the Kairouz woman again.

"Never you mind," said a woman with an Irish brogue. "I'll get himself sat in the study. Come along, Mr. Kairouz. There's a good fellow." Fedosov heard the sound of stumbling footsteps retreating, then silence.

"Tom said he was taking it hard," the black American's voice again.

"Yes, well, it's difficult for all of us," said the Kairouz woman. "Now about your—"

"Where is Tom?" the black American asked. "I expected him to be with you."

"He'll be along," the Kairouz woman said. "He was detained at the church. And I'm sorry, but we weren't expecting anyone. Can I offer you something? Coffee perhaps? I'll ask Mrs. Hogan to brew a pot."

Fedosov looked up to see a car turning onto the street. As it sped past him, he saw Dugan at the wheel and a red-haired woman in the front passenger seat, along with two men in the back he couldn't see well. The car whipped into the Kairouz drive and disappeared from sight around the curve. Seconds later he heard car doors slamming and then the back door to the kitchen banging open.

"KARINA?" bellowed a deep Russian-accented voice, and then—bedlam.

KAIROUZ RESIDENCE
LONDON, UK

Dugan explained the situation as the car raced toward the Kairouz house, his attempts at soliciting ideas for the best way to break the news to Alex and Gillian overwhelmed by the voices of Nigel and Ilya demanding details of the girls' survival. By the time he pulled into the Kairouzes' drive, he still had no clear idea what to do, and his two back-seat passengers were already opening their doors before he'd brought the car to a complete stop in front of the garage.

"Wait," said Dugan to no avail as the men leaped from the car. He shot a worried look at Anna as she wrestled her crutches from between the seats.

"Go on," Anna said. "Go ahead. You probably need to get in there as soon as possible. I can manage the few steps to the back door on my own."

"You sure—"

Anna smiled. "GO!"

Dugan nodded and jumped out. He entered the kitchen to a scene of chaos. Jesse Ward and Gillian Kairouz stood stock still in the kitchen, puzzled looks on their faces. At the end of the hall, Alex stood in the door to the study, leaning against the door jamb, a glass in his hand. He could see Mrs. Hogan behind Alex, standing ready to offer support. Ilya and Nigel were in the hall, calling the girls' names at the top of their lungs.

Dugan heard answering shouts from up the stairway, and the two men thundered up the steps, while everyone else looked on, obviously confused. And then he heard the unmistakable sound of Cassie's happy laughter, and everything happened at once.

There was the sound of glass breaking on hardwood as Alex dropped the brandy snifter and steadied himself on the door jamb. And then the girls were down the stairs, and the hall was crowded as everyone rushed to them, hugging and kissing and clinging together, consumed with the joy of the return of their loved ones, without regard to the WHY of their particular miracle.

Dugan stood in the kitchen doorway with Ward, hoping some of that goodwill would carry over when they realized he'd delayed the moment of joy. He heard the back door rattle and hurried over to help Anna inside. She grinned at him and thumped down the hall on her crutches toward the happy reunion.

As it turned out, it wasn't much different than having them jump out of a cake, now was it?

OUTSIDE THE KAIROUZ RESIDENCE
LONDON, UK

Fedosov listened to the melee in his earphones and cursed at the unexpected complication. The noise was general and of sufficient volume to be coming from several of his bugs at once, so he couldn't pinpoint exactly where the targets were in the house. That was a problem.

Despite the fact the Chief had given him discretion in the area of collateral damage, Fedosov was no fool. This was a posh neighborhood, populated with wealthy people who wielded considerable political clout—a Member of Parliament lived only one door down the tree-lined street. A charge large enough to guarantee the complete and utter destruction of the Kairouz residence might also deal death and destruction to influential neighbors, so Fedosov had been selective in his placement of the charges in the basement. He'd placed the heaviest explosives beneath the living room and kitchen, where he might reasonably expect his three targets to congregate at some point. Smaller incendiary charges were spaced throughout the rest of the house and along the perimeter, to ensure the wreckage from the larger blasts was consumed in a raging conflagration. On the off chance any of his targets survived the initial blast, they would surely perish in the fire that followed it. It was a sound plan, all in all, but one predicated on his ability to determine when his three targets were collected together in either the living room or kitchen.

Fedosov scowled as he listened to the confusion coming from his bugs. The addition of additional voices raised in animated conversation completely overwhelmed his ability to tell who was where, and he cursed himself for not having the foresight to plant video cameras. But then again, he'd wanted to keep his footprint as small as possible, and more bugs meant more possibility of discovery.

He considered aborting the hit temporarily, but no, he'd promised the Chief it would happen today—the man expected results, and neither failure nor delay was an option. Besides, he couldn't just leave the charges in place indefinitely. They'd be discovered sooner or later, alerting his targets and making them even more difficult to kill. He settled in to wait and hoped he could discern when his targets were gathered in one of the kill zones.

CHAPTER THIRTY-THREE

Ilya Denosovitch had his right arm tightly around Karina's shoulders as she hugged him around his waist. He hadn't let go of her since she'd bounded down the stairs into his arms moments before. He knew he was grinning like an idiot, yet was unable to stop, and happy tears leaked down his cheeks, which he brushed away with the back of his left hand. *Spetsnaz* do not cry, he reminded himself, then looked at the scene of happy chaos unfolding around him.

Nigel had released Cassie at the bottom of the stairs, and she'd flown into Gillian's waiting arms before reaching out to include a happy but confused Alex in the family embrace. Mrs. Hogan orbited the group, visibly impatient to fold Cassie in a hug of her own, while Nigel stood nearby, beaming but obviously unsure what to do with himself.

Dyed and Anna stood looking on at the end of the hall near the doorway to the kitchen, while beyond them Ilya saw the CIA agent, Jesse Ward. Ward looked relieved, Anna looked happy, and *Dyed* looked uncertain, as if unsure it was all true. The hallway rang with laughter and a confused babble of voices until Mrs. Hogan finally received her expected hug and then pulled away from Cassie, wiping tears from her own eyes before raising her voice to address the group.

"Right then," Mrs. Hogan said. "Into the kitchen, the lot of ya! Maybe if I put some food in your mouths, you'll all be quiet long enough for Cassie and her friend here to tell us how this blessing came to pass. Though I've no doubt it was God's own miracle, it was." And with that, Mrs. Hogan began to shoo the happy milling group toward the sanctity of her kitchen.

Ilya and Karina trailed the crowd, smiling as they filed down the hall. If only the major were here—oh shit, the major. Ilya glanced at his watch, confirming that he was well overdue for his daily 11 AM email check. He stopped in the kitchen doorway and reluctantly released Karina, nodding her into the kitchen as he dug in his pants pocket for his smart phone.

Karina clung to him and looked up at him. "Where are you going, Uncle Ilya?"

Ilya beamed at his niece. "Do not worry, Karina. I will be near. Join the others, and I will be there shortly."

Karina gave him a hesitant smile and joined the celebration in the kitchen while Ilya hung back in the hall, phone in hand. He'd turned his phone off during the memorial service and powered it on now, surprised by the blinking voice mail icon. His surprise grew when he accessed his voice mail and saw multiple messages from what he recognized as burner phone numbers. This couldn't be good news. He glanced at the celebration in the kitchen and moved in the opposite direction, down the hallway and through the front door to take the call in private—unwilling to put a damper on the celebrations. Once outside, he listened to the last message and called the number as instructed.

"Ilya! Thank God," said Borgdanov. "I've been trying for an hour to reach someone."

"I suppose everyone had their phones turned off for the service—"

"Okay. No problem. I have you now. You must—"

"Andrei," Ilya said, "they are alive. Karina and Cassie are both alive."

"What? But you said your mission was unsuccessful."

"It was, but somehow—"

"That's wonderful," Borgdanov said, "and I want to hear about it, but now you must listen closely. The *Bratstvo* bastards have taken out a contract on *Dyed* and the Kairouzes. The hit is already planned, and it will be soon. You must warn them."

"*Da*," Ilya replied. "How? You have details?"

"I know they have the Kairouz house bugged, and that they plan to use a bomb when they are all gathered there, so you must prevent that from happening—&lrquo;

Ilya shoved the phone into his pocket and turned for the door before Borgdanov finished the sentence.

OUTSIDE THE KAIROUZ RESIDENCE
LONDON, UK

Fedosov nodded as the cook's Irish brogue came through his headphones, urging the group into the kitchen. He listened impatiently to the sounds of the happy crowd moving down the hallway, and he switched between his various listening devices to confirm their transit. Sure enough, the volume of their combined chatter rose in the kitchen as it fell in the other rooms. Soon they'd all be exactly where he wanted them.

He tensed and fingered the detonator, but he hesitated, were all three targets in the kill zone? The Chief would be livid if any survived. Should he wait a bit, to ensure everyone was there? He heard chairs being scraped along the floor, and then a woman's voice he didn't recognize. A British accent, youngish, perhaps the redhead on crutches?

"I propose a toast to the safe return of Cassie and Karina," the woman said.

There was a 'hear, hear,' that he recognized as Kairouz, and then a jumble of other responses.

"Wait. Where's Ilya?" a voice said. Clearly an American, probably Dugan. Good. Only the Kairouz woman left to confirm.

"He went out the front to make a phone call," said someone. Female. Russian accent.

"I'll go get him," he heard Dugan respond. "We can't have a toast without Ilya."

Shit! Don't leave, thought Fedosov. And then he smiled. When everyone was gathered for the toast, he'd know with certainty his targets were all there.

He settled back to wait. How accommodating of them to arrange the signal themselves.

***

Ilya reached for the latch just as the door opened to reveal a smiling Dugan.

"Ilya, come in. We're going to toast the girls' return—"

The big Russian grabbed Dugan by the arm and pulled him out onto the front porch.

"What the hell's the matter with you?" Dugan demanded as Ilya dragged him down the walk away from the house.

"*Dyed*, you are in danger. I think there is a bomb in the house. I must get the others out."

"What? Let's go." Dugan turned back to the house.

"*Nyet*." Ilya tightened his grip on Dugan's arm. "The house is bugged, how extensively I do not know, but I think the plan is to kill you and both

Alex and Gillian at the same time. I don't know why that has not happened, but I think you must stay separate from them."

"So you go in and get them out, and I stand here with my thumb up my ass?"

Ilya shrugged. "I think is safer for the others also, if you are not close."

Dugan hesitated, then nodded. "Okay. Get them out. I'll stay outside."

Ilya nodded back and ran up the walk and through the front door. He moved down the long hallway and into the kitchen. The group gathered there looked up, everyone smiling.

"Okay, now we have you, but where's Tom?" Anna asked.

"*Dyed* will be in soon," Ilya said. "He is smoking a cigarette."

Anna looked puzzled. "But Tom—" She stopped dead at Ilya's finger in front of his lips.

The group fell silent, but Ward and Anna picked up on Ilya's hand signs and quietly scooted their chairs away from the kitchen table and rose, silently urging the others to do likewise, as they all started moving toward the back door.

***

Dugan watched Ilya disappear into the house, his mind racing. If the Russian mob was intent on killing them all in the house, there was likely someone nearby waiting to pull the trigger. It could all be done very remotely, of course, but if they'd gone to such great lengths to kill them together, they'd likely want a witness on site to confirm the deaths. That meant line of sight, which on these tree-lined streets meant close, very close.

He moved off the sidewalk and crept through the shrubbery to the edge of the expansive front yard. He found a good vantage point behind a boxwood hedge and peered up and down the street. There were a few parked cars, but all were unoccupied, so he kept low behind the hedge and moved to the side of the house. Halfway down the yard, he stopped and slowly raised his eyes above the top of the hedge to check out the side street. Sure enough, a hundred yards beyond the entrance to the driveway, a plumbing repair van sat at the curb.

He started forward in a crouching run, keeping the hedge between himself and the van, with no clear idea what he was going to do when he got there.

***

Fedosov sat listening as the ex-*Spetsnaz* announced his arrival, and then cursed under his breath at the news the American Dugan wasn't with him. Then the conversation seemed to die. Something was wrong, but he couldn't tell what. He sat mentally parsing the possibilities, and then it came to him. He was nothing if not thorough, and he always did his homework on potential targets.

Dugan didn't smoke.

His fingers tightened on the detonator, and he pushed the button.

***

Dugan had just cleared the hedge and turned to exit the driveway into the street when the blast took him full in the back, knocking him off his feet. He fell face first on the drive, momentarily stunned, and then felt the hard cobblestones beneath him as rubble began to rain down, causing him to press himself to the ground and cross his arms over the back of his head for protection.

The last bits of rubble still pattered through the leaves above him when he staggered to his feet and looked toward the ruins of the house. His heart leapt into his throat as secondary explosions engulfed the wreckage in flames, and he took a step toward the house, then stopped. Ilya was there, and he had gotten them out. He HAD to believe that, or otherwise it made no difference. He turned back down the drive and stooped to scoop up a fist-sized chunk of masonry as he raced toward the van, murder in his heart.

The van rocked on its springs as he approached and someone moved about inside. Dugan reached the driver's door and yanked it open just as a small rat-faced man slipped into the driver's seat. The man's surprise was short lived, and he immediately slipped his right hand toward his left armpit, but Dugan was already swinging his rock toward Rat Face's nose. It landed with a satisfying crunch.

The pistol dropped to the floorboard of the van, and Dugan dragged the semi-conscious killer from the vehicle and threw him face down in the street, then knelt on the man's back and raised his rock high, ready to smash the bastard's skull. Then he stopped. He didn't want the little fish, he wanted the boss.

He tossed the rock aside and used his necktie to bind the killer's hands behind his back, and then stood. The man moaned as Dugan pulled him to his feet and pushed him toward the drive of the Kairouz house.

"You'd better hope no one's dead, asshole," Dugan said through clenched teeth, "or you're gonna have a lot more to moan about."

CHAPTER THIRTY-FOUR

Borgdanov paced the worn carpet of his hotel room. It had been over six hours since Ilya terminated their conversation so abruptly, and Borgdanov was worried—no news was definitely not good news. He'd already risked compromising them by contacting Ilya openly in the first place and by continuing to try to reach him since their last call, using the same burner phone on the off chance that Ilya's circumstances were such that he may not have access to the other numbers. He fought the urge to try yet again, then jumped at the muffled buzz of a cell phone, momentarily puzzled until he realized it was not the one he'd been using, but one of the others in his suitcase. He threw the bag on the bed and wrestled with the straps, frantic lest he miss the call.

"*Da!*"

"Andrei, this is Dugan—"

"*Dyed*, is everyone all right? Why are you calling me instead of Ilya?"

"First, everyone is all right, though a bit the worse for wear. The bastards tried to blow up Alex's house with us all inside. Ilya got everyone out in time, but he was the last out when it blew. He stopped a couple of flying bricks, one to the head and another to the torso. He has a concussion and some cracked ribs, but the doctor says he'll be okay in a week or ten days. He—and you—saved all our lives, Andrei. I don't know how to thank you."

"*Nyet.* There is no need for thanks, *Dyed*. I am glad everyone is okay. But tell me of Cassie and Karina. Ilya said they are alive? I do not understand. I thought your rescue mission was unsuccessful."

"So did we. Long story short, the guys on the ship rescued them and smuggled them ashore in the US. From there Cassie contacted Ward. I'll bring you up to speed when we have more time, but for the moment, the *Bratstvo* think the girls are dead, and we'd like to keep it that way. We caught the asshole that planted the bombs, and he has no clue who the girls were, nor did he have time to mention it to his superiors, so we think we're all right there for the moment."

"What of Tanya?"

There was a long pause.

"Tanya didn't make it. She died in the container before the rescue."

"She was a brave young woman," Borgdanov said, "so it seems we have yet another score to settle with these *mafiya* scum. But what is your situation now?"

"Officially, we're all dead. That was Anna's idea to buy us a little time while we figure out what to do. We're all in an MI5 safe house."

"*Da.* Is good idea. And soon, I do not think our *Bratstvo* friends will be a problem. Have Ilya call me when he can. I promised I would not start here without him, and I can give him a week, but then he needs to join me in Prague. I have things in motion here."

"How is the recruitment going?"

"Much better since I got some help from an old friend. So tell Agent Ward I will need that favor as soon as possible."

"How many?"

"Just the families for now."

"How many, Andrei?"

"Fifty-seven."

"Uhh… including your shooters?"

"No. Seventy-two with the operators. Plus, of course, Ilya and myself, Ilya's parents and Karina's family. Eighty-two in all. Is this a problem, *Dyed*?"

"Not financially. Alex and I are committed to making it work, and Hanley bitched a little, but he'll come through as well. But Jesse's gonna shit. That's a lot of people to provide with new identities and slip into the country. I think he normally works in ones and twos."

"I think he will be more than satisfied when he sees the intelligence I have for him, but he will have to trust me for now. We need to get all the families out of Russia as soon as possible. The first of them travel tomorrow from St. Petersburg to Helsinki, Finland. It is a short flight, less than one hour. Also, there are flights to Helsinki from other cities, so the travel pattern won't be so noticeable. If I get them all to Helsinki, how soon can you arrange a charter flight to get them to UK or directly to the US?"

"Probably within twenty-four to forty-eight hours, but I think we should bring them to the UK as tourists first. Jesse may need more time on his end."

"Good. I will have them all in Finland in three days, so plan the charter flight accordingly."

"Will do," Dugan said. "What next?"

"We'll hit the *Bratstvo* in Prague. It is their biggest operation outside of Russia itself, and they have less official protection there. Also, it is the center of their human-trafficking operations. I'm finalizing the operation and the extraction plans now. We should be able to execute within a few days after Ilya arrives."

"We'll be there."

"We? No, *Dyed*, not you—"

"They've attacked me and the people I love. I have every right to be there."

"*Da*. You have the right, but I must be truthful, *Dyed*. You do not have the ability to blend in or the military skills for this mission. You are an asset in many places, and if we were going on a ship, I would want you by my side, but here you would be a liability. Besides, we need someone to arrange things on that end."

"Just a damn minute, Alexei—"

"*Dyed*, I would trust you with my life. I HAVE trusted you with my life. But now I entrust you with something even more precious, the lives of all our families. If something goes wrong or for some reason we do not come back, we need to know there is someone we can trust to take care of them. The others there are our friends, but you are our *brat*—our brother—and someone must remain to guard the family, *da*?"

"I don't know whether to be flattered or pissed off."

"You can be either, or both, as long as we know you are looking after our loved ones."

Dugan sighed. "All right. I'll put up a draft email when I have the flight arrangements out of Helsinki. Keep an eye on the email account."

Arsov sat at his old desk, watching a video of the latest whore being seasoned, a nice young brunette from Ekaterinburg in the Sverdlovsk Oblast. She was obviously of Tartar stock, with an exotic look about her that would no doubt make her a moneymaker with the right training. And he had to admit, Beria was doing a good job there. Between brutalizing the girl, and alternating periods of kindness with horrific threats to her family, he already had her broken. The rest would be easy.

Arsov's approval was tempered with caution. Beria was both competent and ambitious, and couldn't conceal his dissatisfaction at the demotion occasioned by Arsov's unexpected return. Arsov had placated him to date with compliments and a bonus paid from his own pocket, but the man had run the Prague operation quite competently during Arsov's absence, and obviously was chafing to do so again. He would bear watching. But that was a worry for another day. Satisfied everything was proceeding as it should, Arsov closed the training video and opened his browser to check out some British news sites.

He'd been elated the previous week to read of the destruction of the Kairouz house and the death of its occupants and assorted guests. He was particularly pleased they'd killed the ex-*Spetsnaz* sergeant, but sorry there had been no mention of Borgdanov. The whereabouts of the Russian former officer was troubling, but not unduly so. Nonetheless, Arzov continued to scout British news reports for any follow-up on the Kairouz bombing or any mention of Borgdanov. He considered contacting the Chief in St. Petersburg directly, to see if he had any information on Borgdanov, but thought better of it. The man frowned on unnecessary contact, and Arsov was doing his best to get back in the Chief's good graces, so perhaps it was best to continue to do a good job here in Prague and to let the memory of the unfortunate situation in London fade. He'd bide his time until another opportunity presented itself.

He glanced at the clock at the bottom of his computer screen—4 PM. He had time to make a run through all the clubs and brothels to keep everyone on their toes. He was sure Beria had everything in hand, but it didn't pay to get sloppy, especially since his own position here was somewhat probationary. He powered down his computer and rose from the desk, just as he heard the distinctive 'sphut' of a suppressed weapon from the living room, followed by a crash.

"Boris?" he called. When his bodyguard failed to answer, he jerked open a desk drawer and retrieved a pistol. "Boris, are you there?" he called again as he moved toward the door.

Arsov burst into the hall, pistol in front of him in a two-handed grip. He swung the weapon right and then quickly back to the left before continuing down the hall toward the living room. He studied the living room over the sights of the pistol, the room deserted except for the very dead body of Boris lying on his back over the smashed glass coffee table, a perfectly round hole between his eyes leaking blood down the side of his face. He felt the stun gun pressed to the back of his skull and stiffened a split second before thousands of volts overwhelmed his nervous system.

***

Arsov's eyes flew open, and he jerked his head back as the acrid smell of ammonia filled his nose. He glimpsed retreating hands in front of his face and struggled to make sense of his surroundings. He was in the 'training' bedroom in the apartment, but the bed had been disassembled and pushed up against the wall. More disconcerting still, he was naked and stretched spread eagle, face up in a half-reclining position, his wrists and ankles tightly bound to something immovable. His genitals rested slightly elevated on a flat piece of concrete shoved into his crotch. He heard movement behind him and tried to turn.

"Careful, Arsov," a voice said. "You might strain your neck, and that can be very painful. We wouldn't want that, now would we?"

The disembodied voice gained a face as a tall man moved into view and stood over him.

"But forgive me. Where are my manners? I am Major Andrei Borgdanov, and this gentleman"—he nodded at another large man that appeared at Arsov's other side—"is Sergeant Ilya Denosovitch."

"Yo-you're supposed to be dead," Arsov said to Denosovitch.

"Sorry to disappoint you," Denosovitch said.

"Wh-what do you want?" Arsov asked, and Borgdanov shrugged.

"Nothing too difficult. Just a little cooperation for now."

"You are insane! Cooperate with you? Do you know what the *Bratstvo* would do to me? And no matter what you do to me, do you think they will let you get away with this? You are already dead, as are your families. But if you release me at once and leave, I will make sure that you are the only ones to die. This is your last chance to save your loved ones."

Borgdanov nodded. "Thank you for your kind and generous offer, but we have already seen to the safety of our loved ones."

"You fool! My men are undoubtedly on the way here now. I suggest you leave while you can."

"Ah yes, your men. By that I presume you mean the forty-three *Bratstvo* thugs that make up your little 'army' here in Prague, spread out to guard your clubs and whorehouses? If so, I regret to inform you that they are all very dead and as we speak are being stacked on the floor of the central warehouse from which you distribute your porn and drugs." Borgdanov looked thoughtful. "It really is amazing how easy it is to take out unsuspecting targets with relatively few trained men and suppressed weapons. Even the former *Spetsnaz* among your soldiers presented little challenge. Surprise really is key, *da?*"

"You're bluffing."

"Oh, but I'm not." Borgdanov glanced at his watch. "And in exactly thirty minutes, their bodies, along with all your porn and drugs, will disappear in a raging warehouse fire."

"You'll never get away with—"

"Yes, I think we will, but before you so predictably threaten me next with the tame policemen the *Bratstvo* has in their pocket, let me save you the trouble. Eight hours ago, Chief Inspector Pavel Makovec was killed by a sniper, and shortly thereafter the other eighteen Prague policemen on your payroll received anonymous phone calls informing them they would be next, should they decide to assist you. They were also provided with details of their involvement with *Bratstvo* and a link and password to a website with full documentation of that involvement, and warned that should they provide any further assistance to your organization, the documentation would be sent to the international news media. Finally, we assured them their 'compensation' would continue to be funded if they would instead cooperate with us. All agreed."

Borgdanov smiled. "So you see, Arsov, your tame policemen now work for me, and I don't think the *Bratstvo* will be back in Prague for a long, long time. Perhaps you should consider cooperation, *da?*"

Arsov studied Borgdanov. The ex-*Spetsnaz* man didn't appear to be bluffing, so perhaps it was time to hedge bets. He'd think of a way to spin it to the *Bratstvo* later, but for the moment his goal was survival.

"Very well," Arsov said. "What do you want to know?"

"Nothing too difficult. Let's begin with the passports. We rescued over a hundred women and children from your little operation. Where are their passports?"

"The passports for the women are in my safe in the office. I... I don't have passports for all the kids. Most were taken on the streets. We normally arrange false papers when we need to move them."

"Very well. Give us the combination." Borgdanov nodded at Denosovitch, who produced a pad and pencil.

Arsov recited the combination as Denosovitch wrote it down and left the room. He returned a short time later and nodded at Borgdanov.

"There are about eighty passports," Denosovitch said.

Borgdanov looked down at Arsov.

"So. That was not so difficult, now was it, Arsov?"

Arsov shook his head. "What more do you want to know?"

Borgdanov looked puzzled. "Know? Nothing. We have all the information we need from you. Now we merely want you to die—slowly and painfully. Unfortunately, it will likely be a bit noisy as well, but given the former use of this room, I suspect it is soundproofed." Borgdanov shrugged. "And if not, I'm sure the neighbors are accustomed to hearing screams and know to mind their own business, *da*?"

Arsov sat, stunned, as Borgdanov nodded to Denosovitch again and the man left the room.

"Wait," said Arsov. "You should not kill me. I can help you. I know things, many things."

"I'm sure you do, but we have much better sources. And besides, WE are not going to kill you. Someone else has claimed that right."

"Hello, Arsov," said a voice to his right, and he twisted his head to see a woman with short black hair enter the room at Denosovitch's side. He recognized the voice, but not the—Karina. Of course, Denosovitch's niece.

"K-Karina? What are you doing here?"

"Oh, it's 'Karina,' now, is it, Arsov? Not 'whore' or 'slut' or any of the other little pet names you called us. I'm so honored you remembered my name. But how about what you called me at first when I could still fight back? Do you remember what you used to say when you beat me and raped me and watched while the others did as well. Because I remember it very well. What was it now? Oh, yes. You would shout, 'That will teach you, you little slut. That will teach you to be a ball breaker.'"

Arsov had been so fixated on the face and the voice, he'd noticed little else, but he flinched now as Karina looked down at his exposed genitals and smiled before she lifted a sledgehammer she'd kept down at her side.

"So finally, Arsov, it seems I really am to become a ball breaker," Karina said as she took the handle of the hammer in a two-handed grip and raised it above her head.

"This is for me and Tanya and all the others," Karina said, and she started toward him.

***

Ilya sat on the sofa in the living room, holding Karina close as she sobbed. Slowly she regained control of herself.

"I-I am sorry, Uncle Ilya."

"Shhh… little Karinka," Ilya said. "Do you think I WANTED you to do this horrible thing? It is only because you insisted that I let you try. But it broke my heart, and I am GLAD you could not. It means the monsters have not conquered you and stolen your humanity. You are our little Karinka still. Brave beyond measure, yes, but not hard. Not brittle and bitter."

Karina pulled back and looked at her uncle. "But what do you mean?"

"I mean that when you take another life, no matter how justified, you lose a bit of yourself. You cannot understand until you do it, and I cannot explain. Sometimes, if you are very angry, it is a good feeling, like a toothache when it stops, but then it becomes an empty feeling. It uses up a little of your soul, I think."

"But, Uncle Ilya, you are a soldier, so—"

"I am not immune, Karinka, but soldiers have tricks. We deceive ourselves and count our enemies only as 'targets,' but in a case like this where the fight is very personal, yes, we pay the price when we kill. It is a price worth paying to protect those we love, but I am glad you did not have to pay it. You have suffered enough, and this is my job, *da*?"

Karina fell silent and hugged him tightly, and Ilya returned her embrace and kissed the top of her head, then gently disengaged himself.

"Stay here now. I must go see the major. It will all be over soon." Ilya stood up.

He walked down the hall and through the door into the training room, closing the door behind him. Arsov lost control of his bodily functions when Karina had started toward him with the hammer, and the stench in the room was almost overpowering. Arsov slumped in the mess, whimpering as the major leaned against the far wall, his arms crossed. Borgdanov looked up.

"I considered finishing him, but I think his fate belongs to you. What do you want to do with him, Ilya?"

Ilya shook his head. "I intended to make him suffer, but he is not worth it. He is only a cockroach, and I will not let him steal anymore of my humanity than he already has."

Borgdanov nodded. "*Da*, you are right. Then step on him quickly, and let's get out of here."

Ilya drew his pistol and shot the cockroach between the eyes.

REGIONAL HQ
FEDERAL SECURITY SERVICE (FSB)
ST. PETERSBURG
RUSSIAN FEDERATION

Vladimir Glazkov looked down, both surprised and annoyed as the cell phone buzzed in the desk drawer. The phone was meant for one-way communication only except in extreme emergencies, so an incoming call couldn't be anything but bad news—or an idiot that would live to regret disturbing him. He yanked open the drawer and looked at the incoming number. Arsov! He should have guessed. He stifled a curse and answered the phone.

"*Da?*"

"Ah. Comrade Glazkov. Good afternoon. Sorry to disturb you," a cheerful voice said.

Glazkov's blood ran cold. No one except those in the highest circles knew his real identity, certainly not Arsov, and that wasn't the fool's voice anyway. He hesitated, torn between hanging up and the need to know more.

"You have the wrong number. There is no one here by that name."

There was an audible sigh. "Very well, then. I will call you 'Chief' if you prefer. It really doesn't matter to me."

"Who is this?"

"Oh, forgive me. I am Major Andrei Borgdanov, formerly of the *Spetsnaz*, but I think you know that. And as you can see, I'm calling from the phone of your late associate, Sergei Arsov."

"I know no one of that name, Major—Borgdanov, is it? I'm sorry, but once again, I believe you have the wrong number."

"And yet, we continue to chat. But perhaps we can end this charade. I presume you're sitting in your office at the FSB, so may I ask you to check your email—not your FSB address, but the 'secret' encrypted one you use to correspond with the rest of the *Bratstvo* leadership."

"Again, Major, I believe you are misinformed." Glazkov struggled to keep the fear from his voice as his fingers flew over the keyboard. In seconds he'd found the single email from an anonymous sender and opened it. He scrolled through it with a growing sense of alarm.

"I think you should have it open by now," Borgdanov said. "And you will see the organizational chart that shows your true identity, along with the identities of the other top *Bratstvo* leaders, along with the positions they occupy in government or legitimate businesses. I emphasize that this is just a small sample of the information I have."

"What do you want?"

"It is not a question of what I want, Glazkov, because what I want, I will take. This is more a matter of an exchange of information to prevent you from making a mistake. A matter of courtesy, so to speak."

"Go on."

"A few hours ago, we destroyed your Prague operation. All of your men there, including Mr. Arsov, are dead. All of your victims have been released and taken to a place of safety, and your warehouse full of drugs, porn, and illegal weapons is presently burning brightly. Additionally, you will no longer enjoy the protection of the Prague police, and should you attempt to make new inroads there, I believe you will find your overtures most unwelcome. Do you understand?"

"You are playing a dangerous game, Borgdanov. You understand, of course, that you are a dead man?"

"Ah, but we are all dead men the moment we are born, are we not, Glazkov? Only the timing and manner of our deaths is in question, and I believe mine will be both peaceful and some time away."

"Believe what you want. You are not a match for the *Bratstvo*. How can you possibly hope to stand against us?"

"Because Glazkov, the information in that email and much, much more is hidden on encrypted servers in several locations worldwide, and in the event of my untimely death by any means, it will be transmitted to every major law enforcement organization as well as to every major news outlet within a matter of hours. The world will know who you really are, what you do, and how you do it, all in sufficient detail to bring your operations to a halt."

"So what? Of course it will be an inconvenience to be so identified, but we are untouchable here in Russia, and do you really think we care about world opinion?"

"No, but I think you care about the money that buys the influence and power you enjoy in Russia, and if I'm reading the data correctly, over 75 percent of that revenue—76.73 percent to quote your latest cash flow report—comes from operations outside of Russia. How long do you think your empire can last even in Russia without the cash to buy the influence you currently enjoy?"

Glazkov sat stunned, imagining the dissolution of all he'd built, until Borgdanov spoke again.

"Glazkov?"

"All right, Borgdanov. What do you want? Part of our operations, I presume?"

"We do not want to play your filthy games, Glazkov. We wish to be neither competitors nor partners. For the moment, we will settle for a truce. Accept that your operations in Prague are finished, withdraw from the UK, and make no attempt to retaliate against anyone connected with this affair, and we will leave you alone."

"For the moment?"

"Nothing lasts forever, Glazkov," Borgdanov replied. "I have no doubt you will begin maneuvering to eliminate us as soon as this call is finished, regardless of what you agree to now. I suggest that if you are so inclined that you first test us in a limited manner, so when I crush your attempts, it will be less painful for you. Remember that I can release information selectively, making sure the damage it does to you is more than proportionate to any harm you might do to me. However, be aware that if any of your actions results in harm to any of my people or their families, the truce is over, and it will be all-out war."

"You are an arrogant bastard, Borgdanov."

"I prefer to think of it as confident."

"And only time will tell if that confidence is justified. Now. Is there anything else we need to discuss?"

"One minor detail. In the email I sent you is the account information for one of *Bratstvo*'s bank accounts in Liechtenstein. As noted in the email, I took the liberty of making a small withdrawal to cover our expenses."

Glazkov turned back to his computer screen and moved his mouse, his blood pressure spiking as he read the note.

"You took it ALL! THERE WAS FIFTY MILLION DOLLARS IN THAT ACCOUNT!"

"A part of which will be used to relocate your victims and their families, as well as to provide counseling. And the rest, well, the rest we'll need to fund ongoing operations. We'll try to get by with what's left, but I suspect mounting a defense against potential attacks will be expensive. A great deal of that depends on you, of course."

Glazkov struggled to compose himself as the silence grew.

"You are a dead man, Borgdanov," he said at last.

"Without doubt. But not tomorrow."

Glazkov sighed. "No. Not tomorrow."

"And may I presume we have an agreement for the moment?"

"*Da.* For the moment."

"Wonderful. It was very nice talking to you, Comrade Glazkov, and do try to keep things in perspective, *da*?" Borgdanov said just before Glazkov heard the click of the disconnect.

He rested his elbows on his desk and buried his face in his hands.

EPILOGUE

Yacht *Sea Tiger*
Atlantic Ocean
East of Jacksonville, Florida
Six Weeks Later

Dugan raised his head as the Orthodox priest finished the Russian prayer, and everyone joined in the collective amen. There was a gentle breeze moving across the swim platform on the stern of the large yacht, and he looked out over the blue sky and bluer sea with a sad smile. It was a beautiful day to say goodbye to a beautiful person.

The priest murmured something to Tanya's parents, and they stepped to the stern rail, Tanya's fiancé, Ivan, at their side. Tanya's father tossed a huge floral wreath onto the surface of the sea, and everyone else in the small group stood silently for a long moment and then began to fade back, leaving Tanya's parents and Ivan some time alone with their grief. The charter captain and his five-man crew had manned the rail nearby, all in crisp white uniforms and standing at attention, but the captain left his position now and moved quietly to Dugan's side, his eyebrows raised in an unspoken question.

"Let her drift here as long as they want," Dugan said quietly. "If they look like they're ready to go, check with me first, and I'll confirm it with them."

The captain nodded and dismissed his crew, who moved away quietly to resume their duties. The captain remained nearby looking over the side but keeping a discreet eye on the grieving family, as Dugan followed the rest of the small group of mourners inside.

The crew had prepared a bountiful buffet lunch in the yacht's spacious salon, and the mourners gathered there in small groups as the steward circulated, taking drink orders. Nigel and Cassie stood in one corner, talking quietly with Ilya, Karina and the priest, while Dugan stood with Alex and Gillian, chatting with Borgdanov. Mrs. Hogan had declined the invitation, on the grounds that she got seasick standing on the dock and didn't feel up to an ocean voyage, no matter how short.

"Alex," Borgdanov said, "it was very generous of you to charter this beautiful boat and fly Tanya's people here all the way from Russia. I know that they appreciate it. It is wonderful gesture, and I thank you for it."

Alex shook his head. "It was the least we could do. I hope it gives them some closure."

Beside him, Gillian nodded and brushed away a tear. She started to speak but then shook her head and smiled sadly, as if she didn't trust her own voice.

"Well, I know it means a great deal to them, and to young Ivan too," Borgdanov said. "Evidently he has been going crazy searching for Tanya. He seems like good boy."

The others nodded agreement, and the conversation drifted towards silence, continuing in fits and starts until the captain appeared at the door to the salon and caught Dugan's eye.

"I think they're ready, Mr. Dugan," the captain said as Dugan reached the door.

Dugan nodded and looked over to where Borgdanov now stood with Karina, and beckoned them over to join him as translators.

They found Ivan and Tanya's parents standing together on the swim platform, looking unsure what to do. Karina hurried to their side, and after confirming that they were ready to leave, gently urged the trio inside to get something to eat. Dugan turned to the captain.

"How long back to Jacksonville?"

The captain looked out at the sea. "Sea's like a mill pond. Four hours maybe, four and a half tops."

"Okay. Let's head back."

The captain nodded and left, and less than two minutes later the engine speed began to slowly increase as the bow of the vessel swung due west. Dugan stood at the stern rail with Borgdanov and looked aft as the breeze washed over them.

"So how is Texas?" Dugan asked.

Borgdanov chuckled. "Odessa, Texas, is very different from Odessa in the Ukraine, so I think whoever chose this name has vivid imagination or strange sense of humor."

Dugan laughed. "I thought it might be a bit of an adjustment. But seriously, are all your people okay? Handley's treating you all right?"

"*Da*. Better than all right, and Mr. Ray Handley's ranch is far from town in middle of nowhere, and we can see anyone coming for a very long way."

He moved his arms in a sweeping gesture. "It is like being here, in middle of ocean, so security is very easy."

Borgdanov nodded. "No, we could not ask for more, *Dyed*. He brought in many of the houses on wheels—how you call them, mobile homes? But they are very big! Woody tells me they are called 'double times,' I think."

Dugan grinned. "I think you mean double-wides."

"*Da*, double-wides. Anyway they are much bigger than anyone's old apartment in Russia. He laid them all out with streets, and somewhere he even found Russian teacher, so we also have school for the children. We have regular Russian village," Borgdanov said. "Of course, is temporary, but everyone is learning English, and the children are learning very fast. We will move in time, but there is no hurry, I think."

"No regrets?"

Borgdanov gave him a sad smile. "Our hearts are Russian, *Dyed*, so there will always be regrets. But we appreciate the opportunity you have all given us to safeguard our families, so we will try to be good Americans too. The children are very happy, especially the younger ones."

"And," Borgdanov continued, "I am happy that thanks to Arkady, we can repay you, Alex, and Mr. Ray Handley for the money you have spent."

"About your friend Arkady—you do know Ward's lusting after that intelligence, right?"

Borgdanov nodded. "I understand, and we will do anything Ward requires of us, as agreed. I will also give him anything he needs to support an operation, or if he wants specific information about something in Russia or elsewhere, I will help him all I can. But I will not turn over everything I got from Arkady, because when we are not working for Ward, we will work on our own." He smiled. "We are Americans now, and I believe in free enterprise, *da*? Also, I am reminded of what Archimedes said about levers."

Dugan thought a moment. "With a lever and a place to stand, I'll move the world?"

"*Da*," Borgdanov nodded. "Arkady gave me a very great lever, and you and the others have given us a safe place to stand. And I don't want to move the world, just Russia."

"So it's not over between you and the *Bratstvo*?"

Borgdanov's face hardened, and he looked at the eastern horizon.

"Oh no, *Dyed*. It has only just begun."

Author's Notes

As readers of my other work know, while my stories are fictional, they are based on real (or at least plausible) events. That wasn't too difficult in the past; both *Deadly Straits* and *Deadly Coasts* are set in an industry I know quite well and (for the most part) in geographical settings with which I'm familiar. However, when I decided to tackle the issue of human trafficking, that required a lot more research, and what I found wasn't pleasant.

The events in *Deadly Crossing* are fictional, but the cruelty of human trafficking and the methods depicted to control its victims are all too real. And while Russia and the countries of the former Soviet Bloc provide the victims for the story (as they often do in real life), human trafficking takes place in every country and every city in the world, including those of North America and Western Europe. Wherever you're reading this, it's likely that there are hidden victims of this horrible crime within a few hours' (or even a few minutes') journey.

Thank You

Time is a precious commodity. None of us truly knows quite how much we'll have, and most of us are compelled to spend large blocks of it earning a living, making our leisure time more precious still. I am honored that you've chosen to spend some of your precious leisure time reading my work, and sincerely hope you found it enjoyable.

If you enjoyed this book, I do hope you'll spread the word to friends and family. I also hope you'll consider writing a review on Amazon, Goodreads, or one of the many sites dedicated to book reviews. A review need not be lengthy, and it will be most appreciated. Honest reader reviews are the single most effective means for a new author to build a following, and I need all I can get.

I invite you to try the other books of the Dugan series listed on the following page, and if you're a fan of post-apocalyptic fiction, I hope you'll also consider my *Disruption* series, beginning with *Under a Tell-Tale Sky* and available on Amazon.

And finally, on a more personal note, I'd love to hear your feedback on my books, good or bad. If you're interested, I'd also like to add you to my notification list, so I can alert you when each new book is available. You can reach me on my website at **www.remcdermott.com**. I respond personally to all emails and would really like to hear from you.

Fair Winds and Following Seas,

R.E. (Bob) McDermott

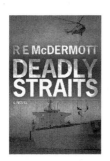

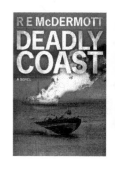

More Books by R.E. McDermott

Deadly Straits - When marine engineer and very part-time spook Tom Dugan becomes collateral damage in the War on Terror, he's not about to take it lying down. Falsely implicated in a hijacking, he's offered a chance to clear himself by helping the CIA snare their real prey, Dugan's best friend, London ship owner Alex Kairouz. But Dugan has some plans of his own. Available in paperback on both Amazon and Barnes & Noble.

Deadly Coast - Dugan thought Somali pirates were bad news, then it got worse. As Tom Dugan and Alex Kairouz, his partner and best friend, struggle to ransom their ship and crew from murderous Somali pirates, things take a turn for the worse. A US Navy contracted tanker with a full load of jet fuel is also hijacked, not by garden variety pirates, but by terrorists with links to Al Qaeda, changing the playing field completely. Available in paperback on both Amazon and Barnes & Noble.

Deadly Crossing - Dugan's attempts to help his friends rescue an innocent girl from the Russian mob plunge him into a world he'd scarcely imagined, endangering him and everyone he holds dear. A world of modern day slavery and unspeakable cruelty, from which no one will escape, unless Dugan can weather a Deadly Crossing. Available in paperback on both Amazon and Barnes & Noble.

Manufactured by Amazon.ca
Bolton, ON

25832269R00149